PATRIOT ACTS

DAVID BAKER

PATRIOT ACTS

Copyright © 2019, 2020, 2021

David A. Baker All Rights Reserved

℗ 2022 End of Vandalism Books; End of Vandalism Books is an Imprint of Jay-Hey Publishers

Print ISBN: 978-1-66786-662-8
eBook ISBN: 978-1-66786-663-5

This book is a work of fiction. Names, characters, places and incidents are products of the author's imagination or are used fictitiously and are not to be construed as real. Any resemblance to actual events, locales, organizations or persons, living or dead, is entirely coincidental. Any historical figures mentioned or represented are used in fictional settings and manners, which are not to be identified as real.

This book is dedicated to the Civitas ChildLaw Center of Loyola University of Chicago School of Law, its Staff and Volunteers, and its Co-Founder and Director, Professor Diane C. Geraghty

TABLE OF CONTENTS

1. You Haven't Lived……..3
2. Do It Like They Do It In The Ten Commandments……....................17
3. Either These Words Mean Something, Or They Don't…… 27
4. Members Of This Community Threaten to Immolate Themselves…………….....................41
5. Nothing Happens For No Reason At All…………... 47
6. Your Government Tax Dollars At Work……….......................57
7. Nobody Here But Just Us Chickens…..................78
8. The Army of God Wants *You*……...............................91
9. Go To The Head Of The Class…...................... 101
10. It's A Human Shell Game…...................... 112
11. You Break It, You Fix It…...................... 128
12. All Prosecution Is Political….... 136
13. Banana Republic Without the Bananas…...................... 142
14. Child Abuse By Proxy…...................... 151
15. Immigrants On Our Shores…...................... 162
16. Welcome To Bully Nation…...................... 175
17. Immunity From Prosecution…...................... 185
18. God Is On Our Side…...................... 196
19. The Rubber Mallet Treatment…...................... 213
20. New Mexico Is Not Part Of Mexico…...................... 229
21. No Such Thing As Bad Publicity…...................... 238
22. Addressing Socially Non-Constructive Behavior…...................... 252

23. A Thousand's A Crowd... 264

24. Give The Man His Earlobes.................. 277

25. You Can All Burn in Hell... 287

26. Everybody's In Custody.. 313

27. I Think We're Supposed To Turn Around.......... 330

28. "Good" Terrorists And "Bad" Terrorists... 342

29. No Such Thing As Free Parking............ 406

30. Thank My Dentist.. 412

1.
YOU HAVEN'T LIVED........

On October 23rd, 2022, the Adolescent Psychiatric Ward of St. Vincent's Hospital, in The City by the Lake, held twenty-three patients, the youngest being a six-year-old, the oldest an emancipated pair not yet discharged to an adult facility. Most of them were anorexic, suffering from severe eating disorders. Eight had attempted suicide; twelve had self-harmed in various ways without overt suicidal tendencies or expressed suicidal ideation; and three were starved to the point of life-threatening malnutrition. Two of those patients were on naso-gastric feeding tubes. The third severely anorexic child refused forced feeding by removing the nostril-mounted tube each time it was inserted. That child was about to get a lawyer.

Philo John Crump, a small-time, sixty-eight-year-old probate attorney, was waiting in the lobby of the Hospital while his belongings were searched for anything a patient might use to self-harm or attempt suicide. He was tall, thin, dark haired and so ordinary looking that when he put on a tie, people asked him for directions, so he attracted no special scrutiny from the staff. He had already checked his flip-phone and house keys at the front desk. The attendants were inspecting the clasp of the watchband on his thirteen-dollar rubber Timex, to see whether, if removed, the clasp could be used to make a lengthwise cut along a child's arm.

"Why don't you just keep it?" Crump asked, annoyed at how long the near strip-search was taking. He was lapsing into irritated wise-guy talk because he wasn't even supposed to be there. He was covering for his partner, Maureen McDougal, who had volunteered to take the starving child's case for free, pro-bono, but she checked out on the assignment because her daughter got caught up in some junior soccer tournament.

While the gate-keepers turned his briefcase upside down, shaking out the contents onto their desk like bank robbers inspecting their loot, two uniformed orderlies walked past, each guiding a large, worn-out looking Alaskan Huskie by harnesses used by people with guide dogs.

"The dogs have Medicare?" Crump asked one of the orderlies.

"Those are comfort animals," offered the woman behind the counter. "A local shelter sends them over and the kids play….." she paused, "….well, not *play*, more, sort of, they *lean* on them. I mean, they like the contact."

"And the fur," one of the orderlies added.

"Can we see your wallet?" prodded the woman rifling his briefcase.

Crump pulled out his billfold. It was old, chunky, overstuffed with junk and harmless as a loaf of bread. "Here, the exploding wallet," he said, handing it over.

"I know—seems like overkill, but they use laminated drivers' licenses and credit cards to cut," the woman said, as she removed Crump's license and cards from the wallet, handing it back over. "You're all set. We'll hold these. Take the elevator down the hall to the fourth floor. Our attendant Giampetro will meet you when you get off."

The place had all the dull personality of the check-in boarding counter at a half-way deserted, mid-sized airport, which made the attendant that much more startling. Giampetro was the largest adult human Crump had ever seen. The man was at least seven feet tall, had to weigh three hundred pounds, was bald as an onion and so stooped over that he could have played

Quasimodo in the local dinner theater's production of The Hunchback of Notre Dame, although from the looks of him, the director would need to scold him for over-acting.

"You the lawyer?" he asked, from somewhere deep down in his chest, as he slowly bent his head in Crump's direction, without straightening up.

"Yeah, I'm here to interview the kid from…..uhh…..from….wherever," Crump responded, since they hadn't been given the kid's name or any background by the clinic that had recruited Maureen for this no-pay, volunteer case.

The elevator lobby was institutional-non-descript, except for the locked entry door to the unit, which was mounted with bullet-proof safety glass that distorted the view of the activities on the other side.

"Stand here," Giampetro ordered, as he slid an I.D. bracelet over a lock pad, and the sliding door whooshed open.

"Holy…Mother…of…*God*," Crump let out, as the inside of the Adolescent Psychiatric Ward came into view. Almost all the kids were female, all of them were emaciated-looking, and while a couple were in wheelchairs, most were wandering aimlessly around the unit. It looked like a scene from one of those old-time horror films, where the young couple move into a haunted house and when they open the attic door, the ghosts of all the prior inhabitants are slowly gliding around, feet barely touching the ground. Crump felt queasy, like if he stared at them too long, he'd be able to see right through the kids. Virtually every child was wearing gauze bandages wrapped around their forearms, covering bony arms from wrist to elbow.

"You haven't lived 'till you've spent time in a Juvenile Psych Ward," Giampetro growled, his chin still buried in his chest.

Everywhere Crump looked, teenagers and young kids were bandaged up, the skin on their arms unseen underneath the gauze wraps.

"They like to cut their arms," Giampetro added. "Some do legs, but it's mostly arms."

Many of them had oblong fanny packs strapped to their waists, with clear plastic tubing running from the packs up to their noses, where the tubes were taped into a single nostril. It looked just like the get-ups he'd seen with old folks who needed oxygen, dragging around inside nursing homes. Every one of them appeared ill, exhausted or just plain wasting away.

"What's with the oxygen packs? They all former chain smokers?" Crump asked.

"Those are….urrr….feeding tubes," Giampetro mumbled.

As they entered the ward, one kid wearing cut-off shorts wandered past. Her exposed legs exhibited a pattern of vertical lines full of angry, red, inch-long scabs, covering her thighs from her knees to her shorts.

"Is that what's under the bandages?" Crump asked, nodding toward the passing kid in cutoffs.

"Pretty much."

Giampetro led Crump to a kiosk off to the side of the unit. A woman stood behind the counter with a phone to her ear, shaking her head silently. She was blonde-haired, round-faced and so cherubic-looking Crump thought she could have passed for a slightly rattled, all-grown-up former child tap-dancer.

"This is the lawyer, here for E.M.," Giampetro announced, as he huffed, then turned and wandered into the ward.

Crump started to speak, but the woman, still holding the phone to her ear, raised a hand to stop him.

"Look, this child has not eaten solid food in three months," she lectured the person on the other end of the line. "You can't just yank out a feeding tube and toss her a hamburger," she argued, frustration rising in her voice. She paused, looking down at a medical chart. "No, we already tried that. She has to stay here until we can get her up to eighty-five percent normal body weight, then we can try initiating a mix of rice and liquids." She hung up.

"Another insurance company, managing length-of-stay," she remarked, as she eyed Crump, disapprovingly. Crump wasn't what she'd expected—too rumpled, collar starting to fray and pill. He looked like he could be almost anybody, maybe the guy driving around the retirees on the motorized luggage cart at the airport. "Sorry. I thought you'd be a woman—"

"My partner got hung up, so she asked me to pinch hit," he said, as he offered her his business card.

"While we're happy for any help we can get here, I'm not sure how 'E.M.' will react to a man."

Crump shrugged. "I know. Maureen McDougal can stay involved. I just need to interview the kid if we're going to file something in court on her behalf. What's with the initials?"

"They don't know her name—it's the I.D. code the Immigration Agents gave her, when they separated her from her parents."

Crump turned to survey the room. There was so much commotion it was hard to single anybody out, but his eyes fixed on the only male child in sight. The kid was seated cross-legged in a wheelchair, his arms resting listlessly on the armrests, his hands hanging in his lap like all the tendons had been cut. Crump figured him for thirteen or fourteen, but with his head hanging down, it was hard to judge. A man and a woman were seated at either side of the wheelchair, the man with his hand on one of the chair's push-handles, the woman smoothing a lock of sandy brown hair over the child's forehead. The kid was all bones and skin, as though if he'd lost another five pounds he'd turn to powder and disappear.

"She's not in the common room," the Doctor spoke up, breaking Crump's train of thought. "We've got her sequestered. She's so intense about not eating she kind of freaks out the other kids," the Doctor added. She glanced at the business card he'd handed her. "Mr. Crump—"

"Just Crump—nobody but the Social Security Administration calls me 'Mister,'" Crump said, turning back to face her. "This is all…. just …..I mean….." He paused, lost for words.

"Never been to an Adolescent Psychiatric Ward, I take it?"

"No. My kids, they eat, and when they got picked on they'd just slug somebody. How did all these kids end up here?"

"Sign of the times, I'm afraid," she said, glancing around. "Thirty years ago, few places—here included—had separate wards for the kids with mental health issues." She paused, watching Crump, who pretty obviously wished he was somewhere else.

"So, what happened? Where'd they all come from?"

"Some of this is from heightened awareness and improved diagnosis, but it's mostly bullying, harassment that takes place in and around schools, and on the internet." She stopped, watching Crump observing the revolving malnourishment exhibition.

"Anyway, I'm doctor Amelia Trimble. E.M. is my patient, and we called Volunteer Legal Services when we got this notice."

She stopped, flipped some papers over on a chart and handed a one-page form to Crump.

The document, dated October 15, 2022, was a form letter, typed on stationery of The United States Citizenship and Immigration Services. It was addressed to "The Parents or Guardians of E. M., a Minor, Currently in Deferred Status". The pro-forma address was pre-printed with "Dear" and then a blank space where "Parents or Guardians of E. M." had been superimposed with a crummy, slightly crooked photocopy job.

It read:

"The child in your custody is currently in deferred status pursuant to 8 U.S. Code 1227, pending deportation during one or more applications of medically-required treatment of a condition which the Secretary of U.S.C.I.S. has determined to be potentially or actually life threatening. You are hereby notified that, due to a recent policy action by U.S.C.I.S., your deferral status has been revoked by the Secretary, retroactive to August 7, 2022. You have

33 calendar days to have E.M. permanently depart the United States, at which time, if E.M. remains in the United States, said E.M. will be deemed illegal status and will face deportation by the U.S. Immigration and Customs Enforcement Division of the Department of Homeland Security. Questions regarding your child's status may be directed to the address printed above. Please have your child's I.C.E. code number, listed at the top of this notice, included in your inquiry."

Crump handed the letter back to Dr. Trimble. "I went to State Schools, so you'll need to help me. What happened here?" he asked.

The Doctor glanced at the letter. "Kind of a sick joke, if you want my opinion. We got this thing after this 'grace' period had already expired. We tried contacting U.S.C.I.S., then I.C.E., and each time the people we spoke to claimed to know nothing about this change in status, or how to fix it. This is a kid who's about to get a semi-permanent feeding tube directly attached to her duodenal—"

"I'm sorry?" Crump interrupted.

"Her stomach and intestines—she's so anorexic she rips out the naso-gastric feeding tube. She's fourteen and has the body weight of a nine-year old. If she leaves the *building,* she's going to die, and the Government's telling us they're going to deport her."

Crump handed back the form letter. "What about the parents? They here legally?"

"We don't even know who her parents *are*—that comes with the initials, 'E. M.' We've been calling her 'Millie,' because she won't tell us her name. We think maybe it's something the parents warned her not to say."

Crump was slowly shaking his head, thinking his partner Maureen had stuck it to him again. He was supposed to be planning his retirement and instead, here he was, in this hospital ward full of kids who all seemed to be slowly, painfully disappearing. The case that brought him here—*Maureen's case*—involved a kid with no name, no parents and some Federal bureaucracy, about to stomp the kid to death.

Crump was tempted to say, "I think I'm in the wrong building," but the Doctor looked like she'd haunt him to his grave if he backed out, and then, there was that Giampetro guy…..

So, he asked, "Where'd she come from and how'd she get here?"

"We don't know much—only that she was one of those kids the Feds separated from their parents when they crossed the Mexican border. The Stuggs Administration was spouting some baloney about needing to isolate the kids because the border crossings were illegal, so their parents were dangerous criminals. They'd scoot the kids away, bussing them all over the Country in the middle of the night. Millie, E. M., came from a group they had holed up in chicken-wire cages set up in the National Guard Armory, over in Edgewater. Once she got there, she just stopped eating. When she became dangerously anorexic, the staffers brought her here."

Crump was thinking that if there truly was a God after all, and the only humane aspect of your child-detention program was using chicken-wire cages instead of razor-wire cages, you were probably going to pay for it someday. Without looking up, he injected, "I still don't get it—then who applied for this, this 'waiver', whatever it is, the thing they're cancelling with this notice? Somebody must have applied to put the kid in this program—"

"I did that," Doctor Trimble interrupted. "One of the best-kept secrets in the world is that the Doctors and Nurses in Adolescent wards become surrogate parents to these kids. Half of them are bullying victims, the other half sent here when they've been injured or sickened in abuse and neglect situations, placed here by the Juvenile Court. We use something we call 'Medically Inappropriate Discharge Orders' to keep the kids in the pediatric hospital wards until it's safe to let them out."

Crump nodded—he'd actually seen that game being played by doctors and nurses. "So, the Court—"

"—Or, just as often, the Hospital Administration—" the Doctor interrupted—

"—they say, 'She's cured. Time to send Itsy-Bitsy-Schmitzy back to her folks', and you guys say, 'That would be a 'medically inappropriate discharge', and Schmitzy stays here until they come up with something better," Crump offered, giving his estimation of the somewhat legit, somewhat illigit, institutional scam.

"Right," Doctor Trimble acknowledged. "So, the first time a D.H.S. squad showed up asking about Millie, she was in no condition to be moved. I sent them packing with a 'no-discharge' order. Then I found out about this Medical Deferral Program on the Internet. I figured if H.H.S. and U.S.C.I.S. had no idea who her real parents were, it'd be none of their business picking apart a deferral application from her surrogate parent. So, I applied, and if anybody asks, the official word is that I did it with no help from the Hospital's lawyers."

"Hmmm," Crump observed, scratching his head. "So, now, the Big Boys in U.S.C.I.S. want to kick her out of the Country?"

"I'm not exaggerating—she'll die if she's forced to leave."

"They can't be serious about this," Crump reflected. "I mean, if this really is a 'policy change', it's got to impact hundreds of kids and adults."

"Try thousands, if you're talking the whole U.S.A."

"The publicity alone would hammer the Administration. Even for President 'The Very Reverend Stuggs', this is a bone-headed move. Ham-fisted, even for *him*," Crump observed.

Dr. Trimble nodded silently, raising an eyebrow in a What-else-is-new? gesture. "They're going to kill thousands of sick people with this thing, and it's got nothing to do with protecting the Public. You ask me, this is an act of *terrorism*. They want the folks in Mexico and Central America who are thinking about heading for the U.S. border to say, 'My God, they're going to take my kids away from me, and then, if they get sick, they're gonna kill 'em'. President Stuggs and his staffers are hoping this'll scare them into staying home."

Crump stepped away, then looked back out into the common room. The ghost kid in the wheelchair was still there, being tended to by his parents. He turned back and asked to see the letter again. "Can you make me a copy of this, this *thing?*" he asked.

Crump stood at the kiosk while Doctor Trimble disappeared into an office. When the Doctor returned, he asked, "So, you want me to find a way to stop this?"

"Right," she answered, nodding.

Crump stuffed the copy into his briefcase. "Here's the problem," he began. "Because she's a kid, she can't personally hire a lawyer, any more than she can open a bank account or go buy a house—no legal capacity to contract. I could represent you folks—the Hospital Corporation—but it's kind of bloodless. Nobody cares what the clanking machinery of the American Healthcare Delivery System thinks about child welfare. I'll need to get a guardian appointed to represent her *as a person*, some adult who can stand in for her and sue the stuffing out of these characters at Immigration Enforcement."

The Doctor cocked her head. "O.K., I'd do that," she offered.

Crump offered a warning. "I feel obligated to tell you that you don't know what you're getting into—"

"I do this kind of stuff all the time."

"O.K., but because she's fourteen, *she* gets to pick: A minor gets to nominate her own guardian, something they do so a kid can choose a parent for cases like divorces. That rule applies to *all* kids, fourteen and over. I'll need to interview her, and then she needs to sign the guardianship petition. That means I'll need to ask her who she wants to appoint."

"You speak Spanish?" Dr. Trimble asked.

"A little….." Crump paused, then held up his thumb and forefinger like he was fishing for flying objects, "—*Un poco*. It's been a while, like high school and college. No hábla Ingles? She speak any English?"

"'Fraid not, but I can help some. I'm semi-literate. Follow me."

Doctor Trimble circled the divider and brushed past Crump, leading him into the common room and past the disappearing kid in the wheelchair. "We can change schools……" Crump heard the child's mother say, leaning into him in a low, pleading voice.

They filed down a surprisingly darkened hallway and turned into an open room with one bed and one child.

E.M., the teenager they called "Millie", was sitting on the bed, wearing jeans and a tee shirt, staring into space. There was an I.V. tube running from a drip-bag into a bandage on the top of her left hand. She had long, brown, dull and lusterless hair, parted in the middle and drooping over her face like she was hiding, peeking out to see if the coast was clear. She looked like a cross between the kids' images Crump had seen pasted on the sides of milk cartons, announcing they'd been abducted, and the quarter profile pictures in high school yearbooks, those fourteen-year-olds staring off into nowhere.

Dr. Trimble spoke first. "Tú tiene un visitante," she announced. "You have a visitor," Dr. Trimble whispered to Crump, not certain he could follow.

The kid didn't move. Crump could barely hear her when she replied, "¿Ha visto a mi madre?"

"I *look* like her Mother?" Crump whispered to the Doctor.

"You are pretty rusty," Dr. Trimble whispered back. "She's asking if you've *seen* her Mother."

Crump realized, just like that, they were at a fork in the road. The kid looked half dead already, her image, classic nightmare fodder for the rest of his life. He figured he could play it straight, get a simple consent and dump the case back on his partner Maureen when she returned, or he could stick his nose into it and almost certainly blow it up. While he was tired down into his bones, daydreaming for hours some days about retirement, there was this thing about a kid searching for her mother that nibbled at a small, dying chunk of his brain that barely remembered the mother he'd lost, the one who'd abandoned him as a seven-year-old kid in a crowded movie theater……

"Sí—" he began, when the Doctor jumped in.

"*Yes?*" Dr. Trimble asked, startled and thinking, What's going on here?

"Está….uuhh…..preocupada por ti," Crump added. Almost to reassure himself that he got it right, he translated, "She's worried about you."

Dr. Trimble shot Crump an angry dagger stare, then grabbed his elbow and yanked him out of the room, closing the door behind them.

"What the *Hell* are you doing?" she began, her arms crossed. "You're *lying* to that child—"

"Yes, I am. If you have a better idea, let me know, otherwise, let me do this."

"I don't think this is ethical—"

"You're absolutely right, and before we leave, I'll give you the number of the Disciplinary Commission, and you can report me and ask them to tag my otherwise worthless law license, but if you want this kid to live long enough for me to sort this out, she's going to need to start eating. She looks like if you put a feeding tube in her belly, it's gonna come out the other side. There's nothing left in between."

Doctor Trimble was practically sputtering. "Look, if you build up that kid's expectations, she's just going to sink deeper into depression," she complained, her head almost vibrating.

Crump raised his shoulders. "Then, I guess I'm just gonna have to find her Mother," he said, as he walked out to the common room and retrieved his briefcase. He took out a stack of forms. "I need to start with getting you appointed her guardian, so I can sue the Federal Government on her behalf. First, we need to stop this deportation thing, then, when that's on hold, I'll try to figure out what they did with Mom."

"I've already asked. The U.S.C.I.S. people say they have no idea."

"You asked *politely*, all doctorly. I'm gonna stick a court order up somebody's….uuhh….." He paused. "Well, you get the idea. Now, you sign here," he said, setting the form against his briefcase.

"We take all the pens away—pens can be used for self-harm. I'll need to go grab one from lock up."

When she returned, they re-entered the child's room. There was a marked change in the kid's demeanor. She was sitting up, looking at them as they entered.

Good, Crump thought. Momentarily forgetting the language barrier, he announced, "I'll need you to sign these forms, so you ask the Doctor here to be your helper. Then, the Doctor and I can bring your Mother back here."

Doctor Trimble interrupted with the Spanish translation, followed with, "¿Puedes escribir su nombre, tu verdadero nombre?"

Crump flattened the stack of forms on the end of the bed and handed the pen to the child U.S.C.I.S. was calling, "E. M.". Doctor Trimble whispered, "I asked her if she could write her real name on the form."

As they both watched in anticipation, the kid took the pen. At first, she fumbled with it, gripping it awkwardly, using coordination she hadn't mustered in months. Then, with a determination that almost punctured the stack of forms underneath the paper, she methodically wrote, "Estrellita Montes," in a kid's fractured version of cursive and printing. She handed the stack of documents to Crump, holding it up with the hand attached to the I.V. drip.

Crump took the forms. "Tell her, we need to make a deal. Tell her, if I'm gonna go find her Madre, then she's gotta let you do the nose tube, then, as soon as she can take it, she's gotta go back to eating. Tell her, otherwise, *No Deal.*"

Doctor Trimble escorted him back into the hallway. "You can't *negotiate* with this child, she's barely *alive*…." She paused, wondering just where the Volunteer Legal Clinic found this reckless cowboy.

"You got a better idea?" Crump asked.

Doctor Trimble was shaking her head, rolling her eyes upward. "I just hope you're serious about this," she said.

"I wasn't, when I came in. I was just kicking the can down the road until my partner could get her butt down here." He stopped, held up the form for her to glimpse the signature. "You see her name? 'Estrellita Montes'—or, if you're a Fed-paper-pusher, 'E.M.' Those *bastards* know her real name. This is essentially a Government kidnapping."

The doctor went back in, Crump in tow. She translated Crump's proposed bargain.

Estrellita slowly nodded.

"Bueno," Crump offered, smiling. He couldn't think of anything else to do, so he offered her his hand, and, remarkably, she shook on it.

When they went back into the common room and Crump packed up, the disappearing wheelchair boy was still there, his parents looking confounded as they tried to console him.

Crump stopped. Looking at the kid was painful. Taking in the entire ward was torture. Somebody was bullying these people, bullying some of them literally to death. The scene was brain poison to Crump, who, after forty-four years as a lawyer, could only muster one thought: There was no way this was all happening without somebody breaking the law.

He walked up to the three helpless-looking victims of *something*. They all looked up.

"What happened to you?" he asked the kid. The boy looked at Crump, silently. His parents seemed alarmed. The Father started to rise, when Crump smiled and added, "You were supposed to say, 'You should have seen the *other* guy.'"

By now the Father was standing, about to ask Crump just what he was doing, invading their space.

"Something bad happened here." He paused. "I'm a lawyer," Crump announced, holding out a business card for the Parents to take. "Call me."

2.
DO IT LIKE THEY DO IT IN THE TEN COMMANDMENTS.......

"**T**HIS IS ALL *YOUR* FAULT."

Crump's relationship with his law partner, Maureen McDougal, hadn't changed much in the twenty-five years they'd been working together: He blamed her for constantly getting him into trouble; she blamed him for the same thing; and, somehow, they seemed to co-exist in this never-ending, music-less opera of cross-accusation.

"*My* fault? You were just supposed to go out there and conduct an intake interview. Now, all of a sudden, we're taking on half the Government in some endless crusade, and to boot, we're not getting paid?" Maureen asked, simmering.

"Probably, it's more like the *entire* Government, if you want to get technical about it."

They were sitting in Maureen's office, debating what to do about the Federal case Crump had impulsively taken on in the course of running an errand for Maureen. Even pushing fifty, Maureen looked like an angry, pissed-off version of the runner up Miss Ireland in some pageant, with floppy, wind-tossed red hair and green eyes so intense her stare seemed radioactive.

"I finally caught up with this Doctor Trimble—you actually *told* her we were going to find the Kid's mother? How're we supposed to accomplish *that*?"

Crump looked out the window. "I don't know—how hard can it be? You Gen X'ers are always livin' it up on the Internet. Why not search for her there? Look, I didn't volunteer for this thing—you did—I'm supposed to be planning my retirement, not taking on bottomless pro bono cases."

"*Crump—*"

"I'm tellin' you, you had to *be* there. This Kid was *dying*. I had to do something, and it's all I could think of, just standing around, feeling stupid. And, that was before I found out President Stuggs and his goose steppers were lying, telling everybody they don't even know the kid's name. Somewhere, there's somebody knows exactly who these kids are, and where they've stashed their folks."

Maureen looked at the U.S.C.I.S. notice from the immigration authorities, threatening to boot the kid out of the hospital and out of the Country. "Yeah? Well, it looks like all they've given her so far is *a number—*"

"Last time around a Country tried this, they tattooed it on their forearms."

"You're not helping—you want me to put *that* in a pleading I'm going to file in Federal Court, under oath?" Maureen asked.

"Maybe."

Maureen rolled her eyes. "Look, I get it. This is obviously part of Stuggs's efforts to slice and dice the Country up by vilifying immigrants, and getting the old guys who love his schtick to spit and sputter along with him. I'm just not sure how to translate that into a Federal Civil Rights lawsuit that will save this kid's life," she complained.

"You're overthinking it," Crump responded. "We don't need to win this thing. The average lifespan of a lawsuit in this country is three years, and by that time, people will be so sick of Stuggs they'll vote for the 'Anti-Stuggs'. We only need to get some publicity, then watch President Stuggs and his Attorney General stand up in open court and tell everybody why they're allowed to torture families and kill kids. Just come up with something so compelling that we survive an early Government motion to toss out the case, then go on to win the injunction hearing, so we can freeze the deportation while we drag it out."

"Oh, great, *that's all*—"

"Hey, you guys put Stuggs in office……" Crump declared, as he lapsed into his recurring argument that Maureen, a devout Catholic, and her fellow bible thumpers were responsible for the Presidential election of a narcissistic crackpot like H. Stennis Stuggs. A former Southern Preacher and Televangelist-turned-Governor, whose unofficial nickname was "Deuteronomy Stuggs," Stuggs had run as a Republican on a Nationalist, Anti-Immigration, Anti-Abortion, Anti-Crime platform. His campaign slogan, abbreviated as an acronym on rallying caps worn by the faithful at his political events, was "**G**et **A**merica **P**raying **A**gain," or "GAPA", something his supporters enthusiastically chanted at his rallies.

Few in the Media had given him a serious shot at winning the Presidential Election, but that viewpoint turned out to be largely the product of scrunched-faced disaffected voters, lying to the exit-polls about their support of the bigoted, glorified talk-show host. He'd run against a candidate with an Ivy-League education and the personality of that annoying, rabbit-handed school kid in the front row who always raised their hand to let everybody know they were smarter than you were, and, unlike *you,* they'd read the homework assignment. Stunned commentators attributed Stuggs' victory to his broad-based media persona, preaching vaguely hateful rants about preserving old-fashioned values and bringing back the Good Old Days. Crump wasn't buying any of it—he just figured the table-pounders who voted for Stuggs wanted to punish everybody else for having views that seemed counter-cultural, an attitude about Government hand-outs that sounded vaguely Socialist and generally, for not being White enough.

"How could people who've supposedly read The Sermon On the Mount, vote for a dangerous, bigoted crackpot like Stuggs?" Crump would ask, peppering Maureen.

"Devout Catholics tend to be single-issue voters," she'd say. "Put anybody—what the Hell, a talking monkey—anybody on the ballot who says they're going to appoint anti-abortion judges, and they line up. Hey, *I* didn't vote for the guy."

* *

After a week of on-again, off-again research, Maureen was stuck. She lacked Crump's reckless disregard for authority and complete disdain for conventionality, which meant that rationality and real-world risk assessment were holding her back.

"I'm stumped," Maureen admitted. "How do you successfully sue these people? Don't the Feds get to set these immigration policies?"

Crump held up a finger, in an "I got it" gesture. "Stuggs is a Preacher, a Man of the Cloth. Why not plead it like he's violating the Ten Commandments: Count One: 'Thou shalt not kill kids'; Count Two: 'Thou shalt not kidnap kids'; Count Three: 'Thou shalt not *lie* about kidnapping kids….' etcetera, etcetera. Zap them with the legal basis for punishing each sin they're committing. Do ten separate counts, and punctuate them with fancy numerals at the top, just like those stone tablets Moses was carting around during the Exodus."

"If you're trying to impress me with your religious training, it's not working—"

"My religious training consists of flunking out of Seminary after one semester," Crump offered.

"How do I get to *ten*?" Maureen asked. "The first five Commandments are all about going to church on Sundays, and then there's adultery—"

"I have to do *everything* around here?" Crump complained. "My copy says, 'Thou shalt not kill,' *not*, 'Thou shalt not kill, unless you go *real, real slow*.'"

"Nice optics, but what laws are they breaking?" Maureen wondered aloud.

"It's not like you're dealing with some jerk in the parking lot of the liquor store—when the Government intentionally does mean, stupid, dangerous stuff to you, they're violating the Constitution," Crump offered.

"Even if you're not exactly a registered green-card holder?"

"Yeah, the Constitution's full of 'personhood' stuff that applies to 'persons', not just citizens."

"Hmmm," Maureen wondered, not fully convinced.

"No, really. I just got off the phone with our old buddy Steve Barnacle, who's looking for a job. He wants to join us. Steve quit the U.S. Attorney's Office as soon as Stuggs got elected. He tells me there's already a class action lawsuit out in California on the family-separation-at-the-border thing. Seems like there's a credible Fifth Amendment, Due Process argument there, and it sounds like the Civil Liberties outfits are winning. Let's check out adding E.M. as a class member in that case. Barnacle says we're on our own for these medical-patient deportations—that policy is too new to have attracted any lawsuits yet. My guess is these medical deportations probably violate Title III and Title VI of the 1964 Civil Rights Act. There ought to be something juicy you can say about kicking a dying kid out of the hospital, when the Government kidnapped her and *made* her into a dying kid."

* *

It had been a little over a week since Crump had visited the Adolescent Psych Ward, so he'd stopped obsessing about the disappearing kid in the wheelchair.

When Sophie, his secretary, called out the names of a couple of callers on hold, he didn't immediately make the connection.

"Who?" he asked.

Sophie wandered into his office. "The Lockwoods--somebody you met out at St. Vincent's—said you gave them your card."

"Oh, yeah. I'll take it in here," he said, as he punched up his speaker phone.

"Mr. Crump, is this a good time? I'm Susan Lockwood, Brian's mom. My husband Bill's on the line, too. You met us at the hospital last week."

Crump strapped on a headset and took them off speaker to keep the call private. "Sure, this is fine. I hope I didn't freak out your son."

"No," she offered. "In fact, right after you left, Brian got the joke about 'the other guy', the same time as my husband, and they had a good laugh over it. It was the first time in over a month we'd heard him laugh about anything."

Crump rubbed his forehead and closed his eyes. "Sorry, I was so shaken up just seeing the place, and then, looking at your son, I felt like I had to say something. The older I get, the worse I am at minding my own business. What happened to Brian, I mean, how'd he get so...." Crump paused. So *what*?

"That's what we wanted to talk to you about. What kind of law do you do, I mean, do you do investigations?"

"Investigations?" Crump asked. "I'm a probate lawyer—decedent's estates, wills, trusts, guardianships for kids and old people, mental health cases and lawsuits over all that stuff. Any legal work starts with basic fact gathering, although for complex cases, I use a private investigator. What do you think you need to investigate?"

There was a pause. "Are you our lawyer?" Mr. Lockwood asked.

After Crump explained that the call was confidential, no matter what, Mrs. Lockwood launched in, sounding like she'd been dying to share this with *somebody*.

"Our son is in eight grade at Carrington Middle School, here in the City. He'd been doing fine, so far as we knew, but for a few months now, he'd been losing weight and then, just refusing to eat. We'd never really known anything about anorexia, but a few weeks ago, my husband held up a single raspberry and begged my son to eat it, and he refused. He hadn't eaten in days.

"We took him to the hospital, figuring it was digestive or something, but when we got there, the doctor at the E.R. asked him what was wrong and he clammed up and wouldn't say a word, so they transferred us to the psychiatric ward. Doctor Trimble started asking Brian what was wrong, and all of a sudden, he just started talking about all these kids and what they were doing to him, calling him 'gay' and 'pussy' and 'faggot'—stuff I hadn't heard *in years*. He said there were a couple of kids who were knocking him around and threatening him, saying things like, 'Tell anybody and we'll kill ya.' I know—these are thirteen and fourteen-year-olds." She paused. "I mean, we never gave him a phone and monitored his computer use, for just this reason."

"Anyway, then Brian reached into his pocket and pulled out a stuffed envelope. The papers inside were pages printed out from the internet, and when we unfolded them, out popped a razor blade. He told Doctor Trimble that the kids were leaving these envelopes in his locker. There was scribbling on the first page that said, 'Why don't you just kill yourself, faggot? Cut along the veins.' The printout was a set of detailed instructions on how to commit suicide by slashing your wrists *the right way*."

She was barely holding it together. "Doctor Trimble explained that Brian was becoming anorexic. When she asked him why he'd stopped eating, he said, 'Cause, I just want to die.'"

She stopped, just long enough to compose herself. Crump took the moment to consider that it was actually humanly possible for him to be even *more* pissed off than he'd been a week ago, his first time at the Adolescent Psych Ward.

Mr. Lockwood chimed in. "When we went to see Ralph Westheimer—"

"Who?" Crump stopped him.

"—the Principal at Carrington, he acted like this was all news to him—claimed neither he nor the faculty knew anything about it, which was weird, since we'd just told him it was happening. So, I asked, 'If we just told you, and you didn't know before that, then how can you possibly say that the faculty are clueless?' He got all defensive. He said, 'Well, if you're going to be like *that*, I guess I'll just have to have our lawyers call you.' We were pretty angry. When I called a couple of parents of Brian's classmates, one of them started to cry. She wouldn't say much, but she admitted that her daughter had complained about what was happening to Brian."

They paused.

"How's your son doing?" Crump asked.

"Not well," Susan Lockwood jumped in. "He seems to barely tolerate a feeding tube, and he's still not eating. My husband thinks this is like a hunger strike. Doctor Trimble says anorexia is a psycho-social disease, and finding out what happened could help in his therapy. When you gave us your card, we decided we'd talk to you about doing an investigation, like, maybe it would help—"

Bill Lockwood interrupted with, "Either way, we're pulling Brian out of Carrington."

Crump sat back and exhaled loudly. "Yes, I can handle this. I think, for now, you need to back out of the process and just focus on getting your son healthy. I'll have my partner, Maureen McDougal, call you to get basic background information. Let us dig into what's happening at the school."

Crump hung up after getting their number. He walked into Maureen's office and relayed the entire scenario, beginning with the kid's appearance at the psych ward. "I just want to thank you, again, for letting me sub for you at St. Vincent's last week. Now we have *two* of these cases."

"Don't *start*….." Maureen warned, tossing her unfinished "E.M." complaint across the desk at Crump.

He sat down across from her, picked up and scanned the complaint. Maureen was suing U.S.C.I.S., I.C.E., a half dozen other Federal agencies, the director of Federal Immigration Services, and, for good measure, the Attorney General of the United States, Warren Handler. Handler was orchestrating the entire process and defending the Stuggs administration, when they took flak for their treatment of people crossing the Mexican border into the U.S.

"Yes, I thought, while we're at it, we'd sue that walking, talking shit-sack, Warren Handler."

Crump nodded silently, as he skimmed the draft. He looked up. "You're up to count ten—I think I've got a tenth commandment to throw at them. Something Doctor Trimble said got me thinking—she called all this medical deportation business an 'Act of Terrorism'. She thought the Stuggs administration was doing this stuff to terrorize folks in Mexico and Central America out of crossing the border, even if they were legal asylum seekers, people who were supposed to get a judicial hearing, not the run-around while we kidnap their kids."

He paused, thinking it over. "Remember all that stuff they passed right after 9-11, bunch of laws designed to punish, deter and prevent terrorism?"

"Sure," Maureen chimed in. "The Patriot Act." She paused. "Didn't that thing expire when some paranoid congressman got worried his cellphone would get pinched by the FBI?"

"Right, parts of it, but not the whole thing. I looked it up once for something, a couple of years ago. One thing I remember is that Title Six of the Patriot Act was designed to allow private victims of terrorism to personally seek civil remedies under the Act. That's still around."

"It's not limited to criminal enforcement by the Feds?" Maureen asked.

"There's that, too, but they also let victims sue for civil remedies, like getting money from the bad guys and dismantling their terror operations. Why don't you toss in another count in the complaint, calling these folks in the Stuggs Administration terrorists and accusing them of violating the Patriot Act? It'll piss them off and get their attention."

Maureen took the draft back from Crump. "You're serious? I mean, nobody thinks The Patriot Act means *that*—"

"Yeah, and before 1954, nobody thought the Equal Protection Clause of the Constitution meant you couldn't send white kids to one school and black kids to another, until Thurgood Marshall had the guts to say that segregation was bullshit. Go ahead, throw the book at 'em, call them all terrorists. It'll eventually get laughed out of Court, but at least for a while, let them think we're going to get mega-damages from the Government and dismantle their Official Shake Down at the Border. It'll be fun while it lasts—If there's one thing the Very Reverend, President Deuteronomy Stuggs understands, it's somebody trying to pick his pocket."

3.
EITHER THESE WORDS MEAN SOMETHING, OR THEY DON'T......

"This is Svetlana Armstrong at the Times. Is this Attorney Crump?"

Crump instinctively held the phone away from his ear. "That didn't take long," he said to himself, and he punched a button, placing her on speaker phone. "Warming up the local economy again? Whose retirement did you enhance this time?" he asked.

"C'mon, Crump. Can we do this, just once, without you giving me shit?" she pleaded.

Reporter Svetlana Armstrong had been bugging Crump for almost forty years, every time he filed any kind of newsworthy lawsuit in the local courts. She'd call, asking for details and backstory not apparent in the public records. Instead of answering, Crump would needle her about just how it was she always managed to pick his heater cases out of the scrum of thousands of traffic accidents and slip-and-falls, filed in the courts every week. Armstrong's under-the-counter payments to the court clerks, designed to give her first dibs on big cases, were so effective that half the time she was on

Crump's phone, on hold, waiting for him as soon as he walked back from the courthouse after filing a complaint. She'd routinely ignore his ribbing about paying off the court clerks, then he'd refuse to answer Armstrong's questions, even though his denials effectively ended up answering them all.

"According to your complaint, U.S.C.I.S., I.C.E. and most of the United States Justice Department are threatening to murder a child they effectively kidnapped, when they separated her from her mother, crossing the border into the U.S.—"

"The complaint speaks for itself, Ms. Armstrong," Crump interrupted.

"So, you expect the Court to enjoin Stuggs and I.C.E., to stop the Government from deporting her out of St. Vincent's, where she's currently receiving critical, life-saving medical treatment—"

"As I said, the complaint speaks for itself," Crump repeated.

"This child—"

"She has a name," Crump offered. "E. M."

"What's with the initials?"

"We customarily only identify minors in lawsuits with initials, although she got those special delivery from U.S. Citizenship and Immigration Services," Crump added.

"About that—your complaint states that the Government actually knows both her true identity, as well as the names and custodial locations of her parents, and they are just keeping it all secret to prevent the re-unification of these families, and I quote: '….to frighten and terrorize potential asylum seekers and others from even attempting to cross the border from Mexico into the U.S., in furtherance of the Stuggs' administration's new 'Zero Tolerance' policy of curbing both legal and illegal immigration—'"

"Again, Ms. Armstrong, you've proved you are an adept interpreter of legal documents."

"C'mon, Crump. Is this for real? You're labelling half the Stuggs Administration as Terrorists."

"You're reading a verified complaint, signed under oath by E.M.'s court-appointed guardian, Doctor Trimble. The Doctor is swearing before God that it's all true. Seems to me, you should be asking the U.S. Attorney's office how they intend to respond to our complaint. In the meantime, just be sure to give Christmas baskets to all those folks down at the Courthouse, who are pulling these heater files for you and tipping you off—"

She hung up.

Crump jogged down the hall to give Maureen a heads-up.

"Better plan to go in the back door at the Courthouse—Svetlana Armstrong just called. She's got her hands on the E.M. complaint, so she'll be there, maybe even with a camera crew," Crump warned, as he walked in to Maureen's office.

Maureen shook her head, looking up at the heavens. "I thought she only had court clerks on the take over in *State* Court. Sounds like she's franchised her operation."

"Yeah, I'm not crazy about this. We got a pretty good draw with the Chief Judge, Sharon Haverhorn. I hope we don't freak her out with a bunch of reporters packed into the courtroom, scribbling down her every word."

"Hmmm," Maureen observed. "You're surprised? You were thinking that labelling half the Stuggs Administration as terrorists was going to fly under the radar? You said you *wanted* publicity." She paused. "And, why is the Chief Judge such a good draw for us?"

"One, she was appointed by the guy four Presidents ago, not Stuggs; two, she's a stickler for detail and follows the law religiously; three, she's exactly my age—we were sworn in together, meaning she's nearing retirement and doesn't give a shit what anybody thinks; and four....." Crump paused.

"You were going to say, 'She's a woman?'"

"You said that, not me," Crump finished, defensively. "Yeah, I'm betting that letting an I.C.E. Goon Squad kill a kid, just to appease the anti-immigrant droolers in Stuggs' political base, is a lever she won't pull."

"As long as she doesn't decide to punish us for your little Patriot Act stunt," Maureen observed, stuffing the files into her bag. "Shall we head over?"

Crump started to back out. "No, you go over without me—I've got an appointment with the school principal at Carrington, and all the U.S. Attorney will ask for today is a continuance to give them time to respond. I'm sure Judge Haverhorn will give you the temporary restraining order and block the deportation, until she can get her arms around the case."

"Thanks loads," Maureen said, as she air-slapped Crump, brushing past him in the doorway.

* *

Maureen McDougal was swearing under her breath, as she struggled through the crowd outside the Federal Courthouse in the City by the Lake. A woman in a fur hat managed to muscle her way through the throng and shove a microphone in her face.

"Svetlana Armstrong, for the Times," she shouted, straining to be heard over the crowd. "Is it true your client, Doctor Trimble, is labeling President Stuggs and his entire Administration as *terrorists*?"

Swell, Maureen thought. It'll be fun while it lasts.......

"No Comment," Maureen shouted, as she shoved and dodged her way into the revolving doors, then practically fell onto the conveyor belt that was running bags through the metal detector.

"Phones, purses, computers and coats on the conveyor," the deputy barked out. "Remove your belts and place them and the contents of your pockets in the doggie dishes, then place them on the conveyor."

Maureen quickly passed through the detector frame, gathering her belongings on the other side. She rode the elevator up to the twenty-third floor, to the courtroom of Chief Judge Sharon Haverhorn, only to find the entrance blocked by a group of people holding over-the-shoulder video equipment, adjusting their set ups to record people coming and going.

"That's *her*," somebody called out, and she was suddenly bathed in artificial light bright enough for dental work. She instinctively covered her eyes with the back of her hand.

"Is your client—"

"No Comment," Maureen called out.

"Can the Federal Government *be* guilty of terrorism?" another reporter shouted, angling a microphone at her.

"The complaint speaks for itself," Maureen shouted, as she turned, grabbed a door handle, and disappeared inside the courtroom.

"I'm gonna *kill* Crump," she swore, a little too loudly, an oath she repeated as soon as she saw the packed spectator gallery inside.

Federal courtrooms were designed to be intimidating in the first place: Dark wood-paneled walls rising to three-story-high ceilings, with the Judge elevated behind a high console surrounded by uniformed guys with guns and official looking people typing away at computers, surrounded by stacks of files. The visitors' gallery was cordoned off, so spectators couldn't get to the front of the courtroom without passing through a swinging gate. The space before the Judge, reserved for lawyers and witnesses, had two massive tables on either side and a microphoned podium in the middle.

On this day, the gallery area was filled to standing room capacity, almost entirely with people scribbling away at notepads and something she'd never seen: One guy, with no coat but a scarf still wrapped around his neck, holding a large artists' tablet. He was sketching away in broad strokes, making a rendering of the courtroom.

This just gets worse and worse, she thought to herself. She'd never been involved in a case where publicity *helped* the outcome.

There was a group of suited, nervous-looking types gathered around one counsel table. The only woman in the group was Regina Debevoise, an Assistant U.S. Attorney she'd known since law school. Debevoise approached Maureen, as she dumped her bag on a seat at the opposite table.

"I see Crump's not here," Debevoise observed. "He set you up."

"Set me up for *what*?"

"The Solicitor General's here, and he's *pissed off*. We're going to ask for sanctions against you, your client and your partner. You're all going to end up paying *our* bills."

Maureen pulled back. "Rule Eleven's pretty clear—to avoid sanctions for untrue pleadings, all we need to do is perform a reasonable inquiry, and have factual and legal bases for the Compliant. I'm comfortable we've done both," Maureen insisted.

"I don't make these decisions. All I can tell you is they think you're out to lunch on the Patriot Act claim, calling the Administration a bunch of terrorists, and they're looking for vengeance—"

"Then," Maureen interrupted, "You'll be consenting to the temporary restraining order, while we brief your sanctions claims?"

Debevoise started to shake her head. "The word on this one is, 'No agreements.'"

Just then, the Judge's clerk stood, and the Chief Judge Sharon Haverhorn entered the courtroom. She was tall, had sandy-brown hair and wore wire-rimmed glasses designed to enhance her authority. As the parties and onlookers all stood, the Judge motioned them to sit by waiving her hands downward.

"Call the first case," she announced.

"Dr. Amelia Trimble, Guardian and Next Friend of E.M., a Minor, versus United States Citizenship and Immigration Services, et. al.,......"

Maureen stood and identified herself as counsel to the Plaintiff Guardian. Then, a procession at the other table began.

"Your Honor, Regina Debevoise, Assistant U.S. Attorney, for U.S.C.I.S and the other defendants."

Half a dozen other attorneys stepped forward, methodically identifying themselves as counsel to the government, followed by the white-haired, older dignitary. "Quentin Peter Meadows, Solicitor General, for the United States," he announced, as the Judge looked up, somewhat startled.

"Mr. Meadows, to what do we owe this honor?" the Judge asked. "I thought your office's charter restricted you to representing the Presidential Administration before the Supreme Court?" The Judge seemed mildly annoyed, probably, Maureen figured, because the case was already drawing a circus to the courtroom.

Meadows, a tall, gray-suited grouch who looked to Maureen like he'd been selectively bred to join an all-male private club started by the crew of the Mayflower, snarled at Maureen as he announced, "We consider this case a libelous affront to the entire Stuggs Administration, the Justice Department and the Federal Government. We'll be seeking sanctions here against the Plaintiff. The claim that we are all 'terrorists', is obviously a publicity stunt, tossed in to prejudice the Court and deflect attention from the weakness of Plaintiff's underlying claims."

Sharon Haverhorn had been a District Court Judge for over twenty years, and the gulf between her politics and those of President Stuggs and his proteges would have made it difficult for them to so much as share a taxi from the airport. She was visibly bristling at the premature sanctions claim.

"Mr. Meadows, you are assuming I've read this complaint, which, up to now, was one of the several *hundred* filed in this District *this week*. I can see it must have something that got under your skin, so if you can allow me to review it, we'll try to address your concerns. Court is recessed."

The Judge disappeared into chambers. Maureen looked around and to her surprise, none of the reporters, not known for their generous attention spans, moved from their spots in the gallery.

Fifteen minutes later, Judge Haverhorn reappeared.

"Your Honor," Maureen said, as she stood, "While my opponent would like to make this hearing into a paid political announcement…." She paused, and glanced over at a bristling Q. Peter Meadows, who was actually trembling…. "We are here on my petition for a Temporary Restraining Order, blocking the deportation of our medically-compromised client's ward--"

Before the Judge could respond, Meadows, who'd been sweating and twitching, in one fluid motion, crossed the aisle to Maureen's side and shoved her shoulder, almost knocking her over.

"This *bogus* claim that a case of dedicated Federal employees, just doing their jobs, amounts to *terrorism*, is itself an act of *treason*, for which counsel and her client should be *prosecuted*—"

The Judge bounded to her feet. "*Mr. Meadows, you have exactly thirty seconds to apologize to counsel and take your seat immediately*," she ordered.

A flustered Meadows turned, trembling, and sat in a huff.

"One thing is clear to me," the Judge announced. "I will be granting your request for admission to practice in my courtroom, *so that if I see another such outburst, I can hold you in contempt, and, make no mistake, I…will…incarcerate…you….*" Judge Haverhorn added, returning to her seat.

The Judge composed herself. "Ms. Debevoise, what is your response to the T.R.O.?"

Meadows was shaking his head in seeming disbelief.

Debevoise rose to address the court. "Your Honor, this complaint is a libelous collection of falsehoods."

"Ms. Debevoise, last time I checked the libel laws, there was a complete privilege for statements made in the course of a court proceeding. Is someone on your team who's admitted to practice in the trial bar in this District, prepared to respond to the T.R.O.?"

"I was hoping to seek thirty days to respond to the complaint and the T.R.O.," Debevoise announced.

Maureen jumped in. "Your Honor, excuse me, but we are asking for a Temporary Restraining Order relating to a child's health and safety, and we noticed it up for this afternoon. I fail to see why Ms. Debevoise can't represent the Government *today*, at least for the T.R.O. hearing. A suspicious person might assume this is a delaying tactic."

There was shuffling in the gallery, while the Government team whispered among themselves at their counsel table, Meadows audibly cursing out the word, "treachery".

"Ms. Debevoise," the Judge asked, ignoring Meadows, "I assume if I give you time to respond to the motion, you'll agree to the entry of the temporary restraining order at least until you are prepared for a hearing?"

"Your Honor, the Government's position is 'No agreements'. As you can imagine, we typically regard doing 'The People's Business' as a sacred trust, and don't take lightly to having third parties interfere with the Wheels of Government."

Maureen started to object, anxiously wanting to say something about Debevoise referring to stopping U.S.C.I.S. from murdering her client as "*Interfering with the Wheels of Government*," but the Judge raised a hand and cut her off.

"I've had the opportunity, courtesy of Mr. Meadows, to review the T.R.O. pleadings. We have an affidavit from the Plaintiff Doctor, telling us that this child 'E.M.' will likely die if she is removed from the hospital, let alone deported. Ordinarily, I conduct T.R.O. hearings by affidavit only. I assume, Miss Debevoise, we can all agree that having a real, living child *die*, is the very textbook definition of 'suffering irreparable harm'?" the Judge inquired.

Meadows stood and smirked, as he spoke up. "Your honor, if I may, this child E.M. is just in a *psychiatric* ward—"

"People don't die in psychiatric wards?" the Judge interrupted.

"I'm not a doctor—"

"No, you're not, and the Court has not yet allowed you to again participate in this argument, given your prior outburst. Ms. Debevoise, do you have a doctor's affidavit, explaining that this is not a critical care situation where I need to concern myself with this child's mortality?"

"Your Honor, I don't, however—"

The Judge cut her off. "*However* will have to wait. Ms. McDougal, prepare an order granting your T.R.O., to remain in effect until we can schedule a hearing on a permanent injunction. Until then, nobody's going anywhere. Ms. Debevoise, give yourself thirty days to respond to all the pleadings. I assume that will set us over for today. And, Mr. Meadows, I'm ordering you, as a condition of appearing in my courtroom, to undergo a series of counselling sessions on anger management. See my clerk before you leave regarding your instructions."

Q. Peter Meadows pulled his Assistant U.S. Attorney aside, cupped his hand in front of her ear and whispered something.

"Your Honor," Debevoise offered, "the Government assumes we will be answering all but Count X of the complaint."

"Count X?" the Judge asked.

"The 'Patriot Act' Count…." She paused. "The one where Plaintiff Doctor Trimble alleges that several officials within the U.S. Government are essentially terrorists, violating the Patriot Act. We assume that Count X is a publicity stunt, and we now move to have Your Honor strike it from the complaint under Rule 12 (B)(6), on our oral motion. We'd also seek Rule Eleven pleading sanctions against Plaintiff Doctor Trimble and the law offices of Crump and McDougal, for including this ludicrous claim in their complaint."

Maureen stepped forward. "Your Honor, we stand behind the entire complaint, and as you have often reminded me, the federal courts do not favor Rule 12 motions to dismiss—"

"Wait," Judge Haverhorn interrupted. "Given the apparent gravity of that claim, allow me to review Count X. Everybody have a seat."

The courtroom went silent. The Judge donned reading glasses and began turning pages. After an agonizing few minutes, the Judge looked up.

"Ms. Debevoise, I assume you and your team have read the complaint?"

"Yes, your honor."

"So, you have seen the allegations—that taking this child away from her parents in the first place was a form of Government kidnapping—."

Meadows was trembling and couldn't control himself. He stood. "The Government is merely implementing sound immigration policy—"

"Wait, Mr. Meadows—let me finish," Judge Haverhorn implored, holding up a hand, "Stop Here" style. "Allow me to read from the Complaint. And I quote: 'The **Patriot Act** defines '**Terrorism**' as 'An attempt to intimidate or coerce a civilian population; to influence the policy of a government by intimidation or coercion; or to affect the conduct of a government; by mass destruction, assassination, or kidnapping.' The claim, as I understand it, is that U.S.C.I.S. and its personnel are attempting to coerce a civilian population of asylum seekers by organized kidnapping of their children." She stopped reading and looked across the courtroom. "If the allegations are true, and in a 12(B) motion I must assume they are true, then it seems to me we have an issue for trial."

Q. Peter Meadows was turning red. Debevoise placed a hand on his shoulder, sat him down and took over.

"Your Honor, it is not *possible* Congress intended that language to apply to the U.S. Government, or any of its subdivisions or officials, let alone allow private parties to sue," she argued. "First of all, from the somewhat circular claims they make, it's reasonably clear the 'terrorist acts' they allege against the Government consist of branding I.C.E. and U.S.C.I.S. agents as 'kidnappers,' for effectuating the current policy of child separations during illegal border crossings. When children are taken into custody with the authority of the State, that *can't,* as a matter of law, be 'kidnapping'. And, in any event, the Government is generally immune from suit, and can only be sued for money damages in the Court of Claims. This Count X should be dismissed, as a matter of law, and Plaintiff and her lawyers sanctioned with the costs of this proceeding."

Maureen's eyes widened. The reporters in the hallway weren't the only people taking Crump's crazy idea seriously. "May I?" Maureen asked, and the Judge nodded.

"Title VI of the Patriot Act is called 'Providing for Victims of Terrorism, Public Safety Officers and Their Families.' It specifically broadens the Victims of Crime Act and ties that statute into the Patriot Act. The *only* purpose of this provision is to allow private, victim-driven lawsuits against terrorists. Your Honor has broad jurisdiction, including power to sit as a Judge in the Court of Claims. Federal Immunity only runs to routine administrative actions by Federal Officials undertaken within the scope of their employment— *intentional* wrongdoing is an exception to immunity under the Federal Tort Claims Act." She stopped, letting it all sink in. "I assume the Government isn't here arguing that alleged acts of terrorism are within the scope of anybody's employment—"

"Your *Honor*," Debevoise tried to intercede.

"Let her finish," the Judge ordered.

"As for her argument that the Feds *can't* be kidnappers, because they act with the power of the State, let me argue this: Suppose a man drives by a school playground, sees a fight breaking out, recognizes a neighbor child about to walk into it all. He pulls up, opens his car door and says, 'Sally, I'm your neighbor—get in—bad things are happening at your school,' and she does and he drives her back to school when things blow over. Now, change things just a little—he notices the same child, doesn't really care about what's happening at the school, he just sees this as an opportunity. He makes the same offer of assistance and the child gets in his car. He drives around for fifteen minutes, planning to do her harm. He then panics, thinking about the consequences and drops her off unharmed in the exact same place. The situations are nearly identical, but the second one is kidnapping, the first one the act of a Good Samaritan. The only difference?" She paused, pointing a finger at her temple. "What's in the man's *head*, his *intentions*. Intent is always a question of fact, and facts get uncovered at trial, so dismissal as a matter of law is uncalled for here."

"Your *Honor*," Debevoise injected.

"I wasn't finished," Maureen complained, barreling on ahead. "As to the argument that Congress didn't intend to apply The Patriot Act to the conduct of individuals employed by the Federal Government, if Congress had meant to distinguish between 'Good' Terrorists and 'Bad' Terrorists, they would have said so…." She paused for effect. "But it's hard to imagine why, in writing sweeping legislation designed to eradicate terrorism, punish terrorists and dismantle their operations, Congress would have given *anybody* a free bite at the terrorist apple."

"Your *Honor, seriously*—" Meadows injected.

The Judge ignored Meadows, speaking directly to his local counsel. "Ms. Debevoise, the allegation here is that the U.S. Government has enacted and then undertaken implementation of *both* policies—separating children from their parents at the border and then deporting sick children in Government immigration custody—to fearfully alter and influence the decisions of those seeking asylum and otherwise intending to migrate to the U.S. Border. This intimidation is alleged to be a form of terror, with the threat of what is, it is argued, kidnapping and then medical abuse and mistreatment. Count X alleges that to effectuate this terror objective, those children of border crossers are then effectively, if not actually, kidnapped. To finish the job, if those children, while in U.S. custody, become ill and dependent on critical medical intervention, they are then threatened with deportation, thrown into near certain life-threatening situations."

"We understand the *allegations*," Debevoise argued. "Those all relate to basic Government functions—"

"Ms. Debevoise, the language I'm reading, defining 'Terrorism', is lifted word-for-word from the Patriot Act's definition of that term, quoted at page thirty-seven of the complaint. You want to argue for dismissal without trial, I must take all the allegations as true."

She paused. The Judge could see the reporters scribbling furiously. "Either these words in the Patriot Act *mean* something, *or they don't*. I'm not dismissing Count X. Have your order reflect that I've denied the Government's 12(B)(6) motion as to Count X. Answer the *entire* complaint within thirty days. Request for sanctions is denied."

4.
MEMBERS OF THIS COMMUNITY THREATEN TO IMMOLATE THEMSELVES..........

C RUMP FIGURED CARRINGTON PREP WOULD look a lot older. It had been around for almost a hundred years, one of the first private schools in the City by the Lake. It was known as a place where parents had to enroll their kids in preschool and give real money at fund-raising benefits, if they had any hope of securing permanent enrollment. Carrington was located in a modern, big-windowed facility in a decent neighborhood north of downtown, and the kids filing in and out looked well fed and carefully dressed. A casual passer-by would never have imagined it could be Hell In A Very Small Place.

When he'd called to set up the meeting with Ralph Westheimer, calling him "the Principal", the man had quickly corrected him: "Head of School" he'd insisted, arguing that "Principal" sent an authoritarian message.

Westheimer's office was decked out with lots of diplomas and citations on the walls, shelves full of books about educational philosophy and a dozen trophies. When Crump was ushered in, Westheimer stood to greet him. He looked like he'd auditioned for the part of headmaster in some exclusive boarding school founded by Pilgrims. He was balding but crew-cut, with a narrow face and a scotch plaid bowtie. He was wearing a rumpled, tweedy-gray-colored suit with suspenders.

"You guys must have some killer athletic teams," Crump commented, glancing at the trophies as he was about to go through introductions, when Westheimer corrected him.

"Those are all for Progressive Bowl. We take first place pretty regularly."

"Progressive Bowl?" Crump couldn't resist asking, thinking it sounded like an eco-friendly toilet of some sort.

"The American Association of Progressive Schools has a competition every year where the students square off, answering questions about the traditions of progressive education—"

"John Dewey pens the progressive bible, 'Human Nature and Conduct'; Mark Hopkins, sitting on one end of a log, with a student on the other end; and all that stuff," Crump interrupted.

Westheimer smiled. "When and where was the first kindergarten founded?" he asked, relishing anybody who didn't find Progressive Education trivia deadly boring and burningly annoying.

"Hmmm…." Crump faked struggling for recall…."Watertown, Wisconsin, 1856?"

"You know your progressive ed history," Westheimer said, smiling.

"I have a photographic memory and I taught grade school for a year before I went to law school," Crump said, offering his hand to shake.

Westheimer shook and said, "Ralph Westheimer, PhD," then left quickly to usher in his attorney, who was waiting in another room.

Crump was left imagining those poor, bored Progressive Bowl participants, pounding their buzzers in answer to utterly obscure brain-teasers, when Johnny Rose, a lawyer Crump recognized from an old case, entered with Westheimer.

"Crump, Johnny Rose here. I'll be representing Carrington Prep. I understand this is about an alleged bullying incident."

"Well, it's more than 'an incident,'" Crump said, as they all sat.

Crump reached in his breast pocket for an envelope, when Rose stopped him, holding out an upraised hand as he blurted, "Wooaaa…..We only agreed to this discussion on the condition it not be recorded," Rose began.

"Uuhh, O.K.," Crump stammered. "I don't think I've ever recorded a meeting in forty-three years of practicing law. Is that a thing now?"

"Just asking," Rose countered.

Crump began. "I assume we're all here for the same reason—there's a kid in the hospital, a student enrolled here, and he's fighting for his life, so we all want to see him get better. Maybe it will help if we can figure out what happened—"

Rose interrupted. "I thought your client was suffering from a self-inflicted eating disorder?"

Odd choice of words, Crump thought, trying to remember if he'd ever heard the phrase "self-inflicted" associated with anything other than a gunshot wound. "Whatever trauma he's suffering from, he's in a psych ward, and the doctors tell me figuring out what happened is the first step to effective treatment."

Rose and Westheimer looked at each other, then Westheimer nodded silently to Rose, like they were whispering kids passing messages under their desks in the third grade.

"What makes you think whatever happened, happened here?" Rose asked.

OK, Crump thought, we're going to play keep-away. "Look, I've already conducted interviews, and no, I'm not going to name names, but there's no question what happened, happened here, and no doubt it was part of a sustained, continuous and aggravated case of bullying. I'd like your cooperation in ferreting out what was done and who was involved, as the Docs at St. Vincent's think it will help them treat young Mr. Lockwood. We can do this by subpoena if you like, but I assumed you'd be more interested in seeing your pupil make a full recovery. So, we talking, or are we suing?"

Westheimer started to stand, but Rose motioned for him to sit back down. "This is a progressive institution. It's not within the School's mission statement to police student behavior—" Rose began, when Westheimer interrupted.

"You know what our bumper magnets say: 'Carrington Prep: Progressive Begins With *Progress*,'" he added, trying, but failing, to deliver that line like he hadn't rehearsed it for hours in front of a mirror.

Crump pulled back and looked at the two of them like they were actors trying to pass an audition. "I think of a mission statement as something that ought to be embroidered on a swatch of cheesecloth and framed for your basement wall, hung up next to the bar and across from the pool table. What about the Prevention of School Violence Act? Doesn't that make it the duty of all 'School Personnel' to prevent and report bullying?" Crump asked.

Both Westheimer and Rose looked prepared. "We believe we are exempt from that statute," Westheimer announced.

"Really?" Crump asked, a little astounded. "How's that?"

"The 'Religious School' Exemption."

"Seriously?" Crump wrinkled his brow like he'd heard him wrong. "This place is as non-denominational as they come," he added.

"We believe our Progressive Idiom is a form of religion," Westheimer offered.

"Wow," Crump answered, clearly dumbfounded. "Johnny Rose here give you that 'legal opinion'? Hope you got it in writing."

"Mr. Crump," Westheimer began, "I've got members of this community who threaten to handcuff themselves to the school gates and immolate themselves, if we so much as offer placement tests. We treat progressive education *religiously*."

"...... That means you're all crazy, not devout," Crump mumbled to himself, almost audibly.

Exasperated, Crump retrieved the envelope from his breast pocket and tossed it on Westheimer's desk. It was marked "Faggot Brian". "Why don't you open it, Johnny," Crump motioned to the lawyer. "I got lots of 'em. They put one in the Lockwood kid's locker, just about every week."

"Crump, I—" Rose began, when Crump cut him off.

"No, read it, just don't cut your fingers on the razor blade inside. It's full of threats and instructions on how to slash your wrists and make it count, together with helpful hints on self-harm from the internet. Go ahead—"

"Is this some kind of *stunt*—"

"No, I mean it. See, the thing is, some of your little progressive progressors were putting this stuff in the kid's locker—the same kids who were knocking him around every day, threatening to kill him if he told anybody."

Johnny Rose opened and read the contents, then he handed the paper to Westheimer.

"Ever seen one of these?" Crump asked.

"What's this prove?" Rose asked, before Westheimer could answer, holding the envelope like it burned to the touch.

"I think you knew all about it, at least, that's what people tell me. The really troubling question is, '*Why?*'"

"Why, *what*?" Rose asked.

"Why it went on for *years*, and you did nothing about it," Crump answered.

Rose and his client silently glanced at each other, figuring it was time to regroup. "I'm certain somebody's confused about this," Westheimer offered, nervously. "Perhaps if you could share what you've been told—"

Crump shook his head. "I came here to do an interview, not to get interrogated."

Rose butted in. "Crump, I'm sure you realize, much of what you're describing, *if it's happening at all,* routinely flies under the radar of the adults in the building. I mean, it's not like the kids raise their hands and ask for permission, before they offer good-natured ribbing to a fellow student."

They're polishing up their defenses, Crump thought. We've gone from, "Not our job," to, "How could we have known?" in the span of five minutes.

"Good natured 'ribbing' is shooting paper clips at the kid who has to recite the Pledge of Allegiance. They were working this kid over with death threats and suicide handbooks. This isn't just a case of mandatory reporters, teachers charged with reporting this stuff, choosing to look the other way. We're talking about incidents of violence directed at a student, conduct that *adults* were bringing to your attention, and the school was actively burying the reports—"

Rose stood up. "O.K., I think we're done here," he announced. "This is obviously not the collaborative process I expected from the representative of a parent, trying to improve the learning environment."

"You're right, Johnny, at this point, I don't care about your 'progressive idiom', or your 'learning environment'. I'm just trying to figure out what happened, so I can maybe stop a kid who's been bullied *into powder*, from disappearing off the face of the planet."

Rose handed the envelope and the contents back to Crump. "I'm sure nobody here had any idea what was going on, so unless you've got more to discuss, I think we're finished," he said, as he and Westheimer stood. "Can you find your way out?"

Crump shook his head as he snatched the envelope. "Your concern for a student in your charge is heartwarming," he said, and he left.

5.
NOTHING HAPPENS FOR NO REASON AT ALL................

"YOU SEE THIS?" MAUREEN ASKED, holding up the front page of the Daily Herald for Crump to inspect.

"JUDGE LABELS U.S. IMMIGRATION OFFICIALS AS 'TERRORISTS'",

the headline read.

"I'd say they're jumping the gun a little," Crump observed. "Couldn't happen to nicer people, though."

"I'll say," Maureen noted. "This publicity is making us all sorts of new friends. Have you seen the hate mail we're getting?"

"Are you reading that stuff? I told Sophie to just box it up and save it for evidence."

Maureen held up an unfolded letter. "Listen to this: 'You guys are replacist elites who deserve to die for helping the internationalists with their plot to dilute the white race through mass immigration. You are the terrorists……'"

"Is it signed by the Attorney General?" Crump quipped.

"It's put together with letters cut out from a magazine and glued all over the paper like a kidnapper's ransom demand," she said, waiving the paper mosaic around in the air.

"Must be from the President himself," Crump added.

"This isn't funny. We're getting bucketloads of this stuff, and Doctor Trimble called and said she's getting some, too."

"Fascinating as opening our fan mail seems to be, we need to go out to St. Vincent's and interview both of our clients, and since you got me into this, you get to go, too," Crump said, brushing off Maureen's hate-mail phobia.

Maureen drove. Crump sat there reading interview notes from the parents of Brian Lockwood's classmates who'd agreed to talk to him.

"I can't figure out why they'd pick this kid out of the crowd—he seems so inoffensive, he's barely even there," Crump wondered, aloud.

"If I believe what my kids tell me, that may be all it takes," Maureen said.

"I don't know—it's hard to believe they'd even notice him. You haven't seen him—even healthy, he'd be practically invisible. There must be something else going on. Nothing ever happens for no reason at all."

As they pulled into the parking lot at St. Vincent's, Maureen asked, "So, now that you've told this 'E.M.' kid that we've talked to her mother, how are you going to pump her for information about her mother?"

Crump shrugged. "I'm not—you are. I'll do the disappearing Lockwood kid. They wanted a woman for E.M. in the first place—figured it'd go better if you interviewed her. I want to find out where they crossed, why she's not asking about the Father, and what C.B.P. did when they first got to the border.

When she asks about Mom, tell her we're talking to the Feds as they move her around—almost true—and we need more info from her to help keep track."

"C.B.P.?"

"Customs and Border Protection, the folks who've been enforcing whatever it is the Stuggs Administration claims, or doesn't claim on a given day, they're doing at the border with these families," Crump added.

"Doing your homework, for a case you didn't ask for and don't really want," Maureen nudged him.

"I just work here," Crump responded, wobbling his head.

"So, my job is to keep spinning the bullshit you laid on this kid last month, while I try to coax useful information out of her that will enable us to make the bullshit come true?"

"You go to the head of the class," Crump said, pointing his finger to the tip of his nose.

When they got inside, Crump guided Maureen through the same fire drill he'd experienced at his first visit, although she opted for just leaving everything with the attendants at the front desk, once they found her Mace cartridge.

"It's easier to do prison interviews at Stateville," Maureen complained.

"Just *wait*," Crump warned.

They were greeted again by Giampetro, who half spoke and half grunted his "Stand Back!" instructions, as Maureen gave in to her instincts and backed away.

When the door slid open, Maureen was paralyzed. The ward was spinning with injured children, many of whom were bandaged like they were shrunken battlefield casualties, set loose before they were healed.

"It kind of hits you," Crump said. "All those kids all bandaged up, and the thing is, it's not an act of God. This isn't unavoidable suffering—somebody is *doing this* to these kids," he whispered.

An emaciated child with translucent skin, dressed in a billowing nightgown, wandered past, gliding noiselessly in slippers. She had a feeding tube taped to her nose and running back to a pack she was carrying around like a purse. The child looked like somebody dug out of earthquake rubble.

"Crump, I can't do this," Maureen said, as she turned away and backed out of the ward, into the hallway, just as Doctor Trimble appeared in the entryway.

"Excuse us," Crump said, as he backed out to retrieve Maureen.

"I should have warned you," he admitted, as she leaned face first against a wall, her forehead resting on the stippled wallpaper.

She stood away. Her eyes were burning. "What's with the gauze bandages on everybody's arms?"

"Covers up the scars and open wounds from self-harming—prevents infection, discourages more self-harm, and seeing the stuff is triggering to those not in the habit, or so the Doctor tells me."

"*Damn it*, Crump, why didn't you *tell* me?" she cried.

"Hey," he said, getting in her face. "I find it helps to get pissed off. I never thought I could kill anybody with my bare hands, but I'm reconsidering that these days. We gotta go in and do these interviews. Can you pull it together?"

She started to nod, wiping her eyes and nose on her sleeve like a six-year-old. "You know, I *hate* you for this," she said, shaking her head like she had cartoon butterflies circling her ears.

"That's the spirit," he said, as they went back into the ward.

"You two O.K.?" Doctor Trimble asked, as they approached her kiosk.

"Allergic reaction to child torture," Crump noted. "This is Maureen McDougal, my partner," he added. "She's going to interview Miss Montes," he explained. "I need to meet with the Lockwood kid. His parents are supposed to be here."

"Yes, they're over by the classroom," Doctor Trimble said, pointing.

"Classroom?" Maureen asked.

"Some of these kids stay here *for months*. Brian is in there now with his parents, who are tutoring him through Algebra."

"Crump says you're fluent in Spanish, which is good, because I'm not," Maureen cautioned the Doctor, as they made their way to Estrellita's room.

When they entered, Maureen was struck by how calm the child appeared. She was sitting in a chair, a feeding tube taped to her nose, the pump box cradled in the chair. She was flipping through a magazine in a pose that made her look like somebody waiting to get her hair done.

"Hola Millie. Esta es la abogada, Senora McDougal, para ayudarla a encontrar a su madre," Doctor Trimble announced.

"Can you help me a little?" Maureen asked.

"I'm telling her you're a lawyer, here to help," Dr. Trimble translated.

"¿Dónde está el hombre que estuvo aquí antes?"

"She's asking about your partner," Doctor Trimble reported.

"He'll be here in a bit," Maureen said, and the Doctor dutifully translated. "Tell her we need to ask a few questions to help get her back together with her Mother."

After Doctor Trimble translated, Maureen asked, "Do you know the place where you and your Mother crossed the border?"

As the Doctor delivered the question in Spanish, E.M. lowered her legs to the floor, closed the magazine and looked at Maureen like she just might be a border agent.

"Chihuahua," she offered, one eye narrowing, as though testing the light.

"Is she talking about a dog?" Maureen asked.

Doctor Trimble shook her head, thinking, This one's not much better than her Cowboy partner. "No, I'm pretty sure she understood the question—that's the region of Mexico where they crossed."

"No, Millie," The Doctor injected. "Donde en los Estados Unidos?" then, to Maureen, "Where in the USA?"

"¿Por Que?" the child asked.

After some back and forth, in which both Maureen and Doctor Trimble assured E.M. that they would only use the information to help, the child the Government called E.M., answered, "El Paso."

With some prompting from Maureen, the Doctor asked, " ¿Tu padre también estaba allí?—"Was your Father there also?" she added, for Maureen's sake.

"No, está muerto."

Maureen understood that much. "Ask her if he died before they crossed the border," Maureen added.

After they established that E.M. and her Mother crossed alone, weeks after her Father had been killed at the hands of Guatemalan gangs, Maureen said, "Ask her what the border guards told them was going to happen to them."

In response to the translation, E.M, offered, "Ellos preguntaron en vientre flota bebé."

Doctor Trimble rolled her eyes. "We're testing my Spanish here—I think it's an idiomatic phrase—it literally sounds like they were asking if she was 'swimming in her belly with a baby', but I'm betting they were asking if she was pregnant."

Great, Maureen thought—Our Government Tax Dollars at Work. "Ask her if they told her anything else?"

After some back and forth in Spanish, E. M. said, "Me preguntaron si estaba teniendo sexo con alguien."

"Yeah," the Doctor translated. "They asked her if she was having sex with anybody."

Maureen rubbed her palm against her forehead. Some goob in the Stuggs Administration with sex hang-ups was probably dictating these stupid, insulting questions. "Did the Border Guards say where they were taking Mom?"

After the Doctor translated, Estrellita gave a one word answer: "Cárcel."

"Jail," Doctor Trimble muttered.

Swell, Maureen thought. "In El Paso?" Maureen asked.

Estrellita, who seemed to understand, answered, without translation, "No lo se. No me lo dijeron."

"They didn't tell her," Doctor Trimble said.

"¿Cuál es el nombre de su madre?" the Doctor inquired, seeking the Mother's full name.

"Elení Montes."

Just then, Crump arrived. "We still have a deal?" he asked. The Doctor translated.

Estrellita smiled. Wow, Maureen thought—no wonder Crump took this thing—kid must be the only creature on Earth happy to see him.

"Sí," the kid said, nodding. "¿La encuentras?"

Crump looked at the Doctor for guidance. "Is that food?" he asked.

"She's asking if you've brought her back here," Doctor Trimble said.

Crump's eyes briefly narrowed, before he offered, "Tell her we're working on it."

He shook her hand again, while the Doctor acted as interpreter.

They said goodbye and went back into the hall, then down to the Doctor's kiosk.

"You got it all wrapped up in there?" he asked.

"You're not gonna like it," Maureen noted, as she summarized the interrogation.

"Sounds like all they did was have some perv ask her about her sex life," Crump commented.

"It's worse than that," the Doctor added. "When she got here, she said some goon at the Armory was asking her to report daily on whether she was having her period—seems they were recording her cycles, for some reason that I, as a Citizen whose safety these jokers are supposedly protecting, can hardly imagine is relevant."

"They're worried the females are pregnant—if the kid is born on U.S. soil, they're automatically a U.S. citizen. My guess is pregnant ones get hustled out of the country pronto, rather than shipped around to dark-site dumping grounds, where they otherwise would hide them from the parents. Policy comes from the top down. Listen to President Stuggs' rants sometimes—it's pretty clear he thinks of women solely in terms of their reproductive capabilities." Crump paused. "Well, at least we know where they entered—that's a start. How's Estrellita doing?"

"We're still calling her 'Millie,'" the Doctor offered. "Force of habit. Anyway, she's been on the feeding tube almost three weeks now."

"She looks lots better than last time," Crump said.

"Yes, I'm just afraid it's temporary—these kids are known for backsliding—anorexia is pernicious. I hope you're actually making some progress."

Crump offered, somewhat defensively, "Hey—we got the restraining order—for now, at least, she's not going anywhere."

The Doctor nodded, somewhat gravely. "Yes, and I don't want to alarm you, but keep in mind Anorexia has a thirty-three percent mid-term mortality rate."

* *

In the car on the way back to the office, Maureen asked if Crump got anything useful out of the Lockwood kid.

In response, Crump said, "Hold on," then took off his jacket and began rolling up the sleeve on his left arm, exposing his biceps, just above the elbow.

"See this?" he asked, flexing his arm and pointing to a nasty scar on the inside of his biceps.

Maureen glanced over. The thing looked like one of the seams on a kid's stuffed toy that was coming apart, the marks from the stitches still plainly visible, the gash pink, angry and bulging.

"Is there a reason you're showing me your battle scars?" she asked.

"Keep your eyes on the road," he said, needling Maureen. "When I was in high school, back in the late Sixties, I got this rebuffing gang recruiting—it was a more civilized time. Street gangs were armed with knives instead of semi-automatic weapons—"

"Crump—"

"So, anyway, when I was at the hospital getting stitched up, they sent a cop in to ask me who did it, and the thing was, there was no way I was going to rat out the guy who did it. At least I still had my arm, and my teeth, and both eyes, and…..well, you get the idea. The cop grilled me pretty good—he was a pro, did a lot of….'This will just be our little secret…'stuff, but I knew what was going to happen if I named names, so I just told him it was too dark, I couldn't tell, etcetera, etcetera—"

"Crump, what about—"

"So, my point is, that Lockwood kid was doing the same dodge, supposedly had no idea exactly who was doing all this stuff, even though a lot of it was pretty obviously done face to face. When I asked him how big his classroom was, he said, 'I don't know—maybe twenty-five?', and I'm thinking, What are the odds he can't pick the perps out of a line-up when the entire classroom is twenty-five kids?"

"So, he's scared shitless?" Maureen observed.

"Right."

"So, what can a bunch of thirteen-year-olds do to each other that has the kid holing up like it's gang recruiting season?" Maureen wondered aloud.

Crump looked out the side window. "Carrington Prep is too hoity-toity to have a gang problem. Not sure, but if I had to guess, I'd bet it has to do more with *who's* behind it than with exactly what evil stuff they're trying out on the Kid, which means Westheimer's lying. He knows."

6.
YOUR GOVERNMENT TAX DOLLARS AT WORK.........

"I WANT TO DESTROY THIS LITTLE prick," Warren Handler, aging, overweight, jowly, leftover preppy Attorney General of the United States of America, announced to Byron Trout, the Assistant U.S. Attorney tasked with digging dirt on Crump. They were sitting in Handler's office, pawing through a file they'd compiled on Crump.

"He has no social media presence whatsoever—hell, he doesn't even have a personal email."

"How's that possible?" Handler asked.

"Don't know—from what we can find, he seems like kind of an oddball. Doesn't vote often, no Party affiliation. Not much if you go way back, but it looks like he was once in State Custody—"

"He's got a record?"

"No, as a kid, he was in Juvie, looks like State Custody for quite a while—hard to say—those files are sealed. The only reason we found any of it was that he got a scholarship to some State University, and his Juvie record was disclosed in the application because he was applying to college straight out of State Custody. Parents seemed to disappear. No siblings. Got scholarships to a couple of State schools, went to law school after teaching for a year, then ended up at some mega law firm."

"Anything good on the teaching job? He get fired for diddling kids, anything like that?"

Trout shrugged, looking through a stack of computer printouts. "No, nothing with the school district, no disciplinary record. There is some weird thing where some parent took a shot at him—"

"*What?*"

"Turns out, it was in a local police station. He reported the woman to Child and Family Services, some deal with her mistreatment of the kid, and she shows up at the station while this Crump guy is being questioned, and she pulls a gun and takes a shot at him."

"What happened?" Handler asked.

"She was prosecuted and the kid was placed in Foster Care, or so the police report says."

"Shit—that's no help."

"I know. Anyway, goes to law school, graduates in '79, then, while he's working at the big firm, place called Bastion, Hughes & Mulroy, he takes on a case suing the D.O.J."

"What?" Handler asked. "Let me see that," he ordered, reaching out for a few pages of the report from his assistant. "Says here," Handler read, "He represented a law-school classmate who was getting disciplined by the Department of Justice, some junior prosecutor who got a judge pissed off because the guy supposedly misused a snitch, going after some gangbanger. This Crump guy filed a 1983 Civil Rights claim, got his buddy re-instated, with back pay and the Gov. paid *his* fees."

"Yeah, one guy we talked to, this Ned Bastion who runs the law firm where Crump worked, Bastion says that case is why Crump left the firm. He ran up a big receivable over three years, and when they pressured him to drop the case, he quit the law firm—"

"I thought you said he got an award of attorney fees," Handler interrupted.

"I know—that Bastion guy really hates Crump. He was laughing it up, remembering how the firm got paid anyway, but not, as he said, before they used the unpaid bill as an excuse to 'Dump Crump.'"

"You got anything better than that?"

"One thing—I checked, he's got no passport, hasn't had one for almost twenty-five years. He had one, back before that, when he started practicing law. His international travel history is fucked up."

Handler wrinkled his forehead. "Fucked up, *how*?"

"So, he takes one trip, down to Pantilla in San Sebastopol, 'The Jewel of Central America', not five years after the invasion down there, and, the thing is, according to State Department records, he never came back."

"What the fuck're you talking about—he's here, he filed this Goddamned lawsuit."

"I know. Peter Meadows checked him out when they were in the City by the Lake, there for the T.R.O. hearing last month."

"So, what? He's a drug dealer, and flies back into Texas with some mule, on a plane in the middle of the night?"

"I don't think so. Our records show that, at the same time he left Pantilla, he'd been deputized by the local branch of the U.S. Attorney's Office—"

"You gotta be kidding me—he was working for us?"

"I know, I had to check it twice," Trout explained. "The A.U.S.A. he got reinstated got him deputized, working on some case, but the file is a mess—some escaped Nazi getting deported, drug dealers, some business with a kid who'd been allegedly kidnapped. There's no terminating report in the file—I can't figure out what happened."

Handler grabbed that set of records. "This guy Barnacle, the A.U.S.A. involved, where's he?"

"Not working for us anymore. He quit when Stuggs took office."

"Find him. He owes us. Given his age, he's getting a pension—a Government pension this asshole Crump got restored for Barnacle when he saved his job. I want to know what Barnacle knows."

"Right." He paused, reading further. "On the personal side, he's been married over thirty years, another lawyer, Mary Haffencamp, does domestic cases, confirms foreign adoptions, lots of bleeding-heart stuff. Three kids, all adults, nothing interesting on any of them."

"I want addresses for all four of them, and any social media presence for any of the kids," Handler noted. "He ever been sued or arrested?"

Trout pulled a fresh sheath of papers from his file on Crump. "No arrests, but, yeah, sued a few times, but not malpractice or ethical complaints."

"So, who's suing him?" Handler asked.

"His opponents—"

"—figures—"

"Well, you ask me, though, it's kind of goofy stuff: 'Intrusion on Seclusion', 'Civil Kidnapping', whatever that means, and one case where they alleged he was a member of a conspiracy of the local 'Power Elite'—"

"Fat chance of that. So, he draws a lot of retaliatory litigation—seems like we're not the first opponents he hit with some wacky claims. What about his partner, Muldoon….McCarthy….."

"McDougal, Maureen McDougal. She's clean and boring. Married to the Lakeside County Coroner, been working for Crump for years. Has two kids of her own, younger than Crump's, still in school—"

"Forget her for now. I want that Barnacle guy in here. If we're paying him a pension, he owes us."

Trout nodded. "Yeah, don't get your hopes up. These two go back pretty far—"

"Then," Handler paused, "he knows where the dirty laundry's buried," he added, badly mixing his metaphors.

"What about the Doc?" Trout asked. "Registered Democrat, does a lot of that Commie Doctor stuff—Doctors Without Borders, stint in the Peace Corps—"

"For now, leave her out," Handler ordered.

"She's the Plaintiff in the Patriot Act lawsuit, signed off on the bullshit terrorist complaint—"

"I know. Just wait. She's the Kid's doctor. And, word is, she's *a blonde.*"

"So?" Trout asked, a little dumbfounded.

"Two things I learned the first day of law school: Don't sue the guy in the wheelchair, and, if you're going to run a smear campaign against an opponent, leave the blonde out of it."

* *

"If I read the Government's initial disclosures correctly, this 'Dennis Ernstmeyer' guy is the reptile who both dreamt up these child separation and hospital deportation scare tactics, and is charged with administering them. Seems like he'd be the first person we'd want to depose."

Crump was in Maureen's office, paging through the documents the Government had dumped on them in response to the lawsuit.

"They filed a general denial of the complaint," Maureen observed, holding up the document.

"You're kidding—"

"Denied every single paragraph, including, 'The United States Customs and Immigration Service is a Department of the Federal Government operated by the Executive Branch, under the authority of the current President, H. Stennis Stuggs….'" Maureen read from the Government's response.

"The legal equivalent of giving us the finger. So, they intend to horse us around, not actually respond," Crump observed.

"It's their usual strategy. Seems to work for them."

"Sure for a while, kind of like jumping off the Empire State Building, and as you zip down past the fiftieth floor, you think, 'Well, nothing bad happened yet…..'"

Maureen pulled her keyboard out from under her desk. "So, you want me to crank out a subpoena for this Ernstmeyer'a deposition?" she asked, already typing away.

"Yeah, but let's do some backgrounding on him first. If he's in the Stuggs administration, he's got to have a screw loose. And, make sure we say we're taking him here in our office—the last time I took a dep in the Federal building, it was an I.R.S. agent, and somebody kept turning the lights on and off, and when that didn't work, they jacked the heat way up and tried to sweat us out."

So it was, four weeks later, Dennis Ernstmeyer, Director of Immigration Policy for U.S.C.I.S., was sitting in Crump's waiting room, with Regina Debeviose, the Assistant US attorney there to defend his deposition. Ernstmeyer looked to be about fifty, tightly cut gray hair and a narrow face, large nose and deep blue eyes.

Maureen snuck a peek out into their reception area. "He's kinda creepy. Looks like one of those chicken farmers that ended up being Hitler's henchmen," she offered. "How does God and DNA cook *that* up?"

"I'm sure his mother loves him," Crump responded, as they entered the reception area together.

Crump and Maureen introduced themselves, then guided the witness and his lawyer into a conference room, where a Court Reporter was seated at the end of the table, setting up her stenography rig. After she loaded a roll of paper into a steno machine, she started setting up a computer and a series of microphones, one taped to the table in front of each chair.

"Wait—" Ernstmeyer injected, to the surprise of Regina Debevoise, who'd told him to keep quiet and speak only when spoken to. "I don't consent to this deposition being recorded—"

"Mr. Ernstmeyer, the rules in the Northern District *require* that depositions be recorded—it's a back up to the stenograph tape," Crump began, when Debevoise interrupted.

"—I'm sure my client was just joking," she said, tossing Ernstmeyer an angry look.

"No I was—" he began, when she interrupted again.

"As I said, we can all understand the ironic humor of the situation," she offered, grabbing Ernstmeyer by the elbow and taking him back into the hallway.

"So, she can barely control the guy," Maureen noted.

When they re-entered the room, Ernstmeyer sat next to the Reporter, with Regina Debevoise to his left. Crump and Maureen sat across from them.

"Can I get you anything?" Crump asked.

"I'd like an American Flag to post next to my chair here, and a Bible," Ernstmeyer noted.

Crump and Maureen looked at each other, barely restrained. "I meant, like, a bottle of water or a cup of coffee," Crump said, purposefully sounding like a bored bureaucrat, desperately hiding his amazement.

"Let's just get started," Debevoise complained.

"Please swear the witness," Crump said, and Ernstmeyer raised his left hand.

"Your right, please," the Reporter asked.

"I'm left handed," Ernstmeyer gently complained.

Wow, Crump thought, this is going to take forever.

"Doesn't matter, we swear with the right," Crump jumped in.

After the witness was sworn, Crump read the case caption into the record, then asked Ernstmeyer a series of background questions. Everything went smoothly until they got to his work history.

"So, you were an accountant, then a consultant, then you went to work for Stuggs—"

"*President* Stuggs," Ernstmeyer interjected. "He's a great man—he's going to Get America Praying Again," he intoned, parroting Stuggs' favorite campaign slogan. He then quickly, in a single fluid motion, produced from inside his suit one of Stuggs' GAPA brimmed baseball caps, which he plopped on the table, the logo staring at Crump like a STOP sign.

"Right," Crump quickly agreed, not wanting to get into it with one of Stuggs' crackpot True Believers. "But, when you started, he was just Governor Stuggs, correct?"

Ernstmeyer nodded.

"You need to give verbal answers—the court reporter can't transcribe you nodding your head," Maureen jumped in.

"Sorry, yes, he was Governor of Alabama at the time."

"We found a copy of your resume from those days on the internet, but looking at it, I'm not clear exactly what you did in his administration," Crump observed. "Your resume just says, 'Senior Policy Analyst.'"

"It's a long story," Ernstmeyer said.

"Go ahead, we've got time," Crump said, egging him on.

"Well, it was sort of a new post, created especially for me. I'd been doing research, and the Governor wanted me to expand on that research, so they created a commission and appointed me its Chief of Staff."

"What was it called?"

"Reservation Reparations."

"What's that mean?" Crump asked.

"It's based on the understanding that the people we routinely call 'Native Americans' are actually descendants of invading hordes that came to America in the late 1600's and early 1700's from South America, and that much of the history of these 'Tribes' is actually propaganda, designed to manufacture a basis for the wholesale land grab we currently refer to as 'Resettlement to Indian Reservations'. The Commission was charged with bolstering research into that demographic phenomenon, so that Indo-European, Anglo-Saxon-Heritage Americans could establish themselves as the true 'Native Americans', and reclaim those reservations and receive reparations for the lands otherwise wrongly taken by these so-called, 'Indigenous Peoples.'"

Crump was staring at the witness, his eyes growing wide enough that he could barely contain his reaction to Ernstmeyer's brief recital of what sounded to Crump like Ku Klux Klan Slam Poetry. "You were getting *paid* for this work?" he asked.

"Of course. We were still developing the evidence when Reverend Stuggs decided to run for President. When he got elected, he asked me to come to Washington and join the Administration. I believe the Commission's work is still underway."

Crump was shaking his head, like he'd heard him wrong. "And, did you uncover any evidence for this *theory*?"

Ernstemeyer shrugged. "As I said, the research is still ongoing. As you, and any casual observer can attest, many so-called 'American Indians' bear striking resemblance to South Americans."

Crump looked over at Maureen, who was gently rolling her eyes. "Are you still engaged in this 'research', at the federal level?" Crump asked.

"No, when I came to Washington, almost three years ago, President Stuggs placed me in charge of immigration policy."

"Can we take a break?" Debevoise asked, looking at her watch, even though the deposition was only twenty minutes old.

"Sure," Crump agreed.

When the witness and his attorney left, Maureen asked, "What do you suppose they're talking about out there?"

"I don't need to suppose," Crump reflected. "She's telling him to lay off the narrative answers sprinkled with his nutjob population drift theories," he whispered, so as not to be overheard by the Court Reporter, who heard him anyway and nodded, silently.

Ernstmeyer and his attorney stepped back in. "OK, we can resume," Debevoise announced.

"You're still under oath, Mr. Earnstmeyer. Can I ask you what you and your counsel talked about just now, out in the hall?"

"You may *not*," Debevoise injected. "It's privileged. Ask him another question."

"OK. Let's get down to the subject at hand. What is the objective of U.S.C.I.S. in separating children from their parents when they cross the Mexican border, as a family?"

"There are many objectives, however, the primary objective is to adopt a 'Zero Tolerance' approach to deter immigration—"

"*All* immigration?" Crump interrupted.

"Virtually all immigration at the Border is 'illegal immigration', Mr. Crump."

"You lumping asylum seekers into that category?"

"One man's 'asylum seeker' is another man's illegal strawberry picker," Ernstmeyer responded, grinning.

"You're saying, that a parent, a father or a mother, grabs up their kids—children as young as four or five—and treks hundreds of miles across the Mexican desert, just to come here to pick strawberries?" Crump asked, allowing his dumbfounded take on Ernstmeyer's snarky answer to leak into his follow-up question.

"I was turning a phrase," Ernstmeyer responded, cracking his first real smile of the deposition.

"Haa….Haa…..Haa….," Maureen whispered, under her breath.

"So, then, why separate the kids from their parents?"

"The parents are criminals—"

"All of them?"

"Yes—by virtue of the border crossing, they are violating U.S. laws."

"Even if they are asylum seekers?"

"Those claims are virtually all bogus," Ernstmeyer testified, smugly crossing his arms and lifting his chin.

"How do you know, if you separate the kids before the parents get a hearing on their asylum claims?" Crump asked.

"Mr. Crump, you can't be serious. Are you expecting C.B.P. agents to close their eyes to the reality of the crisis at the border?"

"I guess it's a question of who's creating that 'crisis'."

"I object—you're lecturing him, not asking questions," Debevoise interjected.

"So, how serious is this *crime*—"

"Why don't you drop the sarcasm," Debevoise objected.

"I was born with it," Crump acknowledged. "Like I was saying, this *crime* of illegal border crossing, the supposed justification for whisking away the children of the immigrant adults—How serious is it?"

"Object to the use of 'supposed,'" Debevoise injected.

"How serious is it?" Crump pressed, ignoring her witness coaching.

"I'm not a lawyer," Ernstmeyer offered.

"Come now—you're the head of a U.S. Government Agency—you must have some idea? Say, more serious than making a bootleg video copy of 'Bloodbath 2—Assault on the Convent', then loaning it to your next-door neighbor?"

"C'mon, Crump, knock it off," Debevoise objected.

"I'm serious—more serious than that, Mr. Ernstmeyer?"

Ernstmeyer tilted his head to the left and right, weighing his options. "Of course, illegal border crossing's more serious," he proclaimed.

"Would you be surprised if I told you the *minimum* fine for that bootleg movie making, *for no profit*, was one thousand times greater than the *maximum* fine for illegal border crossing, two hundred fifty thousand dollars, versus two hundred and fifty?"

Before Debevoise could intervene, Ernstmeyer proclaimed, "I certainly would be shocked."

"Do you think the neighbor who leant you that copy of 'Bloodbath—2' should be arrested and have his children taken away and shipped to another city?"

"You're lecturing him again," Debevoise objected, just to break things up.

"Why not—they're both criminals, *correct,* Mr. Ernstmeyer?" Crump pressed on.

"I agree—there's generally too much disregard for the law," he offered.

Crump paused, covered his mouth and he leaned over and whispered "Good enough?" to Maureen, who nodded silently.

"OK. So, what was the plan—what were you going to do with all those kids?"

"What do you mean?" the witness asked.

"You planning to reunite them? There's a 2015 consent decree in a California Federal Court between the U.S. Government and Immigrants' Rights organizations, requiring you to reunite any family members separated, as quickly as possible," Crump added.

"That was entered into with a prior Administration—that 'Lib' O'Connor. We don't believe that applies to our current program," Ernstmeyer offered, practically spitting out the prior President's name.

"I'll come back to that, but it's my understanding you now claim you weren't even making adequate records, so you now can't track the parents and the kids, making future re-uniting impossible?"

"Don't answer that question," Debevoise spoke up.

"And, the basis for that direction *is?*" Crump asked

"Executive privilege."

"You're joking—"

"I am not," Debevoise replied.

"So, you're saying President Stuggs told you, directly, to not keep adequate records so you couldn't re-unite—"

"I said, he's not going to answer any of these questions," Debevoise insisted.

"Miss Reporter, certify those questions. We'll be taking them to the Judge. Are you going to follow your counsel's direction not to answer?" Crump asked.

"Why wouldn't I?" Ernstmeyer asked.

"Because," Maureen interjected, "it's a bogus direction, and if you follow it and the Court agrees with us, you could be required to return for another deposition—"

"—That's nonsense, and who's taking this deposition, you or your partner?" Debevoise complained.

"Sure, I'm following her direction," Ernstmeyer noted.

"Let's switch gears," Crump offered. "Let's talk about the other 'Policy' we're here to discuss. What was the objective of dumping immigrant kids receiving medical care out of the hospitals—"

"I object to the characterization of '*dumping*'," Debevoise said,

"*Fine*," Crump retreated. "What was the objective of *escorting* those kids out of those hospitals, with the feeding tubes still in their noses and the life-saving I.V. tubes still in their arms—"

"Same objection—"

"Take it to the Judge," Crump snapped. "Miss Reporter, please re-read the question," Crump added.

After the Reporter droned through the question, Ernstmeyer said, "Sound immigration policy."

Crump was gently bobbing his head, wondering if the guy was just stubborn, stupid or evasive. "I get that you consider it 'Sound Immigration Policy'. I'm asking you to explain the objective—what was taking kids with life-threatening conditions out of hospitals, where they were getting life-saving treatment, going to accomplish about immigration policies and what you call 'The Crisis at the Border'?"

Ernstmeyer was rubbing his hands together, looking downward. Crump figured this was both the question he'd been most carefully prepped on, and the one he least wanted to answer. "We felt it was likely that people with compromised children who'd already illegally crossed the border, might be counting on the American Healthcare System to rescue their sick kids on the backs of the Government and the taxpayers," he droned on, pretty obviously giving a rehearsed answer.

"Mr. Ernstmeyer, we've looked at the numbers, numbers maintained by your own U.S.C.I.S.. Only a fraction of these kids came here illegally. Many were brought here at the invitation of teaching hospitals and medical schools, conducting research on rare diseases and conditions where patients willing to participate in controlled studies are hard to find."

"Is that a question?" Debevoise asked.

"I was getting there," Crump answered.

"Well, get there faster, if you don't mind," Debevoise cracked.

"So, if some of the kids were here legally, what was the 'Sound Immigration Policy' behind kicking them all out?"

Ernstmeyer shrugged. "We felt many of them had overstayed their welcome."

"What's *that* mean?"

"Look, not *all* of them were legals. Take your client: She got here through an illegal border event—"

"Maybe. That's the subject of a dispute. But she was healthy when she crossed—she got sick in U.S.C.I.S. custody, being caged in chicken-wire fencing at the Edgewater Armory, like a rabid animal—"

"O.K., Crump, now you're just *arguing* with him. Ask him a question," Debevoise insisted.

"I'm still not clear on the objective of the policy change, I mean, you'd established a classification to let these kids remain under treatment. Why suddenly change it?"

"We felt the program was being abused," Ernstmeyer insisted.

Interesting choice of words, 'abused', Crump thought. You guys ought to be experts. "Abused, *how*?"

"Well, take your case, for example. Your Doctor Trimble made a fraudulent application—she had no parental or custodial authority over E.M.—"

"—she was *confused*," Crump shot back. "Not a lawyer, and didn't understand the legal requirements for guardianship," he tossed out, hoping it would stick. "Anyway, she had apparent authority as the child's doctor, and we fixed any uncertainty about that when we got her appointed E.M.'s guardian—"

"You testifying now?" Debevoise asked. "Perhaps I should be taking *your* deposition."

"Anytime, counsel," Crump hammered back. "So, you couldn't have had that kind of technicality in mind when you dumped this program, '….retroactive to August 7, 2022'," Crump added, reading from the U.S.C.I.S. notification letter Doctor Trimble had showed him on his first visit to the Adolescent Psych Ward.

"You going to mark that as an exhibit, Crump?" Debevoise interrupted.

"Sure. My point is, this is obviously a form letter—look at the copy job where your equipment superimposed the addressee," he insisted, shoving and rattling the letter in Ernstmeyer's face. "This had to be a bucket job—you weren't reacting to abuses in the program."

"Ask a question—"

"Were you?" Crump quickly added.

Ernstmeyer took the notice from Crump and scanned it. "We simply felt the program had become too attractive for the participants. It was too effective, I mean, they were getting care not generally available to them in their home countries."

"So, why is that a bad thing?" Crump pressed on.

"Well, for one thing, this kid's not a citizen, she's not even a resident of the State, and nobody's responsible for paying for the care provided."

Ernstmeyer paused.

"Were you finished?" Crump asked.

"I guess," he said, almost sounding regretful.

Crump sat back, looked up and paused, noodling it over. "Let me pose a hypothetical—" Crump began, when Debevoise interrupted.

"I object to the hypothetical question—this witness is not an expert, and he's not being called or offered as an expert witness."

"Not sure that's correct," Crump offered, "But why don't you wait to hear the question? I think, based on his prior testimony, he can answer it." He paused. "Suppose, Mr. Ernstmeyer, that a man is driving a car through a state—"

"Which State?" Ernstmeyer asked.

"Doesn't matter—any State—and he has a horrific accident. Not his fault, he's hit head-on by a drunk driver going the wrong way on the highway. The cops pry him out of the wreckage, rush him to the nearest hospital and wheel him into surgery. He's half dead, got almost no cash, no insurance and his driver's license shows he's from another State. If they don't operate he's gonna die, and it's pretty clear he can't pay. Does the fact that he can't pay, *coupled with the fact that he's from another State*, mean you wheel him back out of the O.R., and just let him die?"

"I still object," Debevoise injected.

"Duly noted," Crump added. "So, you gonna let him die?"

Ernstmeyer fidgeted. He looked up, over at Debevoise, then back at Crump. "Well, that's a tough question, I mean, sure, I get where you're going, but then, somebody's gotta pay, and if they operate, the cost of that surgery is going to fall on the taxpayers of the hospital's home state, or the federal government, or some of both—"

Crump interrupted. "It's a 'yes-or-no' question."

"I guess, if you have to push me, I'm going to say, no, you don't operate. If you can get him back to his home state—"

"It's five hundred miles away," Crump injected.

"O.K., then I say he should have thought about that before he decided to drive into that other state," Ernstmeyer observed, folding his hands.

"I guess, my question is then, would that be the kind of place most people would want to live—"

"C'mon, Crump, knock it off and ask him a real question," Debevoise barked.

"These are real questions. We're all here for the same reason—to find out the objectives of these policies of Family Separation and Deporting Sick Kids—"

"You're making it a cartoon," Ernstmeyer interrupted.

"How's that?" Crump asked, pleased that Debevoise couldn't really control her client.

"I mean, at least the guy you're describing is a citizen of the Country he's driving through."

Crump nodded. "O.K., lets change the facts. Suppose somebody—heck, let's make it *you*, Mr. Ernstmeyer—you're driving through a foreign country on vacation."

"Which one?" Ernstmeyer asked.

"Doesn't matter. Let's say Romania. Anyway, you're driving through and you have the same accident. No cash on you, no insurance, and there you are, bleeding to death, the car on fire. Should the cops just say, "Oh, wait—it's an American, not a citizen—let's just let him bleed to death and then fry up in that burning car, save everybody a nasty medical bill—"

"Crump, what is the purpose of these questions? If you can't tie all this together, you need to move on," Debevoise objected.

"What's the verdict? Let you die?" Crump asked, ignoring the objection.

"That's different, I'm there legally."

"Why is that different?" Crump interrupted.

"Let him finish his answer," Debevoise heckled, growing impatient.

"I was finished," Ernstmeyer added.

"So," Crump paused….."the standard of conduct is, save innocent lives unless they're illegally over the border, then, let 'em fry?"

"There are bigger issues here," Ernstmeyer began, like he was introducing a lecture. "Somebody has to pay for all this—illegals are a burden on taxpayers. It's the principle of the thing."

"Ahhh," Crump exhaled. "Now we're getting somewhere—the *Principle*—you're saying the policy was revenue driven, protect those overburdened taxpayers. Let's see how that works."

"Are you going to ask him a question?" Debevoise complained.

"He's telling me this policy is designed to lift a burden off the taxpayers. Let's see how his Agency arrived at that '*Policy*'." Crump stopped, pulled a pen out of his pocket and began scribbling numbers on a pad. It took a minute, but then he held the pad up and showed it to Ernstmeyer.

"Mr. Ernstmeyer, do you know how many taxpayers there are in the U.S.?"

Ernstmeyer glanced upward, like he was doing the figures in his head. Crump shook his head—the number was at the top of the page he was showing him.

"Let the record reflect that I'm showing the witness a sheet of hand-drawn computations, I'll label it Exhibit twenty-three." He paused and pointed at the top number on the page. "It's about one-hundred-forty-one million taxpayers, last time anybody checked. How many people are you ripping out of hospitals with this *Policy*? Five thousand?"

Ernstmeyer hesitated. "Not quite, more like forty-five hundred—"

"Close enough—let's stick with my numbers—we'll use five thousand, just to be generous to your argument about those overburdened taxpayers. So, what is each patient costing per year? And, we'll assume the entire cost is borne by the taxpayers—that's nonsense, it's mostly the hospitals and clinics, but let's just run with it. What would you say? Hundred thousand per patient, per year?"

"I…I…uhh, that may be high, more like fifty grand per year. The numbers aren't in—"

"Let's go with my numbers, call it one hundred K a year, per patient. So, that's about five hundred million a year these little devils are costing those taxpayers—"

"Crump—" Debevoise interrupted.

"Stay with me here," Crump bore onward, pointing his pen at the bottom number on his hastily-drawn chart. "So, if we divide that by one hundred forty million taxpayers, that gets us to under four dollars per taxpayer, per year, *for the entire program…..*" He paused. "Or, if you go kid by kid, patient by patient, treat 'em like human beings, it takes about a thousand of 'em before the little buggers cost any taxpayer *a penny*—"

"Crump, if you don't ask him a question, I'm terminating this deposition," Debevoise almost shouted, bending over the table in Crump's direction.

"O.K. So, here's my question: Mr. Ernstmeyer, you think, if average Mr. Taxpayer is driving in his car, and he turns on the radio, and he hears you, explaining this 'Program' on Talk Radio, and you say, 'Having these kids in the hospital is costing you four bucks year', you think that Mr. Taxpayer, he sees one of 'em crossing the street, pushed by some nurse on a rolling stretcher, you think, for the fraction of a penny that kid is costing him, that guy is going to want to run that kid over, just to get him off his tax bill?"

Ernstmeyer tilted his head. As Debevoise started to say, "Crump...." Ernstmeyer blurted out, "Maybe, if the kid is an *illegal*."

Debevoise jumped out of her seat. "O.K. Crump, this has gone far enough. I'm terminating this dep and taking the witness out. You want to keep this up, go ask the Court, 'cause I'll be moving for a protective order."

As they all stood, Crump said, "Be sure to attach a transcript to your motion," and Maureen then helped them out. Crump stayed behind, as the Court Reporter pulled the paper roll out of her stenograph machine.

"You get all that?" Crump asked the Court Reporter. She smiled, then nodded. "Good. I want two copies, expedited."

He met up with Maureen in her office.

"He's lying," Maureen announced.

"Of course, he's lying—this thing has nothing to do with money. They spend more than that on spray washing the U.S.S. Whatever at Pearl Harbor. I guarantee you in a couple hours of research I can find some boondoggle federal program that costs just as much or more—remember the whole 'Snail Darter Research Program', where the feds were looking into mollusk sex life? He can't really get up there and say, 'We just wanted to scare the crap out of those sneaky parents, marching toward the Mexican border, let them know we're going to kill the little buggers once we get our hands on them.' Dr. Trimble's right—it's an act of Terrorism. I just hope Debevoise files for a protective order, so the Judge can see his testimony: 'Yeah, sure, John Q. Public would run over one of these kids for five cents, if he only knew they were *illegals*.....'"

7.
NOBODY HERE BUT JUST US CHICKENS……..

"Where you headed?" Maureen asked, as Crump walked by with his coat and gloves.

"Got another interview with a Carrington Prep parent set up, a name given me by Bill Lockwood, Brian's dad. This is one of the folks who fessed up to knowing something, after the Kid landed in the hospital—said his daughter had complained about the bullying, and she finally said something to her Mother when it seemed to drag on."

"This was before Brian was hospitalized?"

"Yeah, all the stuff between the kid and her parents was, but they first approached the Lockwoods after Brian hit the skids. Anyway, the Father, guy named Tom Lodge, agreed to speak with me about what he knows. I'm not buying all this 'The whole thing was one of the Devine Mysteries of Life' bullshit. Reminds me of the old joke from the Saturday serials we used to watch at the Rockne Theater when I was a kid: The Good Guys go chasing around all afternoon looking for the Bad Guys, and when they get to the abandoned farmhouse where the Bad Guys are hiding in the barn, they shout into the hayloft, 'Anybody home?', and the bad guys yell out, 'Nobody here but just us chickens.' Something happened here, and this guy says he has an idea what it was."

Crump zipped his briefcase. "I'm headed to Lodge's office now," he said, running down the hall.

Tom Lodge was a certified land planner, a man who platted new subdivisions and advised land owners how to get maximum use out of developable land. He had a shop in a small office park on the outskirts of the City by the Lake. Crump pulled into his lot, parked and went into the office, announcing himself to Lodge's secretary, who ushered him in. Lodge was tall, starting to turn gray, and he could have looked like just about anybody, except for a serious, bushy mustache.

"Thanks for coming out my way," Lodge announced, as he stood up to greet Crump.

"No problem," Crump replied. "These are tough discussions—I'm just happy you agreed to share your experiences."

"The Lockwoods are such great folks. When my wife told me Brian was in the hospital, we sat down with our daughter, and based on what she told us, I thought we should say something."

Crump got out a pad. "Mind if I take notes?"

"No—I assume there's going to be a lawsuit—"

"You *do*?" Crump injected, surprised by Lodge's jump to such a confrontational conclusion.

"When I think about what Bill and Susan Lockwood did for that place, there oughta be."

"*Did*?" Crump felt like he was miles behind the guy.

"Bill was on the Board for years—so was I. That's how we met."

Crump looked up, stopped writing. "Mr. Lockwood was on the School Board of Carrington Prep?"

"He's a consultant. They were having a lot of problems when Brian got admitted. They were desperate to get him on the Board. Figured, correctly, that he'd offer a lot of free time and advice to help get them back on their feet—"

"I'm sorry," Crump interrupted, "but I thought Carrington was one of the most sought-after admits in the City?"

Lodge pulled out a drawer and withdrew what was obviously a financial statement, an accounting firm's logo on the top sheet. He handed it over the desk to Crump. "They were—or, *once were*, to be more accurate. When we went on the Board, they were suffering through their fourth straight year of declining enrollment. There was a lot of competition in town, some new private schools opening up, and the Publics were doing a nice job of drawing students back in. Money was tight. They were even having a hard time paying their bills. Westheimer asked both Bill and I to go on the Board. They wanted us to do an assessment, report to the rest of the Board and the Administration with recommendations on how to bounce back. We agreed, and committed a shitload of free time to come up with a comprehensive report...." He paused, pulling another bulky, bound document from his desk drawer. "Here you go," he added, handing it over.

"Carrington Prep Turnaround Report," the cover read. Crump started to page through—it was dense with text, tables and statistics. "What was wrong?" Crump asked.

"You want that list in alphabetical order?" Lodge asked, smiling. "They were skating on their reputation. At the end of the day, there wasn't much teaching going on—some of the Middle School teachers openly refused to teach math at all—found 'memorizing factors' too stifling and boring. There was no oversight or accountability—neither the teachers or the students were getting evaluated. Every time they tried to introduce any kind of standardized testing, even basic reading assessment, the progresso-fascists would have a protest and burn copies of the test blanks on the school building steps—"

"The *whats?*" Crump interrupted, narrowing an eye like he'd heard him wrong.

"'Progresso-fascists', it's what Bill and I called the Progressive Advocates. They were militantly against any changes in curriculum or teaching methods, even though the status quo was killing the place. I'd get these crazy, rambling, twenty-page emails from some of 'em, telling me, in looping, repetitive, sanctimonious text, how the kids' heads would explode if they were given a single page of homework or had to take an evaluative test. We'd started asking tough questions: Turns out some of the Middle School teachers had students—twelve and thirteen-year-olds—who couldn't even read at competent levels. They didn't know that until the administration started pulling kids out of the classrooms and giving them reading evaluations offsite. If they'd done that on site, there would have been protests and Hell to pay."

"Westheimer sort of said the same thing to me when I met him. I thought he was being melodramatic," Crump injected.

"There was this scam going on with associate teachers. Each lead teacher got to pick his or her own associates, and they were hiring their buddies, unqualified folks with no teaching experience or credentials—essentially people who were kissing their fannies. That might not have been so bad, except many of the lead teachers turned the classrooms over to the associates, sometimes for days at a time, while they did personal stuff or went to Progressive Ed seminars. Kids were being taught by folks who were essentially bowling instructors."

"The parents knew this?" Crump asked.

"They were figuring it out and leaving in droves. I remember when Bill and I interviewed a long-standing Middle School English teacher about the whole practice of leaving the kids with unqualified associates, she started screaming at us so loudly that I felt like my hair was getting slicked back on my head, like in the cartoons. Know what she told us?" Lodge asked, shaking his head as though he was having a hard time believing it himself. "She said, 'I have more important things to do than babysit students every day—as long as my master-teacher *aura* is reflected in the classroom, it rubs off on the associates, and the kids are better off if I use my time brushing up on progressive education techniques.'" He paused again and smiled at Crump, who couldn't hide his astonishment. "Yeah," he added.

"This was all in your report?" Crump asked.

"You can just imagine, we were *very popular* with the faculty."

"So, you think this might have made your kids targets?"

"Keep in mind, the report didn't come out until years later. We just think that this stuff was where the focus on Brian started. My daughter's pretty tough, and had her own group to protect her, but Brian was a quiet kid and kind of a loner—a sitting duck."

"So, you think it was your focus on all these academic shortcomings that triggered the bullying?"

"Wait—the thing was, though, the academic stuff wasn't the half of it. Bill was the Treasurer, and as he began doing risk assessments, he told me, 'The folks who run this place have the same attitude about risk management as a bunch of teenagers, hanging out in front of a liquor store on prom night—'We'll never get caught', 'How bad can it be?' and 'We'll show *them*'."

Crump was having trouble keeping up, scribbling as fast as Lodge could talk. This stuff had obviously been on Lodge's mind for a long time and he was pouring it out way too fast. "How did that play out?" Crump asked.

"Let's see: Start with kiddie transportation. All the insurance companies would cover were school busses, but they were taking kids on field trips with parents and faculty members driving them in their cars. They had no idea if some of those folks even had valid drivers' licenses. When we asked why they were doing this, turns out it wasn't even for the money—the bus rentals were cheap. The faculty told us it was 'cozier,' so they preferred it. They were cramming eight, nine kids into small sedans—if anybody got rear-ended, it would have been a mass funeral."

"And—" Crump started to ask, but Lodge was on a roll.

"The building was wide open, with parents wandering in and out all day without checking in or out. Nobody had any idea, at any given time, who was in or out of that building—again, a 'coziness' issue, we were told. They kept pets in the classrooms under heat lamps that were on all night, and of course there was no sprinkler system—they were going to burn down a twenty-million-dollar building just to keep Terry the Tarantula warm overnight. There was nobody lifeguarding the pool, which they turned over to rental outsiders after school hours, people they hardly knew, older kids and adults roaming around the buildings and the locker rooms, and then there was the 'public transit' thing—"

"Slow down, I can't get all this down,' Crump pleaded.

"Sorry—anyway, my wife called me one day, hysterical. Turns out they were taking *preschoolers*, including our four-year-old daughter, on a field trip downtown, and some genius thought it would be a great experience for them to all trundle up on the platforms and take the elevated trains downtown. They'd have forty, three-and-four-year-olds, packed on an elevated platform, with just two teachers and a couple of parent volunteers to corral them. My wife was up there, and she called me afterward to describe the scene. There were kids packed to the edge of the platform, barely staying on, pushing and shoving, and when she complained, know what the teachers decided to employ as a crowd control, safety measure? *They had them all hold hands!*" He paused, this time for effect. "Ever play *Dominoes*, Mr. Crump?"

"And you and Bill complained about all of this?"

"Yes, but actually it was the Hurricane that kind of first clued us in on the craziness," he began.

"Hurricane?"

"Hurricane Sandy, back in 2012. After it hit New York, it came ashore in the Northeast. It wrapped around to the Midwest and headed south, right along the Lake, straight to the Dunes State Park at the South end of the Lake. The thing was, Carrington had a field trip scheduled to that park, the very day the remnants of the Hurricane were scheduled to make landfall at the Dunes. A field trip of six, seven and eight year old's, kids no bigger than fifty or sixty pounds."

"Why do I think I know what's coming?" Crump asked.

"Right—we both had kids scheduled to be on that trip. Keep in mind, at this point Bill Lockwood is the School's Treasurer, the Senior Risk Management Officer of the institution. He's tracking the storm, leaving all kinds of phone messages for Westheimer, his administrators, the teachers scheduled to chaperone the trip, all warning them that readily available, public information says they ought to call it off. They *purposefully* ignore him. Of course, they don't call it off—and, it's like, *a thing*—when my wife calls from the bus, which is about to leave from the school, right into the teeth of the storm, the lead teacher is saying stuff like, 'We can't let you helicopter parents *win*,' like it's some power struggle."

"Jesus—"

"Want to know the kicker? Turns out, that day, I've got a job, one that requires a meeting sixty miles due South of the Lakeshore, right South of where they're headed. Forget that the weather report is for twenty-five-foot waves along the shoreline, lake-front warnings and seventy-mile-an-hour winds, I'm headed to an area that should be safer, straight downwind of the campsite half a hundred miles further from harm's way. So I stop to gas up, and when I get out of the car, the wind immediately blows me over, straight on my ass, and I weigh two hundred pounds. So, I call up Westheimer, and he says, 'Sorry, they left and they're not turning back,' and I said, 'Are you *crazy*?' and know what he says? 'Outdoor education is an important part of our Progressive Curriculum.'"

They *are* all crazy, Crump thought. "Hope they give that answer in their depositions, that'll get them five to ten years for child endangerment. Anybody die?"

"No," Lodge commented. "They got there and daisy chained the kids into barracks, where the kids and teachers hid under the beds for two days until the storm died down. They hunkered down, eating granola bars, drinking sports drinks, singing and shitting their pants. There was no running water and the waves were right to their front doors. It was a complete disaster. This was years before we worked on the report, but, still, I think it could be where the faculty first started to focus on Bill and I. They knew we howled about this to the Board, and then the Board pretended to crack down on the faculty about safety—nothing really changed—the faculty and staff wouldn't tolerate risk management."

Crump stopped writing. "I assume the enrollment report was not well received," Crump observed.

"Hardly, although the senior administration adopted a lot of our recommendations–had to, the place was failing. Many of the folks on the faculty, they're still, to this day, mourning the death of 'Old Carrington', the name they give the pre-reformed school. You can see why some of the faculty and administration may not fondly remember us."

Crump stood up. "But, you both kept your kids there," he commented.

"Yes, we didn't like the alternatives any better. Our local public was hugely overcrowded, neither of us wanted to go Catholic—too many crucifixes, I mean, crosses were everywhere, even the bathroom door handles—and, anyway, Westheimer *begged* us to stay."

Crump paused, stopped putting his notes in his briefcase. "Like, *how* did he beg you to stay?"

"Westheimer kept telling us, 'You're valued families, part of our community, and no hard feelings'. I figured it was because we were full pay, and the help Lockwoods were giving the school—"

"'No hard feelings' about *what*?" Crump pressed.

"Like I said, some of them were *mourning*."

"How long did the begging go on?" Crump asked, sitting back down and adding to his notes.

"It all settled down years later, once we had both enrolled our kids in seventh grade. My daughter thinks it was about two years earlier, fifth grade, that she first noticed the kids starting in on Brian Lockwood, although now we think it could have stated earlier."

Crump began packing up. As he bent over his briefcase, he commented, "I bet this soured your view of the folks you call 'The Progresso-Fascists'?"

"You know, I'd never voted for a Republican *in my life*. If anything, it taught me to distrust people with agendas, regardless of their philosophical bent."

He took the business card Crump offered, then added, "There was a joke we used to tell each other when we were on the Board: 'What's the difference between a Conservative and a Liberal? A Conservative is a crazy fanatic with his hand in your pocket, trying to find your wallet to count your money; A Liberal is a crazy fanatic with his hand up his ass, trying to find his head.'"

* *

Crump pulled into the driveway of the Lockwood home, on the Northern edge of the City by the Lake. It was a modest three-bedroom frame with a front-facing garage, not unlike just about everything else in the neighborhood. It was a pretty quiet neighborhood, the kind of place cops and firemen who had to live in the City, tended to end up.

Susan Lockwood let him in and they retreated to a warmly-lit room in the back of the house, with knotty pine paneling straight out of the Fifties, Crump figured, when the house was probably built.

Bill Lockwood was tall, thin, greying and nervous looking. Susan looked younger and healthier, like the ordeal wasn't yet taking a physical toll on her. They offered him something to drink; he declined. It was getting late and he promised his spouse Mary he'd be home at a reasonable hour.

"I talked to Tom Lodge," Crump began. "Pretty harrowing story," he added.

"Those were tense times," Bill offered.

"Sounds like it. You didn't tell me you were once on the Board of Carrington Prep," Crump asked, trying to not sound accusatory.

"That was a year ago," Susan Lockwood said. "How could that have anything to do with this?"

"Lodge described it as a fairly contentious relationship between you two consultants, and the rest of the community—used words like 'mourning', and 'pretty unpopular'. The bullying went on unchecked for years, and by your own estimates, started about the time of all this business with you two issuing a report about changing the entire culture at Carrington. Cultures evolve very slowly, particularly in places like schools. That's in part because the 'old guard' tends to stick around for a long time in educational institutions, and the cultures are revered, rightly or wrongly. It sounds pretty obvious to me the faculty and administration had to know about the bullying and never did anything—Hell, they must have actively covered it up, from what I've been told."

Bill and Susan Lockwood glanced at each other.

"The thing I don't understand is the means of transmission," Crump began.

"Transmission?" Bill Lockwood asked.

"Yes—I can understand how and why the faculty and administration might be resentful of the changes you and Lodge were arguing for, even if they were essential to saving the school. What I don't get is how that makes its way down to the kids. I mean, it's pretty boring, adult financial stuff, and young kids make for lousy stewards of their parents plans and schemes. And, in this case, the kids would be taking cues from teachers, not from people they eat dinner with each…..night……"

Crump slowed and then stopped as he saw the expression on both their faces. The Lockwoods looked ashen.

"The *waivers*," Susan Lockwood said, almost under her breath.

"The what?" Crump asked, not certain he'd heard her correctly.

"The waiver kids," Bill added. "There's a faculty and staff waiver program at Carrington."

"Meaning?" Crump asked.

"It's pretty expensive—even back then. Tuition was over ten grand a year, even for early childhood—probably out of reach for school teachers and even for the administrators. So the school offers them tuition waivers, and faculty and staff kids go free—they pay a small book fee, but, otherwise, they're pretty much subsidized."

Crump nodded. "How many?"

"I see where you're going," Susan Lockwood commented. "There were at least thirty or forty, at any given time—"

"As a percentage of enrollment?" Crump interrupted.

"At least ten per cent, if you don't count the High School," Bill added.

"So, you've got thirty to forty kids, sitting down to dinner each night, listening to stories about how the evil consultants, the Lockwoods and the Lodges, are destroying the school, wrecking the culture. The dinner-time gossip is that you're doing it at the behest of the money guys, Senior Administration, folks who invited you in to 'fix' the broken culture, the one they all love, the one everybody keeps telling me these folks are willing to publicly immolate themselves over. You know, in any group of thirty to forty kids, there are bound to be a few jerks, maybe even some dangerous jerks, especially if they feel empowered and unregulated......" He stopped.

Susan Lockwood swallowed hard and said, "I think it's potentially worse than that. Bill didn't just issue that report. The school was in pretty bad shape—they'd taken on some debt and were about to default. It was actually on the verge of closing. Westheimer begged us, and we paid off the debt and gave them some working capital to tide them over until they could restore enrollment."

"How much?" Crump asked.

"All told, it was over a million," Susan advised. "We had to raid our retirement accounts, and I dipped into a small stash of inherited funds from my Mom, but I'm sure, to the faculty, it made us look like rich people—"

"It was supposed to be anonymous," Bill injected, "But before long, somehow, everybody knew. And, if there's one thing those folks *hate*, it's people with money, or even, people they *believe* have money—Parents used to jokingly call it, 'The People's Republic of Carrington,' but they were only *half* joking. I'm afraid it put us in kind of a financial bind."

"I'm sticking with our deal—this is a no fee case," Crump assured them. "Do you have a school roster?"

"They circulate one every year. It has the names of the students, as well as the names and addresses for their parents," Susan Lockwood acknowledged. "We've got one for every year, back to the time Bill was on the Board."

"Good—make me a copy," Crump asked. "Just out of curiosity—are there four times as many parent listings as kid listings?"

"You mean—"

"Divorces—are a lot of the kids' parents divorced?" Crump asked.

"Sure, I guess," Susan Lockwood speculated.

Crump stood up. "I can't say I'm sure this is going to help Brian any, but at least we're on the way to figuring out what happened here. I'll bet all the money in my checkbook the bullying had nothing to do with anything Brian said or did."

* *

When Crump got outside, he noticed somebody had tagged Mary's car—there was a bumper sticker pasted to the trunk lid. It was too dark to read at a distance, so he bent down and eyed it up close. The left side of the sticker had the caricature of Uncle Sam, taken from the famous recruiting posters, top hat, star-spangled outfit and all, pointing the "I want you" index finger Crump's way.

Next to Uncle Sam, blood-red lettering announced: "The Army of God Wants *You*......"

8.
THE ARMY OF GOD WANTS *YOU*..........

"**C**RUMP, YOU GOTTA TAKE THESE guys seriously."

Steven Barnacle, all pockmarked face and grimy aviator rimmed-glasses of the reformed alcoholic that he was, sat across from Crump, picking up and inspecting junk from Crump's desk. Barnacle was a former federal prosecutor and law school classmate of Crump's. He was there to warn Crump about the smear campaign quietly being orchestrated by Attorney General Warren Handler.

He hadn't been in Crump's office for a while, and some of the artifacts strewn about the desk reminded him of cases they'd worked on together, over the years. His favorite trinket was a flattened and framed airplane air-sickness bag, with its printed message prominently displayed: "Fine for Unofficial Use: $500.00." He picked it up.

"What's the *official* use of a barf bag?" Barnacle asked, turning it around in his hand like a fine diamond.

"I don't want to think about it," Crump answered. "So, what are they gonna do?" he asked, not convinced the situation was as dire as Barnacle claimed. "Usually, they go after the principals, not the lawyers—too much heat when you mess with the judicial process, even for slathering goobers like Handler."

"You're living in the past. These people don't care. Warren Handler *became* Attorney General so he could promote his crazy theory that the Feds, at all levels—not just the President—can't be prosecuted or regulated, because *they are* the law. He's on some agenda about top-down moralism, and he *hates* you."

"He's hard to take seriously—Handler looks like the giant panda who always wanted to be a real boy, and finally got his wish—"

"Crump, these are not nice people. They will do anything to smear an opponent. Handler grew up at Stenson and Willis."

"My favorite people," Crump noted. "I'm pretty small crackers, so I've only had to face them twice, but, yeah, it was an unpleasant experience. They elevate assholery to an art—everything is jack, jack, jack you around for next to nothing, just to wear you out."

Barnacle nodded. "The Feds flew me to Washington last week, said they had to ask me about an old case. I said, 'Hey, man, I'm officially retired,' and they said it was a condition of my pension—"

"That's bullshit—"

"Yeah," Barnacle acknowledged, "but I'm living on it, so I go, and when I get there, they have this room full of guys, a bunch of A.U.S.A.'s, a couple of private investigators and some nit wits I couldn't figure out. It was all about you: They were grilling me about *everything*, the case where you represented me, that business in '95 with the Nomando kid, and how I got you and Maureen deputized, a list of the cases we'd worked since then." He stopped, looking over his shoulder. "They wanted to know all about your personal life:

Any old girlfriends they could dig up and gin up into saying you misbehaved, maybe moved on them while they were out of it? Ever do any drugs?"

"That's funny," Crump injected. "I'm sixty-eight, most of my 'old girlfriends' are probably *dead,* and I don't even drink."

Barnacle nodded. "I gave them the line: 'Anything that alters consciousness is poison, including alcohol, tobacco and marijuana—"

"—and the word 'poison' and the phrase 'in moderation' cannot be used together in a complete sentence," Crump added, completing their near-slogan. "What'd they say?" Crump wondered.

"Asked me if you'd had that printed on your tee-shirts. I told them your old man was an alkie, and that was partly why you ended up in State Custody. They were all over that—pissed off they couldn't quickly get the juvie files unsealed—but they promised me, they eventually will."

Crump shrugged. "They'll bribe some clerk, but that won't tell them anything—I was in Juvie for an abuse and neglect case, not because I was busting into parking meters."

"I know. That's what worries me. They don't find anything, they're gonna start making stuff up, planting dirt on you, trying to get you picked up and taken in for 'questioning,'" Barnacle offered, using his fingers to put air quotes around "questioning".

"Well, good—I got my own P.I.—"

"Crump, you're not talking about bringing Angelo Turulio into this thing……are you?"

Crump got up and circled the office, looking out the window. "Not *today*—"

"Crump—"

"I know, but that's Angelo's secret weapon. Everybody thinks he's just a meatball, and they keep thinking that until it's too late."

Barnacle stood up and handed a letter to Crump. "That's a file transfer request," he explained. "I'm supposed to deliver it to the current U.S. Attorney for the Northern District. They want all of my files transferred to Washington. This is not going to go away—"

"So?" Crump interrupted.

"So? So, I think you should drop this case."

"I'm ethically bound not to do that."

"C'mon, you know you could give it back to the clinic that referred it to Maureen. They'd stick somebody new on the case."

Maureen walked in, just in time to hear that last suggestion. "That'd be a little tough, now that we've taken on half the World with this thing."

"Hey, McDougal," Barnacle said. "You know, as well as I do, that if you gave it back, whoever took it over would drop all the Patriot Act business and just focus on the medical deportation injunction. That Patriot Act stuff is all Handler and Stuggs care about—it's getting them brutal publicity, on top of all the grief they're getting on the medical deportation cases. They'll quietly retreat on those, at least until the publicity dies down, and then the whole case goes away. In the meantime, Crump here can retire and—"

"And, *what*? I don't play golf. Mary would probably move to another state if I started hanging out at home."

"Yeah, bullshit—last time I saw her, I asked her how things were going, and she said, "Every morning, I wake up, and I ask Crump, 'Did you quit yet?'"

"Not to change the subject, but what do we do about uniting this kid with her Mother? The only thing keeping her alive out there is her newfound belief, courtesy of Crump here, that we are going to find Mom and get them back together," Maureen added.

Barnacle sat back down. "Like I told Crump, there's a consent decree in a Volunteer Civil Liberties case out in California, from before Stuggs adopted his 'Zero Tolerance' program and started jamming these kids by the hundreds into cages. There was a similar program, on a much smaller scale, dealing with immigrant kids whose parents *were* criminals, for some reason other than crossing the border. Even *that* freaked out the courts, so the Government was ordered to re-unite the kids and parents. All you need to do is get your kid certified as a member of that class, then let the Civil Liberties folks help you from there."

Crump sat down. He rocked for a minute in his chair. "O.K., McDougal, this is your case—"

"*My* case?"

"You started it," Crump began.

"I know exactly what you're doing, and we should have this discussion after Steve leaves."

Barnacle stood. "She's right. I'm on my way. I just hope you guys do the right thing and get out of this thing, because these guys are going to get you—"

"About that," Crump said. "You ever heard of a bunch of cockroaches calling themselves, 'The Army of God'?"

Barnacle looked at Maureen, then back at Crump. "Sounds like some crackpot outfit, but no, that's a new one on me. Why?"

"Nothing, just curious."

"I *bet*," Barnacle replied.

"I'll call you," Crump said, as Barnacle showed himself out.

Maureen sat down across from Crump. She was doing her steam-shovel thing, where she used her arms to shove the papers on his desk apart to clear a path so she could glare at Crump unobstructed. As a consequence, Crump knew he was going to get it.

"Look—" Crump started.

"Don't give me this 'Your case' crap. You're the one who dug into a routine guardianship case and came out with a national referendum on Stuggs and his racist-crackpot thugs."

"You know where I'm going," Crump offered. "You've still got young kids. Mine are at least out in the job market—heck, Ben's even a cop—pretty hard to muscle in on one of them. I just want to make sure you're not dragged along by the inertia of this thing. I have no intention of dropping anything or fobbing this off on some stooge of a volunteer."

"Me, neither. I may go to the same church as some of these nutjobs, but I'm not joining the Army of God," Maureen confessed.

"About that," Crump said, as he opened his desk drawer and pulled out the chewed-up bumper sticker he'd scraped off the trunk lid of Mary's car. He handed the droopy sticker across to Maureen. It was still plainly readable. While she turned it over in her hands, he added, "Somebody slapped this on Mary's car when I was out interviewing the Lockwoods."

"Any idea who this is?" she asked.

"No, but the only real question is, are they freelancers, or are they in bed with Handler, Stuggs, and the Crypto-Fascist enterprise we now call the Administration? What I do know is that, whoever it is, they knew Mary's car. Equally creepy, they knew how to find me, interviewing a client at a place I'd never been before, one that I'd decided to visit just an hour before I went."

"Which means?" Maureen asked.

"They were following me."

"Shit."

"So, like I said, you in or out?"

"For now, I'm still in. They touch my family, I'm out," Maureen declared, emphatically.

"Good news, there," Crump offered. "I bought us some protection—"

"Crump, not Angelo Turulio—"

"He might just surprise you—"

"He's, like, sixty-six going on a hndred, and he still looks like one of the Rumble-in-The-Alley-Greaser Extras from 'West Side Story.'"

"I do wonder where he gets those black leather jackets in 2022. I would have thought the environmentalists and vegetarians would have taken care of that," Crump observed.

"Every time I walk into the room, he whips a comb out of his back pocket and combs his hair. He's a dinosaur."

"He may be cold blooded," Crump injected, "but I'm sure the similarities stop there. In any event, he's at the moral center of the universe, and he'll do anything—"

"That's what scares me," Maureen replied.

* *

"Ayy, Boss—long time, no see," Angelo Turulio announced, as Crump ducked under the low doorframe to enter Angelo's cramped office, shoehorned into the crawl space below a Currency Exchange.

"It was *Tuesday*," Crump responded.

"Hey—we're *old*—dats a long time."

Crump and Turulio went all the way back to High School, and while they'd lost and found each other a half dozen times since, Crump had always been a faithful client, ever since Turulio had obtained a private investigator's license. Turulio remained one of Crump's most loyal buddies. Crump had rescued Turulio's dystrophic brother Mario from all sorts of abuse and worked with him until his untimely death at age twenty-five, dedication Turulio never forgot. The West Side of the City by the Lake, where they'd both grown up, was an enclave of Italians, Irish and Pols, and while Crump had lost his West-Side dialect and chops, Angelo had never outgrown his. With his doorknob nose, his greasy, black, short-cropped hair and his hammered face, he looked like a grizzled pianist who'd played one-too-many bars on one-too-many nights.

"What did you do with the chairs?" Crump asked, glancing around at the empty space in front of Turulio's desk.

"Dey got repossessed—"

"Your *furniture* got snagged?"

"S' a long story," Turulio began.

"Well, good news—I got a new job for you."

"Gonna need a retainer," Turulio announced, as he sat on the edge of his desk and pointed Crump to Turulio's own desk chair.

"This's kinda weird," Crump complained.

"Dat's O.K., 'cause, b'cause you got the seat, you gotta take the notes," he said, tossing Crump a notepad.

Crump shook his head in disbelief, then sat down and began writing his instructions to Turulio.

"Ever hear of an outfit called, 'The Army of God?' Crump asked, as he scribbled.

"Yeah, sure—"

"You *have*?" Crump exclaimed, as he stopped scribbling.

"Hey, dis sounds 'mportant, so keep writing—"

"I better be getting minimum wage for this," Crump complained.

"Take it up wid duh Union."

"So, what and who are they?" Crump asked, and before Turulio could answer, he added, "And, how the Hell do you know about these guys?"

"When you gonna start usin' a computer? Is one a dem anti-'bortion outfits," Turulio scolded.

Crump looked up from his note taking. "A 'Right-To-Life' group?"

"You mean, a 'Right-to-Kill-Only-Da-People-We-Wanna-Kill' group, doncha?"

"Gee, Angelo, if this gig doesn't work out, maybe you should go into Advertising—"

"Dees people are dangerous whack-jobs. Dere some uh the folks dat shoot th' 'bortion doctors," Turulio warned.

"So, what do they want with me?"

"Yuh sure it's not at-random?" Turulio asked, walking around Crump to boot up his computer.

"I've been driving for fifty years and never had any car tagged before, and suddenly Mary's car gets tagged by these guys in a neighborhood where I don't live, that I visit for the first time on a whim and that's full of moms and dads pushing around baby strollers. Yeah, it's not random."

"You *are* runnin' round calling Stuggs and his gang a buncha Terrorizers," Turulio said, as he began flipping through screens, standing by his computer.

"How did you know that?" Crump asked.

"Ever'body knows dat," he replied, pulling up a screen with a picture of Crump and Maureen walking into the Federal courthouse, above a caption that read, "Lawyers Go Hunting For Terrorists In Stuggs Administration."

"So, what's the connection? They the first folks to endorse Stuggs' campaign?"

"No, dat was duh Klan, but dere right behind 'em."

"Swell. Look, I don't believe for a minute they just picked my name out of the newspapers."

"Nobody reads newspapers—"

"*Fine*, the Internet, whatever. I think they were put up to this. I'd like you to scope these guys out, follow them around, find out who runs the outfit. Steve Barnacle tells me Warren Handler himself is spearheading the smear campaign on me. I'm betting that he, or one of his henchmen, is behind this."

"Who duh Hell is 'Warren Handler'?"

"He's the Attorney General of the Entire United States of America, the senior legal officer for the Federal government—"

"So's, yur wantin' me to, like, inflate the entire Government?'

"I think you mean *infiltrate*, but, no, just get close to these 'Army of God' types, see if you can link them up to the Stuggs administration, especially Handler."

Turulio logged off his computer and circled the desk. "Hey, mebbe I could 'personate one uh dem folks you see trowin' jars full o' pickled dolls made up to look like dead babies, at the folks goin' inta Planned Parenthood—"

"Don't tell me about it—I'll pay hard cash not to know *how* you get it done."

"Gotcha, skipper."

"Ange, just one more thing: No guns on this job, O.K.?"

"Guns don't kill people, *fingers* kill people," Turulio said, as he ushered Crump out the door.

9.
GO TO THE HEAD OF THE CLASS..........

Chief Judge Sharon Haverhorn surveyed her courtroom. She counted twenty-six for-sure reporters and three sketch artists. We'll be reading purple prose about this tomorrow, she thought to herself, as she asked her Clerk to call the next case, even though everybody in the courtroom knew the name of the next case.

"E.M., a Minor, by her Guardian and Next Friend, Dr. Amelia Trimble, versus the United States Citizenship and Immigration Services, et., al.," the overhead audio system blared out.

Crump stepped up to the podium in the center of the courtroom. He was trying to get the case certified as a Class Action, so they'd be representing all of the thousands of critical care medical patients the immigration authorities, under Dennis Ernstmeyer, were now threatening to deport.

"Your honor, this is our motion for class certification. There are four thousand, six hundred and thirty-two persons, most of them minors, who have been subjected to the Government's forced, Medical Deportation

Program. There is no reason for their cases to be dealt with all over the Country in different lawsuits. We ask that you certify the class of Plaintiffs as all the potential deportees, and designate our client, the Guardian for the minor we call 'E.M.', as the class representative. We are handling the case pro bono, so it is an advantage to the entire class to keep all their cases on a no-fee basis."

"That all, Mr. Crump?" the Judge inquired.

"Yes. I'd like a few minutes of rebuttal time."

"Mr. Meadows," the Judge announced, acknowedging the Solicitor General, who the Judge had purposefully agreed to admit to the local trial bar, to argue on behalf of the Government.

"Thank you," Q. Peter Meadows announced, as he stepped up to the podium and cleared his throat. "As you can imagine, the Government opposes class certification, which we view as an unnecessary and inappropriate escalation of this politically-motivated lawsuit—"

"Excuse me, Mr. Meadows, but who do you see as the 'political motivator' behind this case? Surely, not the fourteen year old child who is the plaintiff, who, as I understand it, is neither a citizen nor a resident of the United States."

Meadows glanced back over his shoulder at Regina Debevoise, the U.S. Attorney handling the case, who had begged him to let her handle the argument. She casually tilted her head in Crump's direction.

"We feel the Plaintiff's attorney and his law firm are on some sort of vendetta, evidenced by the outrageous Patriot Act claim, accusing distinguished officers of the U.S. Government of terrorism."

"Mr. Meadows, it is my understanding we're talking about a two-person law firm that handles primarily decedents' estates and guardianships in State probate court. What possible benefit accrues to Plaintiff's counsel, who are handling the case on a volunteer basis, from suing the Government?"

"We are ourselves not certain of the answer, but I can assure you, the Department of Justice is investigating the matter—"

"And, I'm certain if you discover any irregularities, you'll bring them to the Court's attention," the Judge offered, interrupting what she assumed was another paid political announcement from the Solicitor General. "We have a crowded docket today, so unless you have any substantive objections not raised in your pleadings, I'd like to move on to the next case. I'll rule in the next thirty days."

"We do have two other objections. First, we object to any class certification mixing plaintiff medical deportees who are in the Country legally, with those here illegally."

"What difference should that make to class certification?" the Judge asked. "Your Agency U.S.C.I.S., made no distinction between the two groups, when it issued the blanket revocation of the program allowing deferred immigration status to all patients in the program, did it not?"

Meadows looked down at the podium, flipped a page, then said, "That's correct."

"Does that mean you've reversed the policy, for any class of patients?"

"No, but—"

"Well, then," the Judge interrupted, "how does having at least hundreds, or maybe even *thousands* of these cases, clogging the court systems all over the Country, serve anybody's benefit? That objection is not persuasive. What's your other objection?"

"I'd like to yield to Ms. Debevoise for that argument," Meadows announced, stepping away from the podium.

"Your Honor," Debevoise began, as she leaned into the microphone, "the Government objects to designating the guardian for the minor known as 'E.M.,' as the class representative. That minor child is the true Plaintiff in this case—her guardian is just her caretaker. I've never been involved in a class action where the defendant could not identify the true class representative, let alone, even know that person's *name*," she continued. "Most defendants in lawsuits get to both know and confront their accusers."

Crump rose. "May I?" he asked.

"Go ahead, Mr. Crump," the Judge acknowledged.

Crump spoke from the counsel table, without a microphone, which didn't much matter, given the tone and tenor of his voice. "The reason the Government should be able to deal with our client and her minor charge as class representative, is because they *know* that child's identity."

He paused, waiting for it to sink in, and sink in it did—there was a rumbling of voices and shuffling, as the journalists in the room sat up and began scribbling.

The Judge requested order in the courtroom. "Proceed, please," the Judge told Crump.

"When I first took this case, I interviewed the patient I now represent, just trying to obtain her consent for the state court guardianship appointment. What I learned in that interview was that the Government most assuredly knows my client's true name—which is 'Estrellita Montes'—the name she gave me when she signed a sworn guardianship designation. Perhaps it's purely a coincidence that the U.S.C.I.S. secret code name she was given when they ripped her out of her Mother's arms, just happens to be the leading initials of her proper name….." Crump paused, "Perhaps, but I doubt it."

Crump looked around the courtroom. The reporters were scribbling furiously.

"The single deposition question Mr. Ernstmeyer, the architect of 'Zero Tolerance', was directed by counsel not to answer, was whether the Government was keeping records of the identities and whereabouts of the mothers, fathers and children they were separating when they started ripping these families apart. We believe the reason Ernstmeyer wouldn't answer that question is because U.S.C.I.S. knows *exactly* who the victims of these policies are, and they're only *pretending* that they lack the information and resources to re-unite these families. We hope to prove that the reason they are *pretending* they don't know, is so they can publicly say, '*Gosh*, how can we possibly find them all?' The reason for that charade is that they are intentionally keeping families apart. Their objective is to strike fear and terror into the hearts and minds of their victims and any others who may be considering approaching the U.S. border." Again, he paused for effect. "So, in response to the Government's *drippingly insincere* concern that they won't be able to identify the class representative in this case, well, *now they can't say they don't know*."

The Courtroom was buzzing, but the judge did nothing to stifle the hubbub.

"Thank you. As I said, I'll rule on the motion for class certification within thirty days. Please call the next case," the Judge added, as the courtroom emptied out.

* *

"Was that a good idea?" Maureen asked.

"Outing the kid?" Crump asked, as they walked briskly back to the office. "She's in a pretty secure location—I wouldn't bet against Giampetro in a one on one with an unarmed assailant."

"Yes, but now she becomes more of a target."

"Any more of a target than when the United States Government painted a bullseye on her back and tried to throw her out into the Mexican desert, with a feeding tube trailing behind her?" Crump stopped, turned and asked.

"I just hope you're right," she said. "Everybody in the case identified with a proper noun seems to be getting weirdos following them around."

"You getting tagged with whacko bumper stickers?"

"No, but the hate mail is starting to get nastier, and naming names," she reflected, as they disappeared into the elevator of their office building.

* *

Crump had scoured the Carrington Prep directory, highlighting all the parents who were not on waivers and therefore not working for the school. Figuring they would be the best interview sources to finger the perps harassing the Lockwood kid, he asked Maureen to help him canvass for witnesses.

"I think you might do better with some of the girls," Crump began, when Maureen jumped all over him.

"You mean, '*women*'?"

"They're like, fourteen," Crump argued.

"O. K., *young women*—"

"Humans without 'Y' chromosomes, *whatever*, I just figure the testosterone-free zone is a little more likely place to get honest answers about this stuff."

Maureen looked at him like he was a giant, overgrown toddler. "Boy, are you dreaming. How'd you raise a daughter? You never hear about the 'Mean Girls' phenomena? Once they get to Middle School, they're worse—not as physical, but they're so much better *organized*."

"Yeah, I get that. I just think this thing follows a more traditional path. You talk to the girls, I'll do the boys. Let's see what we get."

Maureen drove. They'd set up interview points for parents, and where the parents would cooperate, the kids. They spent a day getting nowhere, between faulty memories and folks just reluctant to get involved. By early evening, they'd made it to the house of one of the parents who'd first tipped off the Lockwoods that the harassment had been going on for years. The family had a daughter in Brian's classroom and a son in the grade behind.

Maureen took the daughter, with the parents sitting in. Crump peeled off to talk to the son.

"So, your daughter is old enough that her testimony would be considered competent, even though her identity would be shielded from public disclosure. You'd need to consent for it to be used at all in a court proceeding," Maureen began, in response to the Dubrows asking if a lawsuit would be filed and they'd all have to testify. "Not sure this will get to a lawsuit—at this stage, Brian's parents just want to find out what happened—they think it will help the doctors deal with the issues he's having. He seems afraid to even look out the windows at the hospital."

"Well, *yeah*," the kid spoke up. She had shoulder-length brown hair, a tucked chin and dark brown eyes. The kid looked older than the fourteen that she was, and she had an attitude a little like she just might punch somebody.

"Honey, wait—" her Mother cautioned.

"Didi—did I get your name right?" Maureen asked, trying to casually interrupt the parents, who seemed to want to slow the kid down.

"Short for 'Dierdre,'" the Mother answered.

"You were starting to say," Maureen offered, keeping her going.

"He's scared they're gonna get him."

"Who's '*they*'?"

"They don't have like a real, official name, like a gang….." Didi paused. "It used to be more kids, but now it's mostly Parker and Fletcher. They took over when Marianne and Vance got in trouble," she added.

"Honey, slow down. Mrs. McDougal doesn't know these names, or who you're talking about," Didi's Mother cautioned.

Her daughter gave her mother an exasperated look. "Everybody *knows*—"

"Didi, your Mother's right. These names are new to me. Can we back up? When did this Marianne and Vance get into trouble, and who are they?"

"Two years ago," she began, then paused. Her Father had silently walked out.

"This part really upsets my husband," the Mother explained.

They've been discussing this, Maureen thought. Good.

"Twenty Twenty?" Maureen asked.

"No, before, right after Spring break, in fifth grade's when it all began. Marianne started it. She was, like, 'Brian's a dickhead,' and we asked her why, and she said, 'His parents are rich, and they're gonna run the school, and kick us all out,' but we knew that wasn't true. She was mad because she used to look over and copy off all his work, and one day he told her to stop and Miss Ventura heard him, and Marianne got in a bunch of trouble, 'cause copying is not allowed—"

"Slow down, honey," her Mother cautioned.

"Who is Marianne?" Maureen asked.

"She's Marianne Pennebacker—"

"The science teacher's daughter?" Maureen asked.

"Yeah. She's one of *Them*, her and Vance were like, the leaders."

"And Vance is?"

"The gym teacher's kid. They've been at Carrington the longest, so they are the bosses of *Them*."

"*Them*?" Maureen asked.

"It's just a group, it's like all the teacher's kids, except for Winston, who's Westheimer's kid."

"You call them, '*Them*'?" Maureen asked.

"Yeah, only behind their backs. Anyway, they'd put Brian in the elevator and hit that emergency siren button, then they could turn this key they got from the office and he'd be trapped in there until the firemen came, and once it took like half an hour, and while he was in there he wet his pants, and they were waiting in the hall and took pictures when the firemen took him out, but then one of the firemen said, like, 'Hey, what are you guys doing?' and both Marianne and Vance got in a bunch of trouble."

She paused, looked at her Mother as if to say, Is this all right? Her Mother nodded.

"What kind of trouble they get into?" Maureen pressed.

"This was the part that was two years ago. All I know is I saw Mrs. Pennebacker, telling Marianne, like, 'You gotta stop, or they're gonna throw you out,' and some other stuff, but then later, Marianne says to us, 'Parker and Fletcher are gonna take care of that faggot Brian,' and pretty soon after, Fletcher, he's the biggest kid in the class, he was slamming Brian around all over the place......" she paused. "Is this O.K. to tell?" she asked.

"Yes," Maureen assured her. We agreed with your folks to only use this, for now, without attribution—"

"What's *attabution*—"

"Sorry. We won't tell anybody your name. Can you tell me what this Fletcher and Parker did?"

"Bad stuff. They elbowed him in the stomach a lot, they'd push him in the street during outside activities, and they're the ones who put that stuff in his locker, all the kill-yourself instructions and razor blades—"

"How do you know this?" Maureen asked.

"They *told* us, I mean, they warned us not to tell, said they were gonna mess him up, and they could get us thrown out too—"

"Did you believe them?" Maureen asked.

The kid paused and looked up at her mother. "No—nobody gets thrown out—everybody knows that. The really bad part was not wanting to get *Them* to start doing stuff to us."

"So the bad thing was, *Them* starting *what*?"

"I mean, they never let up on Brian: 'You got a faggot face—if I had your faggot face, I'd kill myself—why don't you just do it, I mean, go kill yourself—everybody knows you got no dick in those pants—you don't need a sex change, 'cause you already got yours chewed off giving …….." She paused.

"I think I get the general idea," Maureen said, sparing the Kid from having to finish the menu of insults.

"How could this go on for years, without the staff knowing—"

"—Oh, they *knew*—" the kid interrupted.

"How do you know, they knew?" Maureen asked.

"So, one day, last year, the English teacher, Mr. Farkis, he closes the door, after the four of 'em left the room—"

"The 'four'?" Maureen asked.

"Marianne, Fletcher, Vance and Parker, after they left, Mr. Farkis says, 'Listen, Fletcher, he has it real tough, I mean, his parents are divorced and his Dad left them, and Parker he's got somethin', like epilepsy or somethin', anyway, Mr. Farkis says, 'Don't talk about all this stuff, and don't worry, they sent Fletcher to some doctor, who says he's really OK, so don't worry that he's bragging about going to his uncle's house and getting his guns to shoot kids and stuff, because he's just makin' that up—"

"—Sorry, but a *teacher* said to ignore threats to shoot up the place?" Maureen asked, incredulous.

"Yeah, he said it was just 'talk.'"

"Mr. Farkis mention that these threats were about Brian?" Maureen asked.

"We all knew what he was talking about."

* *

When Crump and Maureen met up outside, she filled him in.

"I guess I was too quick to write off the lack of gang activity at the place—that stuff's classic gang strategy. The older kids get caught and they hand the baton off to the younger, or the dumber, or just the more vulnerable kids, their students in crime," Crump observed.

"Sounds like this Fletcher guy is a gifted student," Maureen said.

"Yeah, but it's not the kids I want. They're not getting paid thousands of dollars a year to keep this from happening. She really describe the waiver kids as a gang?"

"They've even got a tag—'*Them*'—" Maureen noted.

"And a teacher actually told them not to worry about threats to shoot up the place?" Crump asked.

"I guess he just played it down, supposedly to avoid panic. Maybe he still told the Administration, took precautions?" Maureen speculated.

Crump was shaking his head. "Doubt it. Over eighty percent of school shootings involve some sort of at-school bullying. More often than not, the attitude of the faculty is, 'I'm a PhD, not a babysitter—go hire a social worker.' Then, when it happens, everybody wrings their hands and talks about the need for sensible gun control, which won't happen during my adult lifetime. And, these Carrington folks are drunk on Progressive Ed stuff, so the thought of disciplining bullies makes their heads explode—"

"Swell, no wonder this is out of control," she offered.

"Like I said, 'Nobody here but just us chickens,'" Crump replied.

10.
IT'S A HUMAN SHELL GAME........

Maureen McDougal caught a cab out of the San Diego Airport. She was a little jazzed from the landing approach, the way the plane swooped in so close to the downtown buildings that she could see window washers setting up rigs on the rooftops. The cab sped by the nearly endless Naval facilities that dotted the coast South of the airport, glancing past a jarring mix of homeless people camped out in sleeping bags, kids on skateboards doing stunts and massive cruise ships, docked so close to the roadway they looked like they were crossing the intersections. The lakefront in her hometown, which seemed to escape the with-it characterizations of waterfronts on the East and West coasts, was severely underrated, she concluded, as she paid the fare and exited the cab.

She was in town to look into adding Estrellita Montes as a plaintiff in the main class action suit the civil liberties outfits had been using against the Stuggs' Administration's family separation, 'Zero Tolerance' border-crossing policy. The California District Court had long before ordered U.S.C.I.S. and H.H.S. to re-unite any separated families within 30 days, a nearly impossible task once 'Zero Tolerance' kicked in, one that kept the Stuggs administration hopping. While Maureen probably could have accomplished this over the phone, her first interview with their lead counsel, Wade Solley, convinced her she wanted to get directly involved. Solley suggested that his case's thirty-day re-unification order was the reason Stuggs and Ernstmeyer were faking not having family identification and location records, to falsely claim impossibility when ordered to bring families back together.

Solley had thousands of family members he was tracking, while the Stuggs Administration was practicing organized foot dragging to slow him down. Solley told her the El Paso processing center, where the Montes's had entered the U.S., was an indescribable mess. As a result, the El Paso records had been transferred to the San Diego U.S.C.I.S. facilities. Describing the state of the Southern California processing center, Solley then reported, "You gotta see it to believe it," so she figured the trip might also generate evidence for their Patriot Act claims.

She stopped at Solley's office on the outskirts of downtown.

"You're the same Maureen McDougal that's labeled Stuggs and Handler as Terrorists," he said, as he greeted her.

Maureen wanted to confess how completely accidental the terrorism angle had begun, but she was there to find Estrellita's Mother and collect evidence, not to awkwardly answer for her newfound notoriety. "So, how do we get H.H.S.'s records and add my client to your class?" she asked.

"This whole thing is clearly a harassment campaign. We have a couple of injunctions going, so they're supposed to be giving us the records for anybody who's been separated from a parent for more than ten days. That assumes they've got the records, which, most of the time, they claim they don't."

"How's that really possible?" Maureen asked, amazed she could still feel shocked by the Stuggs Administration's mendacious knuckleheads.

"They got 'em," he offered, "They just can't *produce them*. Records assumes you have a process," Solley began. "This thing was carried out like they were gangsters—no, amateur gangsters, rehearsing for real gangster-hood. The entire premise was supposed to be that the border-crossing adults were criminals, but the 'crimes' these people are committing are class-four misdemeanors, the lowest rung on the criminal ladder, with a typical fine of ten to fifty dollars. They literally shuttle them off to a five-minute trial in temporary courtrooms, give them a sentence of time served and fifty dollars, then shuttle them off to Immigration and Customs Enforcement agents for deportation. Their kids, in the meantime, are already gone—"

"Wait," Maureen injected. "If that's all done on such a rocket-docket pace, how do they get the kids separated in the first place?"

"Most of the time, they trick them into giving up their kids," he said, in a deadpan voice that sounded like it was what anybody would expect to hear, describing the acts of a Presidential Administration. "The I.C.E. Agents approach the parents while they're waiting to be 'processed', and tell them they are taking the kids for a bath or to get them something to eat. But the 'processing' takes less than a day, and consists entirely of giving the parents a list of legal service agencies, which they have no way of contacting. By the time the parents are being ushered into courtrooms, the kids are already on a bus to somewhere."

"You gotta be kidding me—"

"No, and it gets worse. On the pretense that they need to protect the kids from their criminally dangerous parents, they whisk the kids off to places where they know they'll be hard to find, and then once they get to a first destination, they bus them around some more. The locations are nowhere near the Southern Border—New York, Seattle, Detroit and City by the Lake, where your client ended up. It's a human shell game they're playing with these kids."

Maureen shook her head. "Why the *busses*?"

"Because, the airlines won't take 'em anymore. They'd show up with one I.C.E. agent and twenty kids at a terminal at midnight for a red-eye flight out of town, and when the stewards asked what was going on, they'd lie and say it was a soccer team, going to a tournament. When the airlines started asking I.C.E. officials tough questions about that bullshit, the jig was up and the airlines said, 'Leave us outta this.'"

"So, how do we add 'E.M.' to your class action and use your court orders to find her Mother? Mom's name is Elení Montes."

Wade Solley slammed a desk drawer shut, picking up a file with loose pages hanging out the sides. "All the recent records from the El Paso cases were transferred here by court order. They're out at the Otay Mesa Border Assembly. Before we head out there to check them out, you just need to sign a joinder motion and we'll get your kid added to the class. That means Department of Homeland Security or Health and Human Services, whichever agency technically has her custody, they'll have just thirty days to re-unite your client with her Mother. We need to go out and dig through the records, because in most cases, they come back to court and say, 'Can't find 'em,' or 'Sorry, they've already been deported.'" We need to stay ahead of them and find her records ourselves, so they don't deport her while they pretend they can't locate her."

The trip out to Otay Mesa Border Assembly from downtown San Diego took over an hour, given traffic congestion and the lack of a direct route. When they arrived, they were told they needed to drive on to the Detention Center, a massive complex closer to the border, where many border-crossing detainees were in temporary custody. When they arrived, the place was all cinderblock pillbox construction, painted bleached-white. It looked like a giant ice cream factory, except for the razor-wire fence surrounding the facility.

As they pulled up to the main gate, there was a protest going on, populated by a large group of oddly-costumed people, holding signs that read, "Don't Jail Babies," and "Shame On You". Maureen could see long lines of men and some women, single file in orange jumpsuits, standing along the fencing inside the facility.

"Can you actually get me into this place?" she asked, as they parked and got out.

"I've got a court pass. For now, you're my partner," Solley noted, flashing a card hanging from a lanyard.

They talked their way through the visitor's gate, then walked to an administration building where they were escorted to a basement storage room and given two large boxes that each looked like half a coffin. They sat at a utility table and flipped the lids off the boxes.

"Supposedly, this is El Paso 2021 and early 2022, which should cover your client's Mother's processing hearing," Solley remarked.

Once they dug in, the impossibility of the task became apparent. The material was in no particular order. It contained everything from medical prescriptions for some of the detainees, to bonding information and receipts for actual fines paid. Near the back of Maureen's box, there were a series of transfer orders that showed a number of detainees were redirected to other facilities, including one outside of SeaTac Airport, near Seattle.

"Figures," Wade Solley said. "Any further away and they'd be in Canada."

"Not all these transfer orders have names," Maureen noted. "Lots of folks are identified with just initials and numbers. What do the numbers mean?"

"We think somewhere, somebody's got a master record of everybody that corresponds to these numbers. Unfortunately, we're still fighting to get those lists, and the folks at I.C.E. claim they don't exist, which, if true, means these numbers are random and meaningless. For now, we just have to search for names and dates. Do you know when they arrived at El Paso?"

Maureen gave him everything she had on Estrellita and her Mother, but they got nowhere. At the back of Wade Solley's box, there was a notation that the remaining records had been moved to the San Ysidro Port of Entry, which was another ten miles south, right on the Mexican border.

"Brace yourself," Wade Solley warned. "The repository there is in one of those temporary detention facilities."

"Can't wait," Maureen grumbled. "Any chance they'll actually have records there that tell us what happened to Elení Montes, back in the Spring of 2022?"

"Maybe—all I know is this is faster than getting a subpoena issued, then having the H.H.S. folks pretend they're searching for her," he said, as they retreated to his car and began the drive to the border. "All the cameras and the Congressmen are gone, so it'll be easier for us to get in. Back when the family separations were front-page news, they kept the holding areas locked up tight. They'll still try to steer us away, but you can't get in and out of the storage areas without going past some of the pens—"

"Pens?" Maureen interrupted.

"You'll see," he said, as he turned into the parking area of the Port of Entry.

Maureen could see the gates off in the distance: It looked like the World's widest toll booth, stretching across two dozen lanes of traffic, with uniformed officers in each cubicle, standing in front of the yellow toll gates as they questioned the people in stopped vehicles. Cars stretched off into the distance on the Mexico side, with a lone gate dedicated to nobody, it seemed, headed the other way. The imbalance of northbound versus southbound vehicles made it look as though Mexico was slowly being emptied of people.

Up a hill to the west of the gates was an endless fence with razor wire curls spooling along the top, as far off as Maureen could see. A line of uniformed, heavily armed and helmeted officers were all standing, arms locked, along the fence, facing a disorganized group of stragglers on the other side. They all seemed to be endlessly staring at each other, as though the first one to blink might lose the game.

"It's a meaningless show of force—if they're going to cross illegally, they won't do it here," Solley noted. "They'd be off in the desert, trying to cross rougher terrain where there are no guards, only unattended fencing. There are stretches of that new wall Stuggs is trying to build further east of here, but there are massive gaps in it. Even crazier, as soon as the news photographers leave and the publicity shoots are over, huge sections of the wall tend to get blown down in the wind."

They parked. Maureen circled the car and followed Solley past the lot to a modern building with a corrugated, white metal roof that made it look like an Art-Deco, drive-in burger joint from the Fifties, except that the building's walls were all windowless, pitted concrete, and they seemed to stretch on forever.

"They threw these things up almost overnight when Stuggs got elected. They're glorified prisons. The only 'windows' are actually ventilation shafts, with electrified bug zappers covering the vents. There are no flying bugs in San Diego—the zappers are there to scare the inmates. The archives are in the basement, which means we get to stroll down the corridors past the holding pens. Like I said, brace yourself," he commented, as they stopped at the entrance.

An I.C.E. officer in a military helmet and fatigue-green uniform checked their papers, then quickly rummaged through their briefcases.

"Not sure what you're planning to do with these," the Guard asked, holding open one of their briefcases. "No copiers inside, and you can't take records out of the building."

"We're note-takers," Maureen offered, pulling a notepad out of her briefcase. "Happy to leave the cases here," she added, as they entered through a steel door the guard propped open.

"Does he not understand how a smartphone works?" she asked Solley.

"Doing his job—a lot of these guys are pretty demoralized. They didn't sign up to be wardens at a makeshift juvenile facility."

They were met by another uniformed officer, with a large keyring and pairs of rubber gloves.

"Put these on," the officer ordered, handing the gloves to Maureen and Solley, who dutifully snapped them on.

As they progressed down a long, dimly lit hallway, they began passing steel doors with glass portal windows at eye-level, the glass lined with chicken-wire reinforcement. As Solley and the guard made their way forward, Maureen stopped to peek through a window. It took her a moment to focus, and even then, she couldn't believe the scene inside. The room looked like the gymnasium where she'd attended high school, except that it was festooned with hastily-erected cyclone fencing, sectioned into roughly eight-by-ten-foot cubicles with blankets tossed on the concrete flooring. Kids of all ages were everywhere: Sitting on floors, lying on the blankets, standing in long, single-file lines, sleeping in the aisles and the cages.

"Looks like a dog kennel," she said, under her breath.

She quickly moved on, so as not to let the guard get too far ahead, but when she passed the next windowed door, she stopped. She could hear screaming and crying, muffled sounds like injured dogs mewing. When she glanced inside, she realized the crying was coming from a group of women, all standing with their fingers in the links of the pen fencing, a few shaking the fences. There were no attendants or guards in sight, and she could see that the pens were locked. There were no children in any of the pens.

She scooted on, stopping at the next windowed door. As she leaned on it, she realized it was slightly ajar and when she pressed, it slowly swung open. She stepped inside. She was looking at an open room that resembled the underwear department of a big-box store, devoid of shelves and merchandise. There were literally dozens of children, some of them diapered infants, sitting or lying in a ring of humanity, centered on the floor of the room. It smelled strangely like boiled cabbage. Virtually all of the youngest kids were crying, some were screaming, a sea of tear-streamed faces that looked like bobbing balloons in a rain storm. The sound was crushing her ears.

Two tables were set up behind the kids. Female attendants wearing surgical masks were handing out bottles and sippy cups, some to standing kids who milled past, some attendants roaming the room to service children sitting or lying on the floor. One child noticed Maureen frozen in the doorway. The child, no more than four years old, had eyes swollen half closed. Her head was rolling slowly on her shoulders, like she might be a little intoxicated. Whenever her head stopped moving, she focused on Maureen, and as Maureen was about to turn away, the child raised her opened hand, fingers splayed. She held her hand up directly to her own face, then slowly turned it outward and extended her arm, reaching out to Maureen.

Maureen started to move toward the child, when the guard approached her from behind and suddenly placed a hand on her shoulder. "These rooms are off limits—records is this way," he announced, as he guided her out. He pointed her down the hallway toward Wade Solley, who'd seen it all before and was already halfway down the corridor.

Her first urge was to strike the guard, but she resisted, shaking off the encounter that was sure to give her nightmares for weeks ahead, as she hurried to catch up with Wade Solley. When they got to the stairwell at the end of the building, they descended and were let in through a locked door at the foot of the stairs. The guard walked away as they entered, the door swinging shut and locking behind them.

"Who *are* they?" she asked, when they were alone.

"Detainees they haven't had time to process or deport yet. Most of them were asylum seekers when they came here. It was bad enough before 'Zero Tolerance,' but once everybody got arrested instead of detained for a hearing, the rooms overflowed. This place was built as a giant storage locker—they used to keep uniforms, weapons and supplies in there—so you can see it's not exactly a Best Western."

"Why separate these people from their kids? I didn't see any family units in there—just kids in some rooms, adults in others, and all of them in cages."

"There's no guarantee that the kids in one room go with the adults in another—more often than not, they're unrelated, since they're shipping the kids off so quickly. These kids are here because they've got nowhere else to send them. You nailed it with your lawsuit—they want word of this hellhole to get out. These folks are all headed back to Mexico and Central America. They want them to tell legendary stories about being imprisoned, not knowing if they'd ever see their kids again. The goal is to have them say, 'No matter how bad gang recruiting or sex slavery may be, this is worse', and *voila*', you've cut the number of asylum seekers in half."

"I need you to testify about this…" she paused, "….I need you to sit for a deposition."

"Gladly, but we only have an hour, so let's dig in," he said, as they began flipping open banker's boxes of manila folders and continuous computer printout.

Maureen started photographing everything with her phone, realizing hand-review was impossible within the hour they were given. After forty minutes, Solley stopped and held up a file.

"I think this may cover the time period, if your kid got it right. Take every page close up," he added. "Looks like most of these folks were sent up to SeaTac, up in Washington State."

When they'd finished, they sealed the boxes and stood inside the door. At just past the hour, the door swung open and their escort guard led them out.

As they walked to their car, a lone protester appeared, facing the line of troops guarding the fence. She was wearing a placard, a sandwich board like she was a fatalist announcing the impending End of the World.

The placard read:

No Christian Family Values

In Concentration Camps

* *

Crump checked back into St. Vincent's Adolescent Psych Ward. His first stop was Estrellita Montes's room. Doctor Trimble escorted him in and he was immediately struck by how much more alive the kid appeared. She was still sporting the naso-gastric feeding tube, but her skin no longer looked shrunken and her hair actually had some shine to it. She was sitting at a table, writing something on a pad of paper.

"Good news," Crump announced, and the Doctor translated. "A Court in California has ordered I.C.E. to help us bring your Mother back here…." He paused, waiting for the Doctor to translate.

"El juez ordenó al gobierno que nos dijera a dónde enviaron a su madre," Doctor Trimble offered.

"¿No está en El Paso?"

"Not now," Crump answered, which the Doctor delivered in Spanish.

Crump and Doctor Trimble then struggled to explain the good news about the court proceedings, concluding with the likelihood that Elení was outside of Seattle.

"¿Cómo?"

"How?" Crump echoed.

"¿Cómo la traes aquí? "

"She's asking, 'How do you bring her here?'"

Crump closed one eye and scratched the side of his forehead. "Tell her, we will bring them together, wherever they are, but she needs to live up to her end of the deal and keep getting better."

The Doctor translated, and Estrellita silently nodded.

"¿Cuando? "

"Thirty days, that's what the Court order says," Crump responded, as Doctor Trimble simultaneously translated.

"Estoy contando los días," she added.

Crump nodded, and as they left her room, he asked, "She's counting on me?"

Doctor Trimble smiled. "No—she said she's counting the days. You'd better be right, or you're in a heap of trouble."

"She looks like she's getting better, like if I screw up she could let me have it—"

"—in trouble with *me*, not her," Doctor Trimble emphasized.

They then circled around the ward to another meeting room, where Crump had invited the Lockwoods to meet with him, as he explained to Brian what they'd learned about his plight at Carrington Prep.

Brian Lockwood was still in a wheelchair, still on the last resort I.V. tube to the hand. His parents were flanking him. Crump pulled up a chair and sat across from them, after closing the door to the room to preserve attorney-client privilege on what he was about to tell them.

"How you doing?" he asked.

Brian shrugged.

"He's feeling a little better, and he's promised to begin taking a naso-gastric tube," his Mother announced.

Crump nodded. "Look," he began. "I don't know how much of this is just fed-up with the abuse you were taking, and how much may be affected by months of starving yourself. The doctor tells me that one thing that happens when you stop eating is you get squirrely—my word, not hers—because your brain is lacking all sorts of stuff it needs to function."

Brian Lockwood nodded again. Crump figured he'd heard this before.

"But, the thing I wanted to tell you today, is that I know what happened to you: I know who did it, and I know why, and it had nothing to do with *you*—"

"Is this a good idea?" his Mother offered, while Crump barreled ahead.

"Stick with me here," Crump said, shaking off Mrs. Lockwood's interruption. "I know more about getting kicked around than you might think—I grew up in State custody, and trust me, in those places, you spent every day looking over your shoulder for who or what was coming up behind you. You start feeling like, 'Hey, must be something wrong with *me*, like, maybe I'm not even worth it, that must be why they're doing this to me'. You try your hardest to fit in, you want to be accepted and instead, they're practically trying to *kill* you. I get it. I know that feeling."

He stopped. The kid was shifting around in his wheelchair, lifting his arms for the first time in any of Crump's visits. He rubbed the palms of his hands on his legs, then sat up straight.

"I've interviewed kids and parents and the folks that run Carrington, and what happened to you was an organized, purposeful harassment campaign, carried out by the waiver kids, the ones whose parents work at Carrington. Then, when the waiver kids got caught, and their faculty parents told them to lay low, the original perps passed the baton off to a couple of thugs—you know who I'm talking about—a couple of kids who were taking orders from those waiver kids. And it wasn't just because they got off on kicking you around, although there was that. It had a purpose—they wanted you *gone*—gone from their classes, gone from the building, gone from the school—"

"Why?" he suddenly asked, and Crump realized he'd never heard the Kid's voice before.

"Because they were retaliating against your folks, mostly your Dad."

"Why?" he asked again, this time in a fainter, pleading voice.

"Do you really think—" Mr. Lockwood began, when Crump interrupted.

"Stay with me. There was no good reason. It was a case of 'No good deed goes unpunished'. Carrington was in trouble—the school was essentially going broke. It had become a playground for the faculty and staff, nobody was teaching much of anything, and your Dad and another parent were brought in to look it over and fix it. They did just that: They gave a lot of their time and even some of their money, to help the place get back on track, but the changes they brought about really ticked off the faculty. Accountability is a real pain in the ass. The teachers and staff weren't used to that and they *hated* it, and they hated your Dad for making it happen. These kids went home every day and listened to their folks complain about how your Dad and Tom Lodge were ruining Good Old Carrington, and the kids took that as an excuse to dump all over you. They figured if you got run out of the place, then your Dad would leave the Carrington Board and they'd get their cushy lives back. They were using you to punish your folks."

"Ahhh…uuhhhmm," the kid started in. "You talked to….." He paused, not certain he wanted to name names.

Crump filled the void. "It was Marianne, Fletcher, Vance and Parker who did it. Don't worry about who told me. I'm right, aren't I?"

Brian Lockwood nodded silently.

"Look at me, buddy," Crump said, and the kid sat up. "This wasn't because you're too short or too tall, or too skinny, or too *anything*. Yeah, I know that's what they said, but that's bullshit—" He paused, looked at the Lockwoods. "Sorry, but whatever they told you, it was just stuff, stuff they were using to get you to *beg* your folks to take you out of the school. They don't even *know you*. It's your parents they hate, and they hate them because your parents did the right thing—they volunteered to help and saved the place from the wrecking ball. Whenever you do that, it brings change, and people who have it easy because they run the place, people like that *hate* change. This is not about *you*."

Crump stopped. They were all staring at him.

"Now, what?" Brian Lockwood broke the silence, startling his parents.

"Good question. I'm your lawyer, and lawyers do a lot of things, but mostly they help people get stuff they can't get on their own. I have an idea that is just the thing for Carrington, but first, you gotta get out of there—change schools—because anything else I can do would just make it worse for you."

"What else can you do?" the kid asked, suddenly taking control of the discussion, while his stunned parents looked on.

"Ordinarily, in a situation like this, people sue the place for money, compensation, pay-back for all the pain and suffering they've caused you. I don't know about you guys, but other than the cost of your treatment here at St. Vincent's, money wouldn't do it for me."

"What else?" the kid asked, again.

"Want to do something for the rest of humanity?" Crump asked, and they all looked astounded.

"No, I mean it—there's way too much of this stuff going on. People like you are getting bullied into hospitals, run out of towns, sometimes even worse. I'd do something about it. The folks who run the place are smug, lazy, self-righteous gas bags and agenda mongers, and they knowingly let this go on *for years*. You ask me, the place is a public nuisance. It oughta be shut down."

"What's a 'public nuisance'?" Brian Lockwood offered, almost under his breath.

"The legal definition is a dangerous act, or a condition, a bad place or just about anything that is illegal because it endangers people or interferes with the rights of the public generally. It's usually applied to bad roads, crumbling buildings or obnoxious or dangerous groups of people—"

"Yeah, Carrington's one of those," Brian offered, and his Father smiled, relieved to see his son's brain functioning.

Crump continued. "So, if it were up to me, I'd sue to have Carrington declared a public nuisance and have it shut down for good."

"I want that," Brian Lockwood said, as he looked over at his Mother, then his Father. "They're going to do this to somebody else, when I leave," he offered.

"I can do that," Crump offered.

The Lockwoods looked at each other for a moment.

"I think we need to talk it over," Mr. Lockwood announced.

"Think of it as a public service," Crump said, as he got up to leave them to debate shutting down one of the oldest private schools in the Country— one that Tom and Susan Lockwood had just spent years of their own time and thousands of their own dollars, trying to save.

11.
YOU BREAK IT, YOU FIX IT..........

WHEN MAUREEN DESCRIBED THE CHAIN-LINK and chicken-wire palace the H.H.S. officials were using to house the detainees at the border, Crump decided they needed an expert witness to testify about just what people hiking through the Mexican desert were fleeing. Educating the Judge about the nightmares compelling the refugees trudging to the U.S. border would demonstrate that only the scare tactics of the Stuggs Administration would out-terrorize the home-grown thugs motivating the immigrants' cross-desert, midnight flight.

As Maureen proclaimed, upon returning from San Diego, "To prove our case, we need to show that whatever these people are fleeing, it's gotta be scary enough that the only thing that's worse is child kidnapping."

Dr. Juan Condrera started his education, like a lot of Crump's classmates at State University, as the reluctant-college-student child of a Nurse married to a Cop, but he stuck with it and eventually obtained a PhD in Latin American Studies. He and Crump had stayed in touch, but over the nearly fifty years since they'd both graduated, this was the first time Crump had actually been able to pay him for his advice.

"What *aren't* they fleeing?" Dr. Condrera asked. "Guatemala is one of the most dangerous places in the World." Dr. Condrera looked like he'd been born in his crème-colored, three-piece suit, working behind the counter of a seedy hotel. At least, Crump figured, nobody'd take him for a stuffy academic.

"Who did what to who?" Crump asked, as Maureen took notes. They were sitting in Dr. Condrera's office, overlooking State University's City Campus, still, to Crump's eyes, one of the most depressing places on the planet. Its architectural design of oppressive stone walkways at rooftop level, blocking out the sky everywhere inside the campus, coupled with its unfinished-concrete block, nearly-windowless buildings, were rumored to have driven the Unabomber, who once assistant taught there, to go on his anti-modernist, anti-technology bombing campaign.

"Where to start?" Dr. Condrera asked. "The Spanish screwed the place over for a century, forcing the native Mayans off their land and essentially colonizing them."

"The child's mother is apparently of part-Mayan ancestry," Maureen interrupted, reflecting on something Doctor Trimble had mentioned.

"No wonder—those people are still marginalized and discriminated against." He paused, gathering his thoughts. "The real catastrophic social churn began in the mid nineteen-hundreds at the hands of Uncle Sam."

Crump leaned forward. "I will confess I snoozed through most of my required history classes. What did we do to enhance the quality of life down there?"

"There was a simmering conflict between the conservative government, which was backed by the Catholic Church and the U.S. Government, versus the popular fronts and students, who leaned Marxist and wanted land reform. Folks in our Government were trying to back U.S.-owned United Fruit Company, which was the chief importer of bananas. U.F.C. controlled much of the land seized from the peasants and indigenous folks. It also controlled most cargo and transport lines in and out of the Country, so it essentially ruled the economy. It all blew up in a couple of revolutions in the forties and fifties, and that led to one of the longest civil wars in history."

"How many civil wars were there?" Maureen asked.

"I meant, in the history of the *World*," he noted. "It went on from 1960 until almost 1996—thirty-six years. The Army killed over two hundred thousand civilians." He stopped to let that sink in. "You want to put that in perspective? The A-Bombs we dropped on Japan had about the same death toll. When it was all over, the new government pardoned all of the Army members of any war crimes, and the ex-Army thugs morphed into the gangs and cartels that control much of Guatemalan society today."

"Our client is the guardian of a fourteen-year old Guatemalan female, who came here through Mexico and was separated from her Mother as soon as they arrived at the border, as part of the Stuggs Administration's family separation, 'Zero tolerance' border initiative. She ended up in a hospital after she essentially went on a hunger strike," Crump explained.

"Well, that's a dangerous demographic. I'll bet the Father is dead—"

"He is. Gang related, we're told."

"One of the highest murder rates in the World, right about now—over six thousand per year, in a country with only seventeen million people. Not as bad as Honduras or El Salvador, but for context, the U.S. has over three hundred thirty million people, and we've only got about seventeen thousand murders per year—twenty times as many people, but only three times as many murders. Violent crime is rampant, but I'm betting Mom's real motivation for the trip to the border is the kid's age."

"I know where you're going," Maureen offered.

"Trafficking—she's just about the age where she'd get snatched off the street, so Mom wisely figured she'd take her chances on migration. Sex trafficking is rampant there, as is plain old violence against women—the femicide rate is one of the highest in the world, and rape is right behind it."

Crump got up and walked over to Maureen. She offered him her notes and he flipped through the pad. "So, here's what I need from you," Crump explained. "After you tell this delightful bedtime story about the paradise known as Guatemala, I need to ask you what, from the perspective of the typical Mother of a fourteen-year-old female child, would stack up against the horrors of dodging gangs and traffickers in Guatemala? What would be so frightening that, against all that, you'd say, "Bad as it is, I'm gonna stay put?"

Dr. Condrera took off his glasses and wiped them with a cloth, replacing them with a shrug. "These 'Stuggs Thuggs', as we like to call them in Academia, they've done their homework. Guatemala is still a heavily Catholic Country. Children are sacred, as sacred as anybody can be in a place like that. So, yes, a parent, one who's facing losing a child to the Gangs or the Traffickers, the one thing that might actually cause that parent to reconsider the trip to the border is this 'Zero Tolerance' program. At least, with the gangs, you've got the element of chance on your side, the possibility that if you run fast and often enough, you might just beat the Devil. If the alternative is a publicly-announced U.S. Government policy of child separation, carried out with the Reich-like efficiency of an outfit like the Stuggs Administration, you might just *rationally* choose to stay home. Add to that the extra horror of learning that if your kid gets sick and needs hospitalization, they'll get deported during the course of medical treatment, you can imagine somebody deciding to stay home."

"Can you testify that, based on your expertise, your knowledge of the region and the culture, you are reasonably certain that the only conceivable purpose for these policies is to scare the stuffing out of potential immigrants?" Crump asked.

"Oh, yes. I know what's going on in their dirty little minds. These 'Stuggs Thuggs' may be a bunch of racist buffoons, but they've managed to hit the cruelty nail on the head. The irony here is that the U.S. contributed mightily to making this mess. Instead of terrorizing these folks who are legitimately seeking asylum, and asylum's what these policies are designed to stop, the U.S. Government should be working on incentives to re-shape Guatemala. We broke it; we should help fix it."

* *

The Lockwoods decided to go forward with the lawsuit to shut down Carrington Prep as a public nuisance. Crump thought they decided a little too gleefully and was going to give them a speech about how revenge was for people with time on their hands, but then he remembered that they were spending most of their days hanging out in an Adolescent Psych Ward, so he figured the parable might not exactly hit home. Instead, he commended them on their civic-mindedness and gave them a series of warnings about what to expect as a plaintiff in a lawsuit.

He didn't think it was possible to generate more fuss than the Patriot Act lawsuit he'd filed on behalf of Estrellita Montes, but as soon as the case was logged in the court docket, he got a call from Svetlana Armstrong.

"Wow. The people in the Court Clerks' Office on your black-market payroll work really *fast*," he said.

"Why do we always have to do this?" Armstrong asked.

"I'm just wondering whether you're going to know about the next lawsuit I file, before even *I* do."

"Care to give me a statement about the story behind the story here?" she asked.

"The complaint speaks—"

"—for itself, I know. I could get that information off your voicemail. C'mon, Crump—you're suing to shut down one of the oldest and most elite private schools in this City, labelling it like it's a toxic waste dump."

"Off the record, but that comparison may not be entirely fair to toxic waste dumps," Crump offered. "At least, when the toxic dump starts to stink, it doesn't actively try to cover its stench, so innocent people continue to stumble in."

"About that," Armstrong started, "the allegations that the faculty and staff actively covered up the mistreatment of your clients' child, due to conflicts of interest—this seems like the most provocative part of your case."

"I thought you were going to say that the Carrington administration's belief that their 'Progressive Idiom' qualifies them for the Religious Exemption from the Prevention of School Violence Act, was the most remarkable part of the case," Crump injected.

Armstrong audibly exhaled, stifling laughter. "Yeah, I can't wait to see how all the Irish Catholics down in Our Lady of the Corned Beef and Cabbage Parish are going to feel about getting schnockered into having to pay, all by themselves, for the lobbyists who cooked up that loophole," she added.

"Can I quote you on that?" Crump asked, giving her back her own stuff.

"You may *not*—Listen, I'd like to interview your clients."

"I'll ask, but don't hold your breath—the Kid's a kid, and the parents aren't the type."

"Look, just ask, O.K.? I've been good to you, all these years, so you owe me," she added.

Crump paused. "The only people that owe you are the courthouse employees whose incomes you've been supplementing all these years, as you singlehandedly raise the minimum wage on the service employee sector by having them skim the court files for newsworthy cases—"

She hung up.

* *

Crump was in Mary's law office, looking out the window at the college campus across the street. They were living in Judson, the first town North of the City by the Lake, in a neighborhood near Mary's office. Crump stopped in mid-day, an unusual event, to deliver a note of caution. Mary looked about the same as the day he'd met her, almost forty years ago. Sandy-blonde hair pinned up in back, now starting to streak with gray; deliberate and sincere Lady-from-Minnesota eyeglasses and take-me-seriously blue suit; all following the advice of law professors in the Seventies, warning the first big batch of female graduates about deflecting chauvinistic jerks in the legal profession.

"I think it's time to take it seriously," Crump began.

"Even if it is a smear campaign or retaliation, what are they going to do with me? I'm running a neighborhood law practice, drawing wills, doing house closings and handling adoptions, divorces and child custody cases. The closest thing I do to all that political stuff you're handling is going to court to recognize foreign adoptions, and the Church sponsors half of those," Mary responded.

"I know. Look, Steve Barnacle went out of his way to rat out the feds who dragged him in to drop dirt on me. He seems to think they looked determined."

Mary flopped a heavy file down on her desk. The door buzzer rang. They were on the second floor of an old brick building, the first floor occupied by a pizzeria popular with the students, so the place was hopping and always smelled like oregano and garlic. You never knew if the folks ringing the bell were confused pizza-goers, picking up a pie, or Mary's clients. She checked the intercom, but it was just a paper and toner delivery. She buzzed the intercom and told the delivery driver to leave it in the hallway.

"See, I can screen visitors—"

"I know, but it's not just the smear campaign I worry about. There's these 'Army of God' fruitcakes running around following me, and they *shoot* people. Who knows what other crackpot organizations Handler and Stuggs are un-officially sending our way. You should not walk alone, even if you're just shuttling the few blocks from here to home."

Mary shook her head dismissively. "I can't start living like this," she protested. "I thought you were about to retire, I mean, that's what you keep telling me."

"Any day now—"

"You just can't let it go," Mary said.

"What's 'It' in that sentence?" Crump asked, feigning ignorance.

"Right, you've got no idea. We'll be having this discussion when you're ninety-nine and creaking around the place in your squeaky wheelchair. What about the kids?"

"Ben's already on it. We figure they don't lean on him—he's a City cop, so he gets to walk around with his gun *showing*—pretty hard to muscle him. He's managed to get the local guys here to park a plainclothes cop in an unmarked car out front here and at home, not all the time, but enough to make it risky for anybody trying to do anything overt. Dr. Tom is always interning at the Hospital, which is crawling with Cops, and Rene's name change makes her pretty hard to track down—"

"You warned her anyway?"

"Sure, yeah." He hesitated. "I also bought us some protection—"

"Crump, you didn't—"

"*Whaat?*"

"You have that, 'Just been to see Angelo' look….."

"This is his *thing*—"

"That's what worries me," Mary said, crossing her arms.

"That's what Maureen said," Crump observed.

"That's because there's no adults in the room when you and Angelo get together…. "

12.
ALL PROSECUTION IS POLITICAL……

When Crump returned to his office, there were two big slabs waiting in his reception area, guys who looked like bouncers at a local strip club. Beefy and crew-cut, wearing tight-fitting jackets barely hiding their shoulder-holstered pistols, they rose as soon as he entered. Sophie tried to head them off, but one of them stuck an arm out as she reached for Crump to guide him past them.

"They've been waiting here for a couple of hours—" she started in, when one of the slabs interrupted.

"You Philo John Crump?" the bigger guy asked.

"Well, yes, but almost nobody uses my first names—"

"We have a warrant for your arrest," slab number two announced, as he reached out with a summons. "Please come with us, and we can avoid any further confrontation—"

"What confrontation, you just asked me my name, and, anyway, what am I being charged with?"

As Crump asked, one of the guys announced "Federal Marshals," then he grabbed Crump's left arm by the wrist and swung him around backwards, grabbing his other wrist and cuffing him with his hands behind his back. The second Marshal quickly patted him down, removing his wallet, his building pass, a wad of Kleenex™, a key ring, four quarters and ticket stubs for a free Cole Slaw Side at Crump's favorite sandwich place.

"Please don't interfere with our attempts to search you," the second Marshal ordered. "I assume you are unarmed?"

"I'm not a gun person. What exactly am I being charged with?"

"Can I hold his stuff?" Sophie offered, as the Marshal bagged it all.

"Sorry, Ma'am, but we'll need to take it with us. He can retrieve it if he bonds out," he commanded, as they led Crump into the elevator.

"Call Steve," Crump shouted at Sophie, as the elevator doors closed and he prepared to do the perp walk he was certain these meatheads had orchestrated outside his building, news cameras and all.

Sure enough, when they got to the lobby, there was a small gathering of reporters and two camera crews. As he was led to an unmarked, boxy black sedan, someone shouted, "Mr. Crump, do you think this is in retaliation for your case against the Stuggs Administration?" He recognized Svetlana Armstrong emerging from the crowd, holding out a microphone for him to answer her question.

"All prosecution's political," he called out, as a marshal placed a beefy hand on the top of his head, and shoved him into the back seat of the car.

* *

"The United States of America versus Philo John Crump," the Clerk of the Court shouted out. Crump and Steve Barnacle stepped forward, Crump cuffed and wearing his orange prison jumpsuit. Across from them, Regina Debevoise approached the bench.

"Regina Debevoise, for the prosecution," she offered.

"Steven Barnacle, for the defendant," Barnacle followed.

"Your honor—" Crump began, when the judge, Reuben Salazar, interrupted.

"Please, Mr. Crump, I know you are an attorney, but let your counsel speak for you."

"Sorry," Crump acknowledged. "A hard habit to break."

The judge nodded. "Miss Debevoise, please read the indictment into the record."

She stepped forward. "On February 15, 2023, at approximately 1:15 P.M. Central Standard Time, one 'Philo John Crump', a Caucasian male approximately aged sixty-eight, did, while crossing the intersection of Polk and Harrison in the City by the Lake, make a hand gesture directed at a horse-drawn wagon emerging from a parked stand immediately adjacent to the Ronald Reagan Federal Building, in direct and contumacious violation of 16 US Code 1338 (a) (3), forbidding unreasonable signs and gestures directed at horses while on or adjacent to National Parks and other Federal Facilities."

She stopped reading. Crump was fidgeting, straining to keep quiet.

"Mr. Barnacle, how does your client plead—"

"Not guilty, by reason of insanity," Crump blurted out.

"Am I to understand your client, who I believe to be a licensed, practicing attorney, is making an insanity plea?" the Judge asked Barnacle.

Before Barnacle could answer, Crump blurted out, "I'm not insane, the statute and this prosecution are—"

"Mr. Crump, I can understand that you might be feeling persecuted by the Government here, " the Judge paused, glancing over at Regina Debevoise, "But you really should let your attorney speak for you. How does your client plead?"

"Not guilty," Barnacle dutifully answered. "We believe, given the somewhat *unusual* nature of this charge—effectively that my client committed a federal crime when, while jogging, he flipped off a buggy driver who practically ran him over while crossing the street—that bond is appropriate, and should be set at a modest level, no more than five hundred dollars."

"Miss Debevoise, what say you?" the Judge said, turning to her.

Debevoise looked like she was struggling to say anything coherent. "Your honor...... the Government believes this crime exhibits a dangerous degree of hostility directed at federal authorities and their related and subordinate actors, and that the Defendant should be held without bond and remanded to federal custody pending disposition of the case," she said, without looking up.

Barnacle cleared his throat, as Crump nudged him forward and whispered something behind him. "Your honor, I reviewed the federal database on prosecutions, and it appears that this particular federal criminal statute, while obviously still on the books, was last prosecuted in eighteen-seventy-one, and has to do with regulating horse-drawn traffic in National Parks. In addition, the 'crime' is gesturing to *the horse*, not the buggy driver or any federal agent or employee—"

"Unless you count the horse as a Fed," Crump injected.

"Mr. Crump, please, allow your attorney," The Judge admonished.

"In any event, my client has a clean record, no prior convictions, and he assures me he would willingly steer clear of all horses, both near and away from federal facilities, pending the course of this prosecution. We believe bond, as requested, is appropriate."

The Judge looked out into the courtroom. There were a dozen onlookers in the gallery, including a few journalists scribbling away.

"Miss Debevoise, while I'm certain the U.S. Attorney *carefully* considered this prosecution before issuing the warrant for Attorney Crump's arrest," he paused, allowing his sarcastic tone to sink in, "I am mindful of the fact that there is a proceeding in a courtroom across the hall, where this defendant is pursuing a highly acrimonious case against several agencies of the Federal Government and its principals. I am troubled by the appearance that this prosecution, under what we can all agree is an anachronistic and rarely used Federal statue, is politically motivated. However strongly your office feels about the dangers of joggers in the City resorting to offensive hand gestures directed at horses parked before Federal facilities, I'm confident this man represents no flight risk or general threat to society. Therefore, I'm setting bond in the case at ten cents—"

"Your *Honor*—" Debevoise interrupted, but the Judge was unmoved.

"—Madame Clerk, please collect a penny from Mr. Crump's counsel, as his ten percent bond deposit, and release him, returning the possessions taken at the time he was arrested. Mr. Crump, you are free to go, but you must report weekly to your counsel, to the bonding agent and Ms. Debevoise, to assure them you have not fled the jurisdiction to avoid offensive hand gesture prosecution. Madame Clerk, call the next case."

* *

"Look at this," Maureen called out, holding up the front page of the Herald.

JUDGE ORDERS ATTORNEY CHARGED WITH OFFENDING A HORSE TO PAY ONE PENNY BOND

"Yeah, I think that backfired," Crump noted. "I mean, it's a pain in the ass for me, but I don't think the hassle factor outweighs how stupid they look to the rest of the world."

"They obviously couldn't find anything else to charge you with," Maureen noted.

"I'm sure, if you dig around in the Federal Criminal Code long enough, you can find a crime for almost any occasion," Crump observed. "Judge Salazar knew exactly what was going on. It'll get dismissed—the stupid thing doesn't even apply here—that horse was owned by a private buggy operator.

It just happened to be stopped in front of the Federal Building when it tried to trample me. What I want to know is, how did the Feds know it happened? I'm jogging in sweats, without a sign on my back that says, 'Here's the Guy Suing the Feds', yet somehow, my random hand gesture makes it all the way up to the U.S Attorney's Office. They've got people following me."

* *

When thirty days passed without any reliable report from U.S.C.I.S. or H.H.S. about Elení Montes's whereabouts, Maureen delivered a motion to Wade Solley, asking him to file it in the California class action lawsuit. She was seeking a rule to show cause for contempt of court against those Health and Human Services Officials who were ordered to find E.M.'s Mother in thirty days and re-unite them.

"They keep telling us the records are 'incomplete', whatever that means," Solley reported. "They checked SeaTac, but it looks like she was moved from there a little over a month ago—"

"After our suit was filed?" Maureen interrupted.

"Looks like it," Solley admitted.

"Does the 'Transfer' look like it occurred after she got added to your class action?" Maureen added.

"Hard to say, but I wouldn't be surprised."

"The 'Human Shell Game' continues," she complained.

"I hear your partner got arrested by the feds for giving a horse the finger," Solley added.

"That news made it all the way out there?" Maureen asked.

"I told you, you guys were big news," he offered.

"Even the nonsense the Government is pulling to bully us out of the case?" Maureen asked.

Solley agreed. "It's the flip off heard 'round the world."

13.
BANANA REPUBLIC WITHOUT THE BANANAS…..

Judge Haverhorn wasted no time in certifying E.M.'s lawsuit as a class action and appointing her guardian, Doctor Trimble, as the class representative. Crump and Maureen were in control of the entire effort to stop the medical deportations all around the Country, for the roughly 4,500 patients facing deportation. As the joinder notices came pouring in, they had to process the applications and review the U.S.C.I.S. termination letters for authenticity. This effort generated a flood of hard-luck stories that were so harrowing Crump, who had a low tolerance for cruelty, gave up after the first hundred and had Maureen and Sophie review the rest.

There were kids with childhood cancers getting treatment not available in their home countries. Excruciatingly painful were the cases of children and adults recruited by teaching hospitals and med schools for their exotic, rare conditions, most of them impossible to study without living patients. Finally, there were immigrants like E.M., felled by a host of deadly medical ailments after they arrived in the U.S. All of them had their deferred deportation status revoked under Dennis Ernstmeyer's new initiative, and all of them faced near certain death if deported.

As Crump filed the joinder notices with the Court, Svetlana Armstrong systematically pulled the information and went looking for victims who would consent to an interview. As she picked off class members, the publicity around the lawsuit spiraled out of control. Entire cable programs were dedicated to showcasing particular patients, and Armstrong quickly became a media sensation.

One teenage victim, who had a non-differentiated mass of tumors growing throughout her body, was interviewed in a wheelchair with her fingers covering the tracheotomy nozzle cut into her windpipe at the neck, so her voice could be heard. Cecilia Raposa calmly explained, in a raspy voice barely making it past her tracheotomy vent, that if she was taken off the treatment regimen at University City Medical Center, she'd immediately die, since the only effective response to her condition was the experimental care she was receiving there. Even with a wheelchair and a tracheotomy, she looked like she could have been anybody's daughter or sister or next-door neighbor. Crump, like everybody else, could barely hold himself together when he observed her media interview.

The viral re-broadcast of the Raposa interview, seen in millions of news programs and internet viewings, made Raposa an unofficial spokesperson for the Plaintiffs, whose ranks quickly swelled to over forty-five hundred.

"This thing is excruciating," Crump complained. "I can't watch these folks without wanting to strangle somebody. I start twitching whenever I see the news coverage."

"You're the one who always told me to just get mad," Maureen reminded him.

"Dr. Hanrahan, your husband's former boss in the Medical Examiner's office, used to say, 'We're all dying, stupid, so get off your ass and do something about it.' It's like we can't even make a dent in this thing. All this Goddamned suffering, and for what? Ernstmeyer and Stuggs, scoring a few points with their rabid supporters, while scaring a few thousand folks away from the border? There's hundreds of thousands more illegals, just overstaying students' and visitors' visas."

"Most of them aren't Hispanic," Maureen injected. "That's what this is really all about."

"Angelo Turulio's on the way up," Sophie shouted, from down the hall.

Maureen rolled her eyes and left. Crump stood up, just as Turulio waltzed in.

"So, you an official, card-carrying member of 'The Army of God'?" Crump asked.

"Ay, boss—dees guys are definitely following you," Turulio offered.

"Thanks for that news flash, but I need proper nouns—names, addresses and some video would be nice. One of these goobers must have been the reptile that reported me all the way up to the U.S. Attorney's Office when I flipped off that horse and offended its sensibilities, otherwise, the Feds would never have the dirt for my indictment. What I really need here is a link between the amateur crackpots and the professional crackpots—I need to show that Handler and his underlings are using folks like this for their smear campaign."

Turulio cleared his throat. "You dinnit let me finish. I got to innerview one a dem today."

"You did?"

"Yeah, she was sittin' in a beater out in fronna your house."

"My house?"

"Yeah, dere following Mary around, dat was one a the things I wanted to tell ya—"

"Shit—"

"I warned Mary 'bout it."

"Good. So how'd you end up talking to the guy?"

"S'was a broad—"

"O.K., so, her?"

"So, I made me one a dem anti-'bortion bumper stickers. Couldn't find a good one, so I made one dat says, 'Guns Don't Kill People—Doctors Kill People.'"

"Why am I not surprised?"

"And, anyway, I parks my car right in fronna her, and I act like I'm de 'lectrician, tool belt and all, and when I come out of yur house from warning Mary, dis broad steps outta the car, and says, 'You a Disciple?'"

"Of *what*?" Crump asked.

"I was getting dere. So, I says, 'You bet,' an before I can say a nudder word, she hands me dis flyer," Turulio said, as he handed a folded paper to Crump. It read:

Pledge Allegiance! Say Your Prayers!

Mongrel Races Out Of America!

March On Lincoln Park! April 30, 1945

"What's *that* mean? April is months away, and 1945—" Crump began.

"I think dats de name udduh organization," Turulio suggested. "It's the day Hitler died."

"Swell, now we got the Fourth Reich involved," Crump grumbled.

"Stuggs is duh Fourth Reich. Dees guys is the Fifth. So's, anyways, dis broad says, Gonna be a rally next Sunday, out at Lincoln Park. Bring yur torches.'"

"She tell you what for?"

"I asked. 'Gonna fight de immigrants,' actually, she calls 'em 'Immigrant *hordes*'. Den, she points at yur house, an she says, 'Dees guys, coupla lawyers, dere workin' to keep de immigrants *on our shores.*' Was everything I got just to keep from laughin' out loud, right in her face. '*On our shores,*' like she's the fuckin' Statute a' Liberty. Den she says, 'Hope you don't do no work for dees guys, cause dere money is *tainted.*'"

Crump shook his head. "You better stay close to Mary."

Turulio nodded. "De only thing worse den a Nazi is a Right-To-Lifer Nazi. You goin' for broke in the piss-off-de-crazies department."

* *

The Lockwoods' suit against Carrington Prep was getting almost as much press as the Patriot Act case against the Stuggs Administration. Westheimer was too with-it to let Johnny Rose handle the case alone. He brought in Stenson and Willis, the mega-firm that was Warren Handler's former employer, a firm he knew would be both ruthless in their defense and, as a bonus, a place where the lawyers collectively hated Crump for going after their on-leave partner, the Attorney General of the United States. The Stenson lawyers piled on motions designed to harass Crump and his clients and buried them with meaningless discovery, asking for documents they knew only the School would have. Crump brought in a raft of volunteers from the legal clinic run by his Alma Mater, State University School of Law, who all gleefully dug into pursuing the case on behalf of their waylaid bullying victim and his parents.

When burying Crump and his staff of volunteers with paper didn't slow Crump's clients down, Gregory Stenson, head of Stenson and Willis, decided to go for broke in the amoral jerk department: He set out to harass the victim. He called Crump for an appointment, then showed up fifteen minutes early and barged past Sophie into Crump's office.

"Crumphuuggh," Stenson began, doing his old, deep-down throat clearing thing that Crump was beginning to think might be taught to these white-shoe types at exclusive prep schools. "I want to depose your client, the kid who started all this—"

"First of all, nice to see you—we don't usually get you high-octane types over here in the bottoms," Crump began. "Secondly, his name is Brian Lockwood, and he's not the plaintiff in this lawsuit, his parents are, and lastly, I interviewed over thirty people before I filed this suit, almost all of whom know more about the issues relevant to the case then the fourteen-year-old kid hovering near death at the hands of your client. I can only assume your request is designed to intimidate and harass the victim of your client's lawbreaking, so I'll be moving for a protective order to block your attempt to continue bullying the kid whose mistreatment brought about this lawsuit. But, thanks for asking."

Stenson plunked down in the chair opposite Crump. He looked like what he was: The senior member of half-a-dozen, male-only, private lunch clubs, with names that sounded like they were founded during the Civil War. He had that sort-of-curly, sort of wavy grey hair these guys always had, with watery blue eyes that made them all look like the Secretary of State or a Supreme Court Justice. Crump figured Stenson's three-piece suit cost more than Mary's nearly antique automobile.

"Look, Crump, this case is a joke—asking the Court to shutter one of the oldest and most sought-after institutions in this City because one kid has a bad experience—"

"Gregory—can I call you Gregory? They say Hell is old and has a lasting reputation—"

"O.K., I can see we're getting nowhere trying to be reasonable about this. Either produce the Kid for a deposition, or we'll see you in Court."

Stenson left, as abruptly as he'd arrived.

"Was that Greg Stenson?" Maureen asked, as she watched him huff and puff his way out the door.

"Yeah."

"What was he so upset about?"

"I didn't ask for his autograph," Crump said, dryly. "Also, that I wouldn't produce the Lockwood kid so he could box his ears in a deposition."

"You think Rebecca Stairs would stand for that?"

"This is the way child traffickers beat the rap. They try to intimidate victims who are barely old enough to testify. I'm betting we can get a protective order from Judge Stairs, given her background in Juvenile Court." Crump stopped himself, realizing he'd overlooked something. "Although, this is State court—"

"Meaning?" Maureen asked.

"Meaning, they can move to substitute judges, for no reason at all. I'm sort of surprised, given Judge Stairs' background, that they haven't done that yet," Crump observed.

"It really pisses off the judges," Maureen added. "If Stenson intends to come back to that courtroom someday, it can haunt him."

"Maybe. More often than not, it's because they're afraid somebody else they might get would be worse for their case. Stairs is pretty highly regarded, her last gig was Chief Judge of Juvenile Court. We'll see how much she's in a hurry to let that old ham-hock Stenson beat up on a skinny kid in a wheelchair."

* *

Maureen and Wade Solly appeared in the U.S. District Court for the Southern District of California, before Judge Jerome Culpepper, to complain about the Government's inability to respond to inquiries regarding the whereabouts of Elení Montes, E.M.'s mother. While Solley had no idea there were dignitaries in the Courtroom, Maureen immediately recognized Peter Meadows, Solicitor General of the United States and their nemesis in the Patriot Act suit, fidgeting at the counsel table with the local U.S. Attorney.

"This guy is following me around," Maureen whispered to Solley, explaining the role of her new chaperone.

"They don't trust you and your partner, so it looks like he's got his finger on all these cases now," Solley whispered back.

"Named Plaintiffs 'F.W.,' 'T.S.,' and 'R.A.,' et. al., versus U.S.C.I.S. and H.H.S. and the U.S., respectively," the Clerk called out, and Solley stepped forward. His opponent also approached the Judge, with Meadows sitting back at the counsel table, glaring at Maureen.

"Your Honor, we are here for a rule to show cause against these Government agencies on behalf of class member 'E.M.', who joined the class two months ago, and two others. We've been over the records we were allowed to review by Health and Human Services, but after an apparent transfer to SeaTac almost a year ago, H.H.S. claims they have no record of the whereabouts of E.M.'s mother, a Ms. Elení Montes. They also have nothing on the other two class members. We'd like H.H.S. ordered to show cause why they should not be held in contempt, for claiming to not have these records and for being unable to re-unite these three individuals in the thirty-day window ordered by this Court."

An ashen-looking U.S. Attorney, undoubtedly fazed by the presence of Peter Meadows, stepped forward. The man looked like he was silently thinking through his resume as he stood in open court.

"Your honor, if I may, the Acting Secretary of H.H.S., Mr. Telemar, informs me that the only records he's been authorized to disclose to Class Members in this case may not fully follow the movements of these particular criminal respondents within the Government's custody."

"What exactly does *that* mean?" the Judge asked, leaning over and peering down at the trembling U.S. Attorney. "I thought we'd been over this—*all* the records on these detainees' whereabouts are subject to the jurisdiction of this Court. What part of '*all*' don't you understand? 'A', or 'L', or 'L'?"

"Your Honor, if I may," Meadows slowly approached the bench.

"Please identify yourself, counsel," the Judge ordered.

"Q. Peter Meadows, Solicitor General, for the United States."

"Mr. Meadows, as you know, I've held your H.H.S. executive director, Mr. Telemar, in contempt already. Why do we not have all the records your Secretary maintains?"

"We believe," Meadows began, casting a sideways glance at Solley, "the records in question are subject to Executive Privilege—"

"Now I've heard it all. You're going to stand here and represent to the Court that this list of where you've parked *thousands* of detainees in your custody has been discussed in *detail* with the President of the United States?"

Meadows lifted his chin and began to speak. "Not exactly—"

"Your honor," Solley began to interrupt, when the Judge raised a hand, palm outward, pausing him.

"Mr. Meadows, it is indeed providential that you've chosen to appear today, as it relieves me of any reservations I may have about incarcerating your Assistant U.S. Attorney, Mr. Peabody here. I'm remanding you to the custody of the U.S. Marshals here in the Southern District. You shall remain in custody until the officers of Health and Human Services charged with maintaining the records regarding the location of detainees subject to this Court's injunction, present to *me,* the exact whereabouts of the three detainees currently subject to this rule to show cause."

As the bailiff approached to secure nylon ties around Meadows's wrists, Peabody stepped forward and announced, "Your Honor, we intend to appeal this ruling directly to the Ninth Circuit, and we request a stay of the custody order pending the appeal—"

"Request denied, Mr. Peabody. Last time I checked, appeals, even emergency appeals in this Circuit, were taking between five months and one year. I would expect that springing your boss here would move considerably faster if you simply produce the records you are withholding from this Court on a truly reprehensible claim of Executive Privilege. The appearance the Government is creating here, that the President can reach out into what is, in essence, a civil suit, and manipulate the outcome for the sake of his political agendas, makes this entire Country look like a banana republic, without the bananas." He paused. "Not in *my* Courtroom."

14.
CHILD ABUSE BY PROXY........

There was a mob scene outside the courtroom of Rebecca Stairs, Senior Chancellor of the Circuit Court of Lakeside County, in the Daniel Burnham Courthouse of the City by the Lake. The press coverage of the Carrington Prep Nuisance Case was so intense that even routine procedural motions drew a crowd. Crump and Maureen arrived early, hoping to beat the packed hallways, but as soon as they exited the elevator, a crush of people began waving microphones and camera lighting in their faces. The courtrooms were off limits to camera crews, but the elevator lobbies were fair game.

"Is it true the Head of School and Faculty were part of the alleged scheme to cover up the abuse of the minor student at Carrington?" one reporter shouted out, as Crump and Maureen shimmied through the crowd.

"Read the complaint," Crump shouted back, as they disappeared inside the courtroom.

Stenson and his crew were already seated at both counsel tables, with stacks of inches-thick, three ring binders spread out all over the tables. Crump and Maureen sat in the front row of the visitor's benches, determined not to appear fazed by the Stenson crew's appropriation of all the work spaces in the courtroom.

As the reporters filed in behind them and filled up the visitor's gallery, Judge Stairs entered the courtroom in a flowing black robe, her clerk trailing behind. Everybody quickly rose, but she just as promptly announced "You can all be seated." Crump hadn't seen the Judge in years, since he'd spent weeks at a time in her old courtroom in juvenile court, where she'd been Chief Judge before becoming a chancellor.

She looked about the same, like a professor who was carrying too many books around, with her glasses slipping down the bridge of her nose as she walked absentmindedly from room to room. She always carried her own files, a stack that had her appearing stooped and harassed. She plopped them down on her dais and asked the clerk to call the first case. She'd purposefully moved *Lockwood versus Carrington Prep* to last on the docket, as an act of mercy to the other litigants in the more routine cases in the courtroom. After an hour of those lawyers maneuvering around the beachhead Stenson and his crew had made of the courtroom, she called the Lockwood's case.

"Your Honor, Crump and McDougal for the Petitioners."

"Good morning, Mr. Crump. Long time, no see," she said, smiling, an almost meaningless courtesy gesture that rattled Stenson.

"Hummpgh…..Gregory Stenson, of Stenson and Willis, and my associate, Paul Montrose, for Carrington Prep, the oldest and—"

"Thank you, Mr. Stenson," the Judge interrupted, anticipating an embellishing speech, way too early in the proceedings. "Remember to give your business cards to the court reporter, so they can reach you for transcript delivery instructions."

Good, Maureen thought—she's reminding everybody that this hearing is on the record.

Crump spoke up. "Your Honor, we're here on my motion for a protective order. Mr. Stenson and his client have noticed up a deposition of the minor student we are here referring to as 'B.L.' We are seeking a protective order to prevent that deposition from going forward."

"You can't work this out?"

"We tried. We had one Rule 201 conference about this matter—" Crump began.

"You could call it that," Stenson interrupted.

"Wait your turn, Mr. Stenson. We'll get to you shortly. Go ahead, Mr. Crump."

"First of all, B.L. is not a party—his parents, as his guardians, are the Plaintiffs, so a simple notice of deposition is insufficient. B.L. should have been subpoenaed, and then we'd be arguing under the rules on protected third-party witnesses. Under those standards, there'd be no reason to depose this witness at this time. This case isn't about this Minor's conduct; it's about the School's. I interviewed over twenty separate witnesses with direct knowledge of the issues in the case before I filed, and Mr. Stenson's client hasn't deposed *any* of them. We believe this action is intended to intimidate this minor witness, who is currently in an extremely compromised medical condition—one, I would add, resulting directly from the acts of by the Defendant institution and several of its employees. We believe the protective order should be granted."

"Thank you. Response, Mr. Stenson."

"Your Honor, that last little act of slander is exactly why we want this witness—"

"Excuse me, Mr. Stenson, but *what* act of 'slander' are you referring to?" the Judge asked.

"That nonsense about the kid they're calling 'B.L.', being in 'a compromised medical condition'—how do we *know* that? And the business about it resulting from Carrington Prep and its employees, which we maintain is pure and simple slander—"

"Mr. Stenson, does the complaint not state, under oath, that B.L. is currently a long-term patient in a hospital, with a life-threatening condition?"

"Sure, it does. We believe that 'hospital,'" Stenson said, making air quotes around the word "hospital" as he spoke, "is nothing more than a juvenile psych ward."

"Mr. Stenson, as you may know, before I moved to the Chancery Division, I spent almost twenty years as the chief judge of the Lakeside County Juvenile Court. During that time, I witnessed first-hand many patients with life threatening conditions in psych wards, many of whom, sadly, never made it out alive. I hardly think the nature of the medical services this witness is receiving bolsters your argument. As I asked, what's the 'slander'?"

Stenson flipped open a binder on the ledge before the Judge's podium. "The mere suggestion that any life-threatening psychological condition can be the result of the sorts of alleged 'bullying,'" again, the air quotes, "is a form of slander. We maintain that the idea that his client—sorry, his client's son—can become dangerously ill as a result of the conduct described in the complaint, is medically impossible. This conduct, even if proven, is just run of the mill, boys-will-be-boys stuff, the sorts of rough fun that we all experienced growing up. The fact that this particular child is the classic 'eggshell-headed plaintiff', the overly sensitive kid who just can't roll with the punches, is exactly the reason we'll be moving to dismiss the complaint."

The Judge looked like she'd heard Stenson wrong, like she couldn't believe her ears. Before she or Crump could respond, Maureen, who'd been bristling and biting her tongue the entire time, jumped into the argument.

"Your honor, I've *seen* B.L.—Mr. Stenson *hasn't*—"

"Now she's *testifying*," Stenson objected.

Before the Judge could intervene, Maureen interjected, "You *bet* I am. While I'm hopeful this child will live long enough to *see* the end of this proceeding, that is by no means a guarantee. I can assure you, whatever B.L. endured at Carrington, this 'Boys-will-be-boys' nonsense is exactly what's wrong here. The conduct alleged here isn't just dangerous and illegal, it's *criminal*—both the conduct and the school's failure to report it and stop it, whether that failure was just lazy and stupid and negligent, or, as we complain, the result of a conspiracy to cover it up. So, now, Mr. Stenson wants to use this deposition to further bully this child and his parents into dropping this suit. You have the power to stop it, and as a simple matter *of decency*, we ask that you do."

"Your honor, I object—"

"To her *argument*?" Judge Stairs asked.

"To the characterization that I would *dream* of using the deposition to bully this child—"

"Oh, *yes*," Crump interrupted. "As you can see, looking around the courtroom at the half-dozen *helpers* Mr. Stenson brought for this routine procedural motion, and the fifty binders they dragged with them, you can just imagine how *gentle* he and his forces will be in deposing this sick child—"

"Enough!" the Judge announced, and the courtroom went silent. "I cannot pretend to be blind to what's going on here," she began. "If there's any chance, and, I mean, *any chance*, that this deposition would be used to intimidate B.L., I must use my power to supervise and regulate discovery to block this deposition from going forward. I will not be party to any form of child abuse by proxy. The protective order is granted."

Outside the courtroom, as Crump and Maureen slipped out, Stenson doubled back to meet them. He'd been giving a bunch of impromptu statements to the reporters, who were making their way to the elevators. Crump set down his briefcase to button up his coat, and when he looked up, Stenson was standing close enough give him an eye exam.

"You think you're something *special* in this courtroom, like this is some little private club?" he asked, as he poked Crump in the chest with his index finger.

"Do I look like the *elevator*, Greg?" Crump asked. "I assume that's why you're pressing my chest like you're picking which floor to get off. Want to borrow my reading glasses?"

"You think just because you and your partner, Maureen O'Sullivan, hang out in this little back alley of the law profession, you can throw street tactics at us and get away with it—"

"Getting old enough that Immediate Recall Memory's becoming a problem, *Greg*? My partner's Maureen *McDougal*—Maureen O'Sullivan's the actress who played Jane in all the Tarzan movies—"

"We'll get to you and your client. This isn't over—"

The door to the courtroom swung open.

"Mr. Stenson, I can hear you all the way up on the bench. I'm trying to review pleadings for my eleven o'clock call," Judge Stairs scolded, as she held the door open, so her clerk and the court reporter could view the scene. "Is there a problem?"

"He was just rehearsing his appeal," Crump jumped in, and the Judge smiled and nodded, as she closed the door.

* *

"This is Doctor Trimble. I've got some bad news."

Don't anybody be *dead*, Crump thought to himself, as he gripped the phone receiver.

"The Lockwood child has taken a turn for the worse," she said.

"Shi-i-it," Crump mumbled, loud enough to be heard by the Doctor. "What happened? I thought he was starting to take a feeding tube?"

"He was. Anorexia is like this—they get starved long enough, it starts to mess with the electrolytes in their system. Changes start to take place in the cerebral cortex—look, the reason I'm calling is when he turned critical, we transferred him up to the I.C.U. His parents asked him if there was anything they could get him, and he asked to talk to *you*. Any way you could make it out here, and, I mean, *quickly*?"

Crump hailed Maureen and they hauled out to the hospital together.

"What are you going to say?" she asked.

"Me? He's the one who wanted to talk to me. I'm supposed to say something?"

"C'mon, Crump—how many kids you raise?"

"Mary did most of the *raising*—"

"You know what difference a sympathetic authority figure can make—"

"Now, I'm an *authority figure*?"

"Crump, you could possibly save this kid's *life*. You gotta go in there with *a plan*."

"Phew, this should be *easy*," Crump said. "While we're on the subject of uplifting communication, you gonna tell Ms. Montes we got that dirtbag Peter Meadows thrown in jail for playing Vegas Shuffle with the records about her Mom's whereabouts?"

"I'll do it if you'll do it—"

"Sounds like we're playing Doctor—"

"Crump, I'm gonna *pound* you," Maureen said, as they pulled into the Hospital parking lot.

They split off as Crump scrambled up to the Juvenile I.C.U., while Maureen went through the miserably protracted intake to the Adolescent Psych Ward. He'd been pre-cleared for I.C.U., given Brian Lockwood's prognosis, and he made it just as Brian Lockwood's parents were taking a break from their bedside vigil. He met them in the outer hallway, away from the buzzing, beeping and gurgling sounds of the I.C.U.

"How's he doing?" Crump asked. They were amazingly dry-eyed.

"Hard to say," Mr. Lockwood answered. "It's like he keeps drifting off, but then he suddenly snaps back to attention and says something. He was doing that when he asked to talk to *you*."

"Any idea why?"

"No," Susan Lockwood began, but then she choked up.

"We think he may realize what's happening," Mr. Lockwood injected, "And there's something important he wants to tell you."

"What *is* happening?" Crump asked.

They both raised their shoulders. "Not sure. This morning, some of his vital signs started to move erratically out of whack. His pulse quickened, and then his blood pressure dropped, and Doctor Trimble said his brain chemistry was changing in a way that might not properly regulate his autonomic nervous system—"

"They can't regulate that stuff from the outside?" Crump interrupted.

"They're trying," Susan Lockwood offered. "We both think you'd better get in there."

Crump entered the ward, with the Lockwoods trailing behind. The place was crawling with female nurses and beefy looking guys in blue scrubs and sanitary hats. Brian Lockwood was sitting halfway up on an inclined hospital bed, a series of I.V. tubes attached to both arms. He seemed awake, but his head occasionally rolled from side to side. He was pale and strung-out looking, like he'd just O.D.'d on something,

"Brian, Mr. Crump is here—"

"Just 'Crump,'" Crump added.

The kid nodded.

Crump got close enough to place his ear next to the kid's face. He looked like he was trying to say something important. When Crump's left ear was practically in the kid's face, Brian Lockwood whispered, "You should have seen the *other guy*."

Crump started to cry, something he hadn't done in years, outside of funeral parlors. He fought it off, thinking intensely, visualizing aggressively bad television from the Fifties and Sixties, focusing briefly on *The Elvis Christmas Special,* which usually did the trick.

"Brian Lockwood, what the *Hell* you doing up here?" Crump asked.

Crump leaned in, close enough to hear the answer. "I'm O.K.," the kid whispered.

Crump glanced over at the Lockwoods. He couldn't tell if they could hear what was going on between them, but he guessed not.

"Your parents said you wanted to tell me something?"

"Are you *my* lawyer?" the kid whispered.

Crump nodded. "Want me to sue somebody?" he asked. "I'm already suing just about everybody at Carrington who's old enough to drive—"

"Closer," the kid whispered, and Crump placed his head near enough so Brian Lockwood could whisper in his ear. "When I told you they were doing some stuff, it was more than just stuff."

Crump pulled away. "The kids, those four the Dubrow kid told me about?"

"Just one," Brian Lockwood whispered.

Crump pulled back again. "Lemme guess—Fletcher?"

"Yeah," he whispered.

"The one who took over when the teachers' kids got in trouble, the one who had 'kind of a tough life'?"

"It wasn't just slamming me into lockers," Brian Lockwood continued, in a tone barely audible to Crump, and obviously designed to be out of earshot of his parents.

Crump briefly thought again about *The Elvis Christmas Special.* "Lemme guess—"

"You don't have to," the kid whispered. "He did it to me twice, in my back end."

Crump pulled back. Not even Elvis could save him. He was starting to crack up. He looked up at the ceiling.

Leaning in, he asked, "Anybody else know?"

"I think he bragged," the kid whispered.

Crump cupped his hand over his mouth. This time, he leaned into the kid and whispered into the kid's ear. "It's just us, O.K.?"

The kid nodded.

Crump leaned back into the kid so he could whisper again directly in his ear. "Look, you gotta get outta here. *I need you to not die. I… need… you*," Crump repeated.

As he pulled back, Brian Lockwood, his head rolling gently left, then right, straightened up.

He nodded.

* *

"How'd yours go?" Maureen asked, when she made it back into her car, where Crump was waiting, sitting at the wheel. "He gonna make it?"

Crump was shaking, visibly. "Fuck," he said, as he pounded the steering wheel.

"You O.K.?"

"No," Crump said, as he started to wail, erupting into a howl, as he began chomping on the top of the steering wheel.

"Crump, you are *biting* the steering wheel—"

"Fuck, Fuck, *Fuck*….," he shouted, this time again pounding the wheel. "Do we have time to go *kill* somebody?"

"What happened in there?"

"It's all comin' back—"

"Uh-oh," she paused. "This is *not* O.K., I mean, if this is bringing all your stuff back, you're not gonna be all right, and you sure as Hell can't help that kid in there."

Crump turned to face her. He was crying, snot running down his face like his head was exploding. "Hire somebody," he choked out.

"You retiring?" Maureen asked.

"No. Going full time on this shit. I am going to fucking *bury* these people. Hire somebody to help with the paying customers."

"Well, my talk was obviously better," Maureen offered.

"You tell her we put that bastard Meadows in jail?"

"Yeah."

"What'd she do?"

"She reached up and slapped me a high five."

"Nice to know somebody in this mess hasn't lost their sense of perspective," Crump said, as he started the car. Then he turned off the ignition and stared on ahead.

"I want all of 'em", he said. "Fucking Handler, and Meadows, and that shit-brained, rat-faced little Nazi Ernstmeyer, and all of those pompous assholes out at Carrington—I want 'em *all*……"

She placed a hand on his shoulder, gave him a shove and said, "Nice to see you're finally getting back down to *normal*………"

15.
IMMIGRANTS ON OUR SHORES………

Mary Haffencamp was about to get into her car when she thought she heard a baby crying. Given that her legal practice primarily consisted of family law, child custody, divorce and adoption, the sound of a baby wailing away in the distance was not unfamiliar, but it was still odd coming from the echoes of the multi-level parking garage of a suburban branch of the Circuit Court of Lakeside County. Those using the lot were not accustomed to anything other than the whoosh of cars ramping up and down, and the recorded robot voice of the electronic gatekeeper, announcing "No Cashiers at the Exits", which came out sounding like "No Cashews After Sex," a slurring Mary was fairly certain was unintentional.

As she was dumping her briefcase in the front seat, she heard the baby crying again, but this time it was louder and repetitive sounding, like it was recorded. She looked around for the source, but the place was dark enough you'd only see moving objects with headlights, and there were none of those in sight. She got in behind the wheel, started the car and began to back out of the parking space, when a hard thud rumbled against the car, like she'd hit something. While it was after five o'clock and dark, she'd just been behind the car and hadn't seen anything amiss back there. She threw the car into park and with the engine still running, got out to look under the wheels.

Mary drew back, seeing legs sticking out from behind her rear wheels. She began to panic but couldn't help herself, so she bent down and let out a yelp when she saw the body of a large man sandwiched under her rear wheels. It seemed impossible that anybody could have landed there so quickly without her hearing anything. Her first reaction was to immediately pull the car a few feet forward, to see if, in fact, the man was dead. She inched the car slowly forward and killed the engine. As soon as she did, she heard the wailing child's voice again, somewhere off in the distance.

She got out and walked around to the back of the car, shining the flashlight from her phone on the man's body. It was only then she realized the "body" was in fact just a man's clothing, stuffed with what appeared to be straw and cotton. It was dressed up in jeans, gym shoes, a plaid work shirt and it had no hands or head.

Just as she began dialing the police, Angelo Turulio came running up the parking ramp behind her.

"You O.K., Missus Mary?" he shouted, short of breath from the back and forth run up four floors to get to her.

"I'm a little buzzed," she started to say, when Angelo placed his hand over her hand holding the phone, and forced it downward.

"Wait—doan call de cops yet—lemme see what dis is," he ordered.

"Angelo—"

"No, wait—"

"Angelo, somebody's trying to freak me out. This lot is usually as boring as the terminal lot at the airport. Whoever put this thing here managed to do it as soon as I got in the car. We have to call the cops—"

"Den I'm never gonna catch de guys what did this," Turulio complained.

"Look, I appreciate what you and Crump are up to here, and it's great that you're following me around, but this is creepy enough that I'm calling the cops—"

"Why doan we jus call Ben?"

"This isn't even his *City*, let alone his beat."

"O.K., but den I'm gonna get lost—doan wanna 'splain what I'm doin' here. You gonna be OK, or you want me to wait?"

They both heard it—the wailing baby, like a cell phone ringer programmed to remind you of….what? Feed the baby? To both of them, it just sounded creepy.

"Yeah, I'm gonna stay," Turulio agreed.

When the patrol car got there, two suburban cops who looked like their regular calls were speeders, drunks and domestics, walked up the stairway and shined flashlights at Mary and Angelo. Mary explained the predicament, while one cop dragged the stuffed, headless torso out from behind the car.

"Could this be some kind of practical joke, like, maybe one of your kids' friends?" the taller cop asked, as he scribbled on a pad.

"They're twenty-three, twenty-five and twenty-six. One's a social worker, one's a med student and one's a police officer—"

"O.K., maybe not," he said.

"Dean, lookit this," the other cop shouted, as he shone his light on the dummy.

There was a hand-written note stuck to the chest of the dummy's work shirt. It read, "Next time kill a real Mexican," and, below that, "Keep Mexicans Off Our Shores."

Turulio explained the connection, the work Crump was doing—which both cops had seen covered in the media—and Mary's work with foreign adoptions. Turulio explained how he had been following Mary around, watching for the nutjobs who were harassing them both.

"We'll make a report, but, in the meantime, if I was you," the cop offered," I wouldn't travel alone, and I wouldn't park in places like this. Just because the neighborhood is usually safe, doesn't mean somebody bent on causing you harm will stay away."

"I tink dis is one a dem 'Hate Crimes,'" Turulio offered.

"Not sure it's even a crime-crime," the cop reflected, as he closed his notepad. "We'll bag this thing and keep it for evidence. We may be able to figure out who did this by checking up on the materials used here. My biggest concern, Mrs. Haffencamp, is that whoever did this, is not gonna stop."

While the cops canvassed the parking garage to see if the source of the recorded baby voice was still lurking around, Mary drove out of the building and dropped Angelo at his car, parked a block from the courthouse garage.

"You gotta be more careful," Angelo began.

"I can't live this way. You and Crump need to wrap up these cases—I'm not going to crawl into a hole and hide, just because everything you guys do seems to attract weirdos."

"Suit yourself Missus Mary, but as Crump always says, 'Duh wheels a justice turn slowly.'"

* *

When Crump exchanged his witness list for the class action with Regina Debevoise, it included a host of federal officials, as well as Dennis Ernstmeyer, mastermind of the medical deportation plan, Warren Handler, Attorney General of the United States, and "H. Stennis "Sten" Stuggs, a/k/a "Deuteronomy Stuggs", President of the United States of America.

"You gotta be f-f-f-ing kidding me," Debevoise demanded, as she half-heartedly swore at Crump over the phone.

"What—you mad at me for outing the President's alias? It's pretty common knowledge."

"C'mon, Crump, I know you're pissed off about the arrest—"

"Me? No, I get that you Feds have emotionally fragile horses knocking around the Federal Building—I should have been more refined in my outburst. I, for one, feel safer knowing that the entire law enforcement apparatus of the Federal Government is ridding the Community of dangerous, horse-offending undesirables."

She did her best to ignore him. "The Judge is never going to stand for this."

"Why not?"

"Why are we even having this conversation? You know the Man is immune from prosecution—"

"When did this become a criminal proceeding?" Crump asked.

"Doesn't matter, he's still immune."

"Remember, 'I did not have sex with *that woman*?' Bill Clinton lost that case, all the way up to the Supreme Court. A sitting President can be forced to testify in a Civil Proceeding." Crump paused. When Debevoise didn't fill the dead air on the call, he added, "My case depends in part on what's going on in all their dirty little minds, and, yes, that includes 'Ole 'Deuteronomy' Stuggs himself. He's a relevant, competent witness, and I intend to take his deposition."

"O.K., we're getting nowhere. See you in court," she threatened, as she hung up.

Sophie was holding a call. She walked in and flashed a card so Crump could read it.

"Why are we acting like K.G.B. agents who think their office has been bugged?" he began, when Sophie silently pointed to the index card she was holding. It read:

Margaret Prendergast from A.R.D.C. on line two

Asking if you got their hearing notice?

Crump picked up the phone.

"Attorney Crump? This is Margaret Prendergast of the Attorney Registration and Disciplinary Commission. We never got a response from you about a preliminary interview regarding your recent arrest. As you know, before any disciplinary proceeding can move forward, we need to conduct an in-person interview with the Respondent."

Crump looked at Sophie, covering the receiver. "You see a complaint from A.R.D.C.?"

Sophie shrugged her shoulders.

"Ms. Prendergast, I'm sorry, but nobody here seems to know anything about this. When did the notice go out?"

He heard papers flipping, then, "Two weeks ago. It relates to your arrest on February 15, for certain violations of Federal law—"

"Where did you send the notice?"

"Your home address, where you're registered."

"I don't think we ever received it, but I assume I can make an appointment now, so let me get a lawyer and call you back. Next week O.K.?"

"Yes. Please check your mail and let us know if you don't have the notice."

After she hung up, Crump called Mary, who'd never seen a hearing notice in their home mail. He then called Steve Barnacle and asked Barnacle to represent him in the A.R.D.C. interview.

Barnacle hustled over to Crump's office.

Crump was hanging up the phone. "Looks like somebody plucked our mail—Mary couldn't find it anywhere in the piles of bills and junk at home, and nothing else appears to be missing. Had to be intentional—who'd want an A.R.D.C. hearing notice? Can't redeem that for a pint at the liquor store."

Barnacle was flipping through a copy of the disciplinary rules. "Somebody must have filed a complaint after you got busted for flipping off the horse. I'll file an appearance and ask for the complaint," Barnacle added. "I'll want to see it before we go over there."

When Barnacle got the complaint, it had been filed by one "Alicia Mae Ludlow."

"Never heard of her," Crump said.

"Well, she's heard of *you*," Barnacle offered, reading the letter of complaint.

"I fear for the safety of the community," Barnacle read, stopping to point out that "community" was misspelled, "when a lawyer with such violent and immoral tendencies is allowed to run loose."

"Another horse lover, apparently," Crump observed.

"—Who writes with a thick, purple crayon," Barnacle added, as he held up the complaint, which was handwritten in juvenile cursive with a waxy, purple crayon that left bits and smudges of purple along the margins.

"A.R.D.C. will take that seriously?" Crump asked.

"They're under tremendous political pressure—everybody thinks lawyers have too much power, and they can get away with murder."

"And, offensive hand gestures," Crump added.

* *

"Please swear the witness," Margaret Prendergast announced, as Crump held up his right hand.

They were sitting around a table at the administrative offices of the Disciplinary Commission.

"Before we begin, may I ask if the A.R.D.C. has done anything to verify the existence of the complainant, Ms. Ludlow?" Barnacle inquired. "She's not, and never was, a client of Mr. Crump's or of Crump and McDougal, and we can't seem to find any record that she's for-real."

Prendergast said, "Off the record," and the court reporter stopped transcribing. "We were able to determine that Mr. Crump's arrest really happened, but we could not find a record of this person in the entire State. We feel we need to do this interview, in any event."

Barnacle narrowed his eyes, like he'd heard her wrong. Crump rolled his eyes.

"Why?" Barnacle asked.

"Still off the record?" Prendergast insisted.

"Sure," Barnacle noted.

"The Commission got a call from a government official, inquiring about the complaint."

"And, that would be?"

"The Attorney General, Mr. Handler."

"Figures," Crump injected. "You ask him how much they paid this 'Ludlow' woman, whoever she is, and whatever her real name is?"

"Can we just do the interview?" Prendergast asked, and they went back on the record.

After Crump described the incident and his stay in the Metropolitan Correctional Center, he concluded with the bit about the penny bond, and how it was all clearly in retaliation for the Patriot Act case. The Court reporter smirked through the entire testimony.

"Can I ask, Ms. Prendergast, exactly what Rule it is my client is alleged to have violated?"

She nodded. "Rule 8.4 (b)."

Barnacle flipped through his rule book and stopped, a look of disbelief on his face. "Criminal Infractions Involving Moral Turpitude?" he asked.

"I assume you will file a response," she offered. Then, "Off the record." The reporter stopped typing and began boxing up her equipment. She'd been through the drill long enough to know when they were done.

"I'm sorry about this, but we need to do this no matter what—"

"I get it," Barnacle interrupted.

"But, if you want to file your own complaint about malicious misuse of the rules in making a false and retaliatory complaint, go right ahead—" she paused. "And, if it's all the same, Mr. Crump, I can't really explain this Complaint. I hope you understand what that means."

* *

Turulio showed up at Crump's office to check in. "Ayy, boss."

"I'm getting horsed around by the A.R.D.C. over this phantom complaint filed by some ghost, supposedly named 'Alicia Mae Ludlow'—"

"Dat's her—"

"Her, *who*?"

"Dat broad what's hanging around outside a yur house," Turulio observed.

"How do you know that? The A.R.D.C. couldn't find her anywhere in the State—"

"Traced her plate. She don't live here. She's from some tiny piss hole in Alabama."

"I shoulda known. What's it gonna take to connect her to Stuggs and Handler?" Crump asked.

"Got my 'sisstant, Charlie Corkscrews, workin' on it. You got a bigger problem, boss."

Turulio shared the story of Mary's close scrape with a stuffed, headless, fake immigrant in the Courthouse parking garage.

"Shit," Crump said. "O.K., let Charlie work on linking these crazies to the Stuggs people. You gotta stay with Mary. She'll never lay low, so you have to follow her everywhere, stay close enough to reach out and touch her. You hear anything from my kids, Ben, Dr. Tom or Rene?"

"No, but dey know to contact me if anything happens."

"You going to that rally by the Baby Hitlers?"

"Wouldn't miss it."

"Let me know if you see anybody you recognize—"

"I'll tell President Stuggs you says '*Hello*'......"

* *

Q. Peter Meadows desperately wanted out of the San Diego Federal Correctional Center, an over-crowded facility with a smattering of drug dealers, illegal alien smugglers, bank robbers and local punks stealing supplies from the Naval Base that occupied much of the downtown harbor. He'd been housed there for almost a week, found in Contempt of Court by Judge Culpepper for refusing to produce the records showing where Elení Montes and others had been stashed by I.C.E.

Meadows's aides were pressuring Dennis Ernstmeyer, the master planner of the human shell game, to come up with the records. Ernstmeyer, a near religious devotee to the "Zero Tolerance" initiatives, at first insisted there were no complete records of anybody's whereabouts in Federal custody. Meadows's aides, fully aware of the game plan involving intentionally keeping the border-crashing families apart, told Ernstmeyer to knock it off and cough up the records. Meadows reminded Ernstmeyer, during a jailhouse interview, that it was *him*, and not Ernstmeyer, who was suffering the indignity of roof-top prison basketball practice. Ernstmeyer then miraculously discovered three lists the Feds maintained that connected up the I.C.E. custody dots of the family detainees.

Once Ernstmeyer produced the records, Q. Peter Meadows was sprung from prison. Wade Solley was then able to locate Ms. Montes the elder, who was parked in detention in Salt Lake City, Utah, and about to be deported back into Mexico, without her daughter.

"This is great," Wade Solley told Maureen. "Not only do we now have a bead on your Lady, but this helps us start putting together bunches of the still-separated families."

"Amazing what an indefinite stay in a contempt-of-court jail cell will do for jogging the memory," Maureen observed, congratulating Solley over the phone. "I'll need you to testify about how the Feds were lying when they claimed they didn't have the records to re-unite these people, and only miraculously discovered them when the Solicitor General got thrown in jail."

Maureen ran the news in to Crump, who was outlining depositions for the President, as well as the main perps out at Carrington Prep.

"You should be the one to give the good news to Estrellita Montes—you started this," Maureen suggested.

When Crump got to St. Vincent's, he was relieved to learn that Brian Lockwood was out of the I.C.U., news Doctor Trimble shared with him as Giampetro deposited him in the Adolescent Psych Ward with a wordless shrug of his massive shoulders. Crump promised to visit Brian Lockwood on his way out.

They walked over to Estrellita's room. "She's finally taking some solid food, and we're mixing her into the general population, so that's good. The language barrier will be an issue, but she's a smart cookie and she's actually picking up some English."

Crump was stunned when he entered the room. Estrellita Montes was up and around, for the first time since he'd met her, almost six months before. More remarkably, she was no longer attached to anything. It was amazing, he thought, how much better humans looked without tubes and bags dragged around behind them.

"Tu madre está en Salt Lake City, Utah," Crump announced, having practiced on the way over in the car.

"¿Dónde está eso?" she asked.

Crump hadn't practiced a response. "You wouldn't have an atlas?" he asked Doctor Trimble.

The Doctor, shaking her head in mildly-incredulous-generational disbelief, pulled up her cell phone and, in an instant, pulled up a map of the United States, with City by the Lake and Salt Lake City, both highlighted.

"Estás aquí," the Doctor said, pointing, "y tu madre está ahí."

"¿A qué distancia está eso?"

Crump, who thought he understood, said "Fourteen Hundred miles, more or less—about two day's drive, a few hours in a plane."

Doctor Trimble translated.

"Vamos," Estrellita announced, as she headed to a closet off to the side of the room, in order to pack.

Crump figured that would be her response, so he offered up another practiced response. "No estás lo suficientemente bien como para viajar, así que íbamos a tratar de traer aquí a usted," he said. He turned to the Doctor.

"Did I say that right—'You're not well enough to travel, so we're going to bring Mom back here?'"

"Yeah, I think you go it."

Estrellita looked profoundly disappointed. "Me siento bien," she said, folding her hands in front of her, like she was trying to catch falling water.

"I know you feel fine," Crump echoed, "but Doctor Trimble tells me you need a few more weeks on solid food. We can get your Mom back here, if you just hang in there a little."

The Doctor translated, all but the slang at the end.

Estrellita sat on the end of the bed, dejected but willing.

"Confío en ti," she said, and even though Crump had no idea what she was saying, he nodded, the way people do when trying to be polite in the face of untranslated speech.

As he turned to leave, she stood up and quickly again shook his hand.

Out at the Doctor's kiosk, Crump said, "I'm almost afraid to ask—"

"She said, 'I trust you,' which, given her circumstances, is a lot. Whatever you do, don't blow it."

16.
WELCOME TO BULLY NATION........

When Crump returned, there were two suits waiting for him in his office's cramped outer reception, a near cubicle with an open window to Sophie's desk.

"You two have an appointment?" Crump asked, as they both stood.

"You Philo John Crump?" one asked.

Here we go again, he thought. "Does anything good happen if I answer that question?"

"We're with Immigration and Customs Enforcement," the taller suit said, as the other guy pulled a manila folder out of a narrow briefcase.

"You guys here to negotiate? I figured you'd bring your lawyer—"

"We're here with a search warrant," the guy with the folder announced, as he handed the warrant over to Crump.

"O.K., fellas, fun is fun, but Maureen, Sophie and I were all born here, and the new guy we just hired grew up in Cedar Rapids, Iowa, and his ancestors came over with Columbus. Whatever you're looking for, it either doesn't involve anybody who works here, or it involves the class action I've got pending against you folks, and a warrant won't cut it there—"

"—this isn't about that case. We have a warrant for files regarding a prior client, a Jack Nomando," the shorter suit said, as he read from the warrant.

"You gotta be kidding me—that file is, like, twenty-five years old."

"Are we going to debate this in the reception of your office, or do we need to get the Marshals?"

"You're going to be shocked to hear this, but even if I thought you had a bona fide reason to be pawing through that file, I don't keep twenty-five-year-old closed files in the office. All that stuff's in storage. And anyway, that case involved a minor, and it was sealed by court order. You can't even get the public record stuff, let alone my file," Crump explained.

"Look, we can take you into custody if you do not produce this 'Nomando' file, wherever it is. The materials we're looking for do not relate to your former client, so they would not be subject to the sealing order. We are looking for the part of the file that relates to *your* involvement."

"*My* involvement? I was the guardian for Nomando's granddaughter."

Junior suit was already calling the U.S. Marshal's Office. Crump sat down and began reading the search warrant. By the time he finished, a U.S. Marshal appeared and cuffed him.

"Call Steve," Crump shouted to Sophie, as the Marshals took him into custody.

* *

Steve Barnacle sat at Crump's desk, flanked by Maureen and Howie Schmeltz, the new associate Crump and Maureen hired to work on their paying cases. They were rifling through a directory of old files Sophie had printed from their stored-file inventory.

"What exactly are we looking for?" Schmeltz asked.

"Some documents that relate to Crump and Maureen getting deputized by the U.S. Attorney's Office in an old case. They'd probably be in a file marked 'San Sebastopol,'" Barnacle answered.

Schmeltz nodded. "This is pretty exciting—I've only been here a couple a days, and already my boss has been arrested—"

"He wasn't exactly *arrested*," Barnacle corrected. "He's in I.C.E. custody for alleged illegal entry into the Country."

"Wow. They gonna deport him?" Schmeltz asked, as he flipped through his pages of the file inventory.

"They can't deport him—deport him to *where*? He's a citizen who's never lived anywhere but here," Barnacle noted.

"So, what's this all about?" Shmeltz asked.

"We were doing something down in Central America for the case, and for reasons we still can't talk about, we returned to the U.S. without going through a commercial airport and we never got our passports stamped on re-entry," Maureen explained. "The thing was, we were working as deputies of the U.S. Attorney's Office at the time."

Schmeltz looked at Maureen with his head cocked and an eye narrowed. "The same people who just picked up Mr. Crump, for the second time in four weeks?"

"Yeah," Barnacle injected. "Welcome to Bully Nation. This is just harassment. Wherever they end up landing this case, I'm going to move to transfer it to Judge Salazar as a related case to the 'Flipping Off The Horse' proceeding. This stupid thing is just the Government forum shopping a bogus enforcement action away from Judge Salazar, so they get a better shot at simple torture."

* *

"So, here we are again," Judge Reuben Salazar announced from the bench, as Crump was led into the courtroom in an orange jumpsuit, this time sporting a four-inch-wide, cream-colored neck brace.

"Ms. Debevoise, clue me in on what's happening here—I just got this case transferred to me by Judge Hoffenbauer, on Mr. Barnacle's motion, so I'm a little behind in the action."

Regina Debevoise stepped forward, glancing only momentarily at Crump. She buckled slightly, seeing the neck brace and noticing Crump was still cuffed with nylon bands.

"Your Honor, this is an immigration enforcement matter. The Government would have no objection if the Defendant's restraints were removed."

Good, Barnacle thought—she senses what's coming.

While Crump held out his arms and the Marshal cut the bands, Debevoise continued. "We are here on Defendant's alleged violation of 8 U.S. Code Section 1227, regarding illegal and unauthorized entry into the territorial United States—"

"Ask her when the alleged 'unauthorized entry' occurred," Crump shouted out, slightly hoarse from the injury involving the neck brace.

"Mr. Crump, we've been through this before—please let your counsel Mr. Barnacle speak for you. Mr. Barnacle, what about that?"

The reporters in the gallery started to sputter, occasional words like "bogus" slipping out audibly.

"The 'event' at issue occurred in Nineteen Ninety-Six, almost exactly twenty-seven years ago, and my client, by definition, can't make an 'illegal or unauthorized' entry—he's a U.S. Citizen, born here, who's never expatriated or renounced his citizenship."

The Judge bent over and asked his Clerk for a hefty volume, which the Clerk passed up to the Judge, who opened it and skimmed a page.

"Ms. Debevoise, help me here," Judge Salazar began. "As a life-long Citizen, what possible criminal statute could this man be violating, by returning from a foreign country to domestic soil?"

Debevoise looked like she was about ready to shout something and head for the exits. "Your Honor, section (d)(2)(B), requires that, upon re-entry, the Defendant was supposed to be processed through Immigration enforcement and have his passport duly stamped with the time, place and date of re-entry—"

"I understand that, and for whatever reason, that didn't happen, but is that anything other than a formality?"

"The Government has the right to determine if the re-entry was somehow linked to an act of espionage—"

"—and, you waited twenty-seven years to decide if this man was a spy?" the Judge pressed.

"There is no Statute of Limitations on Espionage," Debevoise countered.

"Mr. Barnacle," the Judge inquired, turning to Crump's counsel, "I see, from the motion you've filed and the exhibits attached, *including the Government's deputization certificate,* that the alleged re-entry was under the auspices of the U.S. Attorney's Office, on Official U.S. Government business, Mr. Crump then acting as a Deputy U.S. Attorney," the Judge continued.

"That's correct."

"Ms. Debevoise, how is it possible the Government can prosecute this man for doing the Government's business?"

Debevoise shuffled some papers. "Your Honor, we were just served with Mr. Barnacle's motion to quash the indictment and his cross claim for sanctions and malicious prosecution. I'd like time to respond—"

"And, I'll give you that, *after* you answer my question, if you can do so with something coherent. The record before me shows that your U.S. Attorney's Office sent this man on an official government errand outside the Country, and then, twenty-seven years later, you arrest him for what is, essentially, coming home from work—*Your work.* An inquisitive person might think this conduct reeks of a harassment campaign, and that would be true even without knowing you arrested the same man less than a month ago for giving a horse 'the finger.'" The Judge stopped and looked around the courtroom. The reporters were buzzing. The Judge added, "And, that would be true even if that inquisitive person didn't know the defendant was busy suing the Government across the hall, in a high-profile case involving alleged Government misconduct."

The Judge paused. When Regina Debevoise did not immediately answer, the Judge addressed Crump directly. "Mr. Crump, why the neck brace?"

"Your Honor, may we have this line of questioning off the record, in chambers?" Debevoise pleaded.

"*On* the record, *in* open Court," Judge Salazar snapped.

Crump stepped forward. "Excuse my voice," Crump began. "I'm a little hoarse and raspy, due to this injury," he added, pointing to the neck brace. "When I was taken into custody *for the second time*, for this ginned-up immigration prosecution, I was placed in a joint cell at the M.C.C. with another inmate. I was there for about fifteen minutes, when the guy asked me my name—"

"Do you know the identity of this inmate?" the Judge interrupted.

"No—I wouldn't be surprised if he wasn't even a legit inmate."

"Why do you say that?" the Judge inquired.

"I don't know—maybe it was the mechanic's coveralls he had on under his jumpsuit—"

"Your Honor, I object to this testimony—the witness is speculating—" Debevoise offered, only to be cut off by the Judge.

"He's not testifying, he's responding to my questions. I think I can sort out facts from speculation, thank you, Miss Debevoise. You may continue, Attorney Crump."

"So, anyway, I ask this guy why he needs to know my name, and he says, 'You *are* a smart-ass,' and then I say, 'Just Crump,' and then the guy suddenly lunges at me and starts strangling me, and by the time the guards heard the commotion and came in, he'd practically broken my neck. They sent me to the medical ward, put this thing on, then put me in solitary."

"You weren't sent to the Hospital?" The Judge asked.

"Nope."

The gallery was now humming with chatter, as a few additional reporters entered the courtroom. The Judge was moving around, getting off the bench and whispering to his clerk, then returning to his seat. Finally, after some additional commotion and the court reporter resetting her transcription machine, he spoke.

"Ms. Debevoise, if I understand the sentencing guidelines for the *class four misdemeanor* this man is charged with, even if it was a *current*, illegal border crossing by *a non-citizen*, the typical fine is between ten and fifty dollars, and detainees are released on time served. Is that not correct?'

Assistant U.S. Attorney Debevoise cleared her throat. "This is not my usual docket—"

"Fine, I'll answer for you," the Judge interrupted. "I'm releasing this man immediately, and quashing the indictment. We will, however, hold a hearing on Mr. Crump's cross claims for sanctions and malicious prosecution. I want to expedite that hearing to next Tuesday, at ten A.M. Before then, the Government is to produce, to both the Court and to Attorney Crump's Counsel, the video record of surveillance of Attorney Crump's cell, the identity of the inmate who attacked Attorney Crump, the record of the crimes that inmate is being charged with, the identities of the guards on duty at the time of the attack, and I want those guards in the courtroom, prepared to testify. Do I make myself clear?"

"Yes, your Honor," Debevoise answered.

"Mr. Conklin," the Judge addressed the Bailiff. "I want you to direct the U.S. Attorney's office to accompany Attorney Crump to Westside Hospital to have his injuries examined. Any treatment required should be billed directly to the U.S. Attorney's Office. And, Ms. Debevoise, you need to inform your co-counsel, Mr. Meadows, that if these instructions are not promptly followed, those responsible will be held in contempt, and all fines will be assessed against those persons individually and, if not paid within five business days, it will result in incarceration of those held in contempt. Mr. Barnacle, prepare and submit an appropriate order," he said, as he stood from the bench and walked out.

"Nice work," Crump said, nudging Barnacle.

"I hardly said a word," Barnacle replied.

"I know, that was the nice work," Crump added.

* *

Maureen was grinding through interviews of witnesses in the Carrington case, which invariably generated a list of potential additional witnesses each time an interviewee identified somebody else likely to know something important. It was such a common occurrence that she did not, at first, make a priority out of following up on a glancing comment made by one awkward parent who'd said, "You really should talk to the music teacher, Deb Connover."

A week later, by the time she'd caught up with Ms. Connover, the music teacher was in the process of wrapping up her stint at Carrington, having been hired away by a local public school. She was leaving during the school year, conduct so unusual that it peaked Maureen's interest. By the time Maureen could set up an interview, Connover was already teaching at Goodman Public, not far from downtown. She was younger than Maureen expected, and dressed a lot less modestly than Maureen's pre-conceived notions about a grade-school music teacher would have suggested. She couldn't have been much over thirty, had a female-rock-star-mullet hairdo, and gave off the air of somebody who moonlighted in a tribute band on the weekends.

"Thanks for agreeing to speak with me," Maureen began, explaining the broad outlines of the lawsuit, summarizing some of the information she'd been told by other cooperating witnesses. "What we're hoping to learn more about is the type of bullying the Lockwood kid endured at Carrington, and anything you may know about what the School did, or didn't do, to address it."

"Can I ask you a question first?" Connover injected.

"Sure."

"What about indemnity?"

"Indemnity?" Maureen asked.

"Like, indemnity from prosecution—"

"You mean, '*immunity* from prosecution', I think," Maureen posed. "This is a civil proceeding—we're just trying to establish that Carrington has become so dangerous it needs to be shut down. There's no criminal prosecutions in our case."

Deb Connover nodded. "I get that. I'm just wondering, if I help you, can I get this 'immunity' for what I'm about to tell you?"

Maureen was trying not to show her mix of confusion and anticipation, wondering how much of this witness's reaction meant she knew something explosive, or whether she was just paranoid. "We are the civil attorneys for the Lockwoods. If, for any reason, there was any criminal jeopardy associated with the matter, it would be up to the Lakeside County State's Attorney's Office to decide if a given witness should be granted immunity."

"Good. Can you get me in touch with those guys?" Connover asked.

Maureen nodded. "Well, of course, except I don't think anybody in the State's Attorney's Office knows anything about this matter—"

"Well," Connover paused," they *will*, once you hear what I've got to say."

* *

"I've got some bad news," Wade Solley reported over the phone, calling from his office outside of San Diego. "The folks at H.H.S. rejected the transfer request we made to have Elení Montes sent to the facility up by you, so you could get her united with her daughter."

Maureen was sitting at her desk, figuring that Q. Peter Meadows was either as big a fanatic as Dennis Ernstmeyer, or a glutton for punishment. "What basis they give?"

"They claim they are charging her with additional counts."

"She's been in Government custody since five minutes after crossing the border in El Paso. What other offences could she have possibly committed? Failure to brush and floss after meals?"

"I know, these 'offenses' are all contrived," Solley offered. "Looks like it's some kind of drug-related charge, from what they're telling me."

"These people aren't drug smugglers," Maureen complained. "We figure the woman's husband had just been executed by the gangs, for shielding his daughter, who was reaching prime age for trafficking. The Guatemalan Government is covering for the gangs and the war criminals running them. With no man in the house, she just wanted to get her daughter out of the reach of the gangs. Even by current standards, they'd probably qualify for asylum."

"I know," Solley said, sounding dejected. "A lot like every other case that wanders over my desk. Want me to challenge it down here? We got a judge who just finished putting the Solicitor General of the United States in jail for dicking us around—might be the best place to push back on additional Government hijinks."

"Let me see what Crump thinks. He should just be getting out of the hospital today."

"What happened to him?"

"Long story. Let's just say that Ms. Montes is not the only victim of the newly-weaponized Justice Department under the Stuggs Administration. Make sure you don't spit on the sidewalk crossing the street."

17.
IMMUNITY FROM PROSECUTION..........

"WHY DO WE EVEN *HAVE* a land line?" Mary asked Crump, as they surfed through the answering machine connected to their almost-antique, hard-wired home phone.

"Just listen," Crump implored, as he skipped through a dozen robo-calls about air-duct cleaning.

"What's with air ducts? I don't know anybody who's ever had their ducts cleaned. What's in our air ducts?" Mary rattled off, as they flipped through the machine-generated messages.

"Here it is," Crump said, as he stopped the machine and hit "repeat".

"*Beep—Click—*Is this the head of the household? Hey.....Who the Hell do you think you are? You the asshole that's lawsuiting everybody so you can wipe out the white people with all these fuckin' immigrants......" The message seemed to pause, and in the background, a muffled voice said, "Read the rest", followed by, "We know where you are at all times, you and that wife of yours helping all those immigrant babies, we know and we will hunt you down and……*Beep*—" then a pause, followed by the answering machine's voice, "Six O'clock Thursday…..," and then, "Did you know that your air ducts can *kill*………."

"Well," Crump offered, "this is nobody *I* know—"

"You sure about that?" Mary asked. "I mean, so far, the Feds have jailed you for disrespecting a horse, then jailed you again for that crazy Nomando case you handled *for them*, and on a totally bogus charge, thrown you in a cell with some drooling maniac who almost killed you. How do you know that wasn't the Attorney General on the line—"

"I'd recognize his voice—he's a *celebrity*—"

Mary disconnected the phone from the wall jack while Crump was still rambling about the Attorney General, and handed it to him, adding, "Throw this thing away—you'll just have to learn how to use a smartphone."

Crump looked at the boxy phone, complete with built-in answering machine, turning it over in his hands like there might be spying apparatus in the battery pack. "No, I need to turn this over to Angelo for analysis—"

"*Analysis?*" Mary asked. "Angelo? Why not give it to the cops? That's got to count as some kind of crime."

"You mean, the 'Air Ducts' thing?"

"This is not funny. If you're going to keep suing these crackpots, we need to get the local cops involved," Mary ordered.

"I've already asked Ben to help with that. He's working with the local guys here. I'll give this to them, and ask them to shadow you as much as they can. Angelo is already following you most days."

Mary sat at the kitchen table and shook her head. "Most days isn't good enough."

"O.K., I'll have him go full time on you. Charlie Corkscrews can follow the nutjobs from the Army of God," Crump offered.

"What about *you*?" Mary asked. If Crump didn't know better, he would have sworn she was starting to cry, something she almost never did.

"They never hit the lawyers—brings down too much heat."

"You always say that. It didn't stop them from trying to kill you in jail."

Crump sat across from his spouse. She was animating the salt and pepper shakers like they were hand puppets, dancing them around and occasionally crashing them together.

"Given the ass-kicking Judge Salazar gave them, I think that's over—probably explains this nut-cake on the phone—they need to go underground."

"That guy they stuck in the cell with you was some gangster who wasn't even formally charged with a crime. That doesn't count as going 'Underground'?"

"You're probably right—all the video surveillance tapes of the cell seem to have disappeared, and the guards all claim to have not seen a thing. They're saying it's all a coincidence. Sounds to me like they're no longer even trying to hide the harassment campaign. An old machine politician in town used to say, 'Don't worry about when you think I might stab you in the back. Worry when you think I might stab you *in the front*.'"

* *

Maureen decided to fly to San Diego, to help Wade Solley fight the Government's attempt to sandbag Elení Montes with a bogus drug running charge mysteriously tagged on her, as soon as the H.H.S. coughed up her location to the Court. Solley had subpoenaed the stuff I.C.E. had confiscated and bagged when Elení Montes and Estrellita were apprehended at the border. There was an exclusion hearing going on when she arrived. Solley was trying to keep a bag of the alleged-offending substance out of evidence in the hearing. After the Judge concluded there was no provable chain of evidence and that the stuff could have been purchased by the I.C.E. agent off a dealer in the court parking lot, the Government's witness turned up an entirely different, small unmarked bottle of white powder found in the grab-bag of belongings seized from Elení Montes at the border.

"This substance was credibly traced to the Defendant Montes's belongings, seized and cataloged when she was arrested at the border in El Paso," the I.C.E. agent recounted, as he held up the bottle.

Solley objected. "Your Honor, this witness has no qualifications to analyze or characterize the substance in this travel vial. I suggest, before any conclusions are reached regarding this alleged 'contraband,' you await the testimony of my expert, Ms. Carlson, regarding the contents."

Judge Culpepper, who was already leery of the Government's case, asked, "Are you prepared to have your expert testify right now, so we can take her out of order while the Government is still proving its case?"

"Yes, she's in the Courtroom now," Solley offered.

The Judge excused the I.C.E. agent, and a woman who looked to Maureen like a suburban real estate agent, right down to the heels, trench coat and clipboard, rose from behind them and approached Solley, who handed her a folder. She then circled the bench and took the stand. The Court reporter swore her in and Solley identified her as Doctor Sandra Carlson, a research chemist, PhD, and professor at U. California San Diego. After a few minutes of testimony about how she came by the vial to test its contents, she explained it was all done under full view of I.C.E. agents performing chain of custody observations. She then stated that she could identify the contents within a reasonable degree of scientific certainty.

"What's in the bottle?" Solley asked.

"P-E-G 3350," Dr. Carlson testified.

"For those of us not research chemists, can you identify it by its generic name?" Solley asked.

"Polyethylene glycol, 3350," she added.

"And, what exactly *is* 'Polyethylene glycol, 3350'?" Solley continued.

Dr. Carlson paused, then turned to face the judge, while opening the folder and glancing at the report inside. Good, Maureen thought—Solley had prepared her well.

"It's the active ingredient in several common laxatives. It sits inert in the colon and absorbs water from the bowel, then stimulates contractions that force a bowel movement in persons typically afflicted with—"

"Thank you, Doctor," Solley interrupted, not wanting the Judge's focus to be on excrement. "Are these laxatives containing Polyethylene glycol 3350, are they prescription drugs?"

"No, these are typically found in over-the-counter products, commercially available without a prescription, the most common of which is the popular brand, 'Boom-Chocka-Locka.'"

"Yes, uhh…..." Solley paused, trying to redirect the testimony. "So, to put it another way, this substance is not contraband, in any form, delivery vehicle or dosage, correct?"

"That's correct. I've seen it offered in several products, some sold in the PX at Camp Pendleton, so even the Military offers it over the counter. There've been some studies about the long-term, regular use in children and whether any of it is absorbed into the digestive tract, causing cognitive issues, however, so far there's no science on that. But, it's neither addictive, nor habit forming, it's not an intoxicant and not contraband anywhere, so far as that's concerned."

Peter Meadows stood and objected. "That last statement is a legal conclusion this witness is not qualified to make—"

"Mr. Meadows," the Judge butted in. "You're not seriously trying to argue that this commercially-available laxative is somehow a controlled substance, are you? This entire charge has the rancid air of contrivance, something cooked up by the Government to further delay the re-uniting of this parent with her separated child. I'm dismissing the charge currently pending against this woman, and since her asylum case isn't scheduled for another two months, I see no reason why she cannot be relocated to the I.C.E. facility at the City by the Lake, where she can be re-unified with her daughter. So ordered."

The Judge stood, the people in the courtroom stood, and with Dr. Carlson still on the witness stand, glancing around with a "What Did I Do?" look on her face, everybody filed out and congregated in the hallway.

"They're going to try something else," Maureen noted. "There's no good reason for the Solicitor General, who's just been jailed by this Judge for contempt, to be in this courtroom trying to convince this Judge to hold this woman in custody because she had potty-powder in her bag. They're doing this to demoralize us and our client."

As the hallway cleared out, they thanked Dr. Carlson. Then, Solley said," Let me see if I can expedite the transfer order. These things take weeks, and if I can cut that short, we might anticipate and frustrate their next move."

"She's going to disappear again," Maureen said, as they left the building.

* *

Estrellita Montes was having a nightmare.

In the dream, it was her birthday. Thirteen was important, her Mother always said that, things start to happen at thirteen. You change schools, you can help your Father, who manages a farm supply and produce transport building on the edge of Huehuetenango. Father can get paid extra for your time after school. Mother hinted at other reasons to worship thirteen, but those were never explained.

Time got bent and stuck together, the way it does in dreams, but the darkening of the nightmare was the waiting, waiting for her Father to come home from work, waiting to have cena and celebrate, watching as her Mother became more silent, more distressed. Around Ten O'Clock, her Mother called Uncle Caba, had him go to the outpost to check. Her Mother begged her to go to sleep, said she'd wake Estrellita when Father returned, but she could see something was wrong.

They stayed up all night, and in the morning, Uncle Caba came by and hugged her Mother. Nobody had slept. Everything was strange: Quiet, no visitors, and no Padre. Then, at midday, the Sacredote showed up with a card, wearing a purple funeral robe, and he blessed the house and said something in a low voice Estrellita could not hear.

She knew this didn't really all happen the same day, even if it seemed that way in the dream, but when her Mother said they'd never see Father again, she then explained they'd need to move.

"¿Que'?" *Why?*

Mother told her a story. Her Father worked with lots of men at the depot. One of them had a son. Her Father's co-worker was very important, somebody who used to be some kind of government official. His son was part of a group that collected money from other people. Collected money so bad things didn't happen. The son wanted a Novia, a girlfriend, and the son had seleccionado Estrellita, had chosen her. When her Father told this to her Mother, her Mother said it was time to leave, to take the Pan-American Highway to La Mesilla, then on to Mexico.

Estrellita had heard the stories—that these 'Novias' were expected to have relations with all of the Son's gang members, and many of the Novias eventually ended up in a ditch by the roadside. She understood why her Mother had said they needed to leave, but she thought Father would be coming too, at least, thought that before her Father didn't come home.

The next morning, as she and Mother are packing backpacks, the door is kicked in, and she's screaming, and she doesn't remember what happened next, maybe there are shots fired, and then she and Mother are standing in the back of a tractor-trailer truck, in total blackness, stifling heat, and as the truck rolls, she feels she is falling asleep, but her Mother keeps shaking her awake. It is that falling asleep, then being shaken by her Mother, that repeats over and over in the dream, until she is shouting in the darkness of her room, thrashing, unable to drift off without feeling like she is dying, dying and only her Mother can save her.

The light in her room comes on. It is Giampetro. She sits up in her bed.

"What's wrong?" Giampetro asks in English, but then he remembers. "¿Qué pasa?" he repeats.

"Ya vienen," she answers, which he understands to mean, "They're coming."

"¿Quién?"

"Las pandillas. Me harán su esposa," she quickly whispers.

Giampetro knows she's having a bad dream, knows that she does not really think the gangs are coming for her, or that they are going to all try to make her "their bride".

"Me quedaré aquí. Tendrán que pasar por mí. Me los comeré," he says. "I will stay here. They will have to go through me. I will *eat* them," he says, which he repeats and then translates into English, just because he likes the sound of it.

He sits in a chair by the door and turns off the light, leaving the door open.

Estrellita looks at him and thinks, Sí, podría hacer eso…….

Yes, he just might do that…….

* *

Maureen sat in the outer office of Lakeside County State's Attorney Derek Markle. She and Crump had worked with Markle for years. Markle had always been a cross between a bored- bureaucrat career guy and an occasional bulldog, but he was also a quirky, sanctimonious weirdo. "Check out the yellow socks and try to look interested when he rambles," Crump had warned. Still, he was their best contact in the Office of Lakeside County State's

Attorney, so even though the Carrington lawsuit was probably not much interest to him, she figured she'd start with Markle anyway.

"McDougal," he announced, as he came out to greet her. He always looked like a cross between a shoe salesman and an auto mechanic who'd been forced to clean up and put on a too-small, ratty and pilled suit. "How's my favorite Coroner, Mr. Whit?" he asked. He was checking up on her husband, Lakeside County Coroner Whit Wentworth. He was always quick to point out that the bestowing of that name was ample justification for criminal prosecution of Whit's parents.

"Whit's drenched in death," she answered. "I got a weird request," she added, as they retreated to his office and sat across from each other. She noted with a raised eyebrow that Markle was still wearing those yellow socks.

"You want me to indict that nutty boss of yours? You guys can't resist kicking the hornet's nest—"

"You've seen the coverage?"

"Everybody has. Gotta admire you guys for taking on a couple of dirtbags like Stuggs and Warren Handler, but I think you're gonna lose that one. Sorry—I can't arrest the Feds. They'll just claim Federal Preemption—"

"This isn't about the Patriot Act case. We're pursuing a civil case against Carrington Prep—"

"Read about that too," he injected. "That's where you want to shutter the place like it's an abandoned mine shaft."

"Essentially, yes," Maureen offered. "The case is mostly about flagrant violations of the Prevention of School Violence Act, centered on the aggressive and repeated mistreatment of a student who's hovering near death as a result."

"So I hear," Markle observed. "Want me to have the cops swoop in there and take a couple of eggheads away in cuffs? Nothing makes educators into believers like seeing a few of their contemporaries doing the perp walk."

Maureen shifted in her seat and twitched her nose—she could never tell when Markle was joking or serious—he was a little bent, and might do just about anything. "No, I have kind of an odd request. We were questioning a witness—a teacher who's moved on to another school—and out of nowhere, she asks me for immunity."

"You can't do shit there—"

"I know. She's a music teacher, not exactly schooled on the divisions of authority in the legal system. Still, she knows something, wants immunity, so she thinks it's bad and she won't talk to me until I run this down. What'dya think?"

Markle sat back, placed his hands behind his head. He wore Accountant-from-Cleveland daylight-tinting wire-rims, and looked like he'd never learned to properly shave himself. That was the thing Maureen liked most about him: He just didn't care.

"I don't know—I mean, if the place burned down during a secret witchcraft ceremony, and all she did was forget to lock the broom closet, that'd be one thing, but if she's directly involved….."

"It's pretty obviously a matter of a cover-up. The bullying of this kid went on *for years*—they had to know—and I think she knows something about the conspiracy of silence. This kid was targeted because his parents were leading an effort to overhaul the place. It had become a sinecure—"

"Huh?" Markle interrupted.

"A cozy place, run by the faculty with the sole purpose of providing them with cushy jobs, no responsibilities and a clubby sense of self-governance."

"Ahhh, the crime of messing with 'The Good Old Days,'" Markle injected. "Don't mess with my *privilege*," he added. "Want some free advice?" he asked.

Here we go, Maureen thought.

"The World's full of silly people, wishin' it was the Good Old Days again, making life miserable for the rest of us—ain't that what the 'Stuggs Revolution' is all about—The White Guys want their World back? You ask me, I'd say, if you're in a big, crowded room, and a guy gets up to a podium and starts talkin' about bringing back 'The Good Old Days,' get up, leave the room. Call the cops."

Maureen waited, making sure he was done. "So, this being maybe a crime of omission rather than commission, can you offer her something?"

Markle nodded. "Why dontcha bring her in?" he asked, as he stood and unceremoniously, walked out of the room.

18.
GOD IS ON OUR SIDE……..

CRUMP HAD BEEN FIGHTING WITH Regina Debevoise about his plan to depose President Stuggs, when she suddenly resigned from the U.S. Attorney's Office. He figured she wanted to be out of there before the hearing on Crump's cross claims for malicious prosecution and sanctions in the Horse-Flip-Off and Sneak-Into-Your-Own-Country cases. The President's motion to stop the taking of his own deposition was pending before Judge Haverhorn, and the new Assistant U.S. Attorney, there in place of Debevoise, desperately asked for more time to brief it, given Debevoise's departure. While the Judge granted the extra time, she made a point of repeating, in open court, that she was treating the Patriot Act case like any other, and that "She expected the Parties, *all the Parties*, to abide by the rules."

With the delay in the Patriot Act case, the next time Crump was in court was the hearing on his own claims against the Government for the bogus arrests, back before an obviously annoyed Judge Salazar. The local U.S. Attorney's Office sent over a kid who looked too young to sense what was about to happen. Dan Duda, the new A.U.S.A., admitted to Steve Barnacle that it was only his third week on the job, and that he was feeling fortunate to have been given this opportunity, so early on in his career, to try a case.

"If Duda was eight years younger, it'd be child abuse," Crump grumbled to Barnacle, who nodded.

"You wonder if he has any idea," Barnacle said. "They think there's no chance they get tagged, so they send this chump over here," he added.

"Mr. Barnacle, call your first witness," the Judge ordered.

"Your Honor, Petitioner calls Djan Yoveteske," Barnacle announced.

A hulking, burly, buzz-cut of a man in a set of mechanic's coveralls, was escorted to the witness stand by an armed bailiff. Crump looked over the brute that attacked him in his cell, and shook his head.

"Please state your name for the record," Barnacle called out.

"Djan Nevlov Yoveteske," the man announced, as he remained standing.

"You may be seated," Judge Salazar offered, and the enormous chunk of a man, with some difficulty, wrenched himself into the witness chair. "Proceed," the Judge said.

"Mr. Yoveteske," Barnacle began, when the witness interrupted.

"No *Mister*—"

"Sorry. Can I just call you Djan?"

"'It's my name."

"Djan, have you ever seen my client, Mr. Crump, before?" Barnacle asked, as he pointed to Crump, sitting at the witness table.

"Sure—he's the plague guy I roughed up in the cell when the feds tossed me in with him," he offered.

"*Plague guy?*" Barnacle repeated.

"Yeah. The feds picked me up at the shop, earlier that day, an they says, 'Yoveteske, you're operatin' a chop shop,' and I says 'Screw you—this a legit business, auto repair and rebuild,' but they haul me in anyway, say I got connections to the Russian Mob, and I says, 'You stupid assholes, I'm Croatian,' but one of the guys says, 'All the same to me'—"

"Excuse me, Djan, but what day was this?" Barnacle asked, trying to slow him down.

"I dunno, April somethin', the day they tossed me in with that guy," he offered, pointing at Crump, who softly smiled at him from behind the table.

"Go ahead," Barnacle offered.

"So, they book me at the M.C.C.—"

"The Metropolitan Correctional Center, the jail connected to this building?" Barnacle asked.

"Yeah. So, anyway, after they print and snap me, a guy comes in and closes the door, while I'm cuffed to the chair—"

"I'm sorry to keep interrupting, but is that man in the courtroom today?" Barnacle asked.

"Yeah, sittin' over there," he answered, pointing at a Guard seated in a row behind Dan Duda, the bewildered freshman prosecutor, who increasingly looked like he was just trying to figure out what the Hell was going on.

"Then what happened?" Barnacle asked.

"So, this guy, the same one 'ats over there, he says, 'Sorry, but we're gonna hafta hold you without bond, until we can get you a hearing before the judge. Just to be fair, I gotta warn you, we're real crowded, so we're gonna hafta have you share a cell wid a couple a guys, and one of 'em, he's got the *Ebola*', and I says, 'What's the *Ebola?*' and he says, 'It's like the worst, it's this disease, an if the guy spits on ya, or sneezes on ya, your eyeballs turn to blood, and then they *explode,* and then you'll be bleedin' all over, and then, you got the blood pourin' outa your nose, and mouth, and them empty eye sockets, and then, for sure, you gonna die—'"

"Excuse me, Djan, but this man, this guard who's sitting behind U.S. Attorney Duda over there, he told you all this?"

"Yeah, so then I says, 'How do I know if it's the guy with the *Ebola*?' and he says, 'Asshole's name is 'Crump', so be sure to ask', and I says, 'What if he don't tell me, or he lies?' and the guard says, 'Yeah, he's a real wise guy—might do that', so he describes him, then he says, 'Whatever you do, don't let him spit or sneeze on you,' so when I get in the cell, an that guy over there," he paused, again pointing at Crump, "when that guy won't answer me right away, then he wisecracks me off, an I'm figurin', yeah, that's the *Ebola* guy, so I jump him and try to knock him out before he sneezes and my eyeballs explode."

"Thank you," Barnacle said.

"Your witness, Mr. Duda," the Judge called out, Duda's face bristling red.

Duda shuffled some papers, then stood and looked up. "Uuhh..... Mr. Yoveteske—"

"No Mister—"

"Sorry, Djan, uuhh, you don't know whether Mr. Crump here…." He paused, pointing at Crump…"doesn't actually have the Ebola, now, do you?"

"Objection—Relevance," Barnacle began. "Putting aside the absurd notion that the guards may have believed my client had a disease not seen on this *continent in six years*, the purpose of this hearing is to determine if my client's federal custodians set him up to be attacked in his cell. I'm prepared to present evidence that the federal authorities neither tested my client for *any communicable disease* upon taking him into custody, nor—"

"Sustained," the Judge called out. "Do you have any other cross examination of this witness?"

Dan Duda looked a little shell-shocked, "No, your Honor," he announced, and the Bailiff helped Yoveteske off the stand and out of the courtroom.

The offending guard was called, and testified that the events accurately described by Yoveteske were orchestrated and directed by Peter Meadows, Solicitor General, supposedly taking orders from "somebody upstairs." The Judge then cut short the hearing.

"It's obvious to me we are dealing with Government misconduct here," Judge Salazar announced. "Let's set this over for two weeks so, Mr. Barnacle, you can present your case for costs and damages. I'll have more to say then about what I think ought to happen here," he said, as he rose and left the courtroom.

"What's 'Ebola'?" A.U.S.A. Duda asked Barnacle, as they packed up their files.

* *

"What do you mean, 'She's in Mexico'? How's that possible?" a stunned Maureen asked Wade Solley, who was calling from his office.

"When I went to serve my court order on H.H.S., they came back to me and said, "Oh, sorry, but we can't comply with this. There's a new policy: We take them back to their point of entry, and deliver them back into Mexico, while they await their asylum hearings. She's not in Salt Lake City anymore," Wade Solley explained, as Maureen sat silently on the phone.

"That shit-weasel Ernstmeyer's behind this," Crump commented, as Maureen filled him in.

Maureen offered, "I've gotta go back to California and get these guys held in contempt. All it would take is five minutes of Ernstmeyer on the stand, explaining the made-up thinking behind this new, 'Take 'Em Back To Mexico' policy, and Judge Culpepper will have the guy behind bars, with his buddy Peter Meadows—"

"If Judge Salazar doesn't jail Meadows first, although it sounds like a lot of this is coming straight from the Attorney General," Crump offered, recounting the hearing with D'jan, the Chop Shop Guy, who roughed up Crump in jail.

Maureen sat at her desk and flipped though some documents on her computer. "I don't want to complicate the Patriot Act case with this—they're not even trying to lift Judge Haverhorn's temporary injunction on the Medical Deportations. Warren Handler and the Stuggs Administration have become so fixated on not getting labeled 'Terrorists', they've completely forgotten about Ernstmeyer's twisted little medical deportation program. I say we haul 'em all before Judge Culpepper out in California and see if he gives any of 'em the federal death penalty."

Crump looked at his calendar. He was scheduled to go back out and talk with Estrellita Montes next week. "Well, whatever you do, do it *fast*—I got a fourteen-year-old kid out at St. Vincent's, who thinks her Mother is about to walk through the door any day now. I don't even want to think about the impact this will have on her rehabilitation plan……"

* *

Judge Haverhorn ruled that President Stuggs had to sit for a deposition in the Patriot Act case. Both Peter Meadows and Attorney General Warren Handler tried to obtain a stay of the order while they appealed, but they failed, Judge Haverhorn announcing that sitting for a three-hour deposition was not a National emergency. The deposition was ordered to go forward on the first day of June, barring a National Security Alert that required Stuggs to be secreted away in an underground bunker somewhere.

Crump agreed to hold the deposition in the Federal Building, both to sidestep arguing about the location and because, when the Secret Service delivered their security protocols to him, he seriously doubted that the Bagel Joint and Myron's Deli, shops on the first floor of the building housing the offices of Crump and McDougal, could comply.

"You nervous?" Mary asked, the night before the event.

"About what?"

"You're deposing *the President*," Mary said. "There'll be cameras, and guys with guns, and protestors in the Federal Plaza, and half of the U.S. Attorney's Office breathing down your neck."

"Sounds like I deserve a raise—"

"You work for yourself," Mary reminded him.

"Anyway, I'll be sure to wave to the cameras, just in case any of my grade school teachers are alive and watching. They always gave me failing grades on my report cards in all the squishy categories, like, 'Shows Respect For Authority Figures', and 'Completes Tasks In Orderly And Timely Fashion.' This'll show 'em—"

"—Or confirm their worst fears," Mary added.

The next morning, Crump and Howie Schmeltz packed their catalog cases full of exhibits for the deposition of the President of the United States and headed over to the Reagan Federal Building. Mary was right—there were so many protests going on, it was hard to tell where the Anti-Global Warming Vegans started and the Atheists for Godless Currency left off. Reporters were mobbing the place. There were six giant, immaculate, boxy SUVs parked in front of the building, all with drivers nervously waiting, standing beside the hoods. Crump told Schmeltz it looked like a funeral for dead horses.

Crump and Schmeltz submitted, like everybody else in the building, to the virtual strip search ordered by the Secret Service. The crowd inside the lobby was slow moving but smaller than usual, as the Court had agreed to close the courtroom floor of the building to the public as a security measure. Judge Haverhorn offered up her courtroom for the deposition, figuring the size and layout would best accommodate the small army of Secret Service, building security, and lawyers present for the event.

When they got to Judge Haverhorn's courtroom, Stuggs was already there, seated at the end of one of the counsel tables between the gallery and the Judge's dais. Crump stopped for another pat down as he entered, then walked up to the other counsel table like he owned the place. Peter Meadows was there, sitting across from the court reporter, with Stuggs at the end of the table, cradled by Meadows and the Reporter. As Crump set down his catalog case at the opposite end and pulled out his outline, notepad and exhibits, Howie Schmeltz dumped his set of duplicate documents on the table.

"You think it's really *him*?" Schmeltz whispered in Crump's ear.

Great, Crump thought—the guy is going all *Hollywood Walk of Fame* on me, before we even start.

Crump had to admit, Stuggs looked different than the made-up and coiffed character the public was treated to in the media. His dyed-blond comb-over was a lot wispier than it appeared on television. Stuggs was morbidly overweight, a fact successfully hidden from the public using tent-like, billowing suits that were much more revealing of his bulges, up close. He had the appearance of a former football player, grown old and gone to seed, with tanning-bed, spray-on perpetual suntan and the jowls of bulldog. Crump's first thought, on seeing him up close, was that he'd never buy a Florida condominium time-share or a used car from the guy, let alone vote for him to run the Country.

"Who's defending?" Crump announced, as he set up shop. Stuggs was leaning back in his seat, which was literally groaning under the weight.

As Peter Meadows stepped forward to intercept Crump, Stuggs let loose with, "So, this is the fella that's labeled all us hard workin' Administration folks as a bunch of terrorizers."

"Good Morning, Mr. President," Crump replied. "I'd shake your hand, but I'd probably need to go through another pat down, so let me just say it's good to finally meet you. This is my associate, Mr. Schmeltz. He'll be handing around copies of exhibits, as we identify them for your deposition—"

"When do aah ghet to take you'all's deposition?" Stuggs drawled out.

"I can't give you legal advice—that's what Mr. Meadows is here for—but, typically, the lawyers in the case don't depose each other. My client, Dr. Trimble's deposition, is scheduled for next month—"

"Kinda bossy, ain't he, Peter?" Stuggs interrupted, nodding at Crump as he needled Meadows.

Crump and Schmeltz sat downwind and across from Meadows, near the opposite end of the long table, because Meadows was flanked by six guys Crump assumed were either A.U.S.A.'s or Secret Service. None of them, he noted, had any documents or notepads.

"Miss Reporter, can you swear the witness?" Crump asked.

"Please raise your right hand—"

"Certainly, darlin'," Stuggs cut in, as he raised his right hand. His seat moaned, like an injured dog.

The Reporter, a veteran Crump had used before, began, "Do you solemnly swear to tell the truth, the whole truth, and nothing but the truth, so help you God?"

Stuggs smiled. "I do," he paused…."and since you so kindly asked for the Lord's help, why don't we join hands around the table, and begin this here occasion with a prayer."

The people around the table looked at each other in awkward silence. Then, with some flinching hesitation like a circular game of Rock, Paper, Scissors, everybody except Crump joined hands in a circle, as Stuggs offered, "Dear Lord, we ask for your assistance to help these poor, misguided characters, these Secular Humanists who attack us for our Faith, to understand the true meanin' of the Stuggs Agenda, which is to Get America Prayin' Again. Amen."

Crump looked over at Howie Schmeltz, who'd joined in the circle of hands, and gave him a dirty look.

Everybody sat back and resumed their positions.

"You're recording this, too?" Crump asked the court reporter. She nodded. Good—that weird prayer interlude would be preserved for the record.

"Please state your name for the Record," Crump began.

"H. Stennis Stuggs—some folks back home in Greenville Alabama call me 'Sten', and I have, in my earlier days as a country preacher, gone by the nickname of 'Deuteronomy Stuggs.'"

"What's the 'H' stand for?" Crump asked.

"*Henry*, although, in my youth, folks came to be callin' me 'Hank', which I did not like, so I went with a monogram and used my right and proper Christian middle name."

"Where'd you get the nickname 'Deuteronomy'—the fifth book of the Bible—from?"

"It's the source of all the Biblical laws, and my sermons always lay down the law—some folks call me 'The New Moses,'" Stuggs replied, smugly grinning.

Crump quickly explained the mechanics of the deposition—answer verbally, say something if you don't understand the question, don't talk over the question when answering—then they began in earnest.

"President Stuggs, are you on any medications today?"

Stuggs stiffened up and glared first at his lawyer, Peter Meadows, then at Crump. "I'm not gonna answer that—It's privileged, and anyway, just who in the *Hell* do you think you *are*?"

Crump rolled his eyes.

"Withdraw that question—we're not here to help you get headlines," Meadows barked.

"Look, I don't actually care if you are or aren't taking anything newsworthy. I just want to know if we can rely on your answers, or is somebody later going to say, 'He didn't mean that—he was on Prozac—'"

"You can rely on his answers. Ask a real question," Meadows complained.

Crump asked, "Who sets immigration policy in your Administration—"

"I do—"

"Wait, I wasn't finished—you, or Mr. Ernstmeyer?"

"Dennis Ernstmeyer is my loyuhl and trusted director of U.S.C.I.S.," Stuggs responded.

"I get that. My question, though, is where do the objectives behind the Administration's immigration policies originate—with You, Mr. President, or with Dennis Ernstmeyer?"

"I'd say we are a *team*."

"Are you familiar with the answers Mr. Ernstmeyer gave in his deposition in this case?"

"Generally."

Crump had the Court Reporter mark the transcript of Ernstmeyer's deposition as Stuggs Exhibit One. He handed it to Stuggs. "Have you read the transcript of his deposition?"

"It was summarized for me by my Attorney General—ahm the Chief Executive Officer of these United States, so people read for me."

Crump nodded. "This look like a true and accurate copy?"

Stuggs flipped through it like it was a comic book, then said, "Seems like it."

"So, do you agree with the answers Mr. Ernstmeyer gave to the questions I asked him?"

"Dennis Ernstmeyer is a Patriot."

"Yes, but do you agree with his answers? We can re-read the transcript, but I'd prefer not to do that—"

"Objection," Meadows injected.

"Basis?" Crump asked.

"Putting words in the President's mouth—"

"Look, Peter, by *agreement* of the Parties, we have only three hours today. I'd like to not have to ask the President back for another round—"

"Fat chance of *that*—" Stuggs interrupted.

"A critical element of my case is proving the intent behind these policies of Family Separation and Medical Deportation. Mr. Ernstmeyer, one half of the President's *team*, gave us his motives. I'm just asking if the President agrees those are the drivers of those policies." He turned to Stuggs. "So, are they?"

"Mr. Dennis Ernstmeyer is a Patriot, son, somethin' you'll never unduhstand. He has mayh undivided authority to do whatever is necessary, to stop the thrunderin' hordes of illegals bombardin' the Southern Border everuh day, as we speak. As I said, we are *a team*, and if he has to scare up all them illegal Mexicans to trim the tide, he has my blessings, and, speaking of blessings, I think this calls for another *prayer*—"

"Mr. President, these impromptu religious ceremonies are cutting into my three hours, so if we could all just stick to answering my questions, this'd get done a lot faster. Can I take that last answer as a 'Yes?'"

"Yes to *what*?" Meadows asked.

"To whether the President agrees that the rationales Ernstmeyer provided in his dep for the Medical Deportation and Family Separation Policies, are those of the President's and the Official Administration's goals?"

"We are *a team*. How many times I gotta keep telling you that, *boy*?" the President offered.

"So, these twin immigration policies are designed to discourage both legal and illegal immigration, by sending the message that parents will lose their children and sick kids will get deported during medical treatment?"

Stuggs was slowly turning pink. "Let me tell you somethin', Mr. Milo Johnston Crump—"

"Close enough," Crump offered.

"I don't have to answer to you, or any of your Liberalistic, Communistic, Socialistic conspirators. I got elected by a majority of the folks in this Great Country, and we plan to take this Country *back*…." He paused.

"You done?" Crump asked.

Stuggs nodded.

"You have to answer verbally."

"You bet I am."

"O.K. So, who's '*We*' in that sentence, and who are '*We*' taking the Country back '*from*'?"

"Objection," Meadows said.

"Basis?"

"Executive Privilege—"

"You *have* to be joking—"

"I *never* joke," Meadows offered.

"*That*, I believe."

"Miss Reporter, please re-read my question," Crump asked. She did.

"Same objection," Meadows repeated.

"Certify it, and let's move on," Crump said. "Mr. President, your teammate, Mr. Ernstmeyer, testified that he began working for you when you were Governor of Alabama, studying a project he called, 'Reservation Repatriations,' essentially a program designed to make Native Americans pay the Government for the current fair market value of the real estate they occupy as Reservations. Is that correct?"

Stuggs shifted uncomfortably in his chair, which sounded like nuts and bolts were dropping out as he spoke. "Listen, son—I'm from Southern Alabama, sixty miles South of Montgomery. There'd *be* no Southern Alabama if it wasn't for that Great American Patriot Andrew Jackson, who reclaimed my ancestral home from the Indians in the Creek Wars—"

"I don't think he's answering my question—it's a 'Yes' or 'No' question—"

"Let him finish," Meadows ordered, and Crump thought, you mean, let him continue to dig his *grave*....

"As I was sayin', there's more n' one way to look at the predicament of the Red Man—"

"I'm sorry," Crump interrupted. "It really was a 'Yes' or 'No' question—"

"Keep interruptin' me, son, and we're gonna terminate this here deposition," Stuggs proclaimed.

"O.K. let's move on, *again*, Crump offered. "Did you once say, in a speech during a rally in Pine Bluff, Arkansas, that the one language the Bible had never 'passed through', was 'Mexican'?"

"Objection—"

"I have the tape, if you'd like to hear it," Crump offered. "Is 'Mexican' a 'Language'—"

"Look, smart guy," Stuggs started in, leaning forward, his arms on the table. "What do you know about *The Bible?*"

"While I flunked out of Seminary, I'm still fairly certain that the New Testament went from Ancient Greek through a couple of languages, before landing in modern-day English, and the Old Testament meandered through Ancient Hebrew and a dozen or more dead languages before translations into English, and wherever that takes you, I know that 'Mexican' is *not* a language—"

"Ask a question, Crump, or I'll terminate this deposition," Meadows ordered.

"Are you and Dennis Ernstmeyer obsessed with Mexican immigrants, because you think they are infiltrating the so-called 'White Race' in America, and are these policies we're challenging with this lawsuit designed to frighten Mexicans and Central Americans into staying in their home countries, rather than losing their children and sacrificing their sick family members in a maze of Government subterfuge—"

"O.K., Crump, we're done here," Meadows snarled, as he rose suddenly from his chair. "Mr. President, we are terminating this deposition—"

"I don't think I got an answer to that last question," Crump said, as he, too stood away from the table.

"C'mon, Mr. President, we're leaving," Meadows proclaimed. "See you in Court for this, Crump," Meadows added.

"We're *in* Court—"

"Lemme tell you somethin'—" Stuggs began, pointing an arthritic finger at Crump.

"Mr. President—" Meadows tried to intercede.

"Just hole on, Peter. Mr. 'Patriot Acts' Crump, Mr. Smart Ass, we *are* takin' this Country *back,* and you ain't gonna stop us with this here *lawsuit.*" The President glared at Crump.

"Off the record," Meadows ordered, and the Reporter stopped typing.

"You know what's wrong with you?" Stuggs asked, again pointing awkwardly at Crump.

"I didn't vote for you?" Crump suggested.

"Besides that," Stuggs reflected, his starched-up comb-over dancing nervously on his shiny forehead. "You got a hero complex. Think you're standin' up against the big, bad President. Your problem is you *hate* me, and my followers, when all they want is a return to law and order, rightways and things normal, like things used to be before Lefties like you crawled into the spotlight—"

"Sorry to interrupt, Mr. President, but I'm just a tired, old guy—I've just got a client to represent."

President Stuggs huffed, raising his shoulders, smiling his sarcastic, "Yeah, sure" mock expression. He soldiered on, ignoring Crump's response. "The entire Stuggs 'Return to Sanity' pledge is all about bringin' back this great country to the way it was before all you Left-leaning hand wringers and politically correct Secular Humanists, before you started outlawin' 'normal' from all the Great American Institutions—"

"Like what?" Crump injected.

"Public washrooms, for one, like before all that gender-bender business had all those sex-changers in each other's bathrooms, and then there's that 'Me Too' nonsense, where every time a guy pats a woman on the back, they're hauling him off to jail—"

"Probably depends on how far down on that back you're patting," Crump offered.

"And, then there's the damn Communistics in education. You can't even get somebody who preaches Creationism or the inherent superiority of certain peoples, or boys-is-boys and girls-is-girls, onto campuses anymore—they get shouted down and run off. Real Americans can't catch a break, I mean, what the Hell *is* 'Plant-Based Korean Barbeque', anyway?"

Crump wrinkled his lower lip and narrowed an eye. "And, what exactly do you miss about all that?" Crump asked, goading him on, hoping the Judge would overhear them in her chambers.

"Mr. *President*," Meadows pleaded.

Stuggs held up a hand to silence him, before adding, "I mean, people get shot when the police get called, it's just *a thing*. Pretty soon all you ee-ffeminate liberals will be objecting to everything masculine about America, and next thing you know, they'll be banning Westerns and the Sports Illustrated Swimsuit Edition."

Crump's eyes were narrow enough that anybody paying attention would have thought he was in pain. "You're telling me, this whole thing, the entire 'Stuggs Agenda', is all about *nostalgia*?"

Stuggs smiled, then shook his head. "You're a bigger simpleton than I thought. The Stuggs agenda is all about *Stuggs*. For the loyalists, the people at my rallies, for *them,* it's about bringing back The Good Old Days."

19.
THE RUBBER MALLET TREATMENT………..

Judge Reuben Salazar cautioned the spectators in the courtroom gallery to remain quiet and to go out into the hallways if they needed to make deadline-related phone calls. The place was buzzing, in large part due to the presence at the counsel table of Attorney General Warren Handler. He, Peter Meadows and their new underling, Mr. Duda, were all whispering at the counsel table.

The tip of the hat to the press sounded odd to Barnacle, who'd never heard a Judge so openly acknowledge that a large chunk of the gallery was populated by journalists, who were about to hear something newsworthy.

Salazar had a stack of yellow legal pads piled up on the dais, with notes posted and loose pages stuffed haphazardly in the mountain of paper. He was flipping through looking for something in particular, and when he found it, he addressed the courtroom.

"I circulated an order this morning; I hope by now all of you have had time to read it. In it, I quashed both indictments against the defendant,

Attorney P.J. Crump, the original charge under 16 US Code 1338 (a) (3), the so-called 'Horse Flip-Off' case, as well as the superseding indictment on the 'Unlawful Re-Entry to the U.S.' charge. As to the 'Horse' case, whatever the reason may be for that antiquated piece of federal busy-bodying still being on the books, I concluded it could not possibly apply to a commercial, privately-owned animal that simply happened by a Federal courthouse. As to the 'Unlawful Re-Entry' case, as a citizen, I remain mystified that the U.S. Attorney believes that the Federal Government can charge a citizen with the 'crime' of setting his feet upon American soil."

Judge Salazar paused, put aside the stack of yellow pads, and continued.

"Which brings us to the business of today's hearing. I sit today as a District Judge as well as a Judge for the Federal Court of Claims, for this aspect of the case. As you know if you've read my order of today's date, I've concluded that both prosecutions were not only groundless, but that each was retaliatory in nature. These 'prosecutions' were motivated beyond doubt by the Government's and, specifically, the Justice Department's desire to weaponize the federal courts against an attorney who, in the course of representing what is now a class of clients, has accused the Government, and, specifically the Stuggs Administration, of egregious wrongdoing.

"I'm not here today to pass judgment on those claims—that's Judge Haverhorn's job—but I am here to rule on the cross claims for sanctions and malicious prosecution, filed by Attorney Crump. While this process of assessing damages may seem purely mathematical, I want to emphasize that in the thirty-five years I've spent, first as a prosecutor, then as a Judge, I've never witnessed government behavior this unsettling. When the Government becomes a seeker of retribution against a Citizen, and the U.S. Attorney's Office its instrumentality, I feel we've jumped off a cliff, one from which there may be no way to scramble back up the hill. For that reason, all the parties and their representatives should understand that I have no intention of burdening the taxpayers with any damages awarded today—no, these penalties will be assessed against the agents of Government themselves, *personally*. I am as interested in quantifying Attorney Crump's damages as I am with assessing blame. And, let me be clear: Dodging responsibility, 'Just Following Orders', will not be a defense. Any damages not specifically assessed against a particular agent, will be assessed directly against the Attorney General himself, Warren Handler."

As the Judge paused again, the courtroom began to rumble in whispered tones, as several spectators rose and hustled out into the hallway.

"Mr. Barnacle, please call your first witness—"

"Your Honor," Peter Meadows interrupted, "The Government moves to disqualify Attorney Steven Barnacle—"

"*Now?*" Salazar injected.

"Yes, given the admonition that these damages will be personally assessed. Mr. Barnacle is a recently retired member of the U.S. Attorney's Office—"

"Has he worked for the Office on *this case?*"

"No, but—"

"Motion denied. Mr. Barnacle, as I said, call your first witness."

"Your honor, I call Attorney Philo John Crump," Barnacle said, as he rose from his seat.

Crump, wearing a grey, somewhat distressed suit and a striped tie, stood, walked to the witness stand and was sworn in. After a series of preliminary background questions, Crump testified about the aftermath of getting roughed up in his cell by the alleged-mobster, Djan Yoveteske.

"How did the assault come to an end?" Barnacle asked.

"It was the other inmate," Crump responded. "Still don't know his name, but he kicked Yoveteske in the head, and then they started fighting, and when the guy yelled, "This wasn't part of the deal," a guard showed up, entered the holding cell and broke it all up."

"What did he mean, 'This wasn't part of the deal?'"

"Objection," Meadows called out. "Speculation based on hearsay—"

"I'm simply asking if the witness understood the meaning of an excited utterance by this still unidentified inmate," Barnacle noted.

"Overruled. He may answer."

"I just figured I'd been set up, but they guy wasn't expecting two on one. It looked to me like the other guy was gonna kill Yoveteske—it all happened pretty fast," Crump recalled.

"Then what happened?"

"The guard dumped me in another cell, an empty cell, and there was a lot of shouting down the hall in my old cell, and then Yoveteske, the second inmate and the guard walked past my cell and out of the hallway at the M.C.C.," Crump reported.

Barnacle nodded. "Were either of those two inmates—Yoveteske, or the one who attacked him—were either of them in restraints when they walked past?"

"No." Crump paused, briefly. "Looked like they were just taking a stroll," he added.

"Then what?"

"Some kind of EMT, or a paramedic, came in, looked at my neck and handed me the neck brace. He said, 'Here, put this on,' then he left and locked the cell."

"And, that was it?"

"Objection—leading," Meadows said, standing up.

"Overruled," the Judge announced.

"Yes, they left me there in the neck brace, and never sent me for an exam."

Judge Salazar leaned forward. "Attorney Crump, do I understand you to say that, at no time after the assault, were you taken to the infirmary or otherwise attended to by a doctor?"

Crump nodded. "That's right, even after the arraignment—"

"Excuse me?" Judge Salazar interrupted.

"After you ordered the State-sponsored trip to the Hospital, the Marshals released me to counsel here," Crump noted, nodding at Barnacle, "and the guy who released me said, 'You're on your own,' so Steve took me to my doc, who gave me the once over."

Salazar was starting to boil over. He stood. "Mr. Meadows, please approach the bench."

Meadows approached, flanked by Barnacle.

"Why weren't my orders followed? I ordered your office to see that this man was taken to the Hospital. What happened?" Salazar asked.

"The part he left out in that little bit of fiction he was spinning up there," Meadows began, "is that we gave him some forms to fill out in order to obtain Government reimbursed medical treatment, but he handed them back to the marshal, and said, 'Shove these up your....*behind*.'"

"I believe I said, 'Shove these up your *ass*,'" Crump whispered to himself.

"I cannot believe what I'm hearing," Judge Salazar remarked. "Mr. Meadows, I thought I made myself clear—this man was supposed to get immediate treatment for what was, in effect, a Government-supervised assault. As far as I'm concerned, you should have been hitch-hiking barefoot to the hospital, carrying this man on your back. '*Forms?*'" The Judge paused. "Sit down," he commanded.

Once the parties were back at the counsel tables, the Judge began questioning Crump.

"Mr. Crump, do you have any lingering effects from this assault?"

"I gave my medical records to Ms. Debevoise, before she quit the U.S. Attorney's Office. My neck's a little stiff, and my assailant bruised my vocal cords, but it's too early to tell what's hanging around."

The Judge was shaking his head. "Any further questions, Mr. Barnacle?"

"A few," Barnacle said. "Mr. Crump, did you ever find out the name of the other inmate, the one who interceded on your behalf?"

"No," Crump said. "But I did get a chance to talk to him. I ran into him leaving the M.C.C. when I was heading out to the doctor—he was flagging down a cab."

"Flagging down a cab, *unrestrained?*—"

"Yep."

"What did he say—"

"Objection, hearsay," Meadows called out, as Handler nudged him.

"Overruled," Salazar called out. "Go ahead."

"He saw me leaving and he said, 'You got screwed pal—it wasn't supposed to go down that way.'"

"He say anything else?" Barnacle asked.

"No, he just got in a cab and left."

"Your witness," Barnacle announced, as he sat.

The Solicitor General stood. "Mr. Crump, who did you vote for in the last Presidential election—"

"*Objectionnn*," Barnacle shouted. "What possible relevance does this have?"

"We intend to show that Attorney Crump has a long-standing bias against the Republican Party in general and President Stuggs in particular."

"Do I *have* to answer this?" Crump asked.

"Please, Attorney Crump, I know this is difficult for you, being an attorney, but let your counsel make the objections," the Judge admonished. "You may proceed, Mr. Meadows, but you'd better tie this together to something relevant quickly, or I'm cutting this line off."

"I didn't vote."

"Why not?" Meadows asked.

"Do I..." Crump paused. "Sorry."

"Go ahead," the Judge offered.

"I was in the hospital."

"Why?" Meadows followed up.

Before Barnacle could intercede, Crump barreled ahead. "Look, I have a condition that periodically flares up, and I need to go in for a procedure, and I was there that day."

"How do we know that 'condition,' as you call it, wasn't responsible for any so-called 'lingering effects' of the alleged jail-house assault?" Meadows drilled.

"You know," Crump began, "you guys are *amazing*." He paused again. "I grew up in State Custody, and a lot of bad stuff happened there. The condition that landed me in the hospital goes back to an assault I suffered at age twelve—that's how I know it had nothing to do with the injuries I suffered at the hands of your paid conscripts—"

"Your Honor, I insist that the witnesses' reference to 'paid conscripts' be stricken from the record—"

"—Overruled," the Judge ordered.

"Do you seriously expect this Court to believe that the United States Department of Justice would *arrange* to have you attacked in a cell while awaiting arraignment—"

Before Peter Meadows could finish, Crump erupted with, "Sure do, and I got news for you, and your boss over there, Mr. Attorney General Handler. All these creeps and whack-jobs you're throwing at me aren't going to stop the proceedings in the Patriot Act case, or cut down on all the bad publicity you're getting. We're receiving anonymous phone threats and your deputized creeps are following us around, but it's not gonna work—I got clients to represent, and your smear campaign and intimidation tactics aren't going to stop that." Crump paused, but before Meadows could interject, he added, "What are you gonna do? Tie a pillow case over my head and whack me around with a rubber mallet? Too late—it's already been tried—you're gonna have to be more creative. Shove me down the stairs with a sack over my head? Sorry, that's been tried too—State Custody is a real amusement park. You might as well save your energy—"

"Your Honor, I *demand* that all this hogwash be stricken from the record," Meadows bellowed.

"Sorry, Mr. Meadows. Seems to me like *you asked for it*," The Judge replied. "Any further questions for this witness?"

Meadows whispered to Handler, who shook his head. "No, your Honor."

"Call your next witness, Mr. Barnacle."

When Barnacle said they'd been denied any other records or witness identification, the Judge told Meadows he couldn't call any witnesses not identified to Crump's counsel, effectively ending the hearing.

"Ten minute recess," Judge Salazar announced, as everybody stood and he left the bench.

When the Judge returned, he asked everybody to remain seated.

"While the Court has considered the documentary evidence regarding expenses incurred by the Defendant in this matter, it seems like a wholly inadequate remedy to simply order that these medical and related expenses be reimbursed. I consider the Government's behavior here to be so outrageous, the damages awarded must be both a punishment and a deterrent to this sort of misconduct. The contrived nature of the alleged criminal offenses, coupled with the remarkable conduct of government actors once Mr. Crump was in custody, convinces me that this sordid tale is all State-sponsored, or, at least, State supervised. Under the circumstances, I am awarding the Defendant two million dollars, assessed personally, one million each against Attorney General Handler and Solicitor General Meadows. So ordered, judgment to enter—"

"Your Honor," Meadows jumped up. "May we have a stay of enforcement of this judgment, pending appeal?"

"You may *not*—stay of enforcement is denied. Mr. Barnacle, schedule a citation hearing next week so that your client can begin collecting this judgment from Mr. Meadows and Mr. Handler. Gentlemen," he said, as he turned to face the Government lawyers, "be sure to bring all your bank and other account records with you, as well as real property-title records. I'll also want to see your pay stubs—this will be a full-blown Rule 69 enforcement proceeding. Time to pay up," he commented, as he left the bench.

* *

Maureen travelled to Salt Lake City, armed with a fist-full of subpoenas granted to her and Wade Solley by Judge Culpepper, who, in his role overseeing the class action on Family Separations, was as interested as she was in finding out just how and why Elení Montes ended up back in Mexico. Salt Lake City and the entire State of Utah, for that matter, being not exactly contiguous with Mexico, it was obvious to Maureen that somebody went to a great deal of trouble to accomplish this relocation. She was betting there was something more than bumbling involved.

The H.H.S. facility was up on a mountainside near the State University, so she cabbed up to the main gates. On her way up the mountain, she thought about growing up in the flattened Midwest. She was surprised and a little alarmed to see the roadside truck-barrier sidings, festooned with sandbags, designed to corral runaway trucks with failed brakes careening down the mountainside. Equally disturbing were the weather reports on the cabbie's radio, yammering on about "The Runoff": How the water running down the mountainside from snowmelt moved at sixty miles an hour, was sub-freezing, and would paralyze and carry away small dogs and children who wandered into its path. The ride up the mountain left her with a growing appreciation for the boring flatness of the City by the Lake. It may have had its crime and corruption problems, but it didn't shake, rattle, burn or slide, and truck drivers there didn't need Kamikaze road sidings to stop them from crashing, out of control, into restaurants and grade schools.

The guard station at the perimeter of the Health and Human Services Facility looked more like something remote and antique you'd find at an outpost in the Swiss Alps than a secured facility, holding dangerous, law-breaking border crashers. A tiny guard house that resembled a freshly painted, white outhouse, was equipped with just a single pole, candy-cane swirled red and white gate. The guard inside checked her court papers and pass, then let the driver take her to the Administration Building. She took the driver's number, there being no cab stand up on the mountainside.

Maureen hustled into the office of Jack Sandford, the facility head, who, she was surprised to learn, actually worked for I.C.E., Immigration and Customs Enforcement.

"I'm interested in seeing who gave the order to deport this woman, and on what grounds," Maureen asked, more than a little miffed at the endless runaround. "H.H.S. was ordered, weeks ago, to re-unite this woman with her daughter, who's in a hospital in the City by the Lake."

Sandford was paging though a heavy-backed book that looked like the record of deeds in the recorder's office, with pages spindled into a metal-tubed binder.

"This woman, Miss Montes, no longer has any family—"

"What are you talking about? I've *seen* her daughter."

"Says here, 'Family member accompanied crossing April 2022. Minor daughter number 355782, deceased on or about June 2023.'"

Maureen was shaking her head. "Let me see that," she asked, and Sandford turned the book around so she could read the entry. "Where does this information come from?"

"H.H.S. provides I.C.E. status on family members in custody," he answered, looking at the date of the notation. "We would have received this status report on July 12th, the date it was recorded."

Of course, Maureen thought—*after* we got the court order to re-unite these two. "So, where is the record of how she got back to Mexico? I'm primarily interested in where she was taken to cross back over—"

"Mexico?" Sandford asked, puzzled, as he glanced over a computer screen.

"Yes, we were told by I.C.E. in California that she was back in Mexico."

"Says here," he paused, scrolling down the screen, "says here she assaulted an I.C.E. agent upon learning that her family member, number 355782, was deceased. She was charged and is now in I.C.E. custody at Otero Prison in *New* Mexico. Looks like somebody fudged the reporting," he added, turning the monitor around to face Maureen.

Fudged, my ass, she thought. "Can you get me the contact information I need to find her at Otero?"

"Sure, but she's going to need a lawyer—says here she's charged with Battery on a Federal Official."

"Lawyers, we got," Maureen said, as she took the information from Sandford, packed up and called her cab driver.

"I *hate* these people," she said out loud, waiting for her cab.

* *

"Miss Connover," Derek Markle, Lakeside County Assistant States Attorney began, "you understand I cannot make an offer of immunity until I know what information you have to share, and get your assurance that you will cooperate fully in any investigations this office may pursue."

"Can I just ask a question," Crump injected, before Connover could respond.

Markle eyed Crump, his expression a little hard to read, through his self-darkening lenses. "Sure—we're all friends here," Markle noted, the irony not lost on Crump or Connover, who, although a grade-school music teacher, seemed to be tuned in to the world of cops and robbers.

Crump continued. "While I'm fairly certain there were violations of the Prevention of School Violence Act, I'm not yet sure how many of them were by mandatory reporters, so this all may be premature."

"I can tell you that," Connover announced. She shifted in her seat, an uncomfortable, straight- backed number, standard outfitting in Markle's government-issue office.

Crump, who had done his best to caution and prepare Connover, wasn't actually representing her, so he felt a little guilty about not better warning her against completely trusting the Prosecutor. While, in Crump's experience, the Government types tried their best to protect people who ratted out criminal behavior, he knew that if it came down to prosecuting or protecting, informants sometimes got sacrificed.

"We all knew," she began, when Markle interrupted.

"Who's 'we', and what is it 'we' knew?"

"Way back when all this started—"

Crump interrupted. "Let me give you the background, otherwise none of this will make any sense." Crump then filled Markle in on the details he knew—how the bullying of the Lockwood kid had gone on for almost four years, how it began with a few faculty waiver kids and then the baton got handed off to a couple of stooges, when the faculty kids started feeling the heat. The severity of the assaults and the condition of the Lockwood kid, together with the failure of the school to stop it and the alleged cover-up, made the entire mess potentially more serious than just civil penalties.

"So, back in late 2017, when it all ramped up for real, Connie Pennebacker, the middle school science teacher, button-holed a bunch of us. She was pissed off that Bill Lockwood and Tom Lodge were working on a report that would shake up the place—"

'Slow down," Markle cautioned. Who's this 'Bill' and 'Tom'?"

"Sorry—they were parents—"

"Bill Lockwood is the bullying victim's father," Crump offered.

"Yeah, anyway, these parents were hired......no, I guess they volunteered, really, they were asked by the Carrington Higher-Up's to do a study and make suggestions on how to stop the enrollment slide. The place was losing a lot of paying customers, and the old-guard faculty were freaked out," Connover explained.

"Afraid the place was going to close?" Markle asked, taking notes.

Connover smirked. "No—the old guard doesn't think like that. The deal they had was paradise—they get to send their kids to a private school for free, and to boot, they essentially got to run the place, and believe me, *nobody* was putting in a full day's work. The entire set up required a free flow of tuition-paying customers who believed the place was top notch and prestigious. A report that said the model had to change or enrollment would continue to drop would dynamite their sweet deal. *That's* what the old guard faculty was worried about."

"What about everybody else?" Markle asked. "Not everybody's an 'Old Guard', right?"

"The Old Guard bullies the Hell out of the newer faculty—they're afraid to say 'boo', or they get harassed out of the place," she offered.

"OK, so this teacher, Pennebacker, she does exactly what?" Markle asked.

"So, she gets a bunch of us in the Science lab—I still remember the meeting—she's all worked up, and she locks the door, which requires all these special precautions, on account of the Halon release—"

"The *what*?" Crump asked.

"Halon. It's an inert gas they flood the room with in case of fire—this is the science lab. So, you gotta enter security codes to lock the room, and she's taking all these precautions, then, once the place is locked up, she says, 'We gotta do something—they're gonna turn this place into *an Academy*,' she says, like it's a dirty word."

"You'll need to spell it out for me," Markle pleaded. "I haven't been *near* a school building since I almost flunked out of law school, fifty years ago. Why's 'Academy' a bad thing?"

"Academies are all about numbers, testing, ranking and accountability. The whole progressive thing, the educational philosophy that is the Bible at Carrington, is the opposite—no testing, no homework, experiential learning. A crucial part of all that is to have no real structure, where the faculty is self-governed, they're their own bosses. Nobody gets evaluated, there are no work rules, it's essentially a commune masquerading as a school."

"I take it the faculty liked it that way?" Crump asked.

"You don't know the half of it. So, Connie Pennebacker, she gets us in the room and she says, 'We gotta stop this', and we're all, like, 'How we gonna do that?' and, she says, 'Well, one way is to get their kids outta the place,' and the gym teacher, Mike Norwood, he says, 'How we gonna do that—we can't flunk 'em out, I mean, we don't even *give* grades,' and Pennebacker says, 'Well, Lockwood's got a kid comin' down the pike. I can't *wait* to get my hands on *him*.'"

Markle looked up and stopped writing. Crump's mouth hung open.

"Say that again?" Crump asked.

"Right—she says, 'The Lockwoods' got a kid about to enter fifth grade, I mean, if their experience is *real bad*, they'll have to move on elsewhere.'"

"Do you remember the identity of the other people in the room?" Markle asked.

"Sure, but, the thing is, it's not like this was a big secret. Part of the reason I left the place was it made me *sick*, I mean, here are all these educators, supposed to be in it for the love of the job, the feeling for the kids, and they're like, *plotting* to work over this kid, let the other kids bully him *out the door*, just so they don't have to show up for work every day and put in their nine hours. This went on for years, and we all knew it—knew the Lockwood kid was getting picked on, then harassed, then, even, knocked around a little. A couple of us went to Mike Norwood when it was getting out of hand, and we said, 'Mike, this has gone too far,' and he says, 'You want to start punching a time clock every day, lose your associate teachers and start giving standardized tests?'"

Crump was rubbing the palm of his hand on his forehead. Markle looked up from his pad.

"Look, Miss….."

"Connover—"

"Miss Connover, these are pretty serious allegations—"

"It's all true. I can't say that *everybody* in the place knew everything, but mostly everybody knew something was going on, and those people in that room knew *everything*."

"Derek, obviously this testimony would be critical to moving this case along," Crump offered. "If you're willing to take it on, I'd draft a cooperation agreement between your office and Miss Connover here. I seriously doubt you're going to get this information anywhere else, at least, not until you start charging people."

Markle nodded. "Go ahead, draft it up. Include something about surveillance—I may want this lady to wear a wire for us. Can you do that?"

"Remember, I don't work there anymore."

"I know, but you may want to have coffee with a few of 'em. You ever openly complain, other than the approach to the gym teacher?"

"No, not to any of them. I did say something to the Dubows, parents who sniffed it out and started asking questions, but that was it."

"Go ahead, Crump, draft it up," Markle agreed. "Every time I think I've seen it all in this job……"

* *

Outside, waiting for cabs in front of the criminal courthouse, Crump said, "Thanks. That took a lot of guts."

Connover put a hand salute over her forehead to shield her eyes from the sun, as she scanned the street for cabs. "You ask me, anybody who'd engineer something like this is the best excuse there is for bringing back the death penalty……."

20.
NEW MEXICO IS NOT PART OF MEXICO.........

Mary Haffencamp had to make a run to The Cove, a local complex a mile and a half from her office. The place doubled as a private orphanage, something of an anachronism, and a battered women's shelter, run by a local charity. Her legal practice centered on domestic relations of all sorts: Divorce; child custody; adoptions; securing shelter for battered women and their kids, and juvenile court work for abused and neglected children. It didn't pay much, but she'd dropped her high-octane corporate practice when Ben, her first child, was born. Crump always made enough for them to get by, so she figured she might as well do something for somebody, as long as she was going to juggle kids and work.

The case that drew her to The Cove, this early evening, involved an inter-family adoption. Mal Hopkins, a bubbling, sizzling, twitching gob of testosterone and a sometime drug dealer, had allegedly done in his spouse, Melinda, who was found with a needle in her arm, slumped over in their apartment. Melinda was a nurse at the local hospital, and while she'd had a brief history as a user, she'd been clean for years. Her parents therefore insisted that Mal had injected her, as he'd often used her like the Royal Food Taster in the Middle Ages, trying out his stuff on her before using it himself. The cops had been unable to pin the death on Mal, but her death and his record were enough to convince the Juvenile Court Judge that it was time their eight-year-old daughter needed Mal's In-laws as new, permanent guardians.

Mal didn't give two toots about the Kid: He was fighting his In-Laws for custody because the Kid came with a social security monthly check attached, courtesy of his now-deceased spouse. The Juvenile Court Judge had appointed Mary as Guardian Ad Litem for the kid in the custody proceeding. Between Mary and the Judge, they'd been rope-a-doping Mal for two years, waiting for his meth-shortened attention span to give out, hoping he'd eventually walk away from the custody battle. This week, Mal had finally surrendered, and the Kid's Maternal Grandmother was awarded permanent custody.

Mary had arranged for Grandma Stewart to pick up the Kid at The Cove, where she'd been stashed for over a year, once the sun went down. While they weren't certain Mal would still be lurking around, they weren't taking any chances. Mary was to meet Grandma Stewart in the parking lot behind the main building, which looked indistinguishable from the many stone-block buildings of Northern Lakeside University that were spread indiscriminately around the area. Mary preferred using The Cove because it blended in with the Campus, which meant buzzing crackers like Mal knew the place was crawling with University Cops.

As she parked her car and made her way to the back entrance of The Cove, she could have sworn she saw somebody, out of the corner of her eye, scrambling around in the darkened trees off to the right of the lot. Lighting wasn't perfect, so once your eyes left the lights of the building, you were relying on luck, carrots and your optometrist. As she approached the lighted entryway, she again saw, then heard, somebody moving around in the trees off to the side of the lot, which ran up to dense brush and bushes, backstopped by a train embankment. She called the security guard responsible for the handoff, and they connected just as Grandma Stewart pulled into the lot and parked.

As Grandma Stewart exited her car and jogged up to greet Mary, something rolled out of the bushes and stopped underneath the Stewart-mobile. Whatever it was, it immediately began pouring out grey, dense smoke, so that in less than a minute, the entire lot was hazy and impenetrable.

"Mrs. Haffencamp?" the Stewart woman called out, stranded in the smoke and haze.

"I'm here, follow the light," Mary called back.

The Cove security guard, who wasn't taking any chances, retreated with the Hopkins Kid, calling for back up and summoning the local cops.

As Mary reached out to locate Grandma, the smoke began to clear and she could see that both her car and the Stewart-mobile were on fire. As she reached out to offer a hand to the Stewart woman, she was suddenly embraced by a tall man, reeking vaguely of Brylcreem, an outdated hair product that smelled like beef tallow and was used primarily by Greasers in the Sixties.

"Angelo?" Mary asked.

"Where's de udder broad?" Turulio asked, as he let go of Mary. He had a revolver in his left hand.

"I'm here," Grandma Stewart said, as Angelo grabbed her arm and pulled her from the smoke.

"Yuse two stay here. Duh s'curty guard will let you in. I wanna see if I can catch dis asshole," he said, as he disappeared.

As they approached the rear entrance of the Cove, the guard appeared and let them in, just as the fire department arrived and began foaming the burning vehicles.

"I'm keeping both of you for the night," the Guard announced. "You'll need to make a Police report, then it's too dangerous to leave with the child until they can apprehend the estranged Father."

Mary looked out into the chaos in the parking lot, fire trucks with revolving lights, half a dozen cops with cars flashing, and smoke from all directions.

"I would not assume this is the work of Mal Hopkins," Mary said, as they walked up the stairs into the building.

* *

Maureen flew into Alamogordo, New Mexico, County Seat of Otero County, the location of the prison where Elení Montes was being detained. As she took a cab out of the airport, she saw a sign on the edge of town that read,

>Welcome to Alamogordo
>
>Home of the Trinity Bomb Test
>
>Birthplace of the Nuclear Age

Swell, she thought—now we're stashing her in leftover nuclear fallout.

They passed the monument to the World's Largest Pistachio Nut, which she had to admit was larger than your standard-issue subcompact, and the memorial marking the grave of Ham the Chimp, the first space monkey. The driver took her to Chaparral, site of the Prison. The place looked to Maureen like World War II movies' depiction of concentration camps, all fences, razor wire topping, and depressing barracks inside the perimeter.

She was armed with a court order, obtained when she got appointed to represent Elení Montes and convinced a Federal Judge in Salt Lake City that the charge against Elení Montes was fabricated by an I.C.E. official, who, mysteriously, could no longer be identified by the Government. As she entered the Administration Building of the Prison, she got stuck in line behind a small cluster of bald guys in red robes, also seeking admission.

"What's with the College of Cardinals?" she asked the guard, posted at the entrance.

"Those are Buddhist monks, here for Enlightenment Visitation—"

"They fluent?" she asked the guard.

"They're not here for the Border Crashers, they're here for the RSO's."

"'RSO's'?" Maureen asked.

The guard looked down at his feet and stepped on an insect that crunched, loudly. "Registered Sex Offenders," he added, sweeping the mashed bug away with a swipe of his boot.

"You gotta be kidding me," Maureen groused, quietly. "I take it those guys are housed in a separate part of the prison, with the male border crossers—"

"—There aren't any male crashers here, Ma'am, just females," the guard offered.

As the Monks slowly passed through metal detectors and cleared security, Maureen offered the deputy operating the conveyor her bag, then flashed the court order, which stated she was allowed to remove Elení Montes from the facility for transport back to the City by the Lake and the temporary H.H.S. facility there.

"You gotta take this to the Warden, Miss," the guard said, as he read the order. "To the right, fifth door, past the guard's locker facility and rec rooms."

Maureen wandered down the cinderblock-walled hallway. Inside were all-white rooms with gatherings of women, all wearing orange jumpsuits with "NMCD State" printed on the back. Their hair was uniformly tied in buns. They were all watching television. The last room was the same, except the inmates were all men, with a surprising number of them sporting the exact same hair buns as the women.

She knocked on a door with a "Warden Newton" nameplate. A woman in uniform with a sidearm opened the door.

"Maureen McDougal. I'm counsel to inmate Elení Montes. I have an appointment with the Warden," she added, showing the guard the court order.

"Right. The Warden is waiting, he'll see you now," she said, as she walked Maureen into the inner office.

Warden Newton was tall, balding, heavy set and wearing a pale blue suit and yellow shirt that were both much too small. After he greeted her and showed her to a chair opposite his desk, he sat down.

"Hope you've had your chicken pox vaccination, Miss McDougal," the Warden began. "We're having something of an outbreak this week."

Maureen looked up, trying to remember when, and if, she'd been vaccinated, but it had to be decades ago, so instead she said, "This place, in many ways, is not what I expected, right down to the chicken pox. I hope not to be here long enough to catch anything other than my client, who should be leaving with me and an I.C.E. Official, to accompany us back to—"

"About that," the Warden interrupted. "Can I see your Court order?"

Maureen handed over a certified copy of the order.

"This was issued by a Judge in the Northern District of Utah. I'm afraid I've been instructed to only allow the Montes prisoner to be released on an order of the Southern District of New Mexico," he said, turning the copy over in his hands.

"Instructed by *who*?" Maureen asked, impatiently.

"The Regional Director of I.C.E.," the Warden added.

"I don't believe this," Maureen complained. "We went through an entire proceeding in Utah, in which I.C.E. officials appeared and participated. Immigration and Customs Enforcement was ordered to surrender her to me. This is just one more pointless hassle they're putting us through." She paused, thinking over her options. Almost a year of getting horsed around by the Feds finally boiled over, as she said, "Look, either follow this order, *to the letter*—that means she leaves *today*—otherwise, I'm going to ask the Judge to hold you and the local director of I.C.E. in contempt—"

"Not sure where you come off walking into a *New Mexico* facility and tossing threats around with *a Utah Court order*," the Warden asked, abruptly standing up.

"This order is entitled to the Full Faith and Credit of this State under the Constitution—"

"—As long as you get it confirmed by a New Mexico Judge—"

"So, you're telling me that I need to go through the meaningless task of walking into another courtroom, *here*, just to establish that Utah is, in fact, part of the same United States of America, as New Mexico?"

Newton handed her back the court order. "I don't make the rules, Miss McDougal, I just—"

"I know—just following orders. Look, what's it gonna take to get this woman released *today*?"

* *

When Maureen called Crump, she was in temporary custody at the Otero County Prison Facility.

"You did *what*?"

"Just listen, and don't give me any shit—I only get one phone call. You and Wade Solley need to hire a local guy down here in Otero County and spring me and the Montes woman—"

"I get the Full Faith business on your Utah Court order, but tell me again what they're holding *you* for?"

"When I demanded the Warden tell me just exactly *what* I had to do to release her immediately, he did this phony shock and surprise routine and accused me of trying to bribe him, and he had me taken into custody here and dumped me in a cell. I'm sandwiched between the Registered Sex Offenders and the *exclusively female*—of course—border crossers incarcerated here."

Crump cursed—none of this was coincidence, it had to be orchestrated by the folks upstairs in the Justice Department. "I think we'll need connected local counsel. Let me shake a few trees and see what kind of back-slapper falls out. In the meantime, try to stay in your cell as much as possible—"

"I get it—"

"Having just been in your situation, I wouldn't put it past these guys to—"

"—Crump, if you don't shut up, I'm going to *murder* you."

* *

Crump found a lawyer, a former State Rep in Otero County, who took Maureen's case. The process lasted a little over a week, ending in a court hearing at which the Judge finally sprung her from prison. The Judge seemed impressed by the far-fetched nature of the attempted bribery charge against Maureen. This was particularly true once she testified at the hearing that, like many members of her Generation X, she was travelling without any cash, bribery of a public official being extremely difficult to pull off using a credit card.

When Maureen, Crump and their local counsel returned to the prison, the Warden announced that Elení Montes was no longer an inmate.

"We have a court order, now blessed by your local judge, that she's to be surrendered to *us*," Maureen complained. "What happened?"

The Warden was obviously in on the game. "She was relocated this week, while you were incarcerated, I believe," he paused, looking at a computer printout in a gesture Crump was certain was faked. "She's now in I.C.E. custody at the El Paso Del Norte Processing Center."

Maureen was ready to spit. "On whose authority?"

"The C.B.P., Customs and Border Protection—"

"I *know* what it stands for," Maureen popped off, sending the Warden backing away.

"I'd like copies of the transfer orders," Crump asked.

"That would take a Court order—"

"I'll have it here tomorrow," Alan Maclamore, their local counsel, declared.

As they turned to leave, Warden Newton mumbled, under his breath, "We aim to please."

* *

I still believe in God.

I still believed, even after my brothers were taken from us, taken by the gangs. My Mother was still alive then. She lost her faith. I know God is good. God is just. She was one who could not understand such things in a World where God is everywhere. Our Sacredote reminded her that all men have free will, and God is not to blame for the choices men make.

She doubted, and never returned to the faith.

I still believed when they took my husband. He, too, was felled by the gangs, when he was refusing them their due, their nuevas. He was protecting us, protecting his daughter. He wanted more than the life of a simple *puta* for her. You are no longer human, no longer a person, when you become a gang puta. You can no longer take a respectable position, no longer marry, and, if you are lucky, you do not end up in a ditch.

I did not doubt. When I was taken to the Cárcel, and my daughter was taken from me, I still believed in God. My faith is tested by doubt when I do not hear from her. There is an abogado who is helping her, but I only know this because, at one prison camp, a guard who speaks Spanish said, "I don't care what your daughter's abogado does, you're still going back to Mexico." One day I hear she is muerta, next I hear she is alive but has been taken to Mexico, or I hear she is starving in some hospital. I want to believe she will return to me, but one day I am here, and then I awaken and I am moved, we are packed into buses, and then, only a week goes by and I am moved again.

Jesus said, "Blessed are you when men revile you and persecute you and utter all kinds of evil against you falsely." A guard said that this was the end for me, because I am a criminal. I am an infractor de la ley, he said, a breaker of the law.

I knew this would be an end, that night we left our home. I just never believed I would face the end without my daughter.

21.
NO SUCH THING AS BAD PUBLICITY.........

"I DON'T GET IT," A FRUSTRATED, puffy-faced Warren Handler complained. "We tell *everybody* to go after this guy, and all we get are a couple of misdemeanor raps he has no trouble clearing?"

"They weren't exactly Crimes of the Century," Assistant U.S. Attorney Byron Trout observed. "I mean, one involved some crusty statute about disrespecting horses, and the other was a twenty-five-year old immigration violation directed at *a citizen*—"

"That's my point," Handler added. "Dig through anybody's past with a microscope, and you're bound to find a D.U.I., or a domestic battery, or an income tax dodge, or *something*."

"I told you—the guy's kind of a hermit, living in plain sight—no social media, no judgments or liabilities, and, until *we* came along, no publicity," Trout explained.

Handler shook his head. "Tell me about it—he and his partner are portrayed as giant slayers, and we're getting *killed*—so much for 'No such thing as bad publicity'. They've convinced half the Country we're a bunch of thugs, and then Meadows and I get hit with these fucking million-dollar personal judgments."

Byron Trout walked over and closed Handler's office door. "Those'll never withstand appeal—Stuggs has stacked the federal appeals courts with so many right-wingers in the last five years, we're hoping those panels will be like his personal law firm," he said, sitting back down.

"Maybe—Federal Judges are appointed for life—they can be pretty Goddamned independent. In the meantime, we can't get execution and collection of the judgments stayed—these assholes are picking our pockets. And that trial court judge, Salazar, he's a fuckin' sombrero hat rack—"

"I think he grew up in Cleveland—"

"You know what I mean—he should have recused himself, this case being all about fucking Mexicans—"

"He's only on the criminal charges against Crump—the judge in the Patriot Act case is a Methodist from West Branch, Iowa, Herbert Hoover's home town, and I think her somebodies came over on the Mayflower."

"The point is, nothing we do is working. It's like, every time we push back, fuck around with this guy Crump, or jack around his client's mommy, he just digs in a little deeper. Seems to me we need to ratchet up the pressure—"

"—You said, 'hands off' this Plaintiff, this Doctor Trimble, and lay off the partner, McDougal, a mother with young kids."

Warren Handler, Attorney General of the United States of America, stood up and paced to his office window. "This is getting *bad*. The publicity we're getting could force Stuggs out of office. It could kill any chance that kid of his has to be groomed to run at the end of Stuggs's term. The people who put Stuggs," he paused, "…and *us*, in office, expect an endless supply of tax cuts and right-wing judges, not to mention a hand in the face of the Commies and weirdos, trying to muscle into power. This is becoming a big enough shit storm we may need to ramp things up."

"I take it you're worried Stuggs may not be able to win reelection, fair and square?" Trout asked.

"The publicity alone is killing us—those Commies over at MSPBJ are showing round the clock video of the little, shit-faced Hispanic kids crying in their chicken-wire cages, along with weeping teenagers in wheelchairs, whining about their I.V. tubes getting yanked. Stuggs and that weirdo Ernstmeyer—"

"—I recommend keeping *him* off the witness stand as long as possible," Trout injected.

"I know. Stuggs and Ernstmeyer won't back away from the medical deportations—they *want* those Mestizos down in Central America shitting in their pants when they think about asylum. And, winning the Patriot Act case, I don't know—we're not likely to get an amendment to the Statute, expressly exonerating the President and his Administration—"

"—I can just hear the Congressional floor debates: "We need to insulate the President and his advisors from liability when they plot to kidnap innocent children—"

"Right. So, you hear me?"

Trout got up, fidgeted with Handler's phone, pressing and then disconnecting all the lines, so that he heard a dial tone for each line, then he killed the line. He walked over to the door, opened it a crack, looked down the empty hallway, then closed it again. "You want to go down the line?" he asked.

"What about the wife and the kids?" Handler inquired.

"Careful—one of the kids is a local cop."

"Fuck him, then. I thought you said the wife was some kind of Commie?"

"Lawyer, too. Does a bunch of family law and court appointments, foreign adoptions. We've had some observation there already, but that's by splinters—"

"Why don't we have reliable information?" Handler asked.

"Look—these guys, the membership requirements are a little fuzzy. It's hard to know who's in and who's out—it's not like the Council On Foreign Relations—these are Right-to-Lifers, fringe Alt-Right outfits. I mean, some of these outfits are even under investigation by *our* guys."

Handler sat, cocked his head like he'd heard Trout wrong. "I thought we had a protocol in place?"

"You mean, lay off and go easy on the Alt-Right, and the Anti-Abortion types?"

"Yeah, the intelligence agencies have strict instructions not to hassle those guys," Handler opined.

"I'm just saying," Trout added, "it's difficult to get reliable information from those outfits, and nobody effectively controls them—"

"Good. That's exactly what we need here. I assume you can let it be known that turning up the pressure on this guy's family would not necessarily be met with any oversight or interference by the Feds?"

Trout bit his upper lip. "You suggesting, or *telling* me?" he inquired.

"Depends on who's asking," Warren Handler replied.

* *

New Crump & McDougal hire Howie Schmeltz was given the job of responding to the literally hundreds of claims they were getting about violations by the Government of the Temporary Restraining Order, halting the medical deportations. As the drip, drip, drip of these cases wore on, Crump gave up the piecemeal approach and formally filed a petition to make the injunction against medical deportations permanent. Peter Meadows sent over an

Assistant U.S. Attorney, who would meekly argue that U.S.C.I.S. was reconsidering the policy, and Judge Haverhorn postponed the hearing, in the hopes of avoiding a separate trial over a permanent injunction.

"I think Judge Haverhorn is praying the case will go away on its own," Crump observed. "The political heat is getting to her. Some yahoo congressman introduced an impeachment resolution against her last week. It'll never pass, but I think it's gonna take a shove to get her off the dime. She's getting some of the same hate mail we are."

Schmeltz slowly slid a pile of files he was carrying onto his desk. "Where'd you hear that?"

"Her clerk mentioned it, last time we were over there. She was a little rattled, because it's essentially the same folks we're suing that are supposed to look into it and protect her," Crump offered.

"Nothing we can do to move it along?" Schmeltz asked. "I'm worried that one of these patients is going to slip through the cracks, and somebody's going to die in some I.C.E. van while we're fooling around, dealing with the way the Government is nibbling around the T.R.O."

Crump nodded. "That's possible. We just need a couple more things to break for us. The biggest problem now is that the U.S. Attorney's Office won't give us Handler's deposition until we let them take mine—"

"*Yours*?" Schmeltz asked. "Since when do they get to do that? Sounds like harassment."

"My dual arrests, coupled with the million-dollar money judgments we just got against Meadows and Handler, has them arguing it makes me a witness, because this is somehow now *my* vendetta."

"They should be experts," Schmeltz offered.

"Yep. We can continue to fight it, or I can just squirm through my dep and take their last excuse away."

"What do Maureen and Barnacle think?"

"They both had exactly the same reaction. When I asked them if I should sit for my own deposition, they said, in unison, 'I'll sell tickets to that.'"

* *

The first of half a dozen black SUVs entered the visitor's parking lot at St. Vincent's Hospital at about eight o'clock in the evening. Rather than hunt for parking spaces, each drove up to the main entrance and stopped, engines idling. When the last of the six vehicles had lined up single file, blocking any other vehicle access to the entrance, a group of men in suits began exiting the vehicles. When all six men were assembled, they placed orange traffic cones around the main entrance to the hospital, then three went in and three stayed behind.

The lead suit approached Mabel Collier, a volunteer working the information desk in the center lobby.

"We are here to see about a patient," the leader said. He handed a document to Mabel, who didn't know an arrest warrant from a Certificate of Completion from a Canine Disciplinary School.

"Hold on," Mabel said, as she scrolled through a list of patients, and saw that E.M. was in the juvenile psych ward. "I'm sorry, sir, but under H.I.P.A.A. rules, I can neither confirm or deny that this person is even a patient in this institution—"

"We *know* she's a patient. We just need to know which ward, and how we get access to her," he interrupted, annoyance rising in his voice.

Mabel was not yet used to rudeness in this volunteer job. Most visitors were either happy to see a cheerful face or grief stricken. Pissed off and impatient were new. "You don't need to take that tone with *me,* I'm just following the rules—"

The man reached over the booth, grabbed and swiveled the monitor on Mabel's computer, then moved close enough to see that "E.M., a minor," was in the Juvenile Psychiatric Ward, building six, entrance WSW.

"What building is this we're in, and where is Building Six?" the man asked, his chunky jaw and slicked-back hair practically in Mabel's face.

Mabel did not answer—she was busy locating the emergency security alert under her desk. When she finally activated it, the man was already heading out the way he came. She pointed at him and nodded, as two uniformed guards came racing down the hallway toward her. They pivoted and followed the three men out the sliding doors.

"Hold up," one of the guards shouted.

The man in the lead turned to face the guards. "Yes?"

"Whaddya think you're doing? This is a private hospital—you can't just barge in here and start threatening people—"

The suit, a Federal Marshal, slapped the warrant in the guard's face. "We're looking for this person," he said, as the warrant rattled in his hand.

"Look, buddy, I don't care *who* you're looking for, you can't just barge in here without a police escort or sheriff's deputies, trying to arrest a patient. Why weren't we given any advance notice—the authorities always arrange ahead of—"

"Listen, Mister, I know you're just doing your job, but if you don't direct us to Building Six, I'm gonna have to bring you in too, for interfering with an officer of the Federal courts while executing a warrant."

The guard shined a flashlight on the warrant. "This patient is a minor, in a juvenile ward. I can't give you access to a sealed ward. That facility is secured for the safety of the minors residing there."

"Where is Building Six?"

The flustered guard handed the warrant back to the Marshal. "It's over....now, wait just a minute. We get advance notice from the Sheriff and the State's Attorney when they need to see a patient in the psych ward. What's this all about?"

The Marshal was already entering his vehicle, the entourage headed across the lot to Building Six, which, one of them pointed out, was plainly marked. As they slowly crawled through the lot, the hospital guard was on the phone to both the Lakeside County Sheriff's Office and the Mental Health Division of the State's Attorney's Office. By the time the Federal Marshals' armada was at Building Six, a group of guards had assembled at the entry doors.

Again, three of the Marshals approached the main entry. The hospital guards met them, just as a series of squads, sirens going and lights flashing, approached the Marshals' SUVs from behind.

Inside the building, one of the front desk attendants had run up to the Adolescent Psych Ward and alerted Doctor Trimble and Giampetro, who were both still on duty.

"The guards say the guys have some kind of papers, say they can take E.M.," the flustered attendant said.

Doctor Trimble told Giampetro to follow her. When she got to E.M.'s room, she told Giampetro to get somebody to lock it from the outside, once she was with E.M., and not to open it for anybody until she called for him.

"Tenemos que hablar," "We need to talk," Doctor Trimble announced to E.M., who was sitting at a desk reading a Spanish-language comic and listening to music. She closed the door, then waited until she heard the lock fall into place before she sat on the edge of Estrellita's bed.

Outside, the local sheriff's deputies were inspecting the warrant, when Giampetro appeared.

"This's a sealed ward," he announced, seemingly without lifting his chin out of his chest. "You need a court order to enter. Warrant's no good," he added.

He stood blocking the entry, his arms crossed.

"Look, Frankenstein," the lead Marshal began. "I don't know who or *what* you are, but if you don't get out of our way, we're gonna take you with—"

Giampetro, in a sudden move nobody, including Giampetro, anticipated, was on the Marshal, sinking his teeth into the man's outstretched arm. A second Marshal pounced on Giampetro.

"Disengage!" the second Marshal shouted, as he began pounding on Giampetro's immense and somewhat slippery head.

The Marshal suffering Giampetro's bite also swung his fist at the bald giant, then pulled a gun from inside his suit jacket. As he did, two sheriff's deputies simultaneously planted revolvers so squarely on each Marshal's temples, they could almost feel their pulses.

One of the sheriff's deputies shouted, "One more swing, and you're both dead men."

* *

Crump and Maureen were just about to leave the office, when the call came in.

"That was Doctor Trimble," Maureen announced. "We gotta get out to the Hospital. It's chaos. Federal Marshals tried to take Estrellita Montes into custody, and it erupted into an armed confrontation between Lakeside County Sheriffs and the Marshals."

"Now what?" Crump asked. "Where's the kid?"

"Still locked in the ward with the doc. She says there's, like, *dozens* of cops and sheriffs and who knows what out there, sorting it out. I guess they never got very far—apparently Giampetro took a *bite* out of one of 'em," she added, as they ran down to get in her car.

"What are you *smiling* about?" she asked Crump, who had this weird grin on his face.

Crump replied, "I'm just betting Giampetro *swallowed*......."

"Your Honor," Crump began. "Given the events of last Tuesday evening, it is now painfully apparent that the temporary restraining order, blocking any of these so-called 'medical deportations,' needs to be converted to a permanent injunction. On that date, a squad of Federal Marshals, acting on the directions of the U.S. Attorney's Office, descended on St. Vincent's Hospital, and attempted to serve an arrest warrant on my client—my *fourteen-year-old client*, who's been in a hospital ward continuously for almost a year. It was yet another fit of government persecution, one that erupted into violence that threatened the well-being of virtually everybody in that hospital. It was obviously another escapade by the Government in their non-stop effort to circumvent your T.R.O., and *again*, try to deport my client, before we can stabilize her condition and re-unite her with her Mother. It's sick, it's perverse—there's no other explanation—they're *torturing her*. You have the means to stop it. A permanent injunction is the only way to end this."

Crump sat.

Judge Haverhorn was reading Crump's motion for permanent injunction. He'd festooned it with media coverage of the assault on the Hospital, adorned with color news photos and witness descriptions. He'd finished with an affidavit from Dr. Trimble, describing the experience of being locked in with Estrellita as they awaited the federal marshals trying to gain forced entry into a sealed, juvenile hospital ward. It was Dr. Trimble's sworn belief, based on her years of experience as a psychiatrist, that as many as half the residents of the ward suffered general anxiety attacks, and one attempted suicide. Crump could see the Judge was obviously losing it. Her hands were visibly trembling as she flipped the pages in his pleading. When she finished, she looked up. She slowly removed her reading glasses.

"Mr. Meadows, *kindly s*tand and address the court."

Meadows rose.

"Too bad we've abolished the death penalty," Crump whispered to Maureen.

"The Feds still have it," Maureen whispered back.

"Mr. Meadows, what *crime* could this child have possibly committed, *sitting in a hospital ward for the last year*? I thought I ordered your office to stand down on these deportations, pending further ruling?"

Meadows cleared his throat. "This was not about the illegal border crossing this Defendant is party to—"

"By 'Defendant,' you are referring to the minor, here identified as 'E.M.'?"

"Yes, your honor. Our Marshals were attempting to serve an arrest warrant for an entirely separate series of crimes—"

"Which *were*?" the Judge injected, obviously losing her patience. "She's a minor—what would possibly rise above the level of juvenile delinquency, anyway?"

"Perjury, Mail Fraud, Deceptive Practices, Theft of Honest Government Services—"

"Perjury?" the Judge interrupted. "How can a *Minor*, sitting in a hospital, be guilty of perjury?"

Meadows held a document up in his hand. "Your Honor, I hold before you a sworn statement, signed under oath by one 'Estrellita Montes,' the minor we refer to in this proceeding as 'E.M.'"

"Can I see that?" Crump said, standing.

"Me first," the Judge ordered.

After she reviewed it, she offered it to Crump. He reviewed it and returned it to Meadows. It was a copy of the petition he'd had the kid sign that first day they'd met in her hospital room, the petition to appoint Doctor Trimble as the kid's guardian.

"If I may," Peter Meadows continued. "This contains a sworn statement, signed under oath by E.M., although, in this case she 'signed'—well, *printed*—her full name. The attestation reads, and I quote, 'I, the undersigned, being of sound mind and having attained at least the age of fourteen years, do hereby designate the petitioner aforesaid, whose name appears below mine, as a parent or guardian, as my preferred guardian of the estate and person of the undersigned.' Below that, there appears the signature of 'Estrellita Montes.'"

Crump stood. "Your Honor, if you're confused, you're to be forgiven—that document is a routine, form petition for minor guardianship, the one I used to have Doctor Trimble appointed E.M.'s guardian, so, among other things, she could file this lawsuit." Crump paused. He walked over and took the form from Meadows, whipping it out of his hand, just a little too forcefully.

"If he's trying to allege this is a forgery, first of all, I am an eyewitness to this execution—I *saw* this person sign this document—"

"I'm sorry, your Honor," Meadows interrupted. "We are not alleging that she did not actually sign—that would not be perjury by this Defendant. We maintain that the sworn statement was knowingly false—false in a way that de-legitimizes this entire proceeding, which we simultaneously move to dismiss—"

"Mr. Meadows, I'm *lost*," the Judge interrupted.

"It says, 'whose name appears below mine, as a *parent or guardian*.' We maintain that this Doctor Trimble was *neither* a 'parent' or a 'guardian' of this child when E.M. affixed her signature to the document, a fraud on both the state probate court and this Court, that Attorney Crump has now *admitted* he has sanctioned."

"I *don't believe it*," Crump said, as he rose. "That's not what the affirmation says, and not what it means. This is a petition *to appoint* a guardian of a minor. That reference means you're either appointing a parent—the typical case, usually arising during divorces—or *some other person who's asking to be a guardian*—who then, of course, *becomes* a guardian when this is filed and a court order entered."

"Even if that were the case," Meadows offered, "then the application to the medical deferral program U.S.C.I.S. has terminated was fraudulent, since Dr. Trimble was no *parent or guardian* when that application was first filed."

Crump shook his head in abject disagreement. "First of all, that wouldn't justify the paratrooper operation they pulled last Tuesday, which was supposed to be based on this silly argument about the guardianship application, and secondly, the application argument is false, too. Once this child was admitted to the hospital, she could not be discharged without Dr. Trimble's authority—the Doctor became her guardian, as soon as she was assigned as Ms. Montes's primary physician. All this guardianship petition did was allow the state court to recognize and oversee that authority. The S.W.A.T. team raid premised on this argument was still dangerous, authoritarian nonsense."

"Please have a seat, Mr. Crump," the Judge admonished.

Wow, Crump thought, are *we* really in trouble over *their* stunt?

"Mr. Meadows," Judge Haverhorn began, when, unexpectedly, she rose to her feet. "It is my understanding that this…this….*event* you and your Marshals orchestrated over this alleged exercise in disputed *grammar*, resulted in…." she paused, picking up Crump's pleading…."the virtual shut down of a community hospital *for hours*, dozens of anxiety attacks, the calling out of over two dozen local police officers and sheriff's deputies, six damaged vehicles, the resignation of one hospital volunteer, and, for good measure, one patient suffered an epileptic seizure."

She sat. "Mr. Crump, your motion for permanent injunction is granted. In your order, I want you to also enjoin Mr. Handler, Mr. Meadows, the Federal Marshals and any employees of the U.S. Attorney's Office, from coming within one thousand feet of St. Vincent's Hospital." She paused, looked down, then looked out over the courtroom, which was filled with reporters. "I also want your order to reflect that the hearing on Count Ten of your complaint, the so-called 'Patriot Act' Count, is to proceed within sixty days. And, I expect the Attorney General to be in attendance. Provide that if Mr. Handler does not appear, *personally*, we will adjourn the proceedings so that a Capias Attachment can issue against the Attorney General. So ordered."

She stood and began to walk away, when she paused. "Oh, yes—one more thing—I'm taking jurisdiction over this so-called 'Perjury Case', to avoid the appearance that the Government tried to forum shop it away from me. It's definitely a related case. In that regard, the perjury charge against Ms. Montes is quashed and dismissed, with prejudice—costs to the Government. File your fees and costs petition, Mr. Crump, *tomorrow*."

As they all rose, Crump whispered to Maureen, "Well, that couldn't have gone any better."

"What's a 'Capias Attachment'?" she asked.

"They haul him into court in handcuffs," Crump added.

"I'll pay hard cash for the courtroom sketch artists' rendering of that...."

22.
ADDRESSING SOCIALLY NON-CONSTRUCTIVE BEHAVIOR.......

ONCE IT WAS DETERMINED THAT Mal Hopkins, the disenfranchised parent in the custody dispute that ended with the bombing of Mary's car, was in another State the night of the attack, Crump put Angelo Turulio on round-the-clock surveillance of Mary.

"It's jus' me n' Charlie Corkscrews," Turulio complained. "We need a third guy for roun' da clock."

"What about those guys Corkscrews used to work with when he was gunning for sheriff up in Bumpersticker, North Dakota?"

Turulio shrugged. "Tings didn't go so well for Mr. Mahoney up in North Dakota. Remember, dey made da librarian da sheriff and fired Charlie—"

"Get one of the guys who used to work for him. I'm about to collect two million smackers from Handler and Meadows—we can afford it."

So, Charles Mahoney, a/k/a "Charlie Corkscrews," hired Michael Marbarger, a/k/a "Mickey Moneybags", to handle third shift of round the clock shadowing Mary.

"I hope I'm not required to keep all these silly nicknames straight," Mary squared off. "And, won't one of these guys just be sitting all night in a parked car in our driveway?"

"So what?" Crump pushed back. "We're about to get rich, and anyway, this is the way these guys operate. Handler is on leave from Stenson & Willis, but that place is still in his DNA. They never back down, and if they don't intimidate you the first time, they ratchet up the dirty tricks. If it wasn't for their public profiles, they'd be putting a hit out on one of us—"

"Perhaps it's time to reconsider your career choice."

"They say that's a good idea, *every forty years*—"

"I meant, start taking retirement seriously."

"In the middle of this thing?" Crump asked, not really wanting an answer.

"Yeah, if they're seriously considering putting a hit out on you—"

"Hey, they weren't rolling a bomb under *my* car—"

"You don't *own* a car," Mary said, pouncing.

"But, if I *did* own a car, they wouldn't be trying to fire bomb it—brings down too much heat."

"I know—they never hit the lawyers—you keep telling me that. I'll put up with Angelo, and Corkscrews, and Monkeybags and all these other Damon Runyon characters you keep digging up out of some fossil heap, so long as they're following you, too—"

"*Deal*," Crump said, as they turned off the light next to the bed.

Outside, Charlie Corkscrews rounded the house, noted the light was off, and climbed back in his car. He was enjoying a stale donut and some coffee. When he finished, he wiped away the crumbs, then he called police officer Ben Crump, just to remind him it was *his* car in the driveway, so the local cops wouldn't arrest *him*.

✳ ✳

Crump wasn't having much luck deposing the faculty and staff at Carrington Prep.

Most of them were playing scheduling games, guided ably by Greg Stenson, their manipulative lawyer. When Crump persisted and finally deposed the Science Teacher Connie Pennebacker, she took the Fifth Amendment on every question, including, "What is your name?" and "How old are you?".

Crump pulled Stenson aside, during a break in her deposition.

"Greg, have you explained to her that we, and the Court, get to take a negative inference for each question she answers by taking the Fifth? It's a civil case. I mean, if I ask her, 'Did you take out a professional hit against any of the students?', and she answers by taking the Fifth, the Court is entitled to assume her answer to that question is, '*Yes*'".

Stenson shrugged. He couldn't hide his contempt for Crump, who he viewed as the kind of sub-human that any civilized society would have sacrificed at birth, just to preserve natural resources. "Who cares? This entire case is bullshit. There's no way the Judge is going to shut the place down, however many of these little shits pissed on your client's homework—"

"O.K., she's your client's employee."

After cycling through some of the Carrington faculty and staff and getting very little testimony to substantiate the music teacher's conspiracy theory, Crump finally corralled the Head of School, Ralph Westheimer, for a deposition. After swearing in Westheimer, and asking the usual background questions, Crump focused on Westheimer's belief that Carrington was exempt from State law requiring school personnel to take all possible measures to eliminate and control bullying, and to report it to the State Board of Education when it occurred.

"Mr. Westheimer, I know you've mentioned that you believe Carrington is exempt from the Prevention of School Violence Act—and, let's just call it 'The Act', to save time—exempt under the so-called, 'Sectarian' religious school exception—"

"That's correct," Westheimer interrupted.

"I wasn't finished, but, fine, let's go with that," Crump conceded. "The Act says it applies….'to all school districts, and to all non-public, non-sectarian elementary and secondary schools…..' What exactly is your 'sect'?"

Westheimer shifted in his seat, long enough for Stenson to say, "Objection—vague."

"I'll say," Crump mumbled to himself.

"As I believe I first told you the day we met, we at Carrington maintain that our 'Progressive Philosophy and Idiom' are a form of Religion."

"So you did," Crump offered. "The thing is, when I heard that, I wrote a letter to the State Superintendent of Schools, inquiring about your assertion that Carrington, as a *Progressive School,* is exempt from the law as a religious institution." Crump pulled a document out of a jacket, handed a copy to the Court reporter, and a copy to Stenson. "I'm showing you what I've marked as Exhibit One. This is the letter I received from the State Superintendent in response to that inquiry." Crump paused. "Mr. Westheimer, can you read into the record the second paragraph of Exhibit One?"

Westheimer put on reading glasses, scanned the document, and began reading. "Regarding your inquiry, the notion that Carrington Prep falls under the so-called 'Religious Exception' to the Act, is preposterous….." Westheimer pulled back and paused.

"Please, read the entire paragraph," Crump asked.

"….and remarkably ill-informed. The reference in the Act to all 'public, non-sectarian' elementary and secondary schools now subject to the Act', was intended to extend comprehensive anti-bullying protection to all schools other than traditional, parochial schools. I can only assume any contrary opinion was expressed by an inexperienced, non-professional with no real grounding in the manner in which schools in this state are expected to operate." Westheimer stopped reading, and dropped the letter like it was something extracted from the dump.

"So, my question is, Mr. Westheimer, still think Carrington is exempt from the duties to monitor, prevent and report bullying under the Act?"

Westheimer silently glanced at Stenson, like Stenson was supposed to take this one.

"Objection to that question—that letter is just one man's opinion—" Stenson began.

"He's the State Superintendent of Schools—"

"Mr. Westheimer is not a lawyer—that question calls for a legal conclusion."

"Fair enough," Crump agreed. "Is there any question that the Superintendent of all the schools in this State doesn't think your school is exempt?"

"Same objection," Stenson offered.

"Let's move on. Does Carrington have a policy to address school bullying?"

"We don't," Westheimer replied. "We have a behavior modification policy."

"Can you describe it?"

"This is a complicated matter, Mr. Crump."

"That's O.K., go ahead and try—"

"He's telling you it's difficult to describe," Stenson offered.

"Is that an objection? 'This is *really hard*'?"

"Look, Crump, don't take that tone—"

"I got a better idea." Crump pulled another document out of his folder, and handed a copy to both Westheimer and the reporter, then Stenson. "I'm showing you a document I've marked as Exhibit Two—pages fifty-one and fifty-two from the 'Manual for Parents' Carrington passes out at orientation for new students. Let me read from the Exhibit. It's called, 'Addressing Socially Non-Constructive Behavior'. 'We at Carrington do not believe there is any such thing as a bully. We believe there are no bad kids, only confused children who, by virtue of traditional authoritarian and hierarchical conventional education programs, do not understand the adaptations expected of them. We do not believe in 'discipline', as that concept is usually deployed. Instead, we offer suggestions of more positive means of interaction when a student's behavior in some way may appear to be disruptive to members of our Progressive Community," Crump stopped. "For the record, the word 'Progressive' there is capitalized," he added. "Is this what amounts to Carrington's anti-bullying policy?"

Westheimer let the policy statement slip out of his hands. "As I believe I said, we do not *have* anything I would refer to as an 'Anti-Bullying Policy'—"

"That's because you don't believe in bullying?"

"That's because we believe all kids are inherently uncorrupted and positive thinking—"

"I used to believe in Santa Claus, then I grew up—"

"Knock it off, Crump, or I'm terminating this deposition," Stenson injected.

"When did you first learn that Brian Lockwood was subjected to threats by members of the Carrington student body?"

Westheimer again looked at Stenson. This time, Stenson silently lifted his head, nodding in Crump's direction.

"When *you*, Mr. Crump, first made that serious and unfounded allegation—"

"Let the record reflect that Mr. Stenson coached the witness to give that answer, with a gesture—"

"Let the record reflect that this deposition is a work of fiction," Stenson offered.

After a series of questions where Westheimer steadfastly denied any knowledge of the alleged bullying, Crump got around to the music teacher's story, after Westheimer acknowledged Connover's departure from Carrington.

"You're aware, are you not, that beginning in 2017, Bill Lockwood and Thomas Lodge were commissioned by the Board of Carrington Prep to prepare a study and report on the reasons for declining enrollment at Carrington?"

"Yes."

"And, is it also true that by the end of 2017, many members of Carrington's faculty and staff were unhappy with the rumored recommendations they feared were going to be released in that report?"

"With a large group of sophisticated educators, you are bound to get some well-considered disagreements—"

"I'll take that as a 'Yes'—"

"Let him finish," Stenson complained.

"I thought he was," Crump shot back. "And, isn't it also true that several members of the faculty were so distressed about the anticipated report, that they conspired together to encourage bullying of Brian Lockwood, in the hopes that his experience would be so excruciating that his parents would pull him out of Carrington and his Father would then abandon issuing that report?"

"That's preposterous," Stenson interjected, before Westheimer could answer.

Crump shook his head, looking from Stenson to Westheimer. "So, Mr. Westheimer, do you have an answer to that question, other than the one your counsel just coached you to give?"

"I agree, that's preposterous—"

"I was hoping to at least give you points for originality, but I guess not," Crump said.

Crump pulled two more documents out of his folder. "Miss reporter, while these documents look similar, I'd still like you to mark the first as Exhibit Three, and the second as Three-A." He handed the documents around.

"Mr. Westheimer, the document I'm showing you marked Exhibit Three—have you ever seen that before?"

"No," he said, pausing as he looked closely. "I'm sorry—I have—you showed it to me the first time we met."

"That's correct, it's a printout of a posting from a web page, from an outfit called 'Dark Night'. It contains a series of instructions on the best way, using a razor blade, to cut your wrists, to be certain the cutter will bleed to death. I did indeed show it to you. Do you see the hand writing scribbled on this copy?"

"Yes."

Can you read it into the record?"

"It says, 'Why don't you just kill yourself, faggot. Cut along the veins.'"

"Right. Now, look at what I've marked as Exhibit Three-A. Can you tell me what that is?"

Westheimer held it up to the light, turned it a bit, then glanced over at Stenson.

"Crump, is this some kind of—" Stenson started to complain.

"Greg, now, come on—your client has a PhD—all I'm asking him to do is tell me what this is."

"Well, it *appears* to be the exact same internet posting as Exhibit Three, without the handwriting."

"Very good. Do you have any idea where either of Exhibit Three or Three-A *came from*?"

"I know, when you showed me the one with the scribbling, you *claimed* it had been left in young Brian Lockwood's school locker—one of several, I believe you said—that was left there by alleged bullies, with one or more razor blades."

"Yes, again, that's exactly right—several witnesses have now authenticated it as one of many left in the victim's Carrington locker. And, do you have any idea the source of the second copy, the one without the handwriting?"

"Objection—you're asking him to speculate—"

"I am—"

"I assume you went on the internet and pulled up the website yourself," Westheimer concluded.

"That's actually kind of amusing—it suggests I know *how* to surf the internet—but, no. I hired somebody to do this for me. The person I hired is a *Forensic Computer Metadata Examiner*—I know, my partner even had to spell it for me. Anyway, he is issuing a report, one you'll definitely want to read. He traced this posting back to the web administrator for this 'Dark Night' site, and, the thing is, like a lot of web sites these days, they place 'cookies' on the computers of users who land on their sites. We had them check the users that landed on their pages during the date range when this thing showed up in the Lockwood kid's locker. Exhibit Three-A is a print-out taken from the search history of Mike Norwood, your gym teacher. He accessed the Dark Night site less than twenty-four hours before this appeared in the Lockwood kid's locker—"

"Crump, this is highly improper. We should have been given these documents before this deposition," Stenson bellowed.

"You never asked for them—you haven't asked me for *any* documents—but, don't worry, you'll get a complete set when I produce my expert's report. In the meantime, Mr. Westheimer, care to revise any of your answers?"

"Don't answer that," Stenson commanded.

"When we deposed Mr. Norwood, he denied knowing anything about all this—He was lying, committing perjury. You don't know what else I've got, but I'm offering you the chance to not make *his* mistake—"

Stenson bolted upright. "Deposition's over," he announced. "I'd like a transcript, with exhibits," he barked at the court reporter.

Westheimer stood. He looked ashen and a bit shaken.

"You know where to find me, if you change your mind," Crump offered, as the two of them left the room.

* *

Maureen was so jazzed by her experience in New Mexico, what with getting horsed around by Customs and Border Protection and the Warden at Otero County Prison, and then getting jailed, that she took the juiced-up transfer documents C.B.P. used to hustle Elení Montes out of Otero Prison straight to Judge Culpepper in California District Court.

"I want each and every *one* of these characters held in contempt, starting with Mr. Meadows here," she insisted, pointing to the Solicitor General, who'd been brought there by Court order for the hearing. Wade Solley, the Class Representative lawyer for the family separation cases, handed up a sheaf of papers to the Judge, while Maureen soldiered on.

"....and, if that wasn't bad enough, they tossed me *in jail*, just for insisting that your prior orders be followed—"

"Wait one moment, Ms. McDougal, while I review these pleadings. Please have a seat," Judge Culpeper asked.

They waited what seemed like an hour, when the Judge broke the silence with, "Counsel, please, all of you, approach the bench."

Once they were congregated before the Judge, Judge Culpepper began by addressing Meadows.

"Mr. Solicitor General, I should probably ask you for a statement in defense of these actions, but since I find them indefensible, I thought, instead, I'd let you get a good look at Ms. McDougal, because I'm ordering you to be her chaperone, on a journey you, she and Ms. Montes are about to take together. Starting today, you, a C.B.P. officer fluent in Spanish and Ms. McDougal, are to fly, at Justice's cost, to El Paso Texas. Once there, you are to locate and take into C.B.P. custody Ms. Elení Montes, removing her from the El Paso Del Norte Processing Center—to which she has been mysteriously and inexplicably moved—and escort them to the City by the Lake. Once there, Ms. Montes is to be placed by the Court in appropriate custody allowing for reunification with her daughter, one E.M., and together, they can have their applications for asylum adjudicated in Federal Court there in the Northern District—"

"Your Honor," Peter Meadows began—

"Wait—I'm not quite finished. Once in El Paso, the U.S. Attorney's Office is to rent a van, so Ms. Montes does not need to clear T.S.A. security at the airport. You and the Customs and Border Protection Agent will accompany Ms. McDougal and Ms. Montes on the trip from El Paso to City by the Lake. And, if for *any* reason, the two of them do not successfully complete this journey, I will personally hold you in contempt, *again*, only this time, the terms will be that you remain in custody until Ms. Montes has successfully completed her trip. Do I make myself clear?"

"Your Honor, this order is highly unusual—"

"So it is, Mr. Meadows, and I can't *make* you do it, given the limits on mandatory, conduct-inducing injunctions. The alternative is you go back to jail and get fined—I'll give you the choice. We both know why I am issuing this order—it is abundantly clear that, as we sort through the reunification cases the Government has heaped upon this Court, you are applying highly unusual resources to frustrating this particular person's effort to once again become part of a family. I can only conclude this must have something to do with the Government's displeasure with the case the Montes child is pursuing and the possibility it will brand some of your peers as Terrorists. A very human reaction, no doubt, but Government officials don't get to be ordinary people—you don't get to become vindictive or plot out revenge against those in your charge—so now, this Court is going to insure that this revenge saga is about *to end*. Mr. Solley, prepare the appropriate order, and, so we don't have a repeat of the events in Otero County, the Court will have a confirming order entered in the Southern District of Texas. It will be waiting for you when you arrive in El Paso."

Judge Culpepper stood. Meadows began to speak, but he waved a hand at him, silencing him as he left the bench.

23.
A THOUSAND'S A CROWD.......

WHEN MAUREEN AND HER GOVERNMENT Escorts landed in El Paso, a sheriff's van used to escort prisoners to detention met them at the airport. Maureen made it a habit to speak as little as possible to Peter Meadows and their C.B.P. agent, Delroy Tenato, but the prisoners' van made needling communication inescapable.

"This is all you had?" she asked, as the bus bounced along on its crumbling, creaking suspension. "I hope this is not your idea of the transport the Court ordered for our trip up north?"

"Times are hard," Meadows growled, under his breath.

"We use these all the time," Tenato added. Tenato was a balding, fortyish short man who looked like he had a perpetual hangover. Maureen was inclined to doubt his every word.

Maureen was about to say something nasty, when the van turned a corner and stopped.

"Why we stopping here?" she asked.

"This's it," Tenato added.

Maureen stared out the windshield of the van, convinced they were jacking her around again. She wasn't sure what she was expecting—maybe a jailhouse, or a work camp setting like Otero County, or maybe, just a depressing, institutional mega-building with barracks that looked like an Army base. Instead, she was staring at a highway overpass, cars zooming overhead, the wedge beneath the highway crammed with hundreds of people. It would have looked like a crowd leaving a major sporting event, getting caught in the rain and taking shelter under the eight-lane throughway, except for the fencing. The throng of lost-looking people was surrounded by temporary, sand-bag-anchored cyclone fencing, topped with razor wire. The razor wire was falling down, so in many places, it was actually *inside* the fencing, with prisoners, some holding small children in their arms, pressing uncontrollably against the fencing and razor wire. Everybody looked lost, hungry and strung-out, except for the toddlers, who were uniformly crying. Armed guards surrounded the fencing.

"Whooaa…..Where's the *building*?" Maureen asked, as she turned to face Meadows, who was seated behind the driver, filling out a form.

"Building?" Meadows asked, without looking up.

"There's no *building*, like, a major structure. This's a processing center," Tenato explained. "They cross, we bring them here as soon as the guards apprehend 'em, and they stay here until they can get processed."

Almost all the adults and all the kids were wrapped in reflective silver sheeting. Some had cut the stuff and made rain hats out of it. Most of the kids were pressed up against the cyclone fencing, their fingers intertwined in the wires like they'd blow away if they let go.

"What's with the aluminum-foil wardrobe?" Maureen asked Tenato, who, at least, wasn't ignoring her.

"It's the blankets we issue—it can get pretty cool out here at night, and the overpass doesn't completely shut out the rain," Tenato remarked.

"You gotta be kidding me," she said, as she exited the van.

She was staring through the fencing directly into the eyes of a chisel-faced man with achingly high cheekbones, who looked at Maureen, a relatively decked-out, red-headed woman, as though she were a well-dressed messiah.

"Señora Presidenta!" the man called out to her.

"He thinks you're, like, the Governor, or something," Tenato commented. "Let me take you around the overpass—there's a registration tent back there where they got some records…..I guess, if you could call 'em that."

Behind them, Peter Meadows ambled out of the van, carrying a roller-board and a briefcase. He purposefully followed at a distance, sort-of an, I'm not *really* with *them*, kind of pacing.

Everywhere they turned, hundreds of hungry, weather-weary and worn people were crammed up against the fencing.

"How many people are they 'processing' in there?" she asked.

"It varies, usually close to a thousand—"

"My God—"

"Yeah, it's only designed for about one-fifty," Tenato observed.

As they circled the fencing and walked underneath the edge of the underpass, a series of beige-colored, windowless tents came into view, scattered about like they'd been dropped from the sky. In the center was a large, military-green tent built on a half-moon frame, with a door in the middle. A bunch of uniformed guards in fatigues accompanied the snaking line of aluminum-foil, blanket-clad refugees, followed behind the tent. They were all waiting their turn to make their claims for asylum, or otherwise answer for the crime of illegal border crossing.

"How we going to find her in there?" Maureen asked, tilting her head back at the underpass.

"How do we even know if she's still here?" Meadows commented, from over his shoulder.

'She better be—"

"Look, *Counsel*," Meadows said, practically spitting the last word out. "As you can see, this is not exactly the registration line for second semester at some Ivy League College. We hope nobody slips through the fences, and when they do, we usually catch up to them, but on any given day, only about ten percent of those people back there are even officially accounted for."

She glanced back at Tenato, who quickly added, "That's right."

They cut in line and walked through the doorway. Inside, five uniformed officers were sitting at tables facing the entry, filling out forms as an interpreter worked the room. Meadows walked up and whispered something to a man at the end of a table and he rose, waved at them to step between the tables and led them to a second room behind a partition. It was crammed with shoulder-high, pea-green, metal file cabinets.

"You can't be serious," the officer said, as they explained they were there with a court order, authorizing them to take one particular refugee with them. "You saw that crowd—half the time, we just shout out a name for processing when we need somebody, and then three or four of 'em show up at once, all claiming to be Senorita so-and-so. *If*, she's still here, you'll never positively identify her."

Maureen was slowly burning up. The one rule in her job was to never lose it, but she just didn't care anymore. "This is why you guys did this—why you transferred her here. You knew if you deported her, you'd be fined and incarcerated, so you did the next best thing—you dumped her in a place where nobody'd be able to find her," she growled at Tenato.

She turned to face Peter Meadows. She was so close he pulled his head back, craning his neck to avoid touching noses. "This was *your idea*, you *sick fuck*. When this is all over, we are gonna *bury* you...." She paused, then swiped the court order from his hands. "Gimme that—*I'm* gonna find her *myself*," and she turned and marched out of the building, squirming past the snaking line of applicants and guards.

Maureen stomped over to the nearest sagging section of fencing, clutching the court order in her hand. As she dove at the fence, a crowd of detainees stood back, unsure what the crazed woman was doing. She grabbed the fencing where two sections met, yanked a fence post and in one agitated move, tore it clean of a sandbag and peeled away a four-foot opening. As she entered the crowd, they parted enough for her to move in the mass of shoulders and outstretched arms.

Holding the crumpled court order high above her head with one arm, she began shouting, "Elení Montes? Which one of you is Elení Montes, Mother of Estrellita Montes?"

She was making such a commotion, the crowd haphazardly parted for her, but still, she had to rub and bounce off bodies as she fought her way through the crowd, shouting and waving the court order in the air.

"Jesus Christ," Meadows swore. "Go in and get her out of there," he ordered Tenato, who slowly made his way through the fencing, scrunching his shoulders like physical contact would infect him.

As Maureen worked her way through the press of bodies, she bumped into a child, a boy not more than six or seven. He was wearing a stocking cap and a torn, black jacket. He looked up at her wordlessly and she froze. He held up an outstretched hand and she realized, regardless of who she was or what she must have looked like, the kid was offering himself up, willing to be taken away by anybody, taken away *anywhere*. Something hot was running up her spine. She was completely losing control.

"ELENI MONTES," she screamed, loudly enough that two women near her covered their ears.

"Sí," a voice called out, from somewhere in the crowd. As a path cleared away through sheer human resignation, a tall, dark-haired woman approached. She was wearing jeans and a red, bulky ski jacket. She looked like she might not yet be forty, for all the mileage apparent in her wind-burned face.

"Sí," she repeated, "Yo soy ella," she said, just loud enough to be heard.

Maureen took her by the hand and wound their way out of the crush of faces, back through the fencing, with Tenato close behind, moving to where Meadows was standing.

"Ask her if she's the Mother of a young girl named 'Estrellita Montes,'" Maureen commanded.

"¿Eres la madre de Estrellita Montes?" Tenato inquired.

The woman broke into a punctuation-free rattle of uninterrupted Spanish, which to Maureen's ears, sounded like there were a few other languages occasionally mixed in. She talked continuously for minutes, then abruptly stopped.

"Yes," Tenato translated.

"What about the rest of it?" Maureen demanded.

"It's not important," Tenato replied, shrugging it off.

Maureen was steaming. "Translate the rest of it—I want to hear it all."

"I told you, it's not important."

Maureen shook her head and growled mildly, like a dog ripping apart a rag. "Ask her how old her daughter is."

"¿Cuántos años tiene su hija?" Tenato inquired.

Again the woman, this time with increasing agitation, spoke continuously for almost five minutes, her hands gesticulating and offering emphasis at points along the way.

When she stopped speaking, Tenato announced, "Fourteen."

"*Stop...doing.....that*," Maureen insisted, snarling. "What else did she say?"

"It's just a lotta stuff—"

"I *know* that—I'm not gonna take this bullshit—I need to know if it's her."

While Maureen was berating Tenato, the woman reached into her coat pocket and pulled out a small, three-by-four, faded color photograph. She was holding it up for Maureen to see. As Maureen unfolded it and got a good look, even with the crease in the middle, the shot was unmistakably Estrellita.

"Let's get outta here," she said, taking Elení Montes by the hand.

* *

"Please swear the witness," Phil Plint asked the reporter.

Plint had been brought in by Peter Meadows to assist in the defense of the Patriot Act case when Regina Debevoise quit. Big-shot partner at a mega law firm, he'd started life as an Assistant U.S. Attorney, so he was called back into the office now that they needed extra help.

On this day, he was taking Crump's deposition, a concession Crump offered, just to move the case along. Crump had Steve Barnacle defend him, as Maureen was schlepping around the U.S., desperately trying to bring Elení Montes to the City by the Lake. Once Crump was sworn in, Barnacle objected to the entire proceeding.

"Let me just state, for the record, we are giving this deposition under protest: The deposition of counsel representing a party in the case is highly inappropriate, but in order to not have this sideshow delay the hearing on Count Ten of the Complaint, we are offering this witness subject to this standing objection."

"Duly noted," Plint responded.

After almost an hour of background and routine questions about how Crump came by one bit of evidence or another, when Plint figured everybody would be bored by the deposition, he started to dig for dirt.

"Ever been convicted or a crime?"

"No."

"Ever been charged with a crime?"

"Sure. Your client charged me with offending a horse and crossing the border into my own country—"

"Moving right along, in the last ten years, ever had sex with somebody other than your spouse?"

"Object—" Barnacle began, when Crump interrupted.

"What kind of question is *that*?"

"Are you refusing to answer?" Plint asked.

"Look, I'm sixty-seven—no, wait, now I'm sixty-eight years old. I don't know what your Grandpa thinks about when he gets up, first thing in the morning, but for me, it's not whether I get an interlude with some imaginary stranger. It's, 'I wonder if I can get both legs into my pants without falling over on my face.'" Crump paused. "Oh, and I've been married for almost forty years, and I like my spouse—"

"Move to strike that answer as non-responsive," Plint argued.

"Can't wait to see you take that to the Court for a compelled answer," Barnacle cut in. "If it upsets you, Mr. Plint, why don't we adjourn the dep right now and take that question to the Judge?'

Plint ignored him. "It's my understanding you were a ward of the State for most of your minority—"

"Ages seven to eighteen," Crump cut in.

"Were you charged with any crimes as a juvenile offender?"

"Objection—you know those files are sealed," Barnacle offered.

"It's O.K., Steve—not much chance I'll be unfairly treated by the State or by potential employers, at this late stage of the game. I was never in State Custody for anything *I* did."

"What possible relevance does this have to any issue before the Court in this case?" Barnacle asked.

"Is that an objection?"

"Yes, it is," Barnacle continued. "You know darn well these questions are just witness harassment—"

"Are you going to follow your counsel's direction and refuse to answer?"

"I already told you, I wasn't there due to *my* misconduct," Crump offered.

"I need to know *why* you were in State Custody. Your apparent hostility to authority in general and the regulatory power of the State shines a spotlight on your motivation for filing this outrageous claim, labelling the Attorney General, a dedicated government servant like Dennis Ernstmeyer, and several Government Employees, all as *Terrorists*—"

"Now the *Lawyer's* intent matters? This case was referred to my partner by Lakeside County Volunteer Legal Services. We took the case because it needed taking, and because guardianship is something we do. The only 'intent' that matters here is that of *your* clients', and I think we'll successfully show what *that* is."

Plint shuffled in his seat. "Certify that question," he said to the Court Reporter, threatening to take Crump to court to force an answer.

"OK, you want a more complete answer?" He paused, like he was baiting Plint and expected a response.

Plint looked at him in silence.

"My Father ran off when I was six and my Mother abandoned me in a crowded movie theater when I was seven, and then she ran off too. My only surviving grandparents were immigrants who didn't speak much English and didn't understand compulsory education laws. I spent time at a Catholic orphanage, then got tossed around a few foster arrangements and ended up back with my grandparents, but I never left State custody until I went off to college. Need more, or is that good enough for you?"

Plint glanced down, then didn't look up from his notes.

"I bet you're done with *that* question," Barnacle said, needling Plint.

"Came to all this with nothing but the shirt on your back, eh?" Plint asked, smirking.

"Actually, I had to borrow the shirt," Crump responded, dryly.

"Mr. Crump, you claim you were 'Roughed Up' when you were in custody for the immigration violation—"

"*Alleged*-violation. The charge has been quashed by the Court—" Barnacle corrected, when Crump cut in.

"And, the guy who choked me has *admitted* he did it, after your clients lied to him about me having Ebola—"

"I was getting to that—Have you ever had, or do you now have, Ebola?"

"You gotta be kidding me," Barnacle injected.

"There hasn't been a case here *in years*," Crump argued.

Plint moved on. "What is your 'Net Worth'?"

Crump smirked, shaking his head. "I own my bicycle, some furniture I got at a garage sale, my retirement account and a couple of million-dollar judgments against Meadows and Handler, which my lawyer here tells me look to be collectable—"

"We'll see what the Appellate Court has to say about *that*," Plint reflected.

"Sure, in *two or three years*, when they get around to ruling, in the ordinary course of business—"

"Guys," Barnacle interrupted. "This thing's no longer even a deposition—you two are just *talking* to each other. I suggest we terminate this pointless exercise in posturing."

"Just one more question," Plint said. "Mr. Crump, do you think you can ethically try this case, given that you are now a witness in the case?"

Crump smiled, loudly exhaled and shook his head. "So, that's what this is all about? I guess I should be flattered that you guys would go to this length to get me out of the courtroom. Nice try, but ethics questions fall back to State law, and the rules on that are I'm only disqualified from handling the trial if my alleged testimony is material to the case and not duplicated by any other witness. So, unless the Judge concludes the state of my old-guy sex life is indispensable to the case, I'm betting I'll still see you in court."

* *

Cornelius Boofus, unofficial head of the local chapter of "The Army of God," rolled down his driver's-side car window. The drizzle, mixed in with the darkness, made it impossible to see Mary Haffencamp clearly, and he wanted to be certain she was alone. As she walked away from the pizza joint directly below her office, she jaywalked across the street and headed to a parking lot that catered to local tenants, pizza patrons and Northern Lakeside University Staff.

Boofus looked like a skinny, bearded, drugged-out rock musician left over from the Sixties. As he squinted out the car window, he thought Mary's car might be a rental, a maroon sedan with a stick. He figured if any real car buyer would settle for maroon and a stick, it would be a Commie lawyer married to an asshole like this Crump guy they were watching. He'd wanted to do something nasty, annoying and a little dangerous, like pour something in the gas tank, but there was this guy hanging around, this short, punchy looking older guy with tightly wound, curly red hair. Cornelius assumed he was some kind of private security detail she'd hired, since they'd fucked up her last car at the orphanage. He'd seen him before, haphazardly guarding Crump's wife, who looked like she needed security. After all, the woman was a real Commie, a Pro-Choice, Immigrant's-Aid type, the kind that would hire some old chump P.I. for protection detail.

Boofus rolled up the car window, pulled out and drove after her as she sped away. She almost never went straight home, which was a complication. He wanted to ramp it up—word was out they could move on her without getting heat—and he figured her house was the best place to accomplish his mission. Her Commie husband, the pain in the ass attacking Real Patriots like the President and his Attorney General, was almost never home. He seemed to live at the office.

As Boofus followed, he observed that Mary, like a lot of Commies, shopped at one of those hippie co-op health food places, where she picked up a couple bags of groceries from some guy with an earring and no muscle tone. And, there was that redheaded private cop *again*, in the store and then following her out as soon as she left.

She drove a mile and then pulled into the driveway of her townhome. Almost as soon as she stopped the car, a cop pulled up and parked in the driveway behind her. A young guy in uniform got out, said something to her, then got back in the patrol car and drove away. Boofus was about to park and get out of his car, when the other shadow, the guy in the leather coat, quickly drove by, passing directly in front of the townhouse.

"Damn," Boofus muttered. "They said this would be a cinch." He paused. The street was now deserted. "God is on our side," he said to himself, as he got out of his car and walked around the corner, planning to enter her residence from the backyard. He tied a bandana around his head, covering the bottom half of his face, and circled behind the townhouse.

Angelo Turulio pulled up and stopped in front of Crump's place. The only car in sight was dark and empty. He parked and started to turn on his car radio, when the urge hit him. "Shit, gotta pee," he said, as he turned off the ignition and got out of the car. While he didn't want to bother Mary, he knew she'd never mind, and being more civilized than Crump, she would probably even offer him a cup of coffee.

"Sure is quiet around here," Angelo said, as he approached Mary's front door.

24.
GIVE THE MAN HIS EARLOBES..........

Angelo Turulio rang the doorbell. Mary answered the door.

"Angelo—long time no see," Mary commented.

Turulio, who had no real sense of irony, responded, "I'm like a member of da family."

Mary nodded. "C'mon in," she said, as she opened the glass outer door. "Can I get you anything?"

Turulio was at the twitching stage. "Sorry, Missus Mary, but I really gotta see a man about a dog."

Mary, who was used to Turulio's coded language patterns, showed him to the first-floor washroom, just off the main hallway to the kitchen. She went back to cutting up a squash, while Angelo did his business.

Angelo turned on the light in the washroom and closed the door. As he faced the wall and unzipped his pants, he noticed that the wallpaper had pale yellow backing, covered with antique, old-fashioned-guys-with-wigs handwriting. What he was seeing was a wall-to-wall version of the United States Constitution. Turulio sort-of knew there *was* a Constitution, but he'd never really *seen* the Constitution, and his eyes fixed on this clause: "A Person charged in any State with Treason, Felony, or other Crime, who shall flee from Justice, and be found in another State, shall on Demand of the Executive Authority of the State from which he fled, be delivered up, to be removed to the State having Jurisdiction of the Crime."

"Damn," he said, standing there over the Crump toilet. "All dem westerns, where duh bad guys ride dere horses to duh state line to escape da sheriff, musta been done by guys who never read da Cons'tution," he said. He zipped up and was washing, anticipating telling Mary about the valuable insights her wallpaper had given him about the mediocre, inauthentic nature of the American Motion Picture Industry, when he heard a loud crash, simultaneously accompanied by Mary shouting, "Get owwda here!"

"What da fuck?" Turulio shouted back, as he barreled out the door and into the room.

The scene was chaotic: A sliding glass door had been shattered inward, with large spears of broken glass covering the floor and the kitchen table. Mary, who had jumped back, was bending down in the entryway, holding her golden retriever Sanger by the collar. The dog was frantically trying to run into the mess in the kitchen, since the dog was really Mary's protector and she would have gleefully chewed up anybody who got close enough to even smell Mary.

A tall, scraggle-bodied man, his face mostly covered by a bandana, was standing in the exploded entryway. He was wearing an army-surplus jacket, jeans, and amazingly, Turulio thought, a fanny pack. Turulio started to advance on the guy, who appeared to have a small pistol in one hand, but as soon as scraggle-bodied-bandana guy saw Turulio, he bolted, back out the way he came.

"Call Ben, tell him c'mon over, den call Crump!" Turulio shouted, as he ran through the crunching glass shards and out into the yard.

* *

When Crump arrived on the scene, Turulio was standing over a young man who appeared to be alive, but lying flat on his back, immobilized and pant-less. His ears were both bleeding. Turulio kneeled down over him as Crump approached.

"This the guy?" Crump asked. He'd just come out after checking on Mary, who assured him she and the dog were fine.

Turulio nodded.

"What happened?" Crump asked.

"He tried to whack Mary—"

"I know that—I mean, *after* he tried to whack Mary?"

"He tried to whack *me,* but I disarmed da guy, and den I was just questionin' him—"

"Angelo—"

"Well, I was interrogatin' him for *a while—*"

"Then what?"

"He stopped cooperatin' when we got to duh good part," Turulio answered.

Crump leaned in to take a closer look, then he stood up, followed by Turulio. "What happened to his ears, why is he in his underpants and why isn't he moving?"

Turulio shrugged. "So, I was doin' a 'Dick Cheney' on 'im—"

"—I'm sure the former Vice President would be impressed at your appropriation of his name here, so go ahead and tell me what's involved with a 'Dick Cheney.'"

"So's, I put my heel on his balls, then I grab each earlobe and pulls, while I asks him more questions. I guess, somewhere in there, one uh his earlobes musta come off."

"Looks like *both* to me," Crump said, as he knelt down to get close enough to talk at the man's face, which was grimacing in pain. "Why isn't he moving?"

Turulio kneeled next to Crump. "'Cause I stuck his gun up his ass, an' if he moves, it's gonna blow him a new asshole."

Crump looked at Turulio, shaking his head. "Angelo, can you manage to remove the gun from his rectum? It seems to be inhibiting the free flow of information."

Angelo winced. "That'd be a delicate o'pration, but if I gotta," he commented, as he stuck his hand down in the man's underwear. Once he'd extracted the gun, which he held gingerly between a thumb and forefinger, he placed his foot firmly on the man's upturned ankle. The man yelled out in pain.

"Go ahead, boss," Turulio added.

Crump, still bending down over the guy, raised his arm and held out his hand to Turulio, while still staring at the man's upturned face. "Give the man his earlobes back," Crump ordered, wiggling his fingers in a "Gimme here" gesture.

"He don't wear earrings—"

"*Angelo*," Crump repeated, and Turulio forked over the bloody stumps. Crump placed them on the man's chest.

"Please take your shoe off this man's leg, then point his gun at him instead of at me," Crump suggested. When Angelo complied, he addressed the bleeding man. "Let me tell you what's about to happen. A dozen uniformed officers will be here in a few minutes. They've been told you were apprehended by a citizen, one *known to these officers*, in the act of trying to commit a murder. You'll be arrested and booked on attempted first degree murder, and if you're lucky, you'll only do twenty to twenty-five. If I were you, I'd seriously consider cooperating, and in this case, that means telling us who put you up to this."

The man began gesticulating incoherently, grabbing his severed earlobes and holding them in his fist.

"I want a bag of ice," he said, practically in tears. "And, gimme my pants back."

"Who *is* this guy?" Crump asked Turulio.

"One a dem 'bortion guys—"

"*Anti-abortion* guys," the man interrupted.

"Dat's what I *said*," Turulio complained.

"You said '*abortion*' guys—"

"Look, Mr. 'Army of God,'" Crump intervened. "The cops are gonna be here any minute. You have any hope of this not being your last day in the sunlight, I want the names, addresses, social security numbers and blood types of everybody up the food chain, and I don't just mean the guy who gave you the doggie bag full of cash. I want the *suits*."

* *

"This is it?" Maureen asked.

"You complained about the prisoner transport van," Peter Meadows responded, mildly annoyed.

Maureen, Q. Peter Meadows, Tenato the translating C.B.P. agent, and Elení Montes, were all looking at a dust-covered, sun bleached, nineteen-fifties-era elongated school bus, still emblazoned with dark green lettering that read, "El Paso Hospital and Prison Laundry".

"This is just an inmate transport van, recommissioned as the prison's laundry truck," Maureen complained.

"Lotta room, you gotta admit," Tenato added.

The driver was as old as the bus, morbidly overweight with a guy's bouffant of gray, unkempt hair and an equally gray handlebar mustache. He looked to Maureen like the creepy bus driver that always turned out to have kidnapped somebody in Cable-T.V. mysteries.

"Ay, Delroy," the driver called out, through the open, cross-folding passenger door.

"You know this guy?" Maureen asked Tenato.

"Co-worker. Long time ago, he was my parole officer."

The driver nodded in recognition.

"We going anywhere?" Peter Meadows asked, impatiently. "Seems the Court has us on a tight schedule."

Maureen turned to Elení Montes, who was only vaguely aware of who was who and where they were going, in part because Tenato kept doing the bit where he only translated three percent of whatever Elení said. He wasn't much better with Maureen's instructions and explanations.

"Tell her we're taking this rust bucket up North to the City by the Lake, so she can be with her daughter again," Maureen ordered.

"Tenemos que subir al autobús para ir al norte a ver a su hija, para que podamos estar seguros de que no está muerta" Tenato explained.

Elení Montes started to cry. She then broke into a tear-stained discourse that lasted five minutes, and the only words Maureen could pick out were 'Estrellita' and 'muerta'.

"She says, 'O.K.," Tenato offered, when Maureen bit his head off.

"Look, you can just *knock it off*—I know exactly what you're doing— you told her the kid was dead, or maybe dead, or almost dead. If you don't start translating everything we say to each other, *word-for-word*, I'll get a real translator, and you can accompany Meadows here back to Federal prison—"

"Do what she says," Meadows cut in.

"Tell her, Estrellita is alive, in the hospital and we're going to get them back together," Maureen said, and Delroy Tenato finally, fully complied.

They climbed aboard, each dragging bags and roller-boards, except for Elení, who could fit everything she still owned into a shopping bag. The bus smelled like bleach. The seats were all ancient, cracked leather, and most of the windows were stuck halfway down. When the driver started up the bus, it backfired loudly. Elení Montes dove under the seat.

"Tell her it's just the engine," Maureen said. While Tenato helped Elení up and translated, the driver said, "Timing's off," and he got out and popped the hood of the bus. He listened for minutes that featured a few more backfires, each sounding like a firecracker or a gunshot, depending on where you grew up. He then opened a panel on the side of the bus and pulled out a tool kit. With the bus still idling, he flashed a light in the engine and worked on something with a long, angled wrench. Black smoke started coming out the exhaust. He looked up, saw the smoke, said "Shit," then fiddled some more until the smoke subsided.

"All better," he said, as he climbed back into the cab and placed the bus in gear, cranking a long, knobbed stick shift rising off the floor of the bus.

"This trip will *never* end," Maureen said to herself, as they slowly rolled out of the tented-area and onto the roadway.

* *

"Crump, I've interviewed a dozen of your medical deportation class members—"

"I know—I've seen the coverage," he offered Svetlana Armstrong. "You should get the Pulitzer—"

"Look, there's a real story here. Why don't you give me an exclusive statement? I'm sure I can get you media coverage."

"You know I can't comment on pending litigation," Crump offered.

Armstrong blew a mild raspberry into the phone. "Don't you want the weight of public opinion on your side?'

"I'm betting we already have that," he paused. "I mean, you'll never crack the cult of Stuggs worshipers—they think he's saving the World for the White Man—"

"Can I quote you on that?"

"No, you *cannot*, and if you try, I'll give somebody else an interview and claim that *you* said that."

"O.K., suit yourself. I just think, right about now, you could use all the friends you can get. Word is some Nazi-nut-job was arrested last week, trying to take a shot at your wife."

"Word does get around, and do me a favor, if you report on that, don't call Mary 'My wife'—she's so liberal she thinks Bernie Sanders is a Republican, and she hates the term, 'wife.'"

"Got it. If you change your mind, you know where to find me," Armstrong said, and just as she was hanging up, Crump said, "Wait—" but the line was already dead.

* *

"One way we can tell that Brian's getting better, is he asked today if he could come and watch the trial, maybe even testify," Susan Lockwood said, as she sat down in Crump's office. She was there to begin trial prep. She was as upbeat as Crump had ever seen her.

"He eating again, like, real food?" Crump asked.

"You bet—he's finally out of that wheelchair."

Crump paused, scratching the back of his head. "I don't know—I mean, once he's in the Courtroom, Stenson can call him as a witness. While Judge Stairs would never let Stenson run roughshod over Brian, I still wonder how having to go over the whole thing, re-living it before a live audience, while Stenson tries to make him out as a liar—I just don't know how he'd hold up." Crump figured she didn't know all the details of the assaults on her son.

Susan Lockwood nodded like she understood. "But, wouldn't it make the case better, if he were to testify?"

"I suppose so," Crump admitted. "I'll need to prep him, just in case. I think we can win it either way. The State's Attorney has granted Deb Connover immunity, and is seriously considering indicting a few of the main actors. Once State's Attorney Derek Markle starts working over the main perps and they start turning on each other, I think the case will effectively be over."

Susan Lockwood got up and walked over to the window. She looked out and saw a touristy-horse-drawn buggy, just like the one that had landed Crump in jail, a story she knew well.

"I don't think he wants to watch because he thinks it'll make the case better," she said, turning back from the window. "I think he wants to see the whole place *burn*, but mostly, he wants to see you try the case."

Crump raised an eyebrow. "Hmmm. I think he might be a little disappointed—trials are pretty technical and there's rarely a '*Gotcha* Moment'—that mostly happens in the lawyer T.V. shows."

She sat back down. "When I told him about your getting arrested, *twice*, he literally stood up out of his wheelchair for the first time in months and said, 'What are we gonna do about it?'"

"That wasn't in his case, that was in that monstrosity the press is calling the 'Patriot Act Case.'"

"I know. That doesn't matter." She was almost laughing. "You don't get it, do you?"

"Get what?" Crump asked.

"I think that's what my son likes about you—you wouldn't get it if I painted you a picture." She shrugged. "O.K., let's prepare for my testimony. We can do Brian tomorrow."

25.
YOU CAN ALL BURN IN HELL………

THE TRIAL OF THE LOCKWOODS' attempt to label Carrington Prep a Public Nuisance was moving into its third day. Judge Rebecca Stairs was cutting through the procedural motions and preliminary matters quickly, so they'd been in the heart of the case since the first day. Crump and Howie Schmeltz were calling a diverse group of witnesses, and their testimony was building the case that the fabled institution had been corrupted by complacency, cronyism and by reverence for the "Progressive Idiom", a buzz-phrase overused by the Keepers of the Faith, long-serving faculty and staff, desperately trying to preserve the status quo.

After the Lockwoods recounted the story of their gradual discovery of their son's anorexia, followed by the reveal of the chronic school bullying behind it, Tom Lodge, Bill Lockwood's consulting partner, explained the report he and Bill Lockwood had been asked to prepare, about the mess at Carrington that was killing enrollment. He talked about the reaction of the faculty and staff, and how stories had begun to trickle in through his kid and her classmates about how Brian Lockwood had been targeted in retaliation.

The testimony Crump knew would blow open the case, that of Deb Connover, the former Carrington music teacher, came next. Greg Stenson, arrogant, impatient and skeptical about the alleged link between the Lodge/Lockwood Report and the bullying, had delegated following up on Connover's deposition to one of his associates, who'd never succeeded in running her down. She'd never been subpoenaed for her deposition. Stenson had to ask his associate to remind him exactly who Connover was when she took the stand. He was agitated, as Connover had stopped on the way into the courtroom and whispered something to Derek Markle, who Stenson recognized as a Lakeside County prosecutor.

Crump, who overheard Stenson's question, offered, "She's been on the witness list from day one."

"So has everybody else who's ever set foot in the school building," Stenson grumbled, which was true enough—Crump had listed everybody on the faculty and staff, as well as half the parents and kids at Carrington, as potential witnesses in his discovery responses. He figured he'd let Stenson guess which ones he was likely to call at trial. As a result—coupled with the School's choking on Stenson's two thousand dollar-an-hour billing rate—Stenson had not personally taken any depositions other than Brian Lockwood' parents. Stenson and Willis lawyers had interviewed cooperative faculty and staff, but with Connover out of the building, they'd missed her. The Defense-cooperative faculty were all lying, so Stenson had no idea what was coming.

"Please state your name for the record," Crump called out.

Deb Connover arranged herself in the witness chair. She'd dressed for the occasion: In her navy blue suit, she looked like somebody you might see directing a children's choir, tall, young, experienced and ready to peck at you with a baton if you sang out of tune.

"Deborah Joan Connover," she replied.

"I object," Stenson called out, rising from his seat at the counsel table opposite Crump and Schmeltz.

"To *her name*?" Crump responded.

"No—to her conspiring with the Lakeside County State's Attorney," Stenson offered.

"I'm sorry," Judge Stairs answered, "But you'll have to explain yourself."

"This witness was seen, as she entered the Courtroom, whispering with that gentleman in the back row," Stenson said, pausing, turning, and pointing out Derek Markle, who was, in fact, seated in the back row of the spectators' gallery. "I have it on sound authority that man is a representative of the State's Attorney's Office, one who we now believe has in all likelihood interviewed this and other witnesses. On that basis, pursuant to A.R.D.C. Rule 8.4, I object to this witness's testimony."

"Mr. Stenson, isn't Rule 8.4 a rule of attorney discipline? What does it have to do with this witness's qualification to testify?"

"Only that the conspiracy between this witness and the State's Attorney indicates an obvious violation of rule 8.4 by Attorney Crump—'An attorney shall not threaten criminal prosecution to gain advantage in a civil proceeding'—and therefore this witness should be disqualified."

"Your Honor, may I?" Crump asked, rising.

"Go ahead."

"Neither I, nor this witness, have any control over what the State's Attorney does or does not do with this case, or with any of the role-players in it. Mr. Stenson's own objection demonstrates that he just learned of the role, if any, the States' Attorney would have here, watching this witness speak to Mr. Markle *on the third day of trial*. The laws of physics therefore make it impossible that there was ever any *threat* of criminal prosecution to gain advantage. If he wants to report me to the A.R.D.C. with this whacky ethics claim, go ahead—that does not reflect on this witness's qualifications to testify."

Judge Stairs nodded. "Please proceed."

Crump ploughed through the preliminary and background questions, establishing Connover as an occurrence witness at the infamous science lab meeting.

"So, Miss Connover, when did you first learn that there was a faculty expression of dissatisfaction with the expected report about Carrington enrollment declines that Mr. Lodge and Mr. Lockwood were preparing?"

"October of 2017," she responded.

"Tell us what happened?"

"Objection—leading—he's feeding her the answer with his question," Stenson called out, without standing.

"*What happened*? 'Please tell your story', is *leading*?" Crump answered, genuinely annoyed.

"Overruled."

"So, the middle school science teacher, Connie Pennebacker, called us into the science lab and locked the door—"

"I'm sorry—who's 'us'?" Crump nudged.

"Sorry, Pennebacker, Mike Norwood, the school's gym teacher, Brenda Howser, the Middle School English teacher, Carla Wright, Middle School Math, and Victor Holder, the upper-class coordinator—"

"Sorry to interrupt, but Holder, he's a member of the Administration?"

"Leading, *again*," Stenson groaned.

"I'm just making sure she identifies the people present—leading questions are objectionable when the witness could not answer without the suggestion embedded in the question. I think we can all assume that Ms. Connover knew everybody's role, after working at Carrington for what was, at that time, six years."

"Overruled. Mr. Stenson, can we limit our objections to material violations of the rules? I want to avoid the appearance that you were just trying to rattle the witness and interrupt the flow of her testimony," the Judge elaborated.

Stenson, exhibiting his displeasure with the ruling, waved a dismissive hand in the air, without looking up.

"Please continue," Judge Stairs urged.

"Yes, Holder is a member of the Carrington Administration," Connover answered.

"What was the reason for the meeting?" Crump asked.

"Marianne was all worked up about the report that Lockwood and Lodge were preparing. She wanted to talk about it…." she paused, "…..about what we were going to *do* about it."

"Do?" Crump asked.

"Yes. She said, 'We gotta do something. They're gonna turn this place into *an academy—*"

"*Aahhobjection*, hearsay—" Stenson began.

"Your Honor, this is an admission against interest—the entire point of this trial is to show that the faculty and staff *intentionally* condoned and even prompted the mistreatment of my client's son for *doctrinal reasons*— that statement is the same as Ms. Pennebacker saying, "*We gotta retaliate—*"

"This is a bench trial. I'll overrule the objection. I can sort it out. Go ahead."

"So, what happened then?" Crump asked.

"So, then she said, 'We gotta stop this', and I said, 'How we gonna do that?' and, Marianne said, 'Well, one way is to get their kids outta the place.'"

"Did you understand what she meant by that statement?"

"No, not really, but, then the gym teacher, Mike Norwood, said, 'How we gonna do that—we can't flunk 'em out, I mean, we don't even *give* grades,'—"

"More hearsay—it's like a hearsay *festival*," Stenson argued.

"Overruled."

"Then what happened?"

"Then, Connie Pennebacker said, 'Well, Lockwood's got a kid comin' down the pike. I can't *wait* to get my hands on *him*.'"

"Your Honor, I move that the entire testimony of this witness be stricken—" Stenson began.

"Overruled. Please proceed."

"Was that the only discussion you had with any member of the faculty or staff of Carrington about potential retaliation directed at Brian Lockwood?"

"No. As time went on, the harassment of Brian was obviously getting out of hand. I could see some of what was going on, and it had been going on for over a year, so I approached Mike Norwood, the gym teacher—I figured if anybody could do something, he could. I said, 'Hey, Mike, the Lockwood kid is getting harassed and knocked around. This has gone too far,' and he said, 'You want to start punching a time clock every day, lose your associate teachers and start giving standardized tests?'"

"What did you understand Mr. Norwood to *mean* by that?"

"Objection—asking this witness to speculate about what was in Norwood's *head*," Stenson said, standing.

"Her impression is relevant," Crump argued. "They're not discussing the meaning of life or nuclear fusion—this is a discussion about why the Faculty and Staff were *consciously allowing* a student to be bullied, in plain sight, and with the not-so-subtle encouragement of the adults in the room."

"Overruled. Let her finish."

"I knew what he meant. He meant if we didn't look the other way, let them continue to abuse the kid, and Brian Lockwood and his family stayed at Carrington, then that report was going to ruin the sweet deal we all had."

"And, that *sweet deal was*?"

"Faculty self-governance, no accountability, no minimum classroom days, no limits on turning the classroom over to the associates so we could pursue other interests."

Judge Stairs was writing furiously on a legal pad, while most of the courtroom hummed with whispered comments.

"Miss Connover, one more question: Did you share your concerns with anybody besides Mr. Norwood and those at the first meeting with Ms. Pennebacker?"

"I made a few comments to a couple of parents I considered independent and concerned."

"What about other members of the faculty and staff?"

"No."

"Why not?"

"I didn't have to. *We all knew*."

"No further questions," Crump announced.

"Your witness, Mr. Stenson," the Judge said.

Stenson was whispering to Ralph Westheimer, sitting to his immediate right. Westheimer nodded, and Stenson rose.

"Ms. Connover, I'm Gregory Stenson, attorney for Carrington Prep. Let me start with that last statement—'*We all knew*'—"

"Yes—"

"I wasn't finished. Do you expect us to believe that over two dozen teachers and administrators knew about the alleged abuse of this Lockwood individual, for months, even years, and none of them did anything to stop it?"

Connover nodded, tilted her head slightly, and said, "Well, yes, I mean, some knew more than others, some ignored it, some actively encouraged it, and some, like me, thought to ourselves, 'I need this job'. But, yes, *everybody* in the place knew, at some level, that this was going on."

Disappointed with that answer, Stenson moved on. "Ms. Connover, how long were you employed by Carrington Prep?"

"Eight years," she said, looking directly at Stenson and sitting up ramrod straight. Crump had prepared her for this line of questioning.

"And, how many of those years were after this, this allegedly *infamous* meeting you described in the science lab?"

"Almost three—"

"So, you hung around for *three years* after this supposedly jarring, disturbing meeting, the entire time knowing this awful, protracted bullying was occurring?"

"I'd been looking for a job the entire time, and I left as soon as I found something. I support my mother, who is a victim of M.S., and I couldn't afford to leave without another job."

"Your honor, I move to strike that answer as non-responsive—"

"I don't agree, Mr. Stenson—you were asking her why she stuck around, and she's telling you. Proceed."

Howie Schmeltz leaned over to Crump and whispered, "The Judge is responding to objections for you," and Crump whispered back, "Yeah, *how 'bout that……..*"

"So, Ms. Connover, are you expecting this Court to *believe* that a bunch of *dedicated, selfless* educators were intentionally allowing this person to be abused, all in the name of protecting the creature comforts of an undemanding workplace?"

Connover looked at Stenson like he was a cross between the jerk that he was, and someone pathetic and naive.

"Look, I've been teaching long enough to know that the stereotype just isn't true. Teachers are like everybody-elsers—there are good ones, and bad ones, and in-between ones. Just because we're all underpaid—and, *we're all underpaid*—doesn't turn every one of us into Mother Theresa."

Stenson huffed, not satisfied with that answer either, but deciding to move on.

"Ms. Connover, I see you are familiar with Mr. Markle, from the Lakeside County State's Attorney's Office. Have they interviewed you about this matter?"

"They have."

"What did you tell them?"

"Exactly what I just told you."

"I see. And, did they threaten you with criminal prosecution over your participation in this, this alleged *scheme* you've described today?"

"They did not."

"Given that your claims are so, so *harrowing*, did that surprise you?"

"No."

"Why not?"

"Because, they granted me immunity from prosecution."

Stenson erupted. "*Your Honor, I demand* that this witness's testimony be *stricken—*"

"Why?" Crump asked, standing. "Seems to me this is a credibility issue, not a qualification one," Crump argued, glancing over at Westheimer, who appeared nauseated.

"I agree. Ask another question," the Judge ordered.

Stenson composed himself. "Miss Connover, isn't it true you were fired by Carrington?"

Connover sat quietly, shifted in her seat momentarily, then said, "Sort-of."

"What do you mean, 'Sort-of'? Either you were fired, or you quit—which was it?"

"It's hard to say. When I went into Westheimer's office to give my notice, Ralph—Mr. Westheimer—he got kind of weird, and he said, 'Well, it's all the same, because we were about to terminate you, anyway.'"

"You weren't surprised by that, were you?"

"Yes, I was—I'd never been evaluated, although, nobody had, and anyway, nobody ever complained about the job I was doing."

"What did you tell Mr. Westheimer when he said they were going to fire you?"

"I said, 'I wish you'd done it a lot sooner.'"

"You didn't say, "I'll *get you* for this,'?"

Connover smiled. "Do I look like somebody who makes threats like a mobster?"

Crump jumped up. "There's no foundation for the words he's trying to put in her mouth. If he's got a witness who claims those words were uttered by Miss Connover, let's hear about it. I've taken Mr. Westheimer's deposition, and he never mentioned this supposed threat," Crump argued.

"I agree. We'll need to see if he can link it up in his case, otherwise I'll strike the question and answer," the Judge noted. "Any more questions, Mr. Stenson?"

"No, your honor," Stenson offered, and Connover left the witness stand.

Crump then ploughed through a number of additional witnesses, including Westheimer and the other guilty teachers, who all labelled Connover an opportunistic liar. He asked each one of them what "opportunity" was available to Deb Connover from concocting such a story. Only one offered a substantive answer, which revolved around a far-fetched conspiracy theory that Connover was pursuing a career in Hollywood, financed by a mysterious but unnamed Albanian businessman.

Crump finished up by rolling out the suicide-helper web page from Mike Norwood's internet search history and jamming it in Norwood's face, when he tried to deny knowing anything about the threatening letters slipped into Brian Lockwood's school locker.

"Any more witnesses, Mr. Crump?" the Judge inquired.

"One moment, please," he said, as Susan Lockwood leaned over and whispered something in his ear.

"You sure about this?" Crump asked, and when she nodded, he rose and said, "Plaintiffs call Mr. Brian Lockwood."

Stenson shot up. "This '*Mr.* Lockwood' is only fourteen."

"And, therefore, well past the age of qualification and capacity—" Crump began, when Stenson continued.

"And, we were barred from ever deposing him, on the now obviously *false* representation that he was too vulnerable to testify," Stenson added, rounding out his objection.

"That's not true—what we said at the time was that Brian Lockwood was compromised—he was wheelchair-bound and confined to a hospital ward—and that there was no reason to take his deposition *at that time*. There were dozens of other witnesses with better information about what went on at Carrington, many who've testified over the last three days. We simply said that others should be deposed first, and since then, Mr. Stenson has deposed *exactly two* of those witnesses, Mr. and Mrs. Lockwood, the Plaintiffs. It's been months, and Mr. Stenson never again approached us or this court to obtain this witnesses' deposition. He should be allowed to testify," Crump argued.

"I agree. Objection overruled," the Judge ordered, and Susan Lockwood rose, left the courtroom, and returned, steadying a still-gaunt-looking Brian Lockwood, who then walked to the front of the courtroom.

"Please take a seat in the witness stand, Mr. Lockwood," the Judge said, and Brian Lockwood, wearing khaki slacks and a button-down shirt, looking like he was still slightly afraid to be alive, sat down and raised his right hand. After he was sworn in and went through the preliminary questions, Crump focused him on the reason they were all in the Courtroom.

"Mr. Lockwood—I'm going to call you Brian, if that's O.K.—Brian, when did you first notice that you were being targeted for aggressive behavior at Carrington?"

To Crump's surprise, this kid who'd recently barely had the strength to stand up, perked up and glanced around the courtroom, looking the Judge and everybody else in the eye, just as they'd prepared him to do.

"It was October of 2017. It began with Marianne Pennebacker, and then, Vance Norwood."

"Can you describe what you are referring to as 'It' in your prior answer?"

"Yes, but I need to apologize to everybody and to you, Judge Stairs, because some of this is going to sound bad, bad for courtrooms, anyway."

"I'm sure I've heard worse, so please, go right ahead," the Judge responded.

"So, Marianne, she's a year older, she started in with the usual school stuff—'You're a dickhead, you dipshit, why don't you go off somewhere and disappear'—then Vance Norwood started in, and his stuff was a lot more personal."

"Personal, like, *how*?" Crump asked.

"His was all gender and sex stuff—'You faggot….you got a face like a broad…..if I didn't know you had a dick, I'd think you were some horse-faced lesbian….', stuff like that."

"How persistent was this?"

"I had most of my classes with them, so every time I ran into one of them, I'd get a face full of it."

"How often was that?"

"Twenty, thirty times a day. Sometimes more."

"Did it interfere with your ability to get your schoolwork done?"

"It interfered with *everything*. I mean, I couldn't really turn around without one of them being in my face."

"Did this pattern—"

"Objection—characterizing his prior testimony—he never described it as '*a pattern*'—"

"Overruled."

"Did this *pattern of bullying*," Crump dug in, rubbing the word in Stenson's nose, "did this at some point change?"

"Yes. Sometime in late 2019, all of a sudden, Marianne and Vance laid off, and almost like they were a team, Fletcher Goodson and Parker Todd seemed to take over."

"You have any idea why they changed places?"

"Yes. Marianne and Vance were faculty kids, and I heard other kids say that they were gonna get it, because somebody complained, and they were supposed to be extra good, since they were faculty kids. I just figured they got yelled at and so they asked Fletcher and Parker to take over—"

"Objection—this is pure speculation."

"Your honor, he was *there*, we weren't. I think it is safe for us to assume the victim of this abuse had a good idea what was going on—"

"Sustained. Let's stick to what he knew," the Judge said, and Crump thought to himself, "That's bad enough……."

"What did Fletcher and Parker do?"

"For one thing, they were much more physical. Fletcher would grab the front of my shirt in his fist and slam me against my locker—he'd ask me stuff like, 'Want to *die*, faggot?'—and Parker would wait for me outside and shove me face down in the sand pit or trip me when I walked by."

"Did any of these kids ever give you any indication of *why* they were doing this?" Crump asked.

Brian Lockwood lost stride for the first time in his testimony, and glanced at his parents at the counsel table. "Not exactly. But, a few times, Parker would say stuff like, 'Why don't you go home and tell your rich mommy and daddy? Maybe they could buy you a bodyguard?' And, once, Fletcher said, 'Your fucking'….." He paused. "Can I say that?"

"Go ahead, you're under oath, so tell it like it was," the Judge cut in.

"So, Fletcher said, 'Your fucking parents don't get to run the school, asshole,' and I said something like, 'What?' and he said, 'The fucking *teachers* run the place.' I figured it was about what my folks were doing, some studies or something, but I never really understood all that."

"Did you ever tell your parents about this?" Crump asked, wanting to get away from the details of physical abuse.

"No….well, yes, kind of, I mean, I told them at the hospital."

"What hospital?"

"The Psych Ward at St. Vincent's."

"Why were you there?"

"I stopped eating for a long time, and when I was starving—it's called 'Anorexia'—I got taken there, and they said it was like illegal if I didn't say what was going on, so I told Doctor Trimble, and my parents got to hear it."

Crump could see Susan Lockwood starting to tear up. He hoped Brian wouldn't notice.

"Why not tell anybody before that?" Crump asked.

"Mr. Crump, it's hard to explain if you're not there. I mean, when you're twelve and thirteen, you just feel like you're nobody, and you're a screw up, and then everybody around you tells you that you should just go and die, and, I don't know, I can't explain it, but you start to *believe* that stuff, like, maybe they're right, and you should just go and die….." He stopped.

Crump took a folder off the table and opened it. He gave a copy of an exhibit to the Judge and to Stenson, had the court reporter mark it as Exhibit 23, then handed it to Brian Lockwood.

"Brian, I'm showing you what's been marked 'Exhibit 23', Can you identify this exhibit?"

He scanned it, turned it over in his hands. "Sure….well, I think so, I mean, I got so many of these, but this is one of those notes they kept leaving in my locker—there's these vents, so they can slide stuff in—in an envelope with a razor blade, telling me I should just kill myself, and here's how."

"How many of these you get?"

"In the last year, before I went to the hospital, like, one every week."

"What did you do with them?" Crump asked.

"I don't know why, but, mostly, I kept them. I guess I was too embarrassed to let anybody know that people at my school were telling me I'd be better off dead, that I didn't want anybody to see them…." He stopped, noticing his Mother was crying. She stood up and left the Courtroom.

"Should we stop?" Crump asked.

"No—my Mom *asked* me to do this."

"O.K. Brian. Sorry, but I have to ask this: Did you ever follow these directions and try to use one of those razor blades they were leaving you?"

He paused, then nodded. "Once, but, not like in the internet instructions. They tell you to cut the long way, along your veins, instead of straight across. One night, in the middle of the night when I couldn't sleep, I got up and ran the water in the bathroom sink and cut myself, but it was across and it wasn't very deep, so I mostly made a mess. I cleaned it up before my folks woke up and threw the towels away in the neighbor's garbage. I remember thinking I was a screw up, that I couldn't even kill myself the right way….."

He was starting to tear up.

"Sure you don't want to stop?"

"No, we can go…..don't worry, now I'm mostly *mad* about this stuff."

"Why stop eating?"

"It's hard to explain, like I said. Pretty soon, this is your whole life—you know, like how the heavy kids will tell you, 'I'm not the smart kid, or the jock kid, I'm not even the *kid kid*—I'm just the *fat* kid'—it's like that. So, pretty soon, when this is all you hear, all day, every day, you just want to die."

Crump turned to the Judge, then to Westheimer, who looked away when he caught Crump's line of sight.

"Just a few more questions—I promise—Do you know if any of the teachers knew this stuff was going on?"

He nodded silently. "They knew," he said, emphatically.

"How can you be so sure?"

"'Cause, they were doing it right out in the open, and once, I heard a kid complain about it to Mr. Norwood."

"What, if anything, did Mr. Norwood do or say to you?"

Brian Lockwood exhaled loudly. "He said, 'Don't be a wuss.'"

"O.K, just one more—why are you up here, doing this?"

Brian Lockwood nodded. "Because, if I don't stop this, they'll do it again to somebody else."

"No further questions," Crump said.

Brian Lockwood started to stand, when the Judge said, "Hold on—Mr. Stenson, do you have any questions?"

"Yes, a few," and the Judge asked Brian to remain seated and reminded him he was still under oath.

Stenson rose. "Mr. Lockwood, I believe you stated that you got slammed into a locker, tripped and fell a few times—were you ever seriously injured in any of these mishaps?"

"Objection to the characterization as 'mishaps'—*tornadoes* are *mishaps*—"

"Can you answer that question?" the judge asked.

Brian Lockwood squirmed a little. "Yes, I can. It was, not like, *permanently*,"

"So, were those the worst injuries you suffered at the alleged hands of—"

"Your Honor," Crump called out. "We need a side bar conference, outside the presence of any witnesses."

"The Judge stood. "Fifteen-minute recess," The Judge announced. "Be back at 2:45."

"Go see to your Mother," Crump told Brian, as the kid rose and walked over to meet his Father at the counsel table.

Crump, Stenson and the Judge filed into her chambers. She sat down behind her desk. The room was full of pictures of groups of people gathered around the Judge. Turn down the lights, it could have been an Italian restaurant.

"So, we here for a breather for your witness, so his parents can coach him a little?" Stenson complained. Crump ignored him.

"Your Honor, this minor has been through a lot in the last four years—he's just out of the psych ward and eating again. I have knowledge that was shared with me in a confidential attorney/client communication about the degree of physical abuse here, which I cannot share without Brian Lockwood's consent—"

"So, now, the *kid* is your client?" Stenson asked.

"For these purposes, he is. Anyway, I think it is important to shield him from further testimony about this—"

"*Shield*?" Stenson asked, in a mocking tone.

"That's what I said—shield laws would apply here."

The Judge sat up, glanced at Stenson and then Crump, nodded, then asked, "Do we need a foundation for that?"

"Mr. Stenson here will regret that, I promise you. I ask that you order Mr. Stenson to terminate this line of questioning—"

"*No way*—I'm entitled to cross examine him on anything within the scope of his direct—"

Before the Judge could speak, Crump cut in with, "Right now, *Greg*, all your client and its employees face are the fire sale of the campus and having to find new jobs. I'm telling you, it's about to get a lot worse, but if it makes you feel *like a tough guy, then, go ahead,*" Crump stopped. He was leaning forward, his teeth bared and clenched together as he spoke. "*Go ahead, …..I…..dare….you.*"

Judge Stairs pulled back. "I hardly think I need the answer to the pending question to decide this case—the degree of hospitalization is irrelevant. Mr. Stenson, there's no jury here. I think you need to move on. I'll direct you away from this line of questioning."

Back in the courtroom, before Brian Lockwood could take the stand, Stenson rose and said, "No further questions for this witness."

Crump presented his expert witnesses. He then had a whispered debate with the Lockwoods about calling a couple of the perp kids, who he'd subpoenaed, just in case. After convincing the Lockwoods that the kids would lie, and that the lies, even *as lies*, would dilute the impact of Brian's testimony, he rose to his feet.

"Plaintiffs rest," he announced.

Stenson put up a bunch of faculty and parents who all claimed to know absolutely nothing about the alleged abuse of Brian Lockwood or its link to the Enrollment Report or the faculty's role in it. He then rested the School's defense.

Crump called, as his only rebuttal witness, Didi Dubrow, the child that had ratted the faculty out to Maureen and had first drawn the link between the bullying and the faculty-child-attendance waiver program.

Once she was sworn in, Crump asked, "Miss Dubrow, did you ever, in all your time as a student at Carrington, hear any faculty member admit that he or she was aware of what was happening to Brian Lockwood?"

The kid appeared excruciatingly uncomfortable. She looked at the Judge. "Is this O.K. to answer?" she asked.

"Just tell the truth, Miss Dubrow," Judge Stairs said.

"I once heard Mrs. Pennebacker in her office, telling Marianne, 'You gotta stop, or they're gonna throw you out.'"

"How did you know what Mrs. Pennebacker was talking about?"

"Because, right after that, her daughter, Marianne, said to a bunch of us, 'I can't do anything, just 'cause my Mom's a teacher, but that's O.K., because Parker and Fletcher are gonna take care of that faggot Lockwood,' and then, just like she said, Fletcher began slamming Brian around, all over the place."

"Objection!" Stenson shouted. "We are supposed to *believe* these incredible, hearsay statements—"

"It's in the movie…." Didi Dubrow began.

"The *Movie*?" Crump asked, as he narrowed his brow.

"Yeah," Dubrow added.

"Can you be more specific?" Crump inquired, as Stenson rose to his feet.

"So, when I was getting my coat n' stuff, and I heard Mrs. P. telling Marianne she had to knock it off, I stayed back in the coatroom and got my phone and made a movie about it," Didi Dubrow said, as she wriggled in the witness chair and pulled a phone out of her pocket. She held it up and said, "See?"

As the courtroom went silent, the witness held up her phone, turned it horizontal, fiddled with the keypad, then held it out as a video began to play. Nobody could hear it clearly, but before Crump could ask her to raise the volume, Stenson blew up.

"I object to this, this fiasco! We were not given any notice that this person had video-graphic evidence—"

"Your Honor," Crump interrupted, "while Mr. Stenson gave us absolutely no document requests, a matter I reminded him about during his Client Mr. Westheimer's deposition, I had no idea this witness had any such evidence until one minute ago, and I actually have no idea what she's about to show us."

Judge Stairs turned to Didi Dubrow and said, "Miss Dubrow, can you pause this 'movie', bring it back to the start, then hand your phone to the Court Reporter? Counsel, please approach."

As the Reporter handed the phone to the Judge, Crump and Stenson huddled around the dias.

"I'm going to play this video for both of you, and then we can discuss whether there is a proper foundation, whether the content is relevant and admissible, and any other objections you may have."

As the judge held up the phone and activated the recording, a wiggling image of the Carrington Science Teacher and her daughter lit up. "You gotta stop with Brian," the Mother pleaded with her daughter, "or they're gonna throw you out," she added, exactly echoing Dubrow's testimony. As Stenson was about to object, the science teacher continued with, "Let me deal with this, honey. I can get somebody who's not a faculty kid to do it."

The people in the spectators' gallery let out a collective gasp.

Stenson didn't hesitate. "That video's hearsay," he argued, flipping the back of his hand at the phone, still dangling in the Judge's hands.

"No, it's not," Crump responded. "We allow videotaped evidence all the time in this State, from will executions to deposition testimony on cross examination. Seems to me Miss Dubrow has authenticated it, and it matches her testimony, word for word—"

"—not that last part," Stenson cut in.

"You interrupted her, before she could get that part out," Crump responded.

Judge Stairs looked ashen. She mildly shook her head in disbelief, before announcing, "This witness Pennebacker took the Fifth Amendment against self-incrimination, when asked this, and every other question. While we can argue about whether this was an authorized recording, and whether Ms. Pennebacker had a reasonable expectation of privacy from her own students in her classroom, under the circumstances, I find it reliable, probative, and I'm going to admit the recording into evidence."

The Judge turned to Didi Dubrow. "Miss Dubrow, we are going to need to keep your phone for a few days, while the lawyers figure out how to download and preserve this video. It will be returned to you as soon as they can work that out."

"OK," Didi said, shrugging her shoulders in half-knowing acceptance.

"I'm done," Crump announced, returning to the counsel table.

Stenson tried to cross examine Didi Dubrow, but she either didn't understand any of his questions, or she was a very good actress.

"Did Marianne Pennebacker tell you exactly what she meant by, 'I can't do anything'?" Stenson asked.

"I don't understand your question," Didi Dubrow said, as she then did to all the rest of Stenson's questions.

Both sides rested. The next day, they returned for closing arguments, Crump's mostly a summary of how the problem was the culture at Carrington, and it could only be fixed with shuttering the place for good. Stenson called it an "isolated incident", and relied on a re-hash of his "Boys-will-be-Boys", just-learn-to-roll-with-the-punches argument.

Judge Stairs rose. "You all need to take a break while I review my notes. I believe I am ready to rule, so please be back here in an hour. Court is recessed."

Out in the hallway, Stenson buttonholed Crump into a corner.

"Look," Stenson offered. "We can settle this thing—my people are prepared to bargain—"

"Doesn't that usually happen when you don't *know* you've lost?" Crump needled him.

Stenson blew right past Crump's comment. "The Administration is prepared to meet all your clients' original demands: Fire all the faculty and staff directly involved, end the faculty waiver program, adopt a zero-tolerance policy against bullying—"

"—In my experience, 'Zero-Tolerance' *anything* usually evolves into bullying—"

"—and abandon Progressive Education as *a thing*."

"Greg—can I call you 'Greg'?" Crump asked, just to be annoying. "Greg, I have clients to represent here, and they're inclined to let you all burn in Hell. I would have been satisfied with having you all toast in Purgatory, but lately, I'm of the opinion that *this*—" Crump said, as he waived his outstretched arms around the hallway—"*this* is Purgatory, so I'm gonna go with my clients' recommendation. You can all burn…in…Hell."

Greg Stenson actually appeared desperate, which for a rich, powerful old guy, used to getting his way, was not a good look. "I know you think they're all a bunch of Commies, and frankly, they strike me that way too, but we can change all that—sweep the Board, get a few realists involved, get the place back to 'Readin', Writin' and Writhmetic', infuse the joint with some Honest-to-God Capitalists—"

"Greg, no offense, but they're all the same to me, Capitalism, Communism, Nationalism, Socialism—they all eventually lead to Fanaticism. Me, I'm into 'People-ism,' so, I'm gonna go with my clients here—you can all burn In Hell."

* *

"Court's back in session," Judge Stairs announced. "Please be seated." She flipped through a legal pad with stickers stuck to every page.

"I want to thank everybody who participated in this difficult and sometimes challenging trial. I've reviewed the testimony, gone over my notes, considered the opinions of the experts and reviewed again the legal briefs submitted by the parties on the law.

"I recognize that Carrington Prep is one of the oldest and most prestigious educational institutions in this City, and that declaring it, or, for that matter, *any* school a Public Nuisance is an unusual and extreme remedy. Nonetheless, my job is to consider the facts as they are presented to me, and then apply the law.

"It is clear to me that some of the Carrington faculty and staff believe *passionately* in their practices and educational philosophies, but if history has taught us anything, it's that devotion in pursuit of belief is no excuse for endangering the lives of others. I find that doubly true when adults are stewards of children, who, in many ways, are captives of their elders and authority figures—they're not free to simply walk away if they feel a particular environment is not suitable to their liking or otherwise not welcoming.

"There is no question that terrible things happened here, destructive conduct that went on for years. That conduct was blatantly illegal, perhaps criminal—which is not my job to determine—but it was also conduct that nearly killed an innocent child. The principals here on behalf of Carrington urge me to view that all as an aberration, the mistakes of a few misguided individuals, whose failures should not be visited on the entire institution. They ask that I somehow discipline those at fault, and allow Carrington to go on about its business.

"What is obvious to me, however, is that this was no accident. Whether it was the School's legally inadequate and functionally ineffective anti-bullying policy, its complete breakdown in reporting and addressing dangerous behavior, or its oddly sanctimonious belief that its progressive educational philosophy somehow sanctioned this lack of care and decency, in the end, I don't think any of that matters.

"What stays with me about the record here, what is still ringing in my ears, are these things:

--The testimony of Mr. Westheimer, defending his decision to send school children into the *teeth* of a hurricane, with the comment that 'Outdoor Education is an important part of our Progressive Curriculum', which struck me as the equivalent of tying a child to the train tracks in the path of an onrushing train, because mastery of knot-tying was an important part of the curriculum;

--The testimony of Miss Connover, and, *not* her dramatic testimony about the *intentionally, conspiratorial* nature of certain faculty members in their encouragement of the bullying of a student—I'll leave that part to the State's Attorney to sort out—no, the part that struck me was their *motivation*. Once again, the impetus for this shocking, dangerous behavior was a concern over culture preservation—an attempt to drive a family out in the hopes of keeping the status quo;

--Finally, the so-called 'policy' of the school for dealing with this problem of school violence—the pamphlet, 'Addressing Socially Non-Constructive Behavior'. The opening of that document…..let me read it again into the record: 'We at Carrington don't believe there is any such thing as a bully, that there are no bad kids, only confused children who, by virtue of traditional authoritarian and hierarchical conventional education programs, do not understand the adaptations expected of them.' In other words, we turn our backs on the law, on violence to kids, essentially, *on reality*, in reverence to our institutional, educational philosophy.

"I am reminded here of the expert testimony of Mr. Berger, the head of the Education Department at State University, when he said, 'Cultures in educational institutions do not abruptly change, *they evolve*.' I'm sure that's true. The question then becomes, how many more innocent lives can this court allow Carrington to endanger, as its foolish, dangerous and patently illegal culture evolves? I could order all sorts of changes to the school's operations, beginning with my express ruling that the so-called 'Religious Exception' to the Prevention of School Violence Act does *not* apply to Carrington, however devout its faculty and staff's commitment to all things Progressive. But, then, who is there at Carrington to internalize those mandated changes?

"I agree with Mr. Crump—there will be, perhaps forever, too many adults in the building mourning the death of what they call, 'Old Carrington.'

"For those reasons and the other matters stated in the record, I therefore order that Carrington Prep, the institution, the formal, legal entity, be declared a Public Nuisance. The institution is to shut down immediately, and its assets, including its facility and grounds, are to be liquidated by public sale. I am appointing Mr. Berger as Receiver for those purposes. The proceeds of sale are to be held in the not-for-profit corporation that currently operates Carrington Prep, which entity is to become a grant-making foundation, its mission to become funding programs for the prevention and eradication of school bullying and other forms of school violence. I understand this will inconvenience the parents and students currently in attendance, but I feel this action is necessary to protect the health and safety of those minors who currently attend and those that would otherwise attend in the future. So ordered."

The members of the press in the gallery immediately began pouring out of the courtroom. As the Lockwoods stood and turned to file out, Gregory Stenson jumped out of his seat.

"Your Honor, we intend to appeal this order—we'd ask for a stay of enforcement, pending the appeal—"

"Absolutely *not*," the Judge said, in a reprimanding tone. "This is a matter of public safety," she added, as she walked off the bench and into her chambers.

* *

Derek Markle was one of the first people out of the Courtroom. He stood at the end of the hallway leading to the elevators, flanked by two police officers. As people filed out of courtroom, he identified Ralph Westheimer. The officers arrested Westheimer and led him down to awaiting squads, cuffing him in the elevator.

26.
EVERYBODY'S IN CUSTODY……

"What do you mean, 'One of our guys is in custody'?" Warren Handler complained, honking into his cell phone.

"I'm just saying, these people are not exactly a well-disciplined organization—"

"Custody *where*?" Handler asked.

"That's the bad news—not the local Feds. He's in Lakeside County Jail, charged with attempted murder."

Handler paused. "Shit. He know anybody?"

"You know how this works—he knows somebody who knows somebody, on up the line, but I'd be shocked if he knew anybody with *a name*."

"Can we bond him out?"

"Held without bond—"

"How the fuck did *that* happen?"

"Remember, the lawyer's got a kid who's a cop."

"I can't believe how screwed up this is getting. There's gotta be somebody at that County facility that can be reached."

"Dunno—"

"Those places are usually dungeons—"

"I said, 'I…..don't…….know'—"

"Well, find out. Probably no video surveillance, and the staff are all drunks and chumps getting paid shit."

"So, you're saying, *don't* see if we got anybody?"

"I'm saying, fucking deal with it." Handler was about to hang up, when he added, "We got any eyes on that stupid bus detail?"

"They have instructions to take their time. They're snaking their way cross country, staying off the interstates, making lots of stops—"

"But, do we have *eyes* on it?"

"You mean, other than *freaking Meadows*, being *on it*?"

"Yeah—"

"I'll see to it."

* *

"Why are we stopping?" Maureen asked Peter Meadows, as the Prison Laundry Bus pulled into the parking lot at a gas station outside of Enid, Oklahoma.

"Gas up, get some stuff for the road—"

"Why aren't we taking the interstate?"

"Route 81 is the fastest way through the State."

"That *can't* be," Maureen pushed back. "I think you guys are dragging this out as long as possible, although, at this point, I can't imagine why—you're not going to derail this reunion any longer."

Meadows tuned her out, pulled himself out of the seat using the handrail that arched along the edge of the seat in front of him, and climbed out of the bus.

Maureen walked back a couple of rows, past Tenato to where Elení Montes was sitting, staring out the window. She swung in and sat next to her.

"You O.K.?" she asked, briefly spacing out on the language barrier.

"Sí," she said.

Maureen cocked her head. "¿Hablas Inglés?" she asked.

Elení shrugged, unfolded her hands, and said, "No, sólo algunas frases, como '¿Dónde está el baño?' y 'No dispares, no tengo dinero.'"

Maureen poked Tenato, who was watching from the seat ahead of them. "What'd she just say, and don't give me any shit—"

"Mierda," Elení offered, before he could respond.

"She said, 'Only a few phrases, like, Where's the bathroom?', and 'Don't shoot, I don't have any money,' and, at the end there, she translated the word 'shit' for you," Tenato offered.

"Tell her, in about a day, we'll be in City by the Lake, and she can see Estrellita again," Maureen ordered, no longer willing to give Tenato any breathing room.

Tenato dutifully translated, and as he did, she began crying, then wordlessly held up her shopping bag full of odds and ends and loose clothing, offering it up to Maureen in a 'Take this' gesture.

"She thinks she has to give you her stuff, in exchange for you taking her up North," Tenato offered.

Thinking this entire enterprise was the most depressing thing she'd ever seen, Maureen first assured Elení she could keep her clothes, gently pushing the shopping bag back to Elení, then said to Tenato, "I don't know how you do this work."

He looked out the window and nodded. "Yeah, it sucks, but with a record, it's all I could get. Regular law enforcement won't touch you, even if it's a chicken-shit misdemeanor rap."

"Mierda de pollo," Elení said, demonstrating some of the English translation skills she'd picked up crammed into detention centers.

"Tell her it's O.K., she doesn't need to keep translating for me anymore," Maureen commanded Tenato, and she got up to see what was keeping Peter Meadows.

* *

"See if you can find out what's dragging out the reunion bus ride," Crump asked Steve Barnacle. "I'd like to have them here for the Patriot Act trial."

"Sounds like Meadows and the crew are still giving her a bunch of purely sadistic crap, dragging it out as long as possible."

"Crap is right. In a perfect world, I'd like to get Mom back here and get the Asylum hearing tied in with the underlying Patriot Act case. Sounds like Judge Culpepper gave us that option, but I worry Judge Haverhorn won't take Elení Montes's asylum claim if we're done with the trial. Handler and U.S.C.I.S. will do anything to keep these folks apart—the Montes women have become a symbol of the Administration's sick immigration policies, on both sides of the fence, and I worry we may miss our opportunity if we need to try this thing before we can get her back here. Ernstmeyer and Stuggs really are torturing these folks, and now that everybody's watching this case, they want the outcome to be a poke in the eye to the entire family re-unification effort. I want Estrellita's case before Judge Haverhorn, not some Administrative Law Judge back in El Paso, who's got three hundred other asylum cases that week."

Barnacle was sitting across from Crump, flipping through a file. "One thing we could do to add pressure is move on those judgment enforcement citations—pick their pockets for your million dollar judgments. We can't do

Meadows while he's on the court-ordered sightseeing tour with Maureen and Ms. Montes, but we can certainly do Handler."

Crump nodded. "Yeah, he's got to be in town this week anyway—trial starts next week—so let's notice up the Citation before Judge Salazar, and start taking a walk through Warren Handler's bank accounts."

Sophie walked in. "Hey, Steve," she said, glancingly at Barnacle, who was now a regular sight in the office. "Angelo's coming by……just thought I'd better warn you."

Barnacle got up and left, just as Angelo was walking in.

"You get that Army of God, that Cornelius guy, into solitary?" Crump asked.

"Dere workin' on it—County Jail ain't exactly duh place for special treatment. S' pretty overcrowded, and duh County's goin' broke, so extra secur'ty is askin' a lot."

Crump nodded. "Seems like everybody we're dealing with is 'in custody,'" Crump observed. "This Army of God guy is important, and, given what they tried to do to me in the cage, I worry about him."

"Ben says dey got somebody alerted on the inside, but you know how dat goes."

"They get a statement from the guy yet?"

"Says dere workin' on it—"

"What'd they offer him in exchange?" Crump asked.

"Knock duh charges down to ten to twelve, breaking and entering, assault and a hate crime," Tutulio offered.

"Shit—that's not much better than attempted murder. No wonder he's not flipped yet. What's the hate crime? Trying to kill lawyers?"

Turulio laughed, his mouth closed as he tried to downplay his amusement. "No, Mary told th' 'vestigators she's a atheist, and Markle says that qualifies as a religion, an that's why he's chargin' him as a hater—"

"You gotta tell them to drop that hate crime shit—Mary was probably being sarcastic—she used to be a Lutheran. I *want* this guy to flip," Crump urgently interrupted. "What are you guys doing on the Mary watch going forward? This Boofus shitweasel's probably got a crew of conscripts behind him."

Turulio pulled out a pocket calendar that looked like he'd been buried with it. "Still round the clock," he said, opening it up. "Moneybags is dere now. Dis gotta be gettin' expensive," he added.

"That's O.K.. Your buddy the Attorney General is about to pay for the entire undertaking, including your Christmas Bonus."

* *

"Mr. Handler, how old are you?" Barnacle asked.

"Seventy-one."

Barnacle had Warren Handler on the witness stand before Judge Salazar.

"And, before you were Attorney General, you were a partner at the law firm of Stenson and Willis?"

"Thirty-five years as a partner, five as an associate before that," Handler responded.

"And, nonetheless, you expect me to believe your entire net worth consists of two heavily-mortgaged houses and a checking account?"

Judge Salazar was looking at the same questionnaire as Barnacle, one Handler had completed for the citation proceeding in which Crump was to collect his million dollar judgement against Handler. The Judge didn't believe it, either.

"That's correct," Handler responded, somewhat oddly proud.

"Must be tough to support your lifestyle, what with the two houses, on that shoestring?" Barnacle pressed.

"We get by—"

"Mr. Handler, you understand, if you can't satisfy this judgment from current assets, I will need to garnish your wages," Judge Salazar reminded him.

"Don't think you can do that," Handler quipped.

"Why not?" the Judge followed up.

"My Government paycheck is exempt under the Federal Debt Collections Act—I just converted to a Government Pension, which is protected."

"When did you do that?" Barnacle asked.

Handler, obviously trying to be a smart ass, looked at his watch and said, "Ten thirty, this morning."

"Sounds like a fraudulent conveyance to me," Barnacle commented.

"Me, too," the Judge echoed.

"Mr. Handler, have you ever transferred any property to a person, an entity or a trust, for less than full and adequate compensation or consideration?" Barnacle pressed on.

"Once," Handler stated.

"When was that?"

Handler again looked at his watch. "Nine thirty, this morning."

"You have to be joking," the Judge cut in.

"Routine estate planning. Set up a trust with my wife, Priscilla, as trustee."

"How much property did you transfer in trust this morning during this 'Routine estate planning,'?" Barnacle asked.

"Nineteen million, nine-hundred fifty-nine dollars, and some change," Handler said, smirking.

"Your Honor, we will be moving to set aside that transfer," Barnacle announced.

"I expect you will," the Judge said, nodding.

"One more question, Mr. Attorney General. When did you first discuss setting up this trust with your lawyer?" Barnacle inquired.

Handler again looked at his watch. "Eight-thirty, this morning," he said. "But, you can have this," he added, as he took off his wristwatch and handed it to Steve Barnacle.

* *

The rolling contempt citation that was the El Paso County Prison Laundry Bus pulled through the entrance gates of Fort Leonard Wood, outside of Rolla Missouri. It was midnight.

"O.K., now we're stopping at *an Army Base?*" Maureen complained.

"We're on a budget, and this is all we can afford. Don't worry, we'll have separate barracks and bunks for boys and girls, and we'll be in guest quarters—"

"I'd rather keep driving," Maureen insisted.

"I need to sleep," the bus driver said, as he ambled off the bus. Oblivious to any power struggle going on behind him, he walked into the base office and disappeared.

Maureen walked back to check on Elení Montes, who was sound asleep, her arms wrapped tightly around her shopping bag full of clothes.

"Tell her we are stopping for the night and she gets to sleep in a bunk," Maureen ordered Tenato, who woke the woman up and translated.

Maureen and Elení trudged off the bus, checked into the base office and emerged with blankets and pillows. The Visitors' Barracks they were offered was full of empty bunks. Maureen and Elení settled in, both electing to sleep fully clothed.

"Just saying, reveille is at oh-six hundred hours," the night guard said, before she left out the side door.

"That's O.K., we hope to be gone by then," Maureen said, as she pulled the blanket over her head.

In the morning, Maureen and Elení were up and waiting, long before Meadows, the driver and Tenato awoke. They were given their blankets and pillows to keep, caught some breakfast in a chow line, then got back on the bus and waited, swatting at the largest mosquitoes Maureen had ever seen.

They waited over two hours, drifting in and out of sleep, rousing occasionally. There was no sign of Meadows, the driver or Tenato, until the driver eventually emerged from the Fort Administration building.

"You folks sleep well?" the bus driver asked, as he climbed back into the bus.

"It's like, almost lunch time. What have you guys been doing?"

"Sorry," the driver said. "We all overslept, I guess."

"Let's just get going," Maureen ordered, and they swung by the office to pick up Meadows and Tenato.

Tenato got on, followed by Peter Meadows.

"You guys are a day's drive from City by the Lake. I've got to tie up some loose ends here—go ahead without me. I'll commission a base vehicle and catch up with you at journey's end," Meadows announced.

"The Judge said you were our escort—" Maureen began.

"And, I'll get you the last leg—these fine gentlemen can get you over the state line and home. I'll make sure we see you two ladies at the reunification," he said, as he rounded out the folding bus door and off the bus.

The driver and Tenato followed him off. When they got midway to the base office, the trio stopped. Meadows said something to the Driver and Tenato, who both nodded, then they separated.

Maureen watched Meadows walk back to the Base Administration Building, as the driver and Tenato returned to the bus.

"If this bus stops again for anything other than a roadblock, I'm calling Judge Culpepper and swearing out a contempt citation," Maureen said, threatening Tenato, as the bus started up and they passed back out through the gates of Fort Leonard Wood.

Three hours later, they crossed the Mississippi River, finally progressing on the last leg of the trip.

"Tell her we're almost there—six hours, give or take," Maureen ordered Tenato, who complied and translated.

They were driving up a four-lane highway, with a grassy median separating the two Northbound lanes from the Southbound. It seemed like the middle of nowhere, farm country, nothing much to see but rolling fields and windmills. The road had been raised up, with a running ditch to the Northbound side of the road. The only sign of life was an abandoned riding lawnmower, stalled in the grass in the central ditch running parallel to the roadway.

Hours later, as they passed a small river and a stretch of heavily-wooded, undeveloped land, a black, older model, broken-down pickup truck sped past them in the passing lane to their left. It was getting dark. Both Eleni and Maureen were nodding off, when they heard the driver lay into his horn and felt him swerve slightly. He started hollering at the truck driver up ahead.

"Hey, asshole, stay in one lane," he shouted, as he suddenly hit the brakes, tossing Tenato into the aisle, when he jumped up to see what was going on. As Maureen stood to check things out, the bus suddenly accelerated and she and Tenato stumbled backwards, both grabbing the seat handles to stay upright.

"This guy must be *drunk!*" the driver yelled.

Maureen regained her balance and moved forward in enough time to see that the busted-up black pickup was coasting along erratically, just ahead of them. It was slowing down suddenly, so the bus driver had to slam on the brakes to keep from hitting the pickup, then, just as suddenly, the pickup sped up. When the pickup truck again slowed down, it began swerving from side to side and lane to lane, so they could not accelerate to pass the old beater. The bus driver was pushing the limits of their vintage, nineteen-fifties, manual transmission bus, trying to maneuver around the pickup.

"This guy *on* something?" Tenato shouted, as he and Maureen held tight to the corners of the bus seats, rounded, worn handles with ages-old green paint chipping off the piping.

"This is no accident," Maureen said, as she turned to see Elení, who was hunkering down in her seat, hiding behind her brown paper shopping bag and the tote from the base.

As Maureen turned to watch the swerving truck through the driver's windshield, the pickup driver suddenly slammed on the brakes. Their driver, with whatever reflexes remained in his whiskey-drenched, sixty-eight-year old body, swerved to the right to avoid ploughing into the pickup. As the bus turned, Maureen could feel the rough at the edge of the roadway, the undulating pavement on the shoulder of the road vibrating up through what was left of the bus's suspension.

She felt it before she could see it: The bus was careening off the road, taking out a road sign that said, "Compost Preserve, Next Five Miles". As they rumbled down into the ravine along the road, the bus slowly canted at an angle to the right. As it tore into some bushes whipping past, the bus completely listed onto its side. The driver, who like everybody else was not belted in, was thrown sideways out of his seat. His flying body ripped the stick shift out of its floor-mounted casing, and he disappeared through the sliding doors which swung open as the bus kept hurtling on its side.

Maureen was wrenching herself into a position to dive into an open seat, when the bus hit a pile of moraine as tall as a ranch house, slamming to a stop. The last thing she remembered, before she blacked out, was a bumper sticker she glimpsed on that pickup truck, one that read, "The Army of God Wants *You!*"

* *

Maureen McDougal's first thought, being a good Catholic, was, "Damn, I'm dead and I'm in Hell." Her second thought was, "I didn't think it would *smell* this bad."

As she shook herself back into consciousness, she realized the stink was related to the road sign they'd taken out. They were slowly sinking into the dregs of a Green Initiative, a roadside composting project that filled the ravine along the highway with rotting, wet, methane-billowing dead leaves, stagnant water and generally rancid bio waste of all kinds. It was both the reason they were all not dead, and, if they stayed put, the reason they might all die.

The bus was lying on its right side, and with most of the sliding windows stuck halfway open, black, fetid ooze, on the consistency of chunky-style crude oil, was seeping into the bus. Elení Montes, who for the first time in her life had been rewarded for being destitute, escaped the worst of the crash by clinging to her shopping bag full of clothing, a low-tech version of an air bag. She had only a few bumps and bruises. Tenato was still fairly out of it, having hit his head on one of the floor-to-ceiling grip poles straddling the driver's seat and the aisle. He had fallen backwards in between two seats and was still resting there, head first, his boots sticking up and pointing forward, so he looked like a confused rider, occupying the seat upside-down.

Maureen was somewhere in-between: She had broken the last two fingers on her left hand, was darkened all over her face, a mix of ooze and bruise, and her slacks were torn up the side, with some minor bleeding around a bruise on her left knee.

With the bus lying on its right side, the access door was impassable. Maureen wrenched herself up from the slough she'd occupied at the moment of the crash. She climbed, seat to seat, swinging monkey-style, grip to grip, until she got to Elení, who was also pulling herself out of the ooze, which was streaming in through the opened windows.

"You O.K.?" She asked.

"Si', mas o menos," Elení said, nodding.

"Stay here," she cautioned, and to make herself clear, she pantomimed grabbing the seat handles with both hands. "See?" she asked, and Elení nodded, holding tight to the handles.

Maureen climbed back to the front to check on Tenato. She grabbed his feet and turned him on his side, checked that he was breathing and had a pulse, then she picked up his dead-weight head by the hair and slapped him across the face. He recoiled, shaking his head back and forth, like a bee had flown in his ears.

"Whaaaa—"

"Get up, pal. I can't carry both of you out of here, and if it's between you and her," she said, pointing a thumb back at Elení, "you're the one becomes a fossil."

Maureen worked her way across the handles, swinging seat to seat like a child on playground equipment, until she got to the back door of the bus. It was, being a prison vehicle, padlocked shut. She tried kicking out the window in the back door, but being a vintage fifties vehicle, it was not yet equipped with shatter-proof glass with that unique, break-away quality.

"I am going to fucking *murder* Peter Meadows," she grumbled to herself.

"We're going to need to climb out one of the open windows on the left side of the bus," she shouted down the length of the aisle, which Tenato accurately translated, his sense of humor having abandoned him when he was conked on the head. "I'm the smallest one here. Let me try first," she said, as she swung back through the air to the middle of the bus, where one of the windows was almost fully opened, pointing up at a starless, darkening sky.

"Why has nobody spotted us or called the cops?" she asked aloud, but then she could see that they were sunk so deeply into the ravine, they were invisible from the road. "Where's my phone?" she asked, as she patted herself down. Not on her, that was apparent.

"You got your phone?" she shouted up at Tenato, who patted himself and shrugged, holding out his hands in a "Who Me?" gesture.

"That's a new smell," she said out loud, just as she realized it was gasoline leaking into the ooze that was seeping into the bus. "Great," she said. "This wasn't already bad enough, now we're *combustible*."

She climbed up to what was now the inner roof of the bus, the left passenger side, and tried to open the window wider. While the half-opened window, stuck there to keep people *from* getting out, was almost wide enough to let them escape, it was going to be a tight fit for Tenato. Elení Montes was compact enough, but she looked like the last time she had any muscle tone was in high school.

"Mrs. Montes and I got to take our blankets and pillows from the base with us when we left. They're somewhere on this bus. Go find them while I climb out. Once I get out of here, we'll use them to hoist you out," Maureen ordered.

Maureen climbed up to the open window and realized her only hope was to climb out head first and pull herself up by her elbows, once the top half of her body was out of the bus. Her broken fingers were useless and throbbed if she pressed them into service. She pulled herself up and on her second try, she managed to get all the way out, doing a gymnast's leg flare to end up sitting across the half-opened widows. Her broken fingers stung, but otherwise, she could move freely. She looked down into the ooze and saw she'd be useless standing along-side the bus, sinking into the gunk.

"Get me one of the blankets," she shouted to Tenato. When he handed it out to her, she let one end drop lengthwise back into the bus, then hollered, "Tell Elení to grab hold of this, and when I pull her up to the window, she should pull herself out."

She heard the translation and then felt Elení tug on the blanket. She braced her feet against the opening of a window and began to pull. Elení, who hadn't had a balanced meal in over a year, was gloriously underweight, and as she slowly emerged through the window, Maureen was able to give her a hand and pulled her all the way out.

Tenato tossed the other blanket through the window. "This oughta be good," she said, and Elení nodded.

After an unsuccessful try at hoisting him out, complicated by his weight and general circumference, she yelled back, "Tie the blankets together, and toss one end out. Make sure the knot holds—use a slipknot—"

"What's a slipknot?" he yelled back.

"This is what happens when they restrict membership in the Girl Scouts to *women*," she commented to Elení, who said, in response, "Gordo."

"I heard that!" Tenato shouted out.

Maureen looked quizzically at Elení, who offered, "Fat" as the translation.

"Give it to me—I'll do the knot," Maureen shouted, and the second blanket came up through the window.

Once she had secured the knot, she tossed one end down and yelled, "Hold this!", as she signaled to Elení to join her as they, one after another, jumped down off the bus into the ooze.

"Where you going?" Tenato shouted from inside the bus.

"Just wait," she shouted back.

They were standing almost waist deep in the muck, with the bus now half submerged in it. That was the good news: There was solid footing underneath the muck. The bad news was that the bus, and the muck immediately surrounding it, was smelling less and less like death, and more and more like gasoline.

"Stay here and hold the blanket," she said, again pantomiming, which seemed to help. Elení complied, even though she was being instructed by a near-perfect stranger to stand in gasoline-filled muck, just to rescue another perfect stranger who had recently been caging her underneath a highway underpass.

Maureen climbed up the ravine and out to the edge of the road. She tried waving down a few drivers, but nobody stopped, and it occurred to her that if anybody did, that might be a fate worse than rotting in the compost heap. She looked around and eventually found a long, straight branch twice as tall as she was, which she carted back to the bus. She slid down into the ooze and planted it into the hard ground underneath the gunk, then told Elení to hold it up, as she tied the loose end of the blanket around the opposite end of the branch.

Tenato, who was watching from inside the bus, began trying to shimmy up the blanket, but he had to weigh over two hundred pounds, so it wasn't going well.

As Maureen held the branch straight up, she signaled to Elení to push the branch away from the bus with two hands, both of them holding on tight.

"Leverage," Maureen proclaimed.

"Apertura de lata," Elení offered, and from inside the bus, Tenato shouted, "Can opener?"

"That works," Maureen said, as she shouted, "Pull yourself up on the window frame as we pull you out." As they wrenched the branch grindingly away from the bus, Tenato appeared, head first, then made a terribly inelegant spectacle of pulling on the blanket as he squeezed himself through the too-small opening. As he did, his pants peeled off, but as proof that there was in fact a God, his underpants remained on his backside.

As he jumped off the bus into the muck, they turned to climb out of the ravine and flag down a vehicle. Tenato announced, "You people got fucked. You think it's a coincidence that Meadows got off in Rolla?"

While Elení, no stranger to hitchhiking, began waving down a ride, Maureen responded, "My partner Crump always says, 'There's no Hell deep enough for him to hide away in….."

27.
I THINK WE'RE SUPPOSED TO TURN AROUND………

"Are you this Crump guy?" the voice in the receiver called out.

"Uuhh, yes, I—"

"This is the Effingham County Sheriff. We picked up two women and a guy in his underpants, out on Route 45, came out of the compost trench from a crashed bus. One of 'em says she works for—"

"Gimme that," Crump heard in the background, as the phone made a clapping noise.

"Crump, get your ass down here," Maureen shouted into the receiver.

"Maureen, where are—"

"Damn it, Crump, I almost got killed. The bus driver's for sure dead, and we had to climb out of this wrecked prison bus before it caught fire, and it was sinking into *shit*….." and then, she broke down shivering, and couldn't say another word.

Crump talked to the Sheriff when he got back on the line, then to Tenato, and then he asked, "You guys still at the hospital? Stay there," and he ran out of his office to rent a van.

* *

"Wow. You look terrible."

"Thanks," Maureen nodded, looking like a monk, wrapped in a brown, heavy blanket over her shoulders. "I got slammed into a compost heap in a speeding bus—what's *your* excuse?"

"That's nasty," Crump said. "Look, before I drive you outta here, you need to give me the entire story. Wade Solley is waiting for your affidavit, and as soon as he gets it, he's going before Judge Culpepper on an emergency contempt petition, out in the California class action. He thinks the Judge will grind Peter Meadow's *ass*. The Sheriff tells me they found your bus driver's body. Sounds like whatever you did in that bus, it turned Tenato's head around—now *he's* prepared to talk, maybe even testify."

"O.K., let me check on Elení."

"How's she?" Crump asked.

"Mostly shook up and confused."

Maureen limped out of her hospital room, crossing the hall to check on Elení Montes. Crump sat back and slowly realized how much trauma must have occurred. Maureen's face looked like she'd been working on an oil rig when they struck fresh crude, a mix of bruises and sludge the staff still hadn't completely scrubbed away. Her left pinky and ring fingers were taped together and wrapped with a splint, tied to her good fingers. She had a noticeable limp from a couple of banged up ligaments in her right knee.

And, compared to Tenato, she looked *good*.

Crump banged out an affidavit on the Sheriff's typewriter, had her sign it, then faxed it to Wade Solley, together with pictures of all three living victims and a Sheriffs' preliminary report on the dead bus driver.

On the way out to the van, he stopped to speak with the Sheriff, an older guy with a long, weather-beaten face and no sense of humor.

"Look, just keep searching for the pickup—I'm betting this asshole still has his 'Army of God' bumper sticker on it."

The Sheriff looked up from the notes on his clipboard. "We got more of them down here than you might think. A lot of little, single denominational, fundamentalist churches, with lots of Anti-Abortion extremists in the parking lots on Sunday morning—"

"Look, these guys are *killing* people, and they're doing it in league with a bunch of crooked lawyers."

"Rings my chimes," the Sheriff said. "That underpants fella, Tomato, he's stickin' around to give us a hand—says he was pals with the driver. Says he'll join up with you next week in City by the Lake."

Crump, Elení and Maureen all collected what was left of their belongings and walked out to the van Crump had rented. It was getting late and they still had a few hours to drive.

"Meadows was under orders to stay with you. The last leg of the trip was supposed to be to the Edgewater Armory Detention Center, but I'm not taking any more chances," Crump advised. "I sent a message to Handler's lawyers that we'd be taking Elení Montes directly to St. Vincent's."

Maureen threw down her bag of hospital gowns and slippers. "Why'd you do *that*?" she asked, clearly pissed off. "He's gonna try one more time—these guys are *obsessed*."

"Yeah, how 'bout that," Crump responded. "One *last* time," and they all piled into the van.

* *

It was nearing midnight when Crump's rented van approached St. Vincent's Hospital, on the Northwest outskirts of the City by the Lake. While staffing in the Adolescent Psych Ward would ordinarily be winding down to the boneyard shift by this time of night, he'd been calling nonstop from the Effingham Sheriff's Office and the Hospital, making sure Dr. Trimble would be there and staffed up. He particularly asked for Giampetro, who Barnacle had cleared of his brief incarceration on battery charges, by arguing successfully a "Defense of Others" claim, which eventually led Derek Markle to drop all charges against the large, masticating man.

Crump had made a series of additional calls from Effingham, too. What he had planned took a fair amount of coordination.

Maureen and Elení Montes were both snoozing in the second row of the van, as Crump approached the Hospital. As he expected, there was one of those Federal Marshals' black SUVs, parked in front of a fast food joint's lot, across and down the street. A couple of slabs were sitting in the front seat smoking, with another guy sitting in the darkness of the backseat. He wondered how long they'd been there and what they expected to do to get around the injunction, barring them from close contact with St. Vincent's.

He circled the Hospital one more time, checking his watch to see if it was past midnight. At 12:01, he pulled into the biggest lot surrounding St. Vincent's, which was also the one farthest from the Adolescent Psych Ward.

"Wake up guys," he said. After years raising three kids, he had to stop himself from also calling out, "Time to pee."

Maureen was not moving, so as Elení slowly came to, she looked at Maureen, head twisted horizontal like she'd passed out, and said, "Infeliz mujer," which Crump understood to mean, "Poor woman." Given what Elení had just been through, it was a spontaneous gesture that momentarily grabbed Crump, part in sympathy, part in anger at all things *Stuggs*.

"Almost over," he said, then he gently shoved Maureen, who bolted awake, blurted out "Are we there yet?" before she was fully acclimated. This time, Crump couldn't help himself, so he responded with, "Time to pee."

They piled out of the van.

Crump climbed back in when he saw that Elení had left her Effingham County Hospital Tote Bag and the shopping bag with all her worldly possessions, in the van.

"Here, you need to take these," he said, holding it out.

"She going someplace?" Maureen asked. "I thought this was a visit, then she needed to go to the Edgewater Armory?"

"No more chicken wire," Crump said, as he locked up the van.

"Something you're not telling me?" Maureen asked.

"If I told you everything, you wouldn't need me around anymore. Let's go visiting," he added, as they began slowly walking across the parking lot. They had to cross three mostly empty lots, burning with silver-lit mercury-vapor overhead lights, before they got to a lot close enough to still be occupied by parked cars.

As they approached the entry to Building Six, they were met by two bulky looking guys dressed all in black. As the men approached from the side, one of them took out what looked like a simple billfold, held it up, dropped out some unreadable ID cards and announced, "You the parties escorting Elení Montes?"

They stopped.

"Does anything good happen if I answer that question?" Crump asked.

"Just answer it," the guy with the billfold said, stuffing his wallet into the back pocket of his black paratrooper pants.

"Sure, as soon as you tell me who you are," Crump said, pushing back.

"Security," the shorter guy with the pug's face, spit out.

"No, you're not—the Hospital knows we're coming—"

"Why are we talking to these jerks?" Maureen asked, as she started to walk past one of them. As she did, pug-face shot a forearm out and clotheslined her, hitting her neck and stopping her cold, mid-step.

"God damn—" she started to swear, when half a dozen armed police and sheriff's officers came pouring out of the entrance to Building Six. Three of them pointed guns at the phony security guys, announced, "You're under arrest," and cuffed the pair.

"You O.K.?" Crump asked Maureen, who nodded, as she was massaging the front of her neck, while Elení Montes took Maureen by the chin and turned her head from left to right, like a doctor looking into each ear for wax.

"You guys want to tell us who you're working for?" Crump asked. "Who knows, you might get off with simple assault and battery."

"Fuck off," the taller guy said, as the Lakeside County Sheriff's deputy started to turn the cuffed man around, to walk him to a squad.

Bulldog said, "Private security detail," as he too, was turned toward the waiting squad.

"I can help here," Crump announced. "It's not you guys I want—my partner here might *kill* one of you—me, I just want to know who hired you."

"We were told this was a legit security detail," Bulldog offered.

"Why don't you give a statement to these gentlemen," Crump offered. "I *know* who hired you, but if I have to prove it, you get no points for cooperating," he concluded, as he led Elení and Maureen to the door.

"We'll take them to County, Mr. Crump," one of the deputies shouted back their way.

"You know these sheriff's guys?'" Maureen asked, more than mildly annoyed.

"Yeah, I called them out. I knew Handler and Meadows would send somebody new, because they've been ordered to stay one thousand feet away from this place. I'll bet all the money in my checkbook that these frustrated cop-show extras are independent contractors, hired by Meadows and the D.O.J."

"The Court order—" Maureen began.

"The Court order says, 'No Handler, no Meadows, no Federal Marshals, and no *employees* of D.O.J.'—they thought they'd get around it with hired, private security."

"Somebody's going to jail," Maureen said, shaking her head, as they were met at the door by Dr. Trimble and Giampetro.

"Doctor Trimble," Crump began his introduction, then realized he didn't know if "Giampetro" was a first name, a last name or maybe something in between. "And Mr. Giampetro. This is Elení Montes, Mother of Estrellita Montes."

"Señora Montes, soy la doctora de su hija, Amelia Trimble," Doctor Trimble offered, giving the woman a full embrace.

"¿Está enferma?" Elení asked.

"She asking, 'Is she sick?'" Crump whispered to Maureen.

"Al principio, ella estaba luchando, pero ella es mucho mejor ahora," Doctor Trimble responded.

As they went through the search and seizure routine at the front desk, Doctor Trimble pulled Crump aside.

"I just told her Estrellita is doing much better now. She's been on solid food for weeks. She could actually check out any time." She paused. "I know you said your partner went through a lot to get her here, but, my God, she looks like she's been run over by a bus."

"Actually...." Crump started to say, when Maureen and Elení approached them.

"O.K., let's go," Doctor Trimble announced. "The ward is pretty much shut down for the night, so let's all be very quiet," she said, as they boarded the elevator, Giampetro in tow.

When they got upstairs and Giampetro cleared the sliding door, Crump let Maureen lead Elení to Estrellita's room. The two of them opened the door to the darkened room, then, without turning on the light, Maureen showed her to the bed, where her daughter was sound asleep.

Elení slowly and carefully sat on the edge of the bed. She placed a hand on her daughter's resting arm, and the Kid began to roll over.

"Lita," her mother whispered, and through the dim light from the hallway, Estrellita recognized her mother. She sat bolt upright and flung her arms around her mother's neck, squeezing the daylights out of her.

"I think we're supposed to turn around," Crump whispered.

"Go ahead—I'm staying," Maureen whispered back, as she stood over them like a painter admiring her work.

Crump, Giampetro and the Doctor slipped back into the hallway.

"*Damn*, all this time, and we didn't know her nickname was 'Lita,'" Crump observed.

"These are *people*," Giampetro barked, as he turned and walked away.

"That guy should run for President," Crump said.

Doctor Trimble nodded. "I'd vote for him." She paused, crossing her arms. "You know, I thought this was never going to happen. When you first showed up, I thought you were some half-baked, almost retired ambulance chaser, who was fulfilling some kind of ethics-driven pro-bono thing that was required, just to keep your license—"

"Uuhh, yeah, that pretty much describes me—"

She hugged him, mid-sentence, then stepped back.

Crump, who didn't do well with public displays of emotion, said, "Actually, you want to thank somebody, you should be hugging Maureen, who almost got killed getting her back here."

"Yes, and I will, but this whole thing was your idea—"

"Actually, in a roundabout way, it was *your* idea."

Maureen emerged from the room and said, "O.K., you two, break it up. What happens now? We need to take Elení to the Detention Center at the Edgewater Armory?"

Crump laughed. "Give me some credit, McDougal."

"You get me appointed?" Doctor Trimble asked.

"You bet."

"Appointed?" Maureen asked.

"She's now also Elení's guardian. They're both checking out of here and going home with the Doc until we can get them their asylum hearing," Crump explained.

"*Really*?" Maureen asked.

"What'd you think I was doing back here, while you and Mom in there were taking your time, meandering across America?"

"Excuse us, Doctor, but we need to leave now, so you don't get to watch me *strangling* my partner here…."

* *

As Crump and Maureen left the building, Maureen asked, "So, how'd you get the Doc appointed Mama Montes's guardian? The woman seems more put together than *you* are—"

"I used the 'Idleness and Debauchery' clause—"

"That's still in the guardianship code?" Maureen asked, astounded.

"The Good Protestants that put that in, a hundred fifty years ago, haven't left the building yet."

"So, how could she be guilty of either?"

"I relied on 'Idleness'—"

"Crump—"

"*Whaat?*.....when you found her, she was just standing around in a crowd, doing nothing, probably been doing some version of that for weeks.... Look, I wanted her to have a court-appointed private advocate, not just some over-worked social-service agency, and the Doc volunteered."

"Doctor Trimble's a pretty tough character," Maureen observed.

"Watching kids getting driven to suicide probably cooks your DNA a little...." Crump paused. "It's cooking *mine*."

Maureen nodded. "This ending is kind of anti-climactic."

"Hmmhuh," Crump cleared his throat. "Well, there's good news there—we're not done for the evening yet—"

"Crump, I haven't seen my family in over *a week*—Whit is gonna have you *arrested* if I don't get home soon."

"Relax. We're *almost* done," he offered, as he waved at a car off in the distance, sitting on the edge of the parking lot.

It was a sheriff's cruiser. It pulled up next to them, stopped, as the driver's window whirred down.

"You guys ready? Past midnight, so the stuff is effective and official now," Crump opined.

"Yeah," the driver nodded as he put the car in gear. "They still down there?" he asked.

Crump moved to the edge of the block, then craned his neck to see two blocks down the street. "Yes, still there. It's the gray-haired-accountant-look-alike you want—the guys in front are just marshals—your man is the suit in the backseat," he said. "Just wait for me," he added, as they drove out of the lot and down the street.

"You wanna tell me what's going on?" Maureen asked.

"I wanted to surprise you."

Crump and Maureen got in the van and drove slowly out of the lot, down the street after the sheriff's cruiser. They stopped and parked across from the black SUV, which was being approached by the Sheriff's deputies.

"Get out of the car," one deputy ordered. He was carrying a packet of papers.

The two slabs in the front seat climbed out. "What the fuck?" one of them started.

"You, too, Mr. Backseat," the gun-toting deputy ordered.

A very pissed-off looking Peter Meadows got out of the car.

"Look, we were more than one thousand feet away from the Hospital—we measured," Meadows started to say, when the deputy slapped him with the process he was carrying.

"Quentin Peter Meadows, you've been served with a contempt order, issued by the U.S. District Court for the Southern District of California. Pursuant to that order, we have a capias attachment for your custody. You are under arrest. The capias says you're to be extradited to California to answer for the contempt citation. You have the right to remain silent—"

"Save it—I know the drill," Meadows told the arresting deputy.

Crump leaned out the window of the van and waved at Meadows.

He and Maureen watched as Meadows was led away from his marshals. As his SUV sped away without him, the sheriff's deputies did the whole perp-walk thing, cuffing Meadows, walking him to their squad, then placing a splayed hand across the top of his head and forcing him into the back of the car.

"They taking him to County?" Maureen asked.

Crump nodded. "Then the Airport. Warren Handler's going to need a new lawyer for the Patriot Act case."

As Crump started up the van, Maureen looked ahead, down the darkened street, and said, "You know, it was *unbelievable* in there, just watching the two of them hug each other," she paused, "but this was *better*......."

28.
"GOOD" TERRORISTS AND "BAD" TERRORISTS..........

"They said he tried to hang himself—"

"What a coincidence," Maureen injected.

"Look, when Turulio ripped off his earlobes, the guy asked me for an ice bag so he could put 'em back on. He didn't strike me as a member of a suicide cult, Army of God or no Army of God," Crump observed.

"I know, and the States' Attorney was in the process of negotiating a cooperation deal with him," Barnacle added. "I think they want to take a bite out of Handler and Meadows."

Crump, Maureen and Steve Barnacle were sitting around Crump's desk, preparing for trial. They were discussing whether the nearly unconscious Cornelius Boofus, Mary's assailant, could be counted on to testify after an apparent suicide attempt. None of them believed the alleged suicide was legit.

"They get any names out of him?" Crump asked.

"Before, or after, they cut him down?" Barnacle wondered.

"I thought he couldn't talk—bruised windpipe and all?" Maureen asked.

"No, he's comin' back, or so Turulio tells me," Barnacle added.

"Don't tell me Markle's got Turulio in there, participating with the interrogation," Crump moaned.

"Actually," Barnacle offered, "I heard the guy *asked* for Turulio—Markle says Boofus figured Turulio was the only one crazy enough to scare off the people he's really worried about."

Barnacle was looking at his notes from the call earlier that day, alerting him to the supposed "suicide" attempt of Cornelius Boofus. Boofus miraculously managed to allegedly hang himself in Solitary Confinement, using the circular towel from the prison shower-room's hand-washing apparatus. "There was round-the-clock guard watch on the guy, and somebody gets 'confused' about assignments, and faster than you can say, 'Warren Handler and his band of Merry Men,' the guy ends up swinging like a dummy on a parade float—"

"*Names*, can he give us *names*?" Crump wheeled the discussion back around, without looking up from his notes.

"They're working on it," Barnacle reported.

"He's not gonna budge until they get down to three-to-five, and even then, they'd still need to drop the attempted murder charge," Crump predicted.

"Think Mary'd agree to dropping that charge?" Maureen asked.

"I think, if Mary had a building pass at County, she'd be a *suspect*," Crump offered.

* *

As Crump, Maureen, Steve Barnacle and Doctor Trimble walked through the Federal courthouse plaza on the first day of the Patriot Act trial, there were bobbing signs floating above the crowds, with "Impeach Stuggs" and

"Deport Handler" slogans waving in the air. They all four hovered outside the revolving doors, as Maureen fished out her phone and I.D. While they paused, a spontaneous cheer broke out, along with requests for Maureen's autograph. News coverage of her exploits during the bus crash had turned her into a celebrity.

"Hope Handler sees this," Crump mumbled to himself.

The hallway outside Judge Haverhorn's courtroom was packed with spectators, and when they ploughed through the throng and opened the doors, the courtroom was just as overwhelmed. Rows of gallery seating were overflowing with reporters, with a few getting slowly shoved off the ends of the benches.

"Is this a good thing or a bad thing?" Doctor Trimble asked, as they set down their cases on the counsel table on the right side of the courtroom.

"Could cut either way," Crump offered. "The Judge is getting a lot of Cable-News Crank-Talk about impeachment, for not tossing the case out in the first place. I think the news coverage will either turn some heads, or just get more folks calling for her head on the block."

"Looks like they're all reporters," Barnacle observed.

"Not *all*," Maureen noted, as Warren Handler, his new lawyer Phil Plint, and his even newer lawyer, Gregory Stenson, barreled into the courtroom.

"Wonder if Stenson will want to settle *this* case?" Crump mumbled, under his breath. "How 'bout we just fire a *few* of the terrorists?" he added, mocking Stenson's overtures in the Carrington Prep case.

As they all unpacked binders, the Judge appeared in her street clothes, checking out the court reporters and clerks. She asked if everyone had arrived, and when both sides answered "Present", she left briefly, coming back in full robe and taking her place at the top of the elevated platform where she would oversee the proceedings. The lawyers, their clients and the spectators all stood.

"Can I have order?" she called out, but the clamoring and whispering in the gallery hardly died down. After showing some exasperation, she tried again. "Look, I understand there is public interest in this case, but if we can't maintain order in the gallery, I'll need to clear it," she warned. After a tense few minutes, the background noise in the room died down.

"Before we start, I need to remind you all that you cannot use phones or other electronic devices in the courtroom. If you have to leave and re-enter, please do so without disturbing the proceedings." She sat and opened up a laptop, demonstrating that the electronic-gizmo prohibition did not apply to her.

"Madame Clerk, please call the case," she ordered.

"Dr. Amelia Trimble, Guardian and Next Friend of E.M., a Minor, et. al, versus United States Citizenship and Immigration Services, et. al….."

"We all present and ready for trial?" Judge Haverhorn asked, looking away from her laptop screen.

The lawyers all nodded and called out, "Ready."

"Your honor," Crump began, "While I hesitate to do openings in a bench trial, in this case I want to say just a few words."

"Proceed, please."

Crump stepped forward. Without a jury, he knew he was speaking as much to the gallery as the Judge, so he made a conscious effort to move around the courtroom.

"Remember how we all felt, the morning of 9-11?" Crump paused, looking around the courtroom.

"Going to work, or to school, or dropping your kids off at pre-school, only to be told to go home and shelter in place? You want a definition of 'Terrorism'? Well, that's it—an act that makes people shudder and then take cover, because that's what it's *supposed* to do—frighten its victims into changing their behavior, even if they are innocent of the conflict that generated the act of terror. That's why, in the wake of 9-11, Congress decided it needed to do more than just hunt down the perpetrators of the attack on the Twin Towers. They passed sweeping legislation designed to prevent future attacks and to dismantle terrorist operations. That Statute, 'The Patriot Act', gave Courts, Government agencies and the victimized Public the power to cripple those who would inflict terror on innocent non-combatants, to achieve political, philosophical, religious and even personal-obsessive outcomes.

"Why?" he asked, pausing for effect. "Why was the Patriot Act necessary? Criminal Justice traditionally dictates that we find wrongdoers, prove their culpability, then punish them as a means of protecting the innocent and discouraging further lawlessness. Why wasn't plain old Criminal Justice enough of a hammer to use against terrorists?

"If I get drunk during a card game, have an argument and shoot my opponent, that's murder. Bad as that conduct may be, my drunken outburst doesn't threaten to destroy an entire way of life, all across this Country. People living in East McKeesport, Pennsylvania or Bettendorf, Iowa don't wake up in a cold sweat because I shot somebody in a drunken rage. It doesn't rip apart society or rob the entire Country of the freedoms our parents, grandparents and great grandparents fought and died to guarantee. Terrorism is *that* threat—conduct designed to destroy Democracy and our way of life—conduct intended to get innocent people hiding under their beds in the morning, just because *they might be next.*

"So, Congress rightly decided terrorism needed to be dealt with *comprehensively*. In enacting the Patriot Act, the Representatives of the People passed judgment on *all* terrorists: They mandated that any persons who sought to terrorize innocent civilians should be put out of business. Federal, State and Local criminal authorities could still prosecute terrorists for their evil acts, but Congress wanted the Courts, *at the request of any victims*, to be able to dismantle terrorists' operations.

"We will show that the two policies on trial today—intentional, *permanent* separation of parents from their children as they cross the United States

Border, and the more recent action by U.S.C.I.S. of deporting non-citizen minors and adults receiving life-saving critical medical care—these policies are unnecessary, cruel and the essence of terrorism. We will prove that these policies are motivated and designed by the Stuggs Administration solely to inflict terror.

"The **Patriot Act** defines **domestic terrorism** as, among other things, 'An attempt to intimidate or coerce a civilian population by mass destruction, assassination, or kidnapping.' We maintain that all the elements of that statutory definition will be proved as the purpose, the intent and the effect of these twin policies of child separation and medical deportation.

"How do we plan to prove the requisite terrorist intent? While this is not a criminal case, criminal law has shown us that the best way to prove intent is through the actions of those who deny having that intent. In this case, we will show that President Stuggs and his principal architect, Dennis Ernstmeyer, head of U.S.C.I.S., devised both of these policies for one reason, and one reason alone: To terrorize both people already in custody, and those considering crossing into the U.S., including those seeking asylum, a completely legal form of immigration. The purpose of deporting sick kids and of kidnapping—yes, *kidnapping* these children—is to frighten those not yet arrived into staying away from U.S. Borders, and to frighten those already here into returning to the countries they were fleeing."

Crump paused, checking to see if he was losing anybody. Nobody was nodding off in the gallery, while the Judge was typing furiously on her laptop.

"How do these policies terrorize? By letting their victims know that, however horrific their circumstances, a fate worse than political, social and criminal oppression awaits them at the border of the United States. That fate: Lose your children forever, and have the dangerously ill face death from terminating critical medical treatment. In the case of Miss Estrellita Montes, the class representative for the thousands of parents and minors subjected to these policies, both of those terrorist threats were perpetrated by the United States Customs and Immigration Service.

"As you listen to the Government's excuses and justifications for their conduct, I ask you to watch what they do, and scrutinize carefully what they say. Conduct proves intent; excuses are made up after the fact. While almost all things are possible, some things are more possible than others, and these policies cannot have any benign, legitimate purposes."

Crump sat down.

"Mr. Stenson, Mr. Plint, any opening?" The Judge inquired.

Greg Stenson stood.

"Your Honor, U.S.C.I.S. and the other Government parties again raise their objection to this *entire* proceeding. We still maintain that the State, charged with enforcing the Patriot Act, cannot be guilty of its targeted terrorist acts, and that our motion to strike this frivolous lawsuit should have been granted—"

"Your Honor, if I may," Crump said, rising. "If we're going to re-argue their governmental immunity claim, *again,* may I offer this: Suppose the President, or his Secretary of Transportation, simply *hates Canadians,* is really steamed about what those nasty French did to us in the Seven Years' War—"

"Your Honor, *really—*"

"No, Mr. Stenson, you are the one out of order—this is supposed to be an opening statement, not a revisiting of your failed motion to toss out the entire case. Let Mr. Crump finish."

"Thank you," Crump continued. "So, the President says, 'Let's lay some landmines on the roadway just over the border,' and he does, and a busload of Canadian schoolchildren arriving on a field trip is blown to smithereens. The only reason: The President *hates* those Canadians, and wants to see them suffer, never to return to American soil again. Mr. Stenson is arguing, again, *that* can't be an act of terrorism, simply because the President resides at 1600 Pennsylvania Avenue."

"I agree—I'm not changing my ruling on the law," Judge Haverhorn announced.

Stenson theatrically shook his head in mock disbelief. "Your Honor, under the circumstances, the Government parties waive opening statement, other than to say, if Mr. Crump and his clients want to play politics and try to attack this President and his Administration, they should take their complaints to the ballot box—oh, wait, I forgot—*they can't vote*. They're not U.S, Citizens. That's what this case is *truly* about—a misguided attempt by *non*-citizens to harass a popularly elected President, while ignoring the Will of the People. The case should be tossed out as so much rubbish, not given the benefit of a trial, all at the expense of the taxpayers."

Stenson sat.

The Judge appeared completely unimpressed. "Call your first witness, Mr. Crump."

Crump stood: "Your Honor, I call Mr. Dennis Ernstmeyer, head of U.S.C.I.S.."

As Ernstmeyer stood from his place in the gallery behind Stenson, Plint stood and shouted "Objection!"

"Objection?" the Judge asked, obviously confused at an objection before any questions were asked.

"Your Honor, we move to disqualify this witness, on the grounds that everything relevant he could possibly have to say would be barred from disclosure due to Executive Privilege."

Crump stood. "Your Honor, since we've agreed that the transcript of his deposition will take the place of President Stuggs's 'testimony', you'll see that when I asked the President where these U.S.C.I.S. policies originated, with him or with Mr. Ernstmeyer, he answered that he and Ernstmeyer were 'A team'. I won't bore you with the dictionary definition of a 'team', but Vince Lombardi, long-time coach of the Green Bay Packers, who defined teamwork for an entire generation, said, 'Individual commitment to a group effort—that is what makes a team work, a company work, a society work, a civilization work.' I agree with the Coach—each member of a team makes his or her *own* contribution to that team. The argument that everything relevant this witness has to say is essentially protected Presidential mindset flies in the face of the President's own testimony. Mr. Ernstmeyer is the Director of the Agency that cooked all this up—his intent formulates these Policies. He should testify. I won't ask him exactly what the President told him."

"I agree. Motion to disqualify *denied*. Mr. Ernstmeyer, please take the stand, and, Ms. Reporter, please swear the witness," the Judge ordered.

"You're quoting Vince Lombardi?" Maureen whispered to Crump. "Have you ever *seen* a football game?"

"Once, when I was trapped in a hospital bed and couldn't reach the remote," Crump whispered back, as he stood to approach the witness box.

Crump quickly ran through the background questions, then went straight to the Reservation Reparations topic. "Mr. Ernstmeyer, isn't it true you first began your association with President Stuggs doing research on a Policy called 'Reservation Reparations'?

"Yes," Ernstmeyer answered, squaring his shoulders.

"And, isn't it true that policy is designed to force Native Americans to pay reparations for the value of the land under the reservations they now occupy, on the theory that they are not Native Americans but, quote, 'Invading hordes from Central and South America, taking those lands from the indigenous White People once living there?'"

Ernstmeyer squared up once again, made an odd gesture like he was looking at the palms of his hands, then said, "Respected historians and several Geo-Political authorities recognize the academic legitimacy of South American incursion into pre-and post-colonial—"

"Mr. Ernstmeyer, that was a 'Yes-or-No' question—"

"Let him *finish*," Stenson objected.

"Let's move on—I'll take that as a 'Yes,'" Crump cut in. "Isn't it also true that the official purpose behind the Child Separation and Medical Deportation policies was to adopt a 'Zero Tolerance' approach to deter *all* immigration?"

"Yes, essentially, that's true."

"And, that those policies were also aimed at deterring asylum seekers, even though they fall under a category that qualifies as *legal* immigration?"

This time, Erstmeyer seemed to squirm in his seat, folded his hands, read his own palms and said, "The consensus of academics and policy-makers who have studied these issues is that there is an exceedingly large and somewhat impenetrable grey area between what constitutes 'legal' and 'illegal'—"

"Mr. Ernstmeyer, are you *reading* from something?" Crump interrupted.

"Of course not."

"Well, the reason I ask is that, in your deposition, when I asked you the very same question, less than eight months ago, you said, 'Virtually all immigration at the Border is illegal,' and when I asked you if that included asylum seekers, you said, 'One man's asylum seeker is another man's illegal strawberry picker.'"

Before Ernstmeyer could respond, Plint stood and said, "Mr. Crump is objecting to this client having *prepared* for his testimony?"

"Actually, I haven't objected, I was just cross examining him to see *who* prepared him, and whether we are getting the witness's answers or the canned responses of his 'preparers'. Do you deny, Mr. Ernstmeyer, that you referred to asylum seekers as 'Illegal strawberry pickers'?"

"I may have said something like that."

"Actually, you said *exactly* that, but, again, let's move on. Isn't it also true that you refused, during your deposition, to answer when I asked you what U.S.C.I.S. was planning to do with the children it was taking away from their parents at the border?"

"I may have—"

"No, you *did* refuse to answer, citing Executive Privilege—"

"Well, then, I must have had good reason to stay silent."

"So, can we assume that you were separating those kids from their parents on the express direction of President Stuggs—"

"Objection—now he's doing precisely what he said he would not do—putting words in the President's mouth through this witness," Stenson called out.

"Fair enough," Crump cut in. "I'm in this position because they improperly instructed him not to answer this question. Seems that he should, at least, tell us what *his* purpose was in separating kids from their parents, and what he intended to do with these fractured families."

"What if *he can't*?" Stenson posed.

"Then, it wasn't *a team*—"

"O.K., I'm going to order him to answer. Mr. Ernstmeyer, please, without revealing direct discussions with the President, answer Attorney Crump's question," the Judge ruled.

"We were going to do what we do with criminals. They're all criminals," Ernstmeyer offered.

"Who, the kids?" Crump asked. "What 'criminal intent' do they formulate, dragged across the border by their parents?"

"Everybody, anybody crossing illegally is a criminal," Erstmeyer added.

"The *kids?* Without specific intent?" Crump asked, refusing to budge.

"O.K., so maybe the kids, I mean, if they're young, maybe they're innocent, but their parents are still criminals."

"So, what is it you *do* with kids of criminals?"

"We're still working on that part," Ernstmeyer offered up.

"Working, *how*?" Crump asked. Before Ernstmeyer could answer, he added, "Isn't it true, under normal circumstances, if a kid would be displaced when a parent is taken into custody, that law enforcement would place the child with local welfare agencies for foster care, not jail the child?"

Ernstmeyer smiled, as though he'd caught Crump in a trap. "These aren't normal circumstances—those foster children would be the children of *taxpayers*," he somewhat gleefully pronounced.

"So, you're saying, if the parents are up to date with filing their 1040's, their kids go to foster homes, but if they're late filers, or on extension, or just don't have to file, you slap their kids in chicken-wire cages?"

"Objection—characterizing his prior testimony," Plint offered up.

Before Crump could respond, the Judge said, "I think that's pretty much what he said. Please answer the question, Mr. Ernstmeyer."

Ernstmeyer glanced at the palm of his hand, then said, "This is *different*—the parents here are *serious, reprehensible* lawbreakers."

"O.K., let's go there. Isn't it true that the 'crime' those illegal border crossers are committing, is a bottom-of-the-barrel misdemeanor, the least serious crime on the books, and when the parents actually get a court hearing, they're usually fined just a few dollars, then taken back to the border—"

"I'm not a border agent, Mr. Crump," Ernstmeyer cut in.

Good, Crump thought—he's starting to lose control, getting off the script they prepared him to recite. "So, for this 'crime,' this glorified parking ticket, your policy is to rip kids away from their families, with no plan to re-unite them—"

"Objection, the witness never characterized the crime," Stenson argued.

"Right—he said he couldn't tell how serious it was, not being a border agent, so I'm helping him along. I mean, far be it for the *Director of the Federal Agency charged with implementing these policies,* to have any idea how serious a crime he's dealing with when he takes crying babies away from their mothers over it—"

"All right, Mr. Crump, we get it. Ask another question," the Judge ordered.

"Let's switch topics. Isn't it true that the only justification you offer for your so-called, 'Sound Immigration Policy' involving deporting immigrant children in the middle of life saving medical treatments, is allegedly saving the taxpayers money?"

Ernstmeyer did the squaring up and squirming thing again, glanced at his palms, and said, "Medical experts are not fully aware or apprised of the risks and benefits of many of these medical treatments, and there is at least the possibility that the hospital beds and medical equipment commandeered for these non-citizens—"

"Mr. Ernstmeyer, are you sure you're not *reading something*?" Crump interrupted.

"Asked and answered," Plint stood up and objected.

"Well, maybe," Crump began. "It's just, these answers sound rehearsed, and when I asked this witness in his deposition the very same question about this policy, I got an off-handed explanation about how much these kids were costing Joe Taxpayer, and *now* we get this obviously scripted answer about available hospital beds."

"The witness is entitled to consider factors not disclosed in his deposition," Plint argued.

Crump was watching Ernstmeyer, who was holding his right hand at arms' length away from him, like it was contaminated. "Your Honor, I'd like to examine the palms of the witness's *hands—*"

"We object," both Stenson and Plint said, in chorus, both standing.

"I think he's reading something written on the palms of his hands," Crump insisted.

The Judge stood, leaned over and tried to glimpse Ernstmeyer's hands. "Miss Reporter, will you examine the palms of the witness's hands?"

The reporter stood, left her chair and asked Ernstmeyer to offer up his hands.

"Anything there?" The Judge asked.

"Yes," she paused, turning his hands over in hers, like she was a palm reader. "It's writing in blue ink, and it's like, a grid."

"What kind of 'grid'?" the Judge pressed.

"Well, like, at the bottom, there's the word "Medical", and then, across from that word, there's an 'equals' sign and the number '6', written like, 'Medical equals 6,'" the reporter added.

"Your Honor, this is obviously some sort of coaching tool," Crump complained. "Once the Reporter transcribes it into the record, I'd like to ask questions about it—"

"We object—"

"I bet you do—"

"Gentlemen, I'm the referee here. Go ahead and transcribe it, then I'll allow questions, as long as they do not require disclosure of attorney-client privileged communications."

"But, your Honor, of course they will," Stenson pleaded.

"I'll decide that." She looked over at the reporter, who had taken her seat and finished typing. "You have it all?"

The reporter nodded.

"Proceed, Mr. Crump."

"Mr. Ernstmeyer, did your lawyers prepare you for your deposition?'

"Of course."

"And, in the course of that preparation, did they provide you with scripted answers to specific questions?"

"Objection—"

"He can answer that," the Judge ruled.

"Yes."

"And, did you memorize those answers?"

"Sort of—"

"How, *sort of*?" Crump asked.

"Well, I was able to commit them to memory, pretty much, but….." He paused. "Can I say this?" he asked.

"Finish your answer," the Judge ordered.

"I was having some difficulty remembering which answer went with which question, so I made this chart on my hands, so like, if the question was about the medical deportations, that was answer number 6."

"Your Honor, if I might have a moment," Crump asked. The Judge nodded.

"I'm almost inclined to move to strike his testimony as entirely coached and scripted," Crump whispered to Maureen and Barnacle.

"You gotta ask him about the money, and give him the slide show," Barnacle offered, with Maureen nodding.

"He's already come across as a complete stooge for these guys—"

"Yeah, but it's all about intent," Maureen added.

"He's *lying*," Doctor Trimble complained.

"He's also *breathing*—with this guy, they go hand in hand," Crump responded.

"Your Honor, we'll come back to this obviously improper coaching gimmick at close of evidence. In the meantime, I have one more line of questioning for this witness."

"Proceed," the Judge said.

"Isn't it true, Mr. Director, that you think your medical deportation policy is justified because the average American taxpayer would run over one of these patients with his car, just to save a few cents off their tax bill?"

"Well, when you put it that way, I mean, you make it sound so cartoonish—"

"Your honor, move to strike," Crump interrupted.

"Ask him your follow up first," the Judge insisted.

"Mr. Ernstmeyer, when I asked you in your deposition if you thought the typical American taxpayer would run over a sick immigrant kid in the street if he thought it would save him the few pennies the medical deferrals were costing that taxpayer, you said, 'Maybe that taxpayer would kill that sick kid, *if he knew the kid was an illegal*'?"

"Objection," Stenson shot up. "Characterizing this witnesses' prior testimony—"

"Characterizing, *nothing*," Crump shot back. "Allow me to read the question and answer from Mr. Ernstmeyer's deposition transcript," Crump offered, and then he read it verbatim, demonstrating the nearly exact quote.

"Objection overruled. Answer the question, Mr. Ernstmeyer."

"I guess I might have said that—"

"Move, again, to strike as non-responsive—it's another 'Yes-or-No'—"

"Stricken. Mr. Ernstmeyer, yes or no, was that your answer to Attorney Crump's question?"

Ernstmeyer looked briefly at his hands, then said, "I guess so."

"Allow me," Crump asked the judge, as he first handed a report to the witness, to Stenson, Plint and the Judge, then turned on a projector hooked up to Maureen's computer. A lighted image appeared on the wall opposite the witness, where everyone, including the Judge, could see it. The room immediately erupted in laughter.

Two bright box projected images lit up room: On the left, a picture of a toilet seat, hanging as though pasted on the wall, with a bright red, familiar "Do Not Go" warning circle with a line through it, overlaid on the seat, accompanied by a cartoon dialog bubble arising from the seat, with the word "Ouch!" in the bubble.

The lighted square immediately to the right had a nearly identical toilet seat hanging there, without the prohibitive red circle, and this one had a cartoon dialog bubble that said, "Oooohhh…"

"Order, please," the Judge called out, as Crump launched into a question.

"Mr. Ernstmeyer, I've reviewed the records of the U.S. Office of Management and Budget—'OMB', to you—in search of a program that costs the Average American Taxpayer the same per diem amount, person for person, as this program you cancelled, supposedly to eliminate the burden on the 'Average American Taxpayer'. The only one I could find that was a nearly exact match was this one: The General Services Administration, the folks who maintain all the U.S. Government buildings like the one we're in right now, recently replaced all the traditional, hard composition toilet seats in Federal facilities, with so called 'squishy', cushioned toilet seats—"

"Objection," Stenson barreled out, as the gallery buzzed with laughter. "Where is counsel going with this, this ….. 'Stand-Up' Routine?"

"I was getting there," Crump injected. "Mr. Ernstmeyer, while I don't want to be *callous* about the creature comforts of our Elected Officials, still, do you think the Average American Taxpayer would find saving the lives of these medically compromised patients you're jettisoning into the desert, at least as worthwhile as the U.S. Capitol being retrofitted with cushy toilet seats?"

Before Ernstmeyer could answer, Crump added, "Isn't it true that the cost of the entire program to the Average American Taxpayer is about four cents, or less than that taxpayer bears for this cushy-tooshy Federal hardware? If you look at the report I just handed you, isn't the cost even less than the Average Taxpayer's share of the printing bill of the recently-minted, Elvis Presley commemorative U.S. postage stamp?" Crump asked, holding up the Government report.

"That's probably true," Ernstmeyer admitted, not wanting to stick his neck out any further.

"So, you still maintain the purpose—U.S.C.I.S.'s motivation behind this abrupt deportation order condemning these medically compromised patients to near certain death, is to relieve the financial burden on Taxpayers?"

"Objection, asked and answered!" Stenson bellowed, as Ernstmeyer scratched his chin and stared at the images on the wall.

"No further questions," Crump said.

"Any re-direct?" the Judge asked.

"Not on your life," Crump predicted in a whisper.

"No, your Honor," Stenson answered.

"We reserve the right to call this witness for rebuttal in the Defense case," Crump tossed out.

Crump then put on Wade Solley, the lawyer in the California class action. Solley testified about how the 'crime' of border crossing was routinely ignored or disposed of with a few-dollar fine and an escort back to the border. He described how the Judge in his case found that the C.B.P. agents were often getting the kids away from their parents by tricking the parents into believing that they were taking the kids for a shower or a change of clothes. He then explained that there was no plan to reunite the families, that instead the kids were sent to far-flung locations, so re-unification was virtually impossible.

Crump had Solley detail misconduct that H.H.S. and U.S.C.I.S. employed to intentionally "lose" these children. He expressed his opinion, over objections by Stenson, that this practice was designed to send the parents back to where they came from with a message: "Don't cross the border with your kids, because you'll never see them again."

Solley then laid out the sordid tale of Maureen's ordeal to retrieve Elení Montes from the obviously purposeful human shell game Peter Meadows, U.S.C.I.S., H.H.S. and other Federal agencies had been playing. He concluded with the news that Peter Meadows was now in jail, suspected of bringing about the tragic bus ride during the last leg of Ms. Montes's trip to be united with her daughter.

They took a break, then Crump offered up his expert, Dr. Condrera, who explained the gang-driven nightmare that was modern-day Guatemala. He offered his expert opinion that only the fear of losing one's children, or of having them die due to interrupted critical medical treatment, would be sufficient to terrorize victims of oppression in Central America into forsaking their harrowing trips to the U.S. border. He opined that the intimidating child separations and medical deportations, were having their intended effect.

Crump then offered another expert, the chair of the Local Hospital Association, who explained that it was the hospitals, not the taxpayers, who were bearing the cost of the medical treatments interrupted by the medial deportations.

While the Hospital Administrator was on the witness stand, Howie Schmeltz quietly wheeled Cecilia Raposa, the media-favorite, high-profile medical deportation victim, into the courtroom. Crump had trouble keeping the courtroom focused on his expert witness, as between the wheelchair, the gurgling of the ventilation pump attached to Raposa's tracheotomy apparatus and her celebrity status, all eyes were on Raposa, as Schmeltz spun her over to the counsel table.

When the expert witness finished, Crump announced, "Your Honor, Plaintiffs call Ms. Cecilia Raposa," as he maneuvered her wheelchair over to the witness box, parking her in front, so she could stay attached to the life-saving apparatus pumping away on the back of her chair setup.

Cecilia Raposa looked like anybody's kid sister, except for the telltale signs of her condition. She had obviously suffered both stunted growth and misshapen limbs and neck, but through all that, she was perpetually in a doggedly good mood. She gave regular interviews once Svetlana Armstrong had discovered her, and her intrepidly positive attitude made her a media hero.

"Please raise your right hand," the reporter asked, as Raposa looked startled for a moment. She turned her head to face the judge and placed two fingers over her trache vent.

"Your Honor, I'm sorry," she offered, her voice barely audible. "I need to cover my vent in order to be heard when I speak, and I can't reach the vent with my left hand," she explained.

Judge Haverhorn was blushing. Crump looked over at Warren Handler, who looked physically ill.

Good, you reptile, Crump whispered.

"Please, do whatever makes you comfortable," the Judge advised.

Cecilia Raposa kept the fingers of her right hand over her trache vent, and wriggled in her chair so she could raise the elbow of her left arm. "O.K., I'm ready," she said.

The Clerk swore her in, and she said, "I do."

"Miss Raposa, how, and when, did you come to the United States?" Crump asked.

Before she could answer, Greg Stenson shouted out, "Objection, compound question."

Crump was about to respond, when the Judge lost it.

"Mr. *Stenson*, ……first of all, kindly stand up when you object—I'm tired of you simply shouting out objections. Secondly, from here on in, if I think you are making an objection over a routine question just to interrupt the witness, I will hold you in contempt and fine you for each such outburst," she concluded, as she trembled in barely-contained anger.

Stenson, in a move Crump would have paid hard cash to *bribe* him to make, decided to argue back. "Your Honor, with all due respect, the twin questions of 'How' and 'When' she came to the U.S. are material to her status—"

"That'll be a hundred dollars—pay the clerk with a personal check during the next recess," she ordered, still visibly shaken. "Please continue, Mr. Crump."

"As I said, how *and* when did you come to the U.S.?"

Cecilia Raposa nodded. She was remarkably small for her eighteen years, looking like a pre-teen with an adult's face. She shifted nervously in her wheelchair, then said, "When I was four, my mother received a letter from the University Hospital here in town. They'd heard about my condition from a doctor in Guatemala, and asked my mother if they could recruit me for a study involving an experimental treatment here at City by the Lake. My mother moved with me here, and I began receiving treatments at the U., ever since. I've grown up at the Hospital, spending weekends with my mother at her apartment here. I have a rare genetic condition in which tumors grow uncontrollably throughout my body. I don't produce an enzyme that metabolizes cell reproductive proteins, so random parts of my body turn into tumors that, unchecked, would be fatal—"

"Objection to the narrative answer," Stenson called out as he stood.

"—That'll be *two hundred*," the Judge quickly intervened, again fining Stenson, almost gleefully.

"Go ahead," Crump assured her.

She removed her hand from her throat, shifted her head slightly, re-covered her trache vent and said, "It's called Mucopolysaccharidosis, and almost nobody has it, so they wanted to study my case."

"How old are you now?" Crump asked. He realized, from the slight ringing in his ears, that the courtroom had gone stone silent.

"I'm eighteen," she offered. "Without this experimental treatment, nobody with my condition had ever lived past age ten."

"Do you know your immigration status?"

"*Now*?" she asked, straining to be heard.

"Sorry," Crump acknowledged. "When you first came here, fourteen years ago."

"The Hospital arranged to bring us here under a program that let us stay as long as the study and my treatments were still happening," she explained.

"So, you were never illegal status?"

"No. Doctor Stallings says that they'd need to suspend the study without me, and so far, they've treated eleven other children with my condition, based on the experimental treatments they've used on me."

"Tell us what happened to you last year," Crump prodded.

"We received a letter form the Government that said I needed to leave in a month or I'd get deported, along with my mother," she said, her face turning red.

Crump marked a copy of her U.S.C.I.S. notification letter as an exhibit, then offered it to her.

"This the letter?" he asked.

When she nodded, he said, "Let the record reflect that the witness nodded in the affirmative." He then read the form letter, revoking her deferred immigration status.

"How did you feel, when you received this letter?" Crump asked.

Somewhat predictably, Raposa began to cry. "I'm sorry," she said. "But, when I do this, it's almost impossible to hear what I'm saying," she added, struggling to keep her fingers over her trache vent.

"Let's recess for fifteen minutes," the Judge announced, as she swiftly stood and left the bench.

"How's it sound to you?" Crump whispered to Maureen.

"Like, next time he objects, Stenson's goin' to jail," she responded.

Howie Schmeltz offered Cecilia Raposa a bottle of water and some tissue. Once she wiped her eyes, he realized she could neither open the bottle or manage to drink from the narrow-necked opening. Seemingly out of nowhere, he produced a drinking straw from his pocket, popped the cap, dropped the straw in the bottle and offered it to Raposa, who took it and drank.

"I could learn to love this guy," Maureen commented.

"Court's back in session," the Judge announced. "Miss Reporter, re-read the last question," she added.

"How did you feel when you received this letter?" the Reporter recited.

She nodded again. "I was crazy scared. Doctor Stallings told me I wouldn't make it a year without these treatments, and they're not offered anywhere else in the World," she concluded.

"What did you do about it?" Crump asked.

"Before you and Mrs. McDougal helped us?"

"Yes, when you first got the letter," Crump clarified.

"Well, the Hospital found me a lawyer, who called the office that sent it, and he tried to get some kind of exception."

"Did that work?"

"No. First the people the letter said to contact didn't know anything about the change in my program, then when the lawyers found some other people in charge, they told my lawyer, 'No exceptions, unless I was in the military.'"

"What did you do then?" Crump asked.

"I tried to enlist," she offered, straight and deadpan. The spectators began to murmur, unsure how to react.

The Judge asked for order, although she, too, was having a hard time containing herself.

"I take it that didn't work—"

"I flunked the physical," she offered, smiling, then laughing mildly, and the place went up for grabs.

Once the laughter died down, Crump asked, "Were the Hospital's lawyers able to get any kind of reprieve for you?"

"No, I mean, not until you and Mrs. McDougal got my deportation stopped with this lawsuit…." She paused.

"Were you finished?" Crump asked.

"Yes, I mean, I hope you can stop whatever they're doing to me, because, otherwise, I won't make it….." She stopped, her eyes again tearing up and the trachea vent again starting to clog.

Crump couldn't help himself. "Miss Raposa, one more question—You understand that, because they've yanked the rug out from under you and this program you're in, Mr. Ernstmeyer, President Stuggs and their immigration enforcement agency consider you to be a criminal—"

"Objection!" Stenson rose and shouted. "Speculating about the President's motives—"

"I wasn't finished with my question," Crump responded.

"Please do," the Judge ordered.

"Do you consider *yourself* a *criminal*?"

"*Objection*," both Stenson and Phil Plint announced simultaneously, as they both stood.

"I want her to speak to her intent—intent counts here, since U.S.C.I.S. is labelling her a criminal," Crump argued.

"Go ahead and answer, Miss Raposa," the Judge said, sounding like she wanted to adopt the witness.

Raposa was shaking her head. "I was *invited* here," she began. "I'm happy for everything Doctor Stallings and the Hospital have done for me, and I never wanted to hurt anybody or break any laws. My life *matters*. How can that make me a criminal—"

"Objection, another narrative answer," Stenson announced, standing.

"That'll be three hundred dollars," the Judge ordered.

"No further questions," Crump said.

"Any Cross examination, Mr. Stenson?"

"*No*," was all he said.

Crump walked over and thanked her, then he wheeled her out of the Courtroom. As he approached the gallery, it was apparent half the crowd was in tears, while the other half was *seething*. Much of the gallery emptied out behind him, as the reporters lined up to interview Raposa out in the hallway.

"Choke on *that*," Crump said under his breath, as he walked by Handler and his lawyers. "Take her home, will you?" Crump asked Schmeltz.

The Judge adjourned Court for the day, and when they all returned, the crowds in the plaza were larger and louder, and the courtroom even more crammed full of spectators.

Crump stood. "Your Honor, Plaintiffs call Delroy Tenato—"

"Wait a minute," Plint called out, as he stood. "This person is not on their witness list. We object to calling witnesses we have not been allowed to depose."

"Counsel?" the Judge asked, turning to Crump.

"He's right—this man is not on our list. We just learned this morning he was willing and available to testify. Until then, he was, essentially, the Government's witness, unknown to us. He's the employee of H.H.S., who was assigned to accompany my Partner and Ms. Montes on the last leg of their journey back here. He's a security guard, employed by Customs and Border Protection at the El Paso Del Norte Processing Center. They could have interviewed him at any time—the Secretary of H.H.S. signs his paycheck—but we found out this man *existed* all of seven days ago. He should be allowed to testify."

Plint was shaking his head disapprovingly throughout Crump's argument. "So, the Government is supposed to *know* which of its *two million* civil employees might pop up as a witness in this case?"

"While Mr. Plint is breaking my heart, it's not like they would have had to go through an alphabetical list of all Federal employees to anticipate that Mr. Tenato might have something to say here. Mr. Meadows himself assigned Mr. Tenato to this escort detail, and the witness gave his notice to C.B.P. the day that prison bus ended up in the ditch in Effingham, so they might have guessed something was up," Crump argued

"I want to hear what he has to say. Objection overruled. I'll give you all the time you need for cross examination, and you can call him if need be in support of the Government's case," Judge Haverhorn ruled.

Maureen rose and went out into the hallway, then reappeared with Delroy Tenato. He was a little banged up and was walking with a limp, but otherwise seemed put together. He took the stand and was sworn in.

After some preliminary questions, Crump asked, "How is it you came to be associated with Ms. Elení Montes and the effort to locate her at El Paso Del Norte Processing Center?"

Tenato nervously scratched at the lump on his head. "Danny Jackson—he's deceased now—a buddy of mine who's another C.B.P. guy, he told me about the detail, asked if I wanted to do this transport gig, an' I said, 'What's it pay?' an' he said, 'Don't know for sure, but it's scale,' and we get $17.50 an hour, so I figured, 'What the Hell,' and I said—"

"Mr. Tenato," Crump interrupted, "I was really just interested in who recruited you. So, it was Mr. Jackson, the now deceased bus driver for the same detail?'

"Yeah."

"Did Mr. Jackson tell you anything about who you'd be accompanying on this trip?"

"Yeah."

"Can you remember what he said?"

"Objection—hearsay," Stenson called out.

"The declarant's *dead*," Crump argued.

"Overruled," the Judge called out.

"What's 'at mean?" Tenato asked.

"It means, go ahead and tell Attorney Crump what Mr. Jackson told you," the Judge added.

"O.K., so he says, 'Gotta take this stupid broad lawyer—'S'cuse me," he said, looking in Maureen's direction, 'Gotta take her and this border crasher up to City by the Lake in some old tanker prison bus, an' I'm the driver, on accounta it's stick shift,' an' I said, 'Why?' and Danny says, 'Some court order, some big shot fucked up—'S'cuse me again—'an now, the big shot, you an' me's gotta take the lawyer an this crasher up North, but first we gotta pluck the crasher outta the viaduct.'"

Tenato paused.

"The *viaduct*?" Crump asked.

"Yeah, Del Norte's not really a permanent facility, I mean, they just stuck a bunch of border crashers under the Paso Del Norte International Bridge, and slapped a fence around it."

"How many people were crammed under that viaduct, when you had to locate Ms. Montes?"

"Over a thousand."

"Mr. Jackson tell you anything else about the job?"

"Yeah, he said that word from the top was to 'Take our time'—"

"I'm sorry," Crump interrupted.

"Let him finish." The Judge ordered.

"Were you done?" Crump asked.

"Yeah."

"So, what did you take that to mean?"

"I figured the higher-ups wanted the trip to take a while."

"Jackson tell you who the 'top' was?"

"No, but we take our orders from the Chief of C.B.P., Descalso, an' he takes orders from H.H.S. and Justice."

"The U.S. Department of Justice, under the guidance of Mr. Handler?" Crump asked, nodding at Handler.

"Yes sir."

"Mr. Jackson tell you anything else about the job?"

"Yeah, we talked before we got started. I mean, I knew Danny—he'd been my parole officer years ago—an' so I asked him, 'Sounds like a shit assignment?' and he said, 'Pretty major shit, all court orders and this guy comin' with us, this Meadows, he's been moving this crasher all over the place, and so this pain in the ass lawyer goes to court and the judge says, 'Escort this lady North, *or else*', but he thinks he's got it beat, 'cause he dumps her at El Norte, ain't *nobody* comin' outta there, it's all these people and no records, so, figurin' we never get off the ground.'"

"But, you *did* get off the ground, correct?" Crump followed up.

"Yeah, your partner there," he paused and pointed at Maureen, "she grabs the court order from Meadows, who was dickin' her around anyway, and she like *dives* into the crowd, and out she comes with this 'Montes' woman."

"You then did what?"

"We got started, made a couple a stops in Oklahoma and Missouri, then all Hell broke loose."

"Let's slow down," Crump cautioned. "So, where were you when you started the last leg of the trip?"

"The Fort."

"Fort Leonard Wood, outside of Rolla, Missouri, correct?"

"Right."

"And, what happened there?"

"Not much, except for the business with Mr. Meadows."

"What *business*?"

"So, we're about to leave, and Danny says, 'Meadows is bailin' on us,' an' I said, 'I thought he was supposed to go all the way, like, in the court order,' and Danny says, 'Yeah, me too, but Meadows says, 'Fuck the court order, I'm tired of gettin' pushed around by this *cunt lawyer* and her partner—'"

Objection—this is now *double hearsay*," Plint stood up and shouted, hoping to draw attention from the insult. "He's telling you what Meadows supposedly told the bus driver, and then what the bus driver supposedly told *him*—"

"One's dead and the other's in jail," Crump responded.

Judge Haverhorn looked like she'd been slapped. "Objection overruled. Please proceed," she said, shaking her head unapprovingly.

"Did Mr. Jackson say anything else about why Mr. Meadows was leaving the four of you to finish the trip alone?" Crump asked.

"No, only Meadows said, 'Watch the road.'"

"I'm sorry," Crump said. "Those were his exact words—'Watch the road'?"

"Whose?" Tenato asked.

"Mr. Meadows—"

"See what I mean?" Plint said, again raising his double hearsay objection.

"Overruled. Do you understand Attorney Crump's question?"

Tenato again nervously scratched his head. "Yeah, were those Mr. Meadow's words?"

"Right," Crump said.

"Yeah, it was kinda weird, outa nowhere, he says, 'Watch the road.'"

"What happened then?"

"Meadows walks off, heads back into the Ad. Office at the base, and we take off without him."

"What happened then?"

Tenato then described, in detail, the bus crash and the aftermath. Crump had to slow him down several times—his re-telling got faster and faster as the events of that late afternoon and evening became more desperate.

"Did you get a good look at that pickup truck that caused Mr. Jackson to drive off the road?" Crump asked.

"It happened kinda fast, although I did see the same thing your partner, Miss McDougal saw, that the guy had an 'Army of God' bumper sticker on his right rear bumper."

"Did you tell Attorney McDougal anything about the crash, once you were all out of that bus?"

"Yeah. I was sure the whole thing was no accident—that backstabber Meadows *knew* somethin' was up, that's why he bailed on us, and I told her that."

"Objection, mere speculation," Stenson called out.

"Overruled," Judge Haverhorn announced, without looking up.

Tenato looked over at Maureen and nodded.

"Weren't you stepping out of line to tell her that?" Crump asked.

He nodded. "Sure was—look, that woman *kicked ass*," he said, pointing at Maureen. "I mean, you got no idea what it was like, with that old tanker sinkin' into the compost ditch, and fillin' up with gas, and I was knocked out, and Danny was *kilt*, and then she smacks me and wakes me up, and she pulled me and that Montes woman outta the bus. I know when it's time to change sides, and Meadows just set us all up to be kilt, so I figured C.B.P. can stick my paycheck *up their ass*, an' I told the sheriff down there that I'd stick around and go look for Danny's body and help 'em sort it all out, and so I quit, and that's what I did."

"No further questions," Crump said.

Greg Stenson stood.

"Mr. Tenato, I take it you no longer work for Customs and Border Protection, is that correct?"

"Like I said, I quit—"

"Have you been there long enough to draw a pension?"

"Yeah."

"And, is anybody *else* paying you for your testimony?"

"Objection," Crump stood up. "He's suggesting that by simple virtue of his pension, somebody *is* paying this man to testify."

"Sustained. Restate your question, Mr. Stenson."

"Are you currently employed?"

"The Effingham County Sheriff's office gave me a job. Pickin's are pretty slim down there."

"And, is the Sheriff pursuing criminal prosecution of anybody in connection with the bus crash you described?"

"They think they got a bead on that pickup, but we're also lookin' at Mr. Meadows and any Government types that might have put those 'Army of God' types up to it."

"And, you're involved with that investigation, are you not?"

"Yeah, so what?"

"So, on what, other than your own suppositions and biases, do you base your suspicions that Mr. Meadows was somehow involved in that crash?"

"Hey, *I was there*. I saw the look on his face. He was sorta laughin', sorta lookin' at us like we were a couple of chumps—"

"Wait, Mr. Tenato, I thought you said the bus driver, Mr. Jackson told you this?"

"No, we were standin' there together, and Meadows says he's not comin', and he calls Lawyer McDougal over there a couple of names, then he smiles and says, 'Watch the road.'"

Stenson realized he desperately needed to pivot away from the subject. "Mr. Tenato, I believe you said Danny Jackson had been your parole officer. What were you charged with that lead you to have a parole officer?"

"Got involved in drugs for a while when I was twenty-two. Been clean twenty years now. Danny Jackson was great, he was, like……" He trailed off. He looked like he was about to break up.

"A moment, your Honor," Stenson asked, as he whispered with Warren Handler.

"No further questions."

During the recess that followed, Turulio and Derek Markle showed up with Cornelius Boofus, Mary's assailant, in handcuffs. His earlobes were covered in bandages and his neck was bruised, but otherwise, he looked like he'd live.

"Let's go out in the hallway," Markle suggested.

They walked to the end of the hallway to get some privacy.

"Boofus here's ready to talk, "Markle announced.

"What's he got to say?" Crump asked.

"He can talk about who sent him the message," Markle offered.

"There's, a *message*?" Crump asked.

They filled him in.

"We need to ask about your alleged attempted 'suicide,'" Crump said.

"Warn't no suicide," Boofus answered.

"I'm sure," Crump offered. "We'll also need to have you rat out the perps—"

"You bet," Boofus added.

"They're gonna ask if you've been given a cooperation deal," Crump warned.

"Three to five, breaking and entering," Boofus said. "Do I hafta do this in cuffs?"

"Yes," Markle said.

Back in the courtroom, Crump announced, "We call Cornelius Boofus—"

"*Again*," Plint objected. "Yet another undisclosed witness."

"Your Honor, this witness only became available to us today," Crump argued. "He will testify about one very specific set of circumstances. We promise to be brief."

"Let's try not to wander too far afield," the Judge suggested.

Warren Handler looked like he was going to burst. Red faced, he leaned into Stenson, whispered something demanding, and Stenson shook his head.

When Boofus stood up, the crowd in the gallery started to stir. His hands were still cuffed behind his back, and with both ears bandaged and his neck bruised, he made for a spectacle of trauma and intrigue. He was led by a bailiff to the witness stand, and when asked to raise his right hand, he had to turn his back to the courtroom and lift both manacled hands, because Markle refused to un-cuff him. He turned back around and sat down in the witness chair.

"Please state your name for the record," Maureen stood at the counsel table and directed.

"Cornelius Stonewall Boofus," he said, wriggling uncomfortably with his arms still stretched behind his back.

"Are you employed?" Maureen asked.

"I'm an independent contractor."

"What do you do?" she continued.

"Community Activist," he offered.

"Do you get paid by anybody for being a 'Community Activist'?"

"Tithings, mostly, from The Army of God."

"Can you describe for us the organization known as 'The Army of God'?"

"It's a fundamentalist Christian group, mostly made up of recruits."

"What is its 'Mission', if I can call it that?" Maureen asked.

"We try to spread the Word, push for true Christianity where folks are following pagan offshoots of the true Church."

"Like, *who*?" Maureen asked, not exactly sure where this was heading.

"Like, *Catholics*, for one, I mean, with all that instrumental music in church services, and Pope worshipin', and robes and the like."

"Can you better describe for us what your organization stands for?" Maureen asked.

"I thought I just did that—"

"Try again," she prodded.

"Christianity is a *charismatic* religion, I mean, the early disciples went barefoot from town to town, spreading the word, encountering folks on the road and announcing, 'Accept and believe, and you will be saved.' We believe that is still the right way of the Church—each separate church stands on its own."

Crump leaned over and whispered to Maureen, the word, "Stuggs."

"Has President Stuggs ever been in any way involved with the Army of God?"

"Yes, ma'am."

"How?"

"When he was just a preacher at a local church in Buttsville, Alabama, before television and politics and governorships and all that, he led a congregation that became one of the founding members of the Army of God."

"I see. And, does your organization have any current relationship with the President?"

"Not directly, no, ma'am."

"How about, *indirectly*?"

He nodded. "Well, my local chapter, in particular, is run by a fella name of Melbourn Stapes. Stapes has a day job, workin' for an outfit run out of Pineville, Georgia known as Meetinghouse Worship Display—they make all sorts of religious objects used in Church services and the like. Anyway, Melbourn, he's in a local office that is in turn run by Shelby Sinclair, who is second cousin to Deeter Phelps." He stopped, briefly looking around, like anybody in the Courtroom would understand the significance and nod back at him.

"Who is Deeter Phelps, and why should any of us know that name?" Maureen prodded.

"Deeter is half-brother to one of the cousins of Melnee Ernstmeyer."

"And, she is?"

"Married to Dennis Ernstmeyer."

"Aahaa," Maureen said, spontaneously.

"Objection," Plint called out.

"To?" the Judge asked.

"Attorney McDougal's feigned expression, uttered in the record."

It was either that or pack a sandwich and break for lunch, the Judge thought. "Let's move on," the Judge ordered.

"Mr. Boofus, isn't it a fact that your organization is active in the 'Right to Life', anti-abortion movement?"

"We are indeed."

"And, the Army of God is currently listed among groups on an F.B.I. watchlist of domestic terror organizations?"

He was shaking his head in disapproval. "We once was, but it's my understanding President Stuggs had us unofficially taken off any such lists."

"On what do you base that belief?"

"On account of, we heard it through the chain of command."

"What's that?"

"The chain of folks I just described to you."

"I see. Mr. Boofus, can I ask you how you came to be in custody?"

"It's a long story—"

"We've got time," Maureen said.

"So, when word come down that it's now time to focus proselytizing on this lawyer up here and his wife, who are suing to tear down the good works of President Stuggs, I was assigned to interrupt those efforts."

"Interrupt, *how*?"

"That was left up to me, and so, for a while, we mostly followed 'em, then tried to shake 'em up some, but, then, when they weren't gettin' the message, word came down it was O.K. to ramp up."

"'Ramp up, *how*?"

"We were supposed to put 'em in life and limb, get 'em to thinkin', if they don't back off this lawsuit, then, maybe, worse yet was gonna happen. So, one night, I went into Attorney Crump's house."

"How?"

"O.K., I broke in, but I wasn't gonna kill nobody—"

"But you were armed, weren't you?"

"Yes."

"Gun drawn, wearing a mask, and you smashed in their sliding glass door?"

"Yeah, but then there was this guy there, this Turulio guy, and he chased me out and ripped off my earlobes."

"Were you charged with a crime?"

"Attempted murder and a bunch of other stuff."

"And that's why you're here in handcuffs today?"

"Yes, ma'am, but like I said, all I was tryin' to do was do what I was told, scare off them Godless atheists from attacking our President."

"So you've said. And, who was it who delivered the "word" that came down that it was O.K. to 'ramp up'?"

"Like I said, it came down the chain, I mean, I got it from Stapes, but he said it come all the way up the chain—"

"Now, I think we've set a record," Plint argued, as Stenson nodded. "By my count, this is seventh-hand hearsay to Mr. Ernstmeyer, and eight-hand to the President."

"I'll let it stand for his belief," Judge Haverhorn ordered.

"Mr. Boofus, why is it you've just decided today to testify in this case?" Maureen asked.

Boofus squared his shoulders, shifted uncomfortably in his seat. "'Cause I been set up," he began, when Stenson shot up out of his seat.

"Objection, foundation," he shouted out. "I don't even know what that means, out of the blue."

"Can you back up on this line and set the stage, Ms. McDougal?" the Judge inquired.

"Certainly. Mr. Boofus, did anything happen to you while in custody that impacted your decision to testify today?"

"Same objection," Stenson offered.

"He can answer," the Judge ordered.

"Sure did," Boofus began. "When I first come in, I'm in the general population at County, but the first day I got cuffed by a guard in the shower, said I was 'a agitator', an' he hits me while I'm cuffed, so I asked for a lawyer, and next thing I know, I'm in solitary—"

"Another narrative answer," Stenson began, when the Judge cut him off.

"I don't think there's any other way," Judge Haverhorn proclaimed. "Let him finish."

"Go ahead," Maureen prodded. "I think you were in the toilet—"

"You ain't never been in the can—toilet's in the cell. I'm in solitary, and I'm there for a week, only getting' out to shower and to meet with my court-appointed lawyer and Markle over there—" He paused, and nodded over at Derek Markle, sitting in the front row. "On account of, we're all negotiatin' for my plea bargain. After a week, we're gettin' close, but then, I'm let go to the shower, and I'm in the shower-john and suddenly there ain't no guard there, and next thing I know, I'm knocked out silly, and I can't breathe, and as I'm wakin' up, I'm back in solitary but there's a towel wrapped 'round my neck and I'm hangin' from one of the window bars in the cell—"

The room went up for grabs. Boofus stopped short, as the Judge called for order.

"Were you finished, Mr. Boofus?" the Judge inquired.

"Well, no, not exactly, I mean, Missus Lawyer here was askin' me why I chose to come here today, and like I was saying, when I kicked over the bedstand and a guard come in and cut me down, and he says, 'Jeesus H. Christ, and how'd you get back in here and where'd you get this fucking towel?' I know'd I'd been set up."

"Objection, hearsay as to the guard and speculation," an increasingly worked up Stenson shouted out.

"I think the man knows whether he tried to kill himself, and certainly the guard's comment is an excited utterance, not just casual chit-chat," Maureen argued.

"Proceed, Ms. McDougal," the Judge ordered.

"Set up by *who*?" Maureen prodded.

"By the same people who told me it was time to ramp it up, goin' after me now that I was in the bucket and threatenin' to talk—"

"Your Honor, this is outrageous speculation, with no foundation—" Stenson argued, when Boofus cut him off.

"Speculation *my ass*. There weren't nobody in these United States except your boss there, Mister A-ttorney Gen'ral, who could reach me in County, *in solitary*—"

"Mr. Boofus, are you completing your interrupted answer?" the Judge asked.

"Yes, your Honor Ma'am, I am. There ain't nobody in there what knows me, or cares about me, or has any reason to say 'Hello, you cracker,' except the folks what put us all up to harrassin' that lawyer over there an' his Commie-lawyer wife."

The courtroom again went up, and the Judge again ordered quiet.

"Mr. Boofus, how can you be so certain of who was behind this attempt on your life?" Maureen asked.

"'Cause they done it before, only to others," he answered.

"Rank speculation and imbedded hearsay," Stenson shouted out, his neck straining and turning red around his collar.

"I'm not even sure what he's talking about," the Judge injected. "Can you be more specific, Mr. Boofus? '*Who*' did '*What*' before?"

"It was one of our guys they sent out after that prison bus—" he began, when the courtroom erupted.

"Order, order!" the Judge cried out.

When the room quieted, Maureen asked, "What are you referring to?"

"I was one a' the guys they wanted to go to downstate and mess with that prison bus with you and that border crasher, but on account of I was gettin' so close to the two Commie attorneys, I stayed and they got a guy from downstate to do it. It come direct from Stapes, who says, 'This is straight from the top, that bus is never 'gonna get where it's goin.'"

"Your *Honor*—" Stenson began.

"Let him finish," Judge Haverhorn ordered.

"So, that's why I figured the only way to stay alive was to come here and tell all this, so there'd be no more reason for Mister A-ttorney General and Ernstmeyer to keep tryin' to off me."

Judge Haverhorn was sitting straight-backed and stiff, her mouth hanging half open.

"No further questions," Maureen McDougal announced.

"Let's recess for five minutes," the Judge ordered. She sat and typed furiously for the entire time.

"Mr. Plint?" the Judge offered. "Your witness."

Plint stood. He looked rattled and red-faced. "Mr. Boofus, you said you'd been 'charged'. That by the Lakeside County State's Attorney?"

"Yes, sir."

"Attempted murder, and, what else?"

"Breaking and entering, assault, bunch of other stuff and a hate crime, on account of Mr. Crump's wife being a Atheist."

"And, isn't it true that, before you agreed to testify here today, you were offered a reduced sentence to fewer charges?"

He nodded. "That's right. But we're not done negotiatin'—"

"I see. So, you've been told to come here and say this, and *then* the State's Attorney will reduce your sentence?"

"Objection, characterization of his prior testimony—that's not what he said—" Maureen started.

"Sustained," Judge Haverhorn said. "Ask another question."

"I just wanna say, I got a public defender, and she's handlin' all the negotiatin'—" Boofus began.

"There's no question pending," the Judge offered.

"I know, Your Honor Judgeship, but this guy here is tryin' to say I'm lying, just to get off the hook."

"I understand, that's insulting, but wait until you're asked a question," the Judge affirmed.

"Mr. Boofus, have you ever spoken to Dennis Ernstmeyer?"

"No, don't believe I have."

"How about his wife?"

"Nope."

"Her cousin, or Mr. Deeter Phelps?"

"No, but it don't work that way. The message comes down when the message comes down, and we know when the heat is on, and when it's O.K to ramp it up."

"Move to strike that last answer as non-responsive," Plint argued.

"Overruled."

"Mr. Boofus, you actually have no idea whether you were attacked in prison, and, if so, who's the culprit, isn't that so?" Plint more argued than asked.

"I *know—*"

"The official report says, '*attempted suicide*', does it not—"

"Mister Attorney, the Bible says suicide's a sin—a *mortal* sin. I may of done a lot of questionable stuff, but I ain't 'gonna burn in Hell just for you people and your attemptin' to keep all the Mexicans out," Boofus shot back.

"No further questions." Stenson waived further cross examination, but reserved calling Boofus in his case.

"Quit while you're ahead," Crump whispered to Maureen.

"Plaintiffs rest, your Honor," Crump announced.

"We'll begin the Defense case tomorrow," the Judge responded.

Boofus was led out by a bailiff. When Crump stood and turned, he realized the Courtroom gallery was almost entirely empty. "When did *that* happen?"

"Right after he essentially said that the current Administration told him it was O.K. to put a hit on you and Mary, and then they put a hit on *him,*" Barnacle said.

The next day, Crump and his team could barely get into the courtroom, the place was so crowded. They'd watched some of the news coverage the night before, which was punishing to Handler and the Administration, accusing them of being a glorified crime syndicate. That mood was again present in both the protests going on all over the courthouse plaza, and in the gallery, where Maureen got asked for her autograph, over and over.

"How can Handler and Ernstmeyer possibly think they're going to prevail?" Dr. Trimble asked, as they took their seats and the Judge called the case to order.

"That'll all change once the Government puts on its case," Crump whispered. "It always sounds like a winner when you've only heard one side. I gotta believe they have a bunch of rebuttal witnesses, and they'll put Ernstmeyer in a walk-in freezer somewhere, claiming he's mysteriously unavailable, when we want to re-call him."

As those words were leaving Crump's lips, Gregory Stenson was taking the mind-numbingly stubborn move of calling, as his first witness, Dennis Ernstmeyer, back to the witness stand.

"Whaaaa??" Maureen exclaimed, just loud enough for her team to hear.

"Either arrogant, or stupid, or they just feel that they need to rehabilitate him, after he was labelled as a crackpot and a crime boss," Crump whispered.

"I'm going with arrogant *and* stupid," Doctor Trimble weighed in.

Ernstmeyer was sworn in.

"Mr. Ernstmeyer, can you describe the task you were given when you were appointed head of U.S.C.I.S.?" Stenson asked.

Ernstmeyer seemed agitated. Crump figured that the loss of coaching cues tattooed to his hands and the accusation that he was connected to a yahoo-conspiracy of militant Right-to Lifers, had rattled him.

"Yes," he offered, trying visibly to calm himself. "When I took on this position, there were half a million people entering the Country illegally each year, and half of them were crashers at the U.S. and Mexican border. They annually contribute to a total of over ten million unauthorized, illegal immigrants living in this country. My charge was to find a way to stem this influx, this….." He paused. "This *invasion* of the Country, in the face of a Congress unable to do its job and pass reasonably restrictive legislation, and prior administrations who were advocating for open borders—"

"Objection to the non-responsive answer," Crump offered.

"It's a complicated subject," Stenson argued.

"He's giving a scree about the Immigration State of the Union. The question was, 'What *task* were you given?', not, 'Can you give us a paid political announcement from the Stuggs administration, justifying invoking terrorism in the name of these policies—"

"I object to his objection," Stenson rebutted.

"Mr. Ernstmeyer, can you bring it around to what you *did*?" the Judge nudged him.

Ernstmeyer was obviously struggling, annoyed by Crump's breaking up his phony, academic-sounding scripted answers. He was sweating, rubbing his palms together. "Yes, of course. We were charged with finding a way to impose rationality to the chaos at the Mexican border, where every stray alien who wandered near the U.S. was given an administrative hearing by over-taxed Judges, who, we believed, were allowing cases to go forward just to clear their overcrowded dockets—"

"He's doing it again." Crump complained.

"No, he's *not*," Stenson responded.

The Judge offered, "I asked him what he *did*, Mr. Stenson. He is, I believe, again describing the problem he was facing. Let us assume immigration at the Mexican border was a problem. What was it this person, this agency, *did* to try to remedy that problem?" the Judge suggested.

Ernstmeyer was again visibly flustered. "You're not letting me *finish*," he complained. "You cannot understand the solutions we fashioned without understanding the *infestation* we faced."

"That may be, Mr. Ernstmeyer," the Judge continued, not pausing over his use of the term *infestation*. "But, still, it would be helpful for the court to hear about the actual steps you devised and then how they were carried out. The issue in this case is about your Agency's actions, and the intentions behind them, in implementing child separations and medical deportations."

"O.K.," Ernstmeyer rattled off, his growing annoyance bubbling up. "We'll dissect this problem in *a vacuum*, without a realistic appreciation of the scourge illegal immigration represents—"

"Mr. Ernstmeyer, let me ask the question this way: 'What actions did you take when you were appointed Director of U.S.C.I.S., and what were your reasons for taking them?'" the Judge almost pleaded.

Ernstmeyer was completely unprepared for random, unrehearsed questioning, and felt cornered by the Judge asking him questions. His head was shaking, like he was shivering in the cold. Stenson, recognizing the problem, started to rise, when Ernstmeyer blurted out, "At least, I'm not like these replacist elites, Mr. Crump and his clients, trying to aid and abet the internationalists with their plots fostering mass immigration—"

"Hey, hey, *heyyy*," Crump cried out as he stood. "Say that again?"

"Your Honor, that's not even a proper objection," Stenson cried out.

"Say what?" Ernstmeyer asked, looking confused and unaware he'd gone off the rails.

"Ms. Reporter, could you please re-read the witness's last answer?" the Judge pleaded.

Before Stenson could intervene, the Court Reporter called out, "He said, 'At least I'm not like these replacist elites, Mr. Crump and his clients, trying to aid and abet the internationalists with their plots fostering mass immigration....' And then, he didn't finish," the Reporter concluded.

"Your Honor, I request an adjournment until this time tomorrow," Crump called out.

"This is highly irregular," Stenson argued.

"Your Honor, the Government improperly terminated this man's deposition before we could get to this topic. I'd like just one day to prepare to cross his defense testimony."

"We're all a little fatigued," Judge Haverhorn observed. "Let's break until ten o'clock tomorrow. Court is adjourned," she said.

"What are we *doing*?" Maureen whispered, as the parties packed up, while the press and observers shuffled out of the courtroom.

"*Biology*," Crump whispered back.

* *

"Sophie, find me that box of hate mail we've been getting about the Patriot Act case," Crump called out, as soon as they entered the office.

"We're taking a day off to go read our hate mail? You had him *unglued*," Maureen chided.

"Unglued is right," Crump said.

"You gonna fill us in, or make us guess?" Barnacle asked.

"Here it is," Sophie announced, as she hauled in the box of crackpot messages they'd begun receiving, as soon as Judge Haverhorn refused to dismiss their complaint branding Stuggs, Ernstmeyer and their Government Agencies as Terrorists. Sophie was about to dump it all out on Crump's desk, when he cried out, "*No, wait*, just leave it here. Can you scrounge around and finagle me a pair of rubber gloves?"

Barnacle looked at him like maybe he'd finally lost it and gone over the edge.

"O.K., Crump, now you're even weirding *me* out," Maureen said

"Remember, way back in the beginning, when we first started getting this stuff, you got one that was made out of letters, cut out of magazines and glued to the paper like a ransom demand?"

"I guess—"

"What'd it say?"

"Crump, that was *a year ago*—"

"It said, we were *replacist elites,* conspiring to dilute the white race through mass immigration. I'd never heard that phrase before, so I looked it up—well, I had Sophie look it up for me. Anyway, it's a catchphrase of these crazy white nationalist outfits, who view immigration into the U.S. as a plot to 'dilute' the white race. The thing is, it's fringe, or it used to be, before Stuggs got elected and started signaling to the cable news crank talkers that is was time to mainstream it. But even for these white-nationalist guys, it's kind of new, so it stuck with me and jogged my memory when Ernstmeyer blurted it out. It's not just the use of that phrase, though—the statement in the letter is virtually *identical* to Ernstmeyer's outburst today. Either he's plagiarizing one of his fellow-traveler nutjobs, or it's *him.* How much you wanna bet that Ernsty," he nodded over toward the courthouse, "Ernsty sent us that letter?"

"Wow, you are really reaching," Barnacle offered.

Sophie came back with the rubber gloves, but they were obviously the used, dishwashing type. "No—I need those medical kind, unused, fresh out of the box," he insisted.

Sophie shook her head and waltzed out to run to the pharmacy across the street.

"Thanks," he called out, then added, "While you're out there, can you also scan your rolodex and find me the current number for Alison Hawley?"

As Sophie disappeared, Maureen asked, "Who's Alison Hawley?"

"An old girlfriend."

"*Crump*—"

"What? You're shocked I could have an 'old girlfriend', or just amazed I could dig one up now, after all these years?"

"You're gonna connect all this up?" Barnacle asked.

Crump sat back like it was lecture time. "So, a million years ago, in high school, I wanted to get into cross-country bike racing, so I joined the Old Town Bike and Track Club, the only way I could get my hands on a racing bike. It was a bunch of hippies that ran this bicycle co-op, and they did bike racing on the weekends. One of my co-operative partners was this incredible woman, gritty counter-culture type, tough as nails. She could weld a bike frame and true a thirty-six spoke rim in an hour, with her bare hands. We had a thing going, but then she went away to college while I was stuck here, dumped at City College, which was all I could afford on my State scholarship—"

"Crump, we only have a day—" Maureen interrupted, rolling her hand in a circular, hurry-up motion.

"O.K., so, anyway, Alison was a bio-and-genetics major, and she eventually traded in the tie-dyes and weird beads for suits and sensible shoes, and she started a place called Cell-Bred Technology. Cell-Bred was one of the first DNA testing outfits—they pretty much pioneered DNA testing, the standard used in evidentiary proceedings these days. She'd easily qualify as an expert, and I'm betting she can examine that letter and tell us if it was assembled and mailed by our buddy, Dennis Erntsmeyer."

Sophie popped in with a box of medical-grade Nitrile gloves. "You *owe* me," she said, as she turned and went to get Alison Hawley's number.

As Crump started fishing through the hate mail with his gloved hands, Maureen asked, "O.K., so far, I'm not yet ready to have Character and Fitness yank your law license, but assuming this woman can pull a DNA sample off that letter and run a test that fast, how's she going to get a sample to match from Ernstmeyer?"

Crump looked up from his dig through the box, holding up the letter and attached envelope in his hand like he'd won the lottery. "I'm telling you, if anybody can do it, she can."

✳ ✳

An hour later, Alison Hawley was sitting in Crump's office, turning the letter over in her Nitrile-gloved hands. Maureen thought she looked just about as advertised—former hippie turned capitalist. She was wearing a dark blue dress-for-success suit and had real-person hair and glasses, but you could still picture her with long, unruly wild hair, beads and a police record.

"You got the guy's full name and address?" Hawley asked.

"Yeah, I'll pull it—it's the first background question we always ask, so it'll be in his deposition transcript," Crump noted.

"Good. There's a one thousand percent chance, if he really is one of these cuckoo supremacists, this guy's paid one of those DNA search places, the ones that sell kits as Christmas gifts, to see if he really is related to the King of Prussia."

"How would you get that information?" Barnacle asked.

"That stuff's proprietary—you execute this massive wavier when you sign up. Those places sell your results to *everybody*—Crime labs, other databases, and, of course, outfits like mine. If he's searched in the last ten years, we have it. If we don't, can't you ask the Court to make him cough it up?"

"Yeah, but for a bunch of reasons, I'd prefer not to ask the Judge," Crump noted.

"Wait, I'm sure I'll have it. It's likely self-authenticating. These DNA ancestry search companies make them sign an affidavit buried in the fine print when people order their DNA background."

She put down the letter. "Who here has handled this with their bare hands?" Alison Hawley asked.

"Just Maureen and Sophie," Crump answered.

"Good—I'll need samples from them, so I can eliminate them from the test results."

She pulled a couple of envelope-sized packets out of a bag and removed a sealed bundle of swabs from each, handing one each to Sophie and Maureen. "Take these swabs, do the insides of your cheeks, then place the swabs in these envelopes and sign the pre-printed affidavit on the side of the envelope."

While they complied, she added, "I'll check out the entire letter, including the adhesive on the back of the stick-on letters, the envelope glue and stamps."

"We'd need to prep you and offer you as a witness for tomorrow morning," Crump warned.

"I'll have an answer before ten tonight," she said, as she went out with Maureen and Sophie to collect their samples.

"I owe you," Crump called out.

"This'll cost you twenty-five hundred bucks, plus five hundred an hour for the testimony," she replied, calling out over her shoulder.

"The Sixties die hard," Barnacle commented, listening to Hawley leave the office. "So much for 'Free Love, Collective Economies and The Age of Aquarius,'" he added, once he was sure she was out of earshot.

* *

The next morning, inside the packed courthouse, Stenson tried desperately to rehabilitate Ersntmeyer, who couldn't stick to script and kept lapsing into diatribes about the corrosive impact of unchecked immigration.

When Stenson finished with Ernstmeyer, the Judge asked Crump if he had any cross examination or rebuttal questions for the Director of U.S.C.I.S..

"I'd still like to reserve cross examination," Crump offered. "I do have affirmative matter I'd like to introduce—"

"Your Honor, how many of these stunts are you going to let him pull?"

"*Gentlemen*," the Judge began, as a visibly relieved Dennis Ernstmeyer quickly left the witness stand. "I'll decide how far he goes with impeaching this witness."

Crump announced, "Your Honor, I'd like to impeach this witness with forensic evidence and expert testimony."

"You Honor, this is just one surprise party after another. We object to the offering of previously undisclosed expert testimony, in the middle of trial," Stenson griped.

"Your Honor, all of this could have been avoided if they hadn't improperly terminated Mr. Ernstmeyer's deposition. I learned a few new things yesterday about this witness, and I believe, once you've seen this evidence, you'll agree it impeaches this witness's testimony about his *intent*, which is the key to proving my case."

"Please proceed. We'll consider this an offer of proof until it's completed. I'll rule on admissibility when you're done."

Stenson threw his hands up in the air and muttered, "See you in the Appellate Court," a bit too loudly.

"Mr. Stenson, I'd advise you to keep your 'Contempt of Court' utterances to yourself," an irritated Judge Haverhorn scolded.

Crump silently offered a copy of the hate-mail letter to the parties and counsel, then offered the original, in a clear, sealed, full-sized plastic envelope, up to the Judge, marked as Exhibit twenty-nine.

"I'm offering this as Exhibit 29," Crump explained. "I'd like the Reporter to read it into the record," he added.

"Is this some kind of joke?" Stenson asked, waving the copy of the letter around like a flag.

"Please, Ms. Reporter, if you can," the Judge ordered.

"You guys are replacist elites who deserve to die for helping the internationalists with their plot to dilute the white race through mass immigration. You are the terrorists……'" the Reporter read from the letter. She stopped to type the content into the trial transcript.

"Your Honor, this is one of several pieces of threatening hate mail we received when this case started. I'd like to have my secretary, Ms. Sophie Dohringer, take the stand to authenticate it and set the date of its receipt by my office."

"Where's the link up to *this case*?" Stenson bellowed. "For all we know, this is a stage prop."

"I'll get there," Crump offered.

Once Sophie had authenticated the letter, Crump introduced Doctor Alison Hawley and asked her to take the stand. After the Judge overruled Stenson's objections, Crump read Doctor Hawley's eighteen-page resume into the record and qualified her as a DNA expert, over the continuing objections of Stenson and Plint, who were going from red to purple. Warren Handler removed his glasses and pinched the bridge of his nose.

Crump had the Doctor describe the chain of evidence, tracing the letter from Crump's office to her testing lab. She explained why she tested Maureen and Sophie, then elaborated on her testing regimen.

"I use a spectrograph that checks thirteen identifiable sequences on five diffident human chromosomes, all sites with no statistically significant random nucleotide sequences. In other words, there is no chance of random or accidental matches of DNA samples, using these markers."

"Doctor Hawley, were you able to obtain any useable DNA from this letter, and the envelope in which it was mailed?" Crump asked.

Some members of the press in the gallery were standing. The judge asked them all to sit.

"Yes, I was. There was a residual trace of DNA from both Ms. McDougal and Ms. Dohringer, who I tested ahead of time, as it was expected that they'd leave some DNA, having handled the letter."

"Anybody else?" Crump asked.

"Yes. Several of the cut-out and adhesive letterings bore DNA from the same person, who also left large amounts of DNA on the envelop flap, some around the edges of the glue, and traces on the backside of the stamp—which, by the way, was self-adhesive—he didn't *need* to lick it."

"How many trace samples from this person?"

"Thirty-seven."

"And, were you able to match that person's DNA to any living person, in any existing national database?"

"I was. Dennis Ernstmeyer, who has sent in his own DNA samples to two commercial testing laboratories, searching his ancestry, matched all thirty-seven."

The gallery erupted into rambling commentary, which the Judge quickly ordered silenced.

Crump had Doctor Hawley authenticate Ernstmeyer's DNA sampling, from two commercial sites. She offered up both of the test results Ernstmeyer had obtained, as well as one affidavit he'd signed, on the later-dated of his two searches.

"Please read Mr. Ernstmeyer's affidavit from 'Not Your Grandfather's DNA' into the record," Crump asked.

"Hearsay," Stenson almost hollered.

"It's an admission," Crump responded.

"Please," the Judge offered, as curious as everybody else in the courtroom.

Doctor Hawley slipped on reading glasses. "'My name is Dennis Ernstmeyer. I have already paid one ancestry firm to confirm that my paternal ancestors originate from the Caucasus Mountain Range in modern-day Russia, the birthplace of the Caucasian Race. That outfit was unable to confirm my claim of being directly descended from the first, 'True White Race.'" She paused. "Those words all had leading caps," she added. "I'll continue reading. 'I would hope your firm can confirm my claim.'" Doctor Hawley finished, looked up and removed her reading glasses.

"Doctor, did you use the results from the sample Mr. Ernstmeyer submitted with that affidavit, to seek a match against your test from the letter?" Crump asked.

"I did."

The courtroom went up for grabs like it was a party.

"Order, please. Order," the Judge called out, clapping her gavel for the first time in the trial.

"And, do you have an opinion regarding who prepared and mailed this letter?"

"I do. Dennis Ersntmeyer assembled and mailed this letter to your office, based on the DNA sampling, immediately upon the date it bears."

"Is there any possibility that these conclusions are in error?"

"No. The DNA match is 99.9999978 percent accurate. Put another way, there is less than a hundred million to one possibility anybody else could have assembled and mailed this letter. If they had, it would not be covered with Mr. Ernstmeyer's DNA, with no other samples except traces from the recipients."

"And, can you express that opinion within a reasonable degree of scientific certainty, based on all your experience and training?"

"I can."

"Doctor Hawley, can I ask you to do me one more favor—"

"*Favor* is right," Stenson called out.

"Mr. Stenson, that'll be four hundred dollars," The judge called out.

"One more *task*," Crump continued, "Can you hold up the original of Exhibit twenty-nine, and read its contents into the record? I want no confusion about which letter you are describing, or about what it says."

The Doctor held up the letter, extending it directly before her eyes. "It says, 'You guys are replacist elites who deserve to die for helping the internationalists with their plot to dilute the white race through mass immigration. You are the terrorists......'"

"And, for the record," Crump announced, "Ms. Reporter, please read Mr. Ernstmeyer's last recorded answer at the close of evidence yesterday."

The court reporter spooled through her stenograph tape. "At least I'm not like these replacist elites, Mr. Crump and his clients, trying to aid and abet the internationalists with their plots fostering mass immigration....." the Reporter repeated.

"Thank you. No further questions."

When Crump turned around, the gallery was emptying. All the reporters and journalists were filing out.

Stenson tried desperately to trip up Doctor Hawley, but she was unfazed. The judge ruled that Dr. Hawley's report was admissible in evidence. Stenson then put on a dozen additional witnesses, all arguing about the legitimate purposes behind the dual policies of Family Separation and Medical Deportation. The Courtroom remained nearly empty, with the reporters and journalists all out trying to get the jump on each other, telling the story of the crackpot white supremacist behind the Administration's immigration policies.

"Your Honor," Crump offered, "At this time, I'd like to re-visit the President's failure to answer those two questions he refused to answer in his deposition—Who's he taking the Country 'back' from, and did he create these policies just to terrorize border crossers?"

Stenson, who looked defeated, stood and said, "I thought we agreed, there'd be no putting words in the President's mouth?"

"Mr. Crump, Mr. Stenson, I'm not inclined to subpoena the President for a return trip, so why don't you both assume for your closing arguments, that President Stuggs and Mr. Ernstmeyer are the 'Team' the President proclaimed they were. I'll allow whatever reasonable inferences flow from that. Please proceed to close."

Maureen handled the closing argument. Summarizing the evidence, she began by reminding the Judge to look at what they do, not listen to what they claim they're doing. She characterized the hate mail manifesto from Ernstmeyer as one of those telltale acts.

"The Stuggs Administration and its ringleader, Mr. Ernstmeyer, offered only one explanation for their separation of children from their parents when they crossed the U.S. Border—'They're all criminals,' Mr. Ernstmeyer said. When we asked him how serious was the crime they were committing, he claimed he didn't know. So, let's help him out: Illegal Entry is, under Federal Criminal Law, a misdemeanor, punishable by a fine of fifty dollars and no more than six months in jail. Mr. Ernstmeyer suggested that such *severe, dangerous* criminal activity, justified *permanently* taking kids away from their law-breaking parents.

"Ignore the nonsense he sputtered about whether the parents were taxpayers: There's nowhere in the United States where your careful adherence to the Internal Revenue Laws determines whether you get to keep your children. Let's look at what *else* is the type of misdemeanor that subjects you to these penalties.

"I scoured the lawbooks, and here's what I found: Reckless Driving—you make a left turn without using your turn signal; Public Intoxication—another way of saying, you just left a Major League Baseball game; Petty

Theft—you shoplift an apple at the grocery store; Vandalism—you carve your initials into a tree in a public park; Trespassing—you cut through your neighbor's yard to retrieve your tennis ball, without permission; or, my favorite, Reckless Conduct—you cross the street against the red light, with the 'Don't Walk' sign flashing away.

"Try to imagine law enforcement officers *permanently* taking your children away from you for any of these admittedly illegal infractions, and you can see that Mr. Ernstmeyer's excuse is just that—something made up on the spur of the moment, when he was asked the question, because it sounded better than, 'We just want to scare the parents *to death*'.

"Ernstmeyer and his Boss, President Stuggs, will undoubtedly cry 'No Fair—those are *State Crimes*. We're talking violations of *Federal Law* here.' O.K., so I scoured the books to find a similar Federal Law, carrying the same penalties as illegal border entry. I confess, I could only find *one*: Illegal appropriation of a Federally-protected national symbol or image. That's right—walking around in a bootleg Smokey the Bear tee-shirt has been tagged by Congress as an offence in the same class as illegal border entry. 'Sorry, Ma'am, but that there Smokey-the-Bear tee-shirt is a bootleg, we're gonna hafta take your kids away, *for good*.'" She paused, before adding, "*Right*," dripping with sarcasm.

"So, Ernstmeyer's and his Agency's solution to illegal immigration is to *keep* illegal border crossers—those children—*in* the Country, while they deport their parents. Sound like an effective way to address what Mr. Ernstmeyer called '*the infestation*?' There's only one possible explanation for this behavior—to inflict terror. Since their offered justification for child separation is nonsense, there is only one other explanation: Terrorize those border crossers, and make sure word gets out to those who might follow in their footsteps.

"At least they *tried*, when asked for a justification for medical deportations. Some gibberish about taking up available hospital beds, although, the testimony you heard from one of the victims made it painfully apparent that almost none of them are *in* hospital beds. Then, there's the excuse Ernstmeyer coughed up in his deposition, that he tried to walk back in his trial testimony: Cost savings. The expert testimony of Doctor Sharpe, who said it was the hospitals, and not the taxpayers who were bearing the cost, undercuts the truth and even the logic of *that* excuse. Mr. Ernstmeyer had to admit that the average American taxpayer is charged more for cushy Government toilet seats or the printing costs on the Elvis Presley commemorative U.S. Postage Stamp.

"The only possible explanation for medical deportations is betrayed by that kidnapper's ransom note Dennis Ernstmeyer sent my partner and I when this case started: Stopping *all* forms of immigration, to prevent the feared *dilution* of Ernstmeyer's beloved White Race. Or, as he called it when he asked for his own DNA test: 'The *First, True White Race*.' This is what terrorists do: They can't achieve their goals through the political system, so they blow stuff up. I would submit to you that this is the mindset of a Terrorist, not some beleaguered Federal bureaucrat, just trying to do his job. It's also a mindset shared by the President of the United States—"

"Objection," Stenson called out, standing.

"Sorry, it's a fair inference, Mr. Stenson," the Judge ruled. "Continue, Ms. McDougal."

"Ernstmeyer and his Attorney General maintain that the Patriot Act's reach cannot be extended to their conduct, because they are fighting their dreaded 'infestation', another way of saying, 'The Ends Justify the Means.' If the last hundred years of worldwide atrocities haven't consigned that argument to the Dustbin of History, then this case *should*. Our Democracy is just as threatened by characters like Dennis Ernstmeyer, kidnapping innocent children with Government authority, as it is when fanatics blow us up. You can't effectively condemn the bombers, and expect to be taken seriously when you're openly, *proudly*, a kidnapper.

"Intent is what matters here. You heard about the sick, persistent, twisted attempts to thwart us from re-uniting just one child, the lead plaintiff here, Estrellita Montes, with her Mother. That saga alone should be enough to convince you this is Stuggs' and Ernstmeyers' *obsession*, not some legitimate Government policy. But you don't need to stop there—Mr. Boofus, their amateur hit man, told you what was really going on here—a concerted effort to harm or even kill, just to keep one, lone immigrant from re-uniting with her child. Obsession is the earmark of a terrorist. We've proved their sick, twisted intent beyond a preponderance of the evidence."

Maureen concluded with, "I don't know what the right immigration policy is, and I'm not some activist, pleading for open borders. I just know it can't be *this*."

Stenson, in his closing argument, tried his best to rehabilitate his side, arguing that U.S.C.I.S. couldn't be roped in and punished, even if they decided to *shoot* the folks illegally crossing the border. He recoiled some when the gallery *whooshed* at that statement, but mostly, he sounded like he was just biding his time, waiting to go out into the hallway to strangle Dennis Ernstmeyer.

The judge took the case under advisement and promised to be back with a ruling before the end of the day.

Stenson walked over to the Plaintiff's counsel table and offered, "We could try to negotiate this like civilized human beings, instead of all this glorified *name calling*—"

"Sorry, Greg," Crump said, cutting him off. "I thought the official Government position was, 'We don't negotiate with Terrorists'. Seems like a sound policy to me."

* *

When the Clerk called the case and Judge Haverhorn announced that court was back in session, many of the journalists had returned, and the gallery was packed.

The Judge looked out over the courtroom. She was holding the pasted-together hate-mail letter, now identified as the work of the President's senior advisor on immigration. She held the letter up, theatrically waving it around so that everybody in the courtroom, including the sketch artists, could see it.

She began to address the Courtroom.

"While I am personally shocked to see how a man, a dangerous bigot like Dennis Ernstmeyer, could rise to the level of an Agency Director under President Stuggs, I can only assume that for a white nationalist conspiracy theorist like this to occupy such a position, his views must reflect those of his employer, the President of the United States."

She paused. She was now looking directly at Warren Handler, the senior legal officer of the United States of America.

"What I find truly amazing, though, is how remarkably wrong-headed and self-defeating these white-supremacists and their agendas truly are. Think about this: The supposed reasons these race-baiters fear and target the so-called "non-white" immigrants, is their belief that these immigrants are not only racially inferior, but also *culturally* inferior. The theme in their rants seems to be that the quality of life we Americans enjoy—the relative freedom from Government and criminal oppression, the championship of private property rights and civil freedoms, will be threatened with destruction if we allow too many people from the 'inferior' races and cultures to immigrate. They will, it is argued, dilute the White-Race gene pool, and with that, they argue, dilute the civic culture that defines the quality of life in America.

"The ultimate irony about this wrong-headedness, I fear, is in the measures Ernstmeyer and his followers—and, yes, those of his boss, President Stuggs—the measures they resort to in an effort to throttle the 'invasion' of these allegedly inferior peoples. Those very efforts undermine that civic culture to the point where they threaten to make the U.S. mimic the allegedly corrupt, dangerous cultures that these targeted immigrants are fleeing. Did it ever occur to you, Mr. Handler, and to your fellow staffers and administrators, that it is your conduct, and not the influx of the people you so fear, that threatens the very way of life you claim to be striving to preserve?"

Handler tried to rise, but she cautioned him to sit.

"Almost every day, I empanel juries in this courtroom, juries that are increasingly made up of cross sections of the very diverse urban populations you fear are destroying the America you are sworn to protect. More often than not, they are made up of equal parts recent immigrants and first-generation descendants of the people you are targeting with these abusive policies directed at immigrants. You know what I see in those jurors? Not contempt, not disregard for our laws and civil norms—I see people honored to experience a system of laws and norms designed to treat people fairly and protect them from both the oppression of their neighbors, and yes, the oppression of their Government."

She paused, again waving Ernstmeyer's threatening letter in the air. "In my opinion, it is *you*, Mr. Ernstmeyer and *you*, Mr. Attorney General, and your Senior Administrators and followers, who pose the greatest threat to our civic culture. Turn this country into a glorified crime syndicate, designed to empower some with oppressive ideals and allow them to target the innocent, and you become the instruments of your own worst fears—destruction of the civil society you claim the influx of 'the wrong kind of people' will bring about." She paused. "What worries me, truly *scares me*, is what will happen when the decision makers in this Administration are faced with a true crisis, be it war, or storms, or disease or pestilence. How will they respond? Will these crackpot conveyors of hate, who act on silly, infantile, ingrained prejudices, have any hope of saving us from the thundering tides?"

She stopped. The reporters were scribbling furiously, trying to get down her every word. She knew her words, almost verbatim, were going to end up pasted all over the media by the end of the day. She let them sink in. Knowing there'd be renewed calls for her impeachment, she decided it was time to circle back to her ruling in the case.

"But, I'm not here to spout philosophy or to try to sweep away all the wrongs of the Stuggs Administration—I'll leave that job to the voters. All I can do is rule on the facts and the law before me. I am here reminded of the words of Attorney McDougal—who has suffered more for the Plaintiffs in this case than any person has a right to expect. She said it best: 'It's hard to imagine why Congress would have tried to distinguish between 'Good' Terrorists and 'Bad' Terrorists, in legislation designed to deter and eliminate Terrorism.' Like Counsel, I don't know what the right way is to deal with border security, but, as counsel said, it can't be *this*. Mr. Handler, this ends *now*.

"So, based on the evidence presented and the law which governs my ruling, I conclude that the Defendant parties are guilty of all the illegal conduct, and all the violations of law, alleged in the complaint, including those of Count Ten, the violations of the Patriot Act. In my opinion, those violations are no longer merely 'alleged'. They are proven.

"And, so, I hold Mr. Ernstmeyer, as the Director of U.S.C.I.S., and Mr. Handler, and the agencies that enforce and carry out these policies, liable to the Plaintiff, the Guardian of 'E.M.', as she is called here, as well as to the rest of the Plaintiff class. I order that the twin policies of U.S.C.I.S., so-called 'Family Separation' and 'Medical Deportation', as enforced by U.S.C.I.S., H.H.S. and C.B.P., be immediately terminated and dismantled. While the parallel case in the Southern District of California will continue to call for re-uniting these families already separated, no new separations are to occur. No deferred medical deportations are to occur. Those programs are declared to be illegal acts of Terrorism.

"Given the tragic and perverse efforts of the U.S. Attorney and the Stuggs Administration to block the prior orders of this and other courts in this effort to remedy the damage inflicted by these illegal policies, Mr. Handler, if you, or any agent of the Federal Government, so much as lifts a finger or twitches nervously to circumvent my order, I will immediately order your, or that person's, incarceration.

"I will promptly set a hearing to determine damages the Defendants must pay to all victims of these terrorist acts, sitting, in that hearing, as Judge in the U.S. Court of Claims. In the meantime, I also find Mr. Ernstmeyer, Mr. Meadows, and you, Attorney General Handler, to be in contempt of court of my prior orders, and, while not my job, also in contempt of the consent decree blocking much of the prohibited treatment of immigrants like E. M., said decree entered in the Southern District of California, in related case number 2018 cv 3681. I therefore direct Mr. Handler, and all of his agents and employees, as well as all of the other Defendants, to refrain from further contact with any of the Plaintiff parties or their counsel. Local, civil authorities are to take custody of the impacted parties. All further Government activity in these matters shall be conducted and supervised by a Commission I will empanel, beginning tomorrow.

"Mr. Crump, Ms. McDougal, please approach the bench."

Crump and Maureen both stood and walked to the front of the courtroom, standing side by side.

Judge Haverhorn shook her head, noticing the splint on Maureen's broken fingers. "I apologize, on behalf of the Federal courts—I'm well aware of the tactics brought to bear on both of you personally, and on Ms. Montes the elder and Ms. Montes the younger, in this case. The least that can be done for Doctor Trimble and her ward, is for me to take jurisdiction of their asylum case in this Court. We're not moving them again."

The Judge looked out across the courtroom. Reporters were filing out in a mass exodus. Handler was steaming. She stood. "Mr. Crump, submit your order for judgment and enforcement, tomorrow at 9:00 A.M."

29.
NO SUCH THING AS FREE PARKING............

CRUMP HAD DRIVEN MARY'S CAR to Court, given the boxes of exhibits and catalog cases he knew they'd need to bring back after the trial ended. Maureen, Steve Barnacle and Howie Schmeltz all wanted to go out and celebrate. Doctor Trimble agreed to meet them after she delivered the good news to the Montes women, who were now crashing at her house, awaiting their Asylum hearing. Crump told them he'd join up with them after he'd carted all their stuff back to the office.

He'd parked in the underground garage of an office building across the street from the courthouse, like most everybody else visiting the court by car. He was almost the last person out, hauling the final box of files and exhibits to Mary's car, when he heard somebody approaching in the otherwise empty, echoing, nondescript concrete basement. He looked over his shoulder, but he didn't see anybody. He opened the trunk and started dumping files inside.

Warren Handler was halfway up the slanting, opposing ramp, about to get in and drive away. He looked across the garage and spotted Crump, loading up his car. Handler walked down the ramp, crossed the unfinished concrete floor, marched over and suddenly grabbed Crump's shoulder from behind. Crump jumped, hit his head on the trunk lid and spun around to face Handler, expecting instead some punk about to roll him.

Handler was red-faced. "This means *nothing*," the Attorney General began, his head trembling, small dribs of spittle flying sideways out of his mouth.

"You're *foaming*," Crump noted.

"You think stopping us from shit-canning just one toothless Mexican kid is going to stop us?" he asked, not really interested in the answer.

"For whatever it's worth, she's Guatemalan, not Mexican—if you're going to sputter racist, xenophobic bullshit, might as well get the unfairly marginalized national origin right—"

"Why do you think all these fucking mestizos are climbing the walls to get in here? Civil Rights lawyers and bleeding-heart church groups, giving them false hopes of fitting in? They're coming here because they want a piece of the action, they want to live in a civilized country, they want what you and your liberal hand-wringers *hate* about us. They want to share in the good life our ancestors built here— capitalism, safety and security, a culture that values hard work and capital preservation—our respect for private property. And we intend to keep them from diluting our culture until the whole fucking country is an unrecognizable mix of mongrel nationalities. Either we have a country, *or we don't*. That's what this is all about: We're gonna stop all these taco-benders and gang-bangers you want us to absorb, just because they manage to walk here, or swim here, or hop in a van run by some mule. Congress will never get it done—all they care about is extending their voting base, waltzing in a bunch of extended family members, offering chain-immigration to a bunch of laborers who reproduce like cockroaches. You may think you've won, but we are going to push, push, push back, so the prevailing culture that built this Country can survive, and yes, make this place the great nation it once was, before all these illegals started to infest the place—"

"You know," Crump interrupted, "I always pictured you as this towering, crypto-fascist, racist bigot, bent on destroying the Country and the Democracy, just to lock yourself and your buddies into power, but now, as I get to see you up close, I realize I was wrong about you—you're *shorter* than I expected."

Crump paused, long enough for Handler to say, "You can *eat* me."

"Warren, *Warren*," Crump scolded. "On top of all your other fine qualities, now we're encouraging cannibalism?" He paused, shaking his head. "Like it or not, you're fighting a demographic battle you can't win, and sooner or later, all that'll be left of the Good Old Days you're fighting to preserve is gonna be some guy in a 'Drain the Swamp' tee shirt, grumbling nonsense to himself as he pushes around a shopping cart, daydreaming fantasies of revenge you've helped him conjure up. Sure, there'll be a few guys like you and your prep-school buddies, scattered around in Country Clubs here and there, but eventually, that guy is all you, and your kids, and your grandkids, are going to have left to 'protect'. That's the America you're fighting to save with all this ethno-centric bullshit."

Handler was turning red. "I'm sure we'll get this nonsense reversed on appeal," Handler claimed.

"You need to sharpen up on your lawyering. The case isn't over yet—can't appeal before we have our damages trial. The only thing you can appeal now is the Judge's contempt findings against you guys, but, for right now, you're still in Contempt of Court. Know what that means? It means, if you step out of line, even while you're up on appeal, she can do more than fine you. Ever been to prison? No, I bet not. I've been over there, couple of times actually with your help, and all I can tell you is that with your hundred-dollar haircut and your tassel loafers, the inmates are gonna *love* you……"

"We should have let that gangster finish you off in that cell. I *saved* your *life*, you ungrateful bastard—"

"Only because you figured I'd gotten the message, and you didn't want the extra heat killing a lawyer would bring down—"

"Yeah, and I was *wrong*," Handler said, as he turned and walked away.

* *

Crump was sitting in his office later that night, having unpacked, deciding whether he wanted to join Maureen and the group for their celebration. They'd called, letting him know they'd moved on to a restaurant, bugging him to show. Crump always had trouble with ceremonies and celebrations: He'd collected College and Law School diplomas in the mail, skipping out on both graduations, and he and Mary had eloped, getting married before a Judge. A shrink friend of Mary's once told him that, in her opinion, he had issues with childhood *compliance*, that he was endlessly wanting to be acknowledged as just a plain old human being. The shrink feared he couldn't handle social customs and ceremonies.

Maybe she was right. Maybe he was so screwed up he couldn't have the kinds of normal, human, emotional responses—

The phone rang.

"This the attorney that had that big case today? You the guy, this, ...wait a minute...." The man paused. He was reading something. "I got this number off our card reader. You used a credit card to pay today. We got phone numbers for the corporate cards. Anyway, I read online one of the stories about you whippin' that dirtbag Handler's butt—"

"Who *is* this?" Crump cut in.

"Sorry. I work in the security booth at 191 South, the building where you parked today. I wanted to tell you, we got the entire building under video surveillance—cameras, sound equipment, heat sensors, water sensors. Anyway, wanted to let you know we got that whole, entire thing between you and Mr. Attorney General himself, we got that whole thing on video. Sound's pretty good, too—you can hear him, right up to the part where he says he was gonna kill you in jail—"

"*Where* are you?" Crump interrupted.

"Downstairs, the lobby of your building. The guards won't let me up. I got a copy of the video for 'ya—actually, got it on both stick drive and I cut you a DVD. Can send it to your phone too—"

"I'll be right down," Crump said, desperately digging through his wallet, finding only a five and some singles. "I gotta tell you, though, I only have, like, seven dollars—"

"You kiddin' me? I woulda walked across the desert in my bare feet to give this to you."

* *

"I gotta admit, when I heard you called, I figured it must have been an accidental butt-dial."

"I don't have a smart phone," Crump said.

"So, why are we meeting at the Monkey House of the Zoo?" Svetlana Armstrong asked, as they walked over to the cage populated by the nasty, long-armed monkeys with the angry, red behinds.

"I'm reconsidering my approach to a few important things these days, and now that I've freed that Montes kid and her mother, I need something else to keep me busy."

"Good for them," Armstrong said, as they both leaned over the railing.

The monkeys appeared agitated, like they were about to throw something. "Looks like everybody's getting into the act," Crump observed, watching one simian wind up to sling something like a pro. "Let's move," he added.

"What about all those other poor folks they got caged up? I mean, I know the court is busting it all down, and you guys *technically* represent them too, but let's face it, they don't have a dedicated team of private lawyers personally plugging to save each one of them."

Crump dug into his jacket pocket and held out a stick drive and a DVD. "I've changed my mind about the publicity thing," he said, offering the objects to Armstrong. "Starting with this."

"What's *this*?"

"You'll see. And, if it's not on every T.V. monitor and computer screen in the World by six-o'clock tonight, you really should hang it up. Once you get this spread around the planet, we meet here once a week, Thursday nights at seven, the only late night they got here. We do that for as long as it takes for you to get the entire story. You promise to publish it, and I won't give it to anybody else. You'll probably need to publish it under an alias—these right-wing nutjobs will come after you—"

"What about you?"

"They're already all over me."

Armstrong looked him over, like he might be dying of some mysterious disease, or maybe he'd just seen God in his fireplace. "Why're you doing this, and why now?"

"It's a rotten job, but somebody has to do it," he said.

"Sounds noble—"

"It's not—I was lying—I *hate* these people......."

30.
THANK MY DENTIST…………..

Angelo Turulio was heading out to a neighborhood Southwest of Downtown in the City by the Lake, to check out a rally of Anti-Stuggs protesters. The area was home to many Hispanic residents, most of them multi-generational, legal immigrants, but it was also a safe haven for illegal immigrants who were related to residents, and for folks just looking for a place to hide out. U.S.C.I.S. and I.C.E. immigration enforcement troops, under the unbowed, direct supervision of the Attorney General, had taken to knocking on doors there without warrants, hoping to shake down residents for identification, in an effort to capture and deport illegal residents.

Turulio was hoping to catch a glimpse of some I.C.E. squads doing more than just knocking on doors, figuring it might give him additional visuals Steve Barnacle could use in the enforcement and damages aspects of the Patriot Act case against the Stuggs administration. He parked in front of a Taqueria near the main drag, got out and began winding his way to the crowds gathering near the Statute of Our Lady of Guadalupe, a shrine in the main town square.

As he made his way toward the shrine, he saw a white panel van careening down a side street, swerving erratically, like it was driven by a drunk or somebody having a stroke. Abruptly, the van jumped a curb and began accelerating on the pavement, headed for a woman and two kids who were walking, holding hands and carrying "Stop Stuggs" protest signs. They saw the van and started running. By the time the woman realized the driver was going to run her down, Angelo was already sprinting to catch up to the swerving vehicle. As the woman tried to dive with her kids into the entryway of a storefront, Angelo drew parallel to the driver's side of the van. The cab was open on both sides, and the driver was standing at the wheel.

"Stop!" he huffed, regretting his sedentary lifestyle. He was trying to hop in the cab and disable the driver, who he thought might be on something. He changed his mind when he caught a better view of the guy, who was bearing down on the family of three with an intensity that did away with any possibility he was impaired. It was the "Get America Praying Again" hat the driver was wearing that finally tipped off Angelo, who was in the throes of interrupting an assassination attempt.

"Stop duh truck, asshole!" Turulio barked, his head buzzing.

Gripping the steering wheel with his right hand, the standing driver suddenly stuck his left arm out of the driver's cab and took a shot at Angelo with an angry little pistol. Turulio hugged the side of the truck as he dodged the shot. He grabbed the handle of the van's sliding door and whipped it shut on the driver's hand. The pistol flew free and out into the street, and as the door swung back open, it was obvious Turulio had broken the man's hand. He was now driving with just his right, his left arm hanging as he bore down on the fleeing trio.

The mother dove into a storefront entryway, but her kids, confused and panicking, continued to run, erratically fleeing ahead of the swerving van. As the driver slowed to better focus on running down the now separated kids one at a time, Turulio ran in front of the van and grabbed first the girl, then the boy. Angelo executed a flying tackle into the stairwell of a garden apartment. He landed first, breaking their fall.

"Stay here," he ordered, then, anticipating a possible language barrier, he added, "Recuerda el Álamo", which translates to "Remember the Alamo", not particularly useful under the circumstances, but the only Spanish phrase Turulio knew. He deposited the kids in the well, then ran out and after the van. The driver was now crawling along, still navigating the pavement, looking for an opportunity to re-enter the street, a matter complicated by the parking meters aggressively spaced close enough to maximize revenue, but not far enough apart to allow a safe trajectory off the sidewalk.

Turulio entered the cab of the van off the open passenger door and struck the driver in the jaw. The startled man turned, just in time for Turulio to send his "GAPA" hat sailing off his head, while he grabbed the hair on the back of the man's head and slammed his face into the truck's steering wheel. The driver lost control and the van swerved into a lamppost, crashing to an abrupt stop. The driver tumbled out the open door onto the pavement, with Angelo directly on top of him. As he started to rise, Turulio silently apologized to God as he mercilessly kicked the driver in the groin.

With the driver immobilized and steam rising from the fracture in the front grill of the van, Turulio noticed a wiring harness of some sort, casually draped from underneath the van's dashboard, running into the rear cab of the van through a sliding panel like the security pane in police cruisers and taxi cabs. He jumped back into the cab and tried to see what was in the back of the van, but there was no entry to the cargo area from the cab. He ran around to the back of the van, but the doors were locked. Jumping up into the cab, he tried to pull the wiring harness away from the dash, then back through the security panel, but it was secured at both ends. The cargo area was dark and windowless. The only things he could see through the security panel were a bunch of boxes and a few barrels, two with blinking red lights on top.

Turulio began to panic. He pulled up the wiring harness, which had four, color-coded, gauge-twelve electrical wires bundled together. He tried wringing the wires into a knot, in a two-handed, back and forth compression, designed to break them apart. When that didn't work, he began biting through the cables, first as a bundle, then, determinedly, one at a time. After a tense few minutes of getting his tongue shocked, he was able to break two of the wires in half, just as the police arrived and cuffed the driver, then escorted Turulio from the van.

It being 2023, the final events were recorded on a half a dozen cell phone videos, which quickly became the most transmitted and viewed communications in any of the cell phone carriers' histories.

* *

"Is it true," one of the reporters called out, "that the bomb Mr. Turulio disarmed was a Nuke?"

The Mayor held up a hand as if to say, "Hold on there".

"The FBI has confirmed that the device in the back of the Terrorist's van was, in fact, laced with radioactive material—a so-called 'Dirty Bomb,' so, not a conventional thermonuclear device. Still, it was a weapon with devastating potential to blanket much of the city in radioactivity," the Mayor announced to the swarm of reporters and cameras at the press conference.

"Mayor Haygood, can you elaborate on the potential force and effect if the bomb had been allowed to detonate?" one reporter shouted.

The Mayor paused. She looked over at Angelo Turulio, who was seated at the makeshift table in the press room of City Hall, Crump to his immediate left, the Chief of Police on his right, and FBI agents at either end. As she glanced at Turulio, he quickly, in one fluid motion, took a comb out of his back pocket and in two hasty swoops, combed his hair.

"Look, this is all still being analyzed, but it was a dirty bomb—yes, an amateurly constructed device, but, still, an A-Bomb of sorts. In addition to the destruction in the blast zone, nobody knows which way the wind will blow after one of these bombs detonate, so I think it's fair to say that just about every man, woman and child in this City owes their lives to Mr. Turulio here," she said, nodding to her right.

Angelo combed his hair again.

"I guess," the Mayor added, "the birds and the squirrels owe their lives to this man."

"What do we know about the assailant?" Svetlana Armstrong blurted out.

An FBI agent spoke up. "So far, only that he was not acting alone. We believe he obtained the materials to construct the bomb from an underground terrorist network who stole the components from a munitions plant in South Carolina. He was definitely affiliated with two splinter groups, the anti-abortion guerilla underground known as 'The Army of God,' and the white supremacist legion calling itself 'April 30, 1945,' which takes its name from the presumed date of death of Adolph Hitler—"

"—Isn't it true that both factions are at least loosely affiliated with the President, the Stuggs Administration and Attorney General Handler?" Svetlana Armstrong pressed on.

Go get 'em, Crump thought, as he slowly nodded.

"As you know, the Stuggs administration vehemently denies any formal connection to either group," the FBI agent continued. "We are examining all ties either outfit may have to any domestic organizations, including pockets within the Government."

"Mr. Turulio," one reporter shouted, straining to be heard over the clatter of the room. "Did you have any idea that you were disarming the timer on a deadly nuclear device when you chewed through those wires leading to the bomb?"

Turulio squared his shoulders and sat upright. "A 'course not—who'da think such a thing?"

"Then, why go after those wires with your bare teeth?" the reporter followed up.

"I'd jus' seen da guy try ta run down a broad—s'cuse me, a woman—an' her two kids, jus b'cause dey was Hispanic, an for all da guy knew, dey was headin' to church after dat rally. I had good cause to b'lieve he wasn't microwavin' a bagel back dere."

As one reporter questioned, out loud, why anybody would microwave a bagel, another shouted out, "How can we ever really thank you?"

Turulio cocked his head. "Thank *me*? You's should thank *my dentist*," he paused, like he was scanning a mental rolodex. "Guido Farracci, D.D.S., Thirteen Twenty-two Washington, Suite Ten-o-Five," he said, then he stopped, when he couldn't remember the man's phone number.

The Mayor was signaling that she wanted to wrap up the press conference, when Crump poked his head into the space of Turulio's microphone and grabbed it. "Mayor Haygood, I just wanted to say that I've known Angelo Turulio for almost sixty-years—we grew up together—and I always thought that, someday, Angelo was going to Save the World."

As they were all about to stand, Turulio grabbed the microphone back. "I wanna say somethin'....he paused. "Dis is what happens when you got Government by gang bang. You sell hate to people, tell 'em it's an O.K. thing, and pretty soon, th' people yur back-slappin' inta action, dey gets *good* at it. This guy was no lone wolf—he b'lieved he had Stuggs and da Feds on his side. R'member dat 'GAPA' hat I sent spinnin' offa da guy's head? He was makin' *a statement*."

Turulio, once again, silently combed his hair.

Mary was watching the press conference at home.

"Enough of this," she said, as Ben, Rene and Dr. Tom got up and Mary turned off the monitor.

"Where you going? Ben asked, as they walked out of the house together.

"Downtown, to play adult in the room, one more time."

They each drove away. When Mary got to the reception area of Crump & McDougal, Sophie guided her into Crump's office, where he was watching a replay of the press briefing on a computer screen at his desk.

"You actually buy a computer?" she announced, as she walked in and sat down.

Crump closed the screen. "No—borrowed this from Maureen," he said, sheepishly, like he'd been caught scanning internet gossip.

"I think it's time," Mary said.

"Time?"

"Look, any day you can announce to half the country that Angelo Turulio has 'Saved the World,' it's time to pack it in—"

"What about the appeal of the Patriot Act case?" Crump argued.

"They can't appeal until the Judge completes the damages trial and finishes dismantling those border programs. Even then, the appeal will take *years,* and these Stuggs Thuggs will be gone, long before that's over. The video of Handler's parking garage Neo-Nazi-rant has been viewed so many times, it's burning a hole in peoples' video monitors," she offered.

"About that," he offered, pausing. "I'm secretly dictating my memoirs to a friend—" he said, when Mary cut him off.

"Sure, *sure* you are," she said, as he got up and looked out the window. She walked over and grabbed his chin, turning his head around. "*Look at me*—I've decided you're officially retired. Maureen and Angelo can give you a commemorative rubber Timex, and then you can scoop all this stuff off your desk and ride out of here. Steve Barnacle wants to join up full time, so he and Maureen can handle the fallout phase of this case. Looks like both the Montes and Lockwood kids are going to survive, and now the rest of the captives are going free. Time to hang it all up."

Crump sat down. "What will we *do?*"

"You're sixty-eight. You've been working since you were six years old. Why do we always have to be *doing* something?"

He looked upwards. "Do you think it would be O.K. if I still occasionally *sued somebody*?"

"You're a *sick man*," she said, as he stood and she took him by the arm and walked him out of his office.

* *

It began with dozens of spontaneous protests.

First, crowds began to form in major cities, placard-bearing citizens with signs that read, "Impeach Stuggs and Handler", or "Resign", with images of the President and his Attorney General, separated by a mushroom cloud. Soon, the crowds had swelled so that downtowns were paralyzed, people choking off traffic and making passage impossible. Then, major strikes and work stoppages erupted, bringing commerce to a halt.

The Administration tried desperately to contain it all, but the local authorities were unwilling to curb any of it. After a nasty exchange with National Guard troops in Columbus, Ohio, where the soldiers put down their weapons and began joining the protests, Stuggs and Handler, along with their families, fled the Country. While the reports were spotty and unreliable, the consensus of opinion was that the two disgraced officials were living in villas somewhere in either Austria or Hungary, or maybe even Russia, places run by regimes more sympathetic to their social agendas.

A moderate politician with a reform agenda, Marshall Treadway, was elected President, soundly defeating Stuggs' Vice President Stanton Anderson, who tried rescuing one last gasp of the 'GAPA' Nationalist movement. Treadway immediately installed Angelo Turulio as head of the Secret Service, and Angelo promptly changed the name of the organization to "The Shadows of Night," after one of his favorite greaser bands from the Sixties.

Several commemorative tee-shirt makers sprung up, selling millions of message-bearing tops with many of Angelo Turulio's Greatest Hits emblazoned on peoples' chests. Even without a formal count, the undisputed sales winner was the tee that read, "Thank My Dentist."